THE SOUL STEALER

GRAHAM MASTERTON is best known as a writer
of horror and thrillers, but his career as an author
spans many genres, including historical epics and sex-
advice books. His first horror novel, *The Manitou*,
became a bestseller and was made into a film starring
Tony Curtis. In 2019, Graham was given a Lifetime
Achievement Award by the Horror Writers Association.
He is also the author of the Katie Maguire series
of crime thrillers, which have sold more than
1.5 million copies worldwide.

THE SOUL STEALER

GRAHAM MASTERTON

HEAD
OF ZEUS

An Aries Book

First published in the UK in 2022 by Head of Zeus Ltd
This paperback edition first published in 2022 by Head of Zeus Ltd,
part of Bloomsbury Publishing Plc

9 7 5 3 1 2 4 6 8

A catalogue record for this book is available
from the British Library.

ISBN (PB): 9781801103954
ISBN (E): 9781801103961

Typeset by Divaddict Publishing Solutions Ltd

Printed and bound in Great Britain by
CPI Group (UK) Ltd, Croydon CR0 4YY

Head of Zeus Ltd
First Floor East
5–8 Hardwick Street
London EC1R 4RG

WWW.HEADOFZEUS.COM

THE SOUL STEALER

I

'Trinity? It's Margo. I have to see you. I'm so scared. I've never been so scared in my life.'

'Margo? What's wrong? Where are you?'

'You remember Peyton's Place, on Reseda? That bar where we all got together for Trudy's birthday? Do you think you can meet me there?'

'I have to pick up Rosie from school right now, but sure, after that. Say four o'clock?'

'Okay, then. Four. I'll see you there at four. But you *will* be there, won't you? Please promise you'll be there.'

'Yes, I promise.'

Margo hung up without saying anything else and Trinity was left staring at the blank screen of her phone. She hadn't heard from Margo Shapiro in over a year, when she had last attended a reunion party at John R. Wooden High School. Margo had been sparkling then: red-headed and eye-catchingly attractive, and bursting with excitement about her walk-on part in Howard Bright's latest comedy, *Hilarity Jones*.

What could have happened to frighten her so much? Trinity had never heard anyone sound so panic-stricken.

She went through to the narrow hallway, stepping over the boxes that were ready to be returned to Amazon. She took down her denim jacket from the peg by the front door and called out to her father, 'Dad!'

There was no answer. She could hear Steve Wilkos on the TV, with the volume turned low, so she called out again. 'Dad! I'm just going to pick up Rosie from school!'

There was still no response, so she went into the living room. Her father was slumped sideways on the worn-out red couch, with an open can of Rolling Rock wedged between his hairy thighs, and softly snoring. She went up to him and shook his shoulder.

'Dad – I'm just going to pick up Rosie!'

He opened his eyes and stared up at her for a moment as if he couldn't think where he was, or who she was, or even who *he* was, himself. His wiry grey hair was sticking up as if he had been electrocuted, his eyes were puffy and his chin was prickly with silver stubble. The front of his blue Chargers T-shirt was ribbed with diagonal brown lines. His breakfast had been last night's leftover burger and he had used his T-shirt to wipe the barbecue sauce off his fingers.

'Trinity—' he said, trying to sit up straight without tipping his can of beer into his lap. 'You're an angel, Trin, I swear to God. I shoulda – I shoulda picked her up myself – but after yesterday – you know what day it was yesterday. Honestly, I swear to God, I'll pick her up tomorrow. I'll even get up early and *fetch* her to school. How about that?'

'Tomorrow's Saturday, Dad.'

'Well, there you are. The Lord's looking after me. But I'll fetch her Monday. I swear.'

Trinity nodded and said, 'Okay, Dad, whatever.' She didn't remind him that he had taken Rosie to school only once in the past three and a half years, and on that occasion he had been stopped for backing his car up into the Arby's Roast Beef Sandwich sign on Reseda Boulevard and causing over $400 worth of damage.

But she was forgiving. Yesterday would have been her mother's birthday if her mother hadn't been taken by ovarian cancer three years ago, at the age of forty-seven.

Her mother was looking at her even now, from the oval picture frame on top of the air conditioner, with her cropped brown hair, her high Slavic cheekbones and her turned-up nose, which her father had always called her 'ski-jump' nose. Her mother was smiling but her smile was somehow apprehensive, as if she had secretly suspected that her happiness couldn't last for long.

In looks, they could have been sisters, Trinity and her mother, although Trinity's hair was shoulder-length and sweeping, and she was much skinnier than her mother had been. But they shared those Slavic cheekbones and some of that constant caution in their eyes, like a deer stepping through a forest.

'You'll be passing the market on Vanowen, won't you?' her father called out, as she opened the front door.

'Dad, I just paid the rent. I got dust.'

'Jim'll let you have a six-pack. Tell him I'll pony up next Friday.'

'Well, I'll ask him. But I'm in a hurry. I promised to meet my friend Margo at four.'

'Margo? Who's Margo?'

Trinity didn't answer but closed the door and crossed over the driveway to her father's Mercury Monarch with its faded silver paintwork and its one green passenger door. As she was climbing into the driver's seat, Kenno came strutting over from next door, where he had been washing his orange Challenger.

'Trinity! How's it hanging, doll?'

Kenno was a keen bodybuilder and his sleeveless maroon T-shirt showed off his balloon-like biceps, densely decorated with tattoos of skulls and gorillas and bosomy women. He was handsome in a Josh Hutcherson way but he looked younger than his twenty-seven years because of his acned cheeks and his tawny man-bun, and his legs in his ripped denim shorts were disproportionately spindly for his pumped-up torso.

'I can't stop, Kenno. I have to pick up Rosie from school.'

'You've lost weight, baby, do you know that?'

'It's these skinny jeans, that's all,' said Trinity. She slammed the door shut and started the engine but she wound down the window.

Kenno leaned on the roof of her car, squeezing out his sponge. 'Do you know what I'm going to do? I'm going to take you up to the Tamales House and treat you to all the wet chicken burritos you can eat. That'll give you some oomph.' He held his hands out in front of his chest to show her what he meant, his sponge still dripping.

'Kenno, I'm a vegetarian. And I have to go, or else I'll be late.'

Kenno grinned at her, showing her his missing front tooth. 'Okay, okay, forget the chicken burritos. Rajas con queso.'

'Chillies give me heartburn. Goodbye.'

She backed out of the driveway with a squeal of worn-out tyres and drove to Kittridge Street to Reseda Charter High School. It was a hot, brass-bright afternoon and she had forgotten her sunglasses so she had to drive with her eyes narrowed because of the reflection from the hood. She also had to drive carefully because the Monarch's transmission fluid was leaking and the gearbox kept unexpectedly downshifting, jolting her forward behind the wheel.

Rosie was waiting for her under the trees on the corner of Etiwanda Avenue, talking to two of her girlfriends. Trinity blew her horn, turned around and drew up beside her. Rosie opened the back door and tossed her school bag onto the seat, and then she climbed in next to Trinity. The first thing she said was, 'What's for dinner?'

Rosie could not have been more different from Trinity. She was fourteen years old, short and plump, and bore a strong resemblance to their paternal grandmother, Lily, with curly blonde hair and windflower-blue eyes. She had been an exceptionally pretty baby, and Trinity guessed that when she lost the weight she had put on at puberty, she would be turning all the boys' heads. In the meantime, she compensated for her lack of looks by being snippy and opinionated and endlessly demanding.

Trinity didn't tell her that with thighs like hers, Rosie's navy-blue skirt was hitched up far too short. That would have started a tirade that might still have been carrying on at bedtime. 'Why? Why do you say it's too short? Are you saying my legs are too fat or something? Is that what you're saying? Be honest!'

'For dinner? I don't know,' said Trinity, as she pulled into the kerb beside the market on Vanowen Street. 'I was thinking spaghetti.'

'*Again?* We had spaghetti Monday.'

'Rosie, until Dad's unemployment comes in, spaghetti's about all we have.'

'So why have you stopped at the store?'

'Why do you think? Dad wants to borrow some beer.'

Trinity climbed out of the car and went into the market. It was frigid in there and smelled of cheese and she gave an involuntary shiver. She was hoping that genial Jim would be there behind the counter, but instead it was his young assistant Jesús, with his shiny black pompadour and his shirt open over his medallions, sticking price labels on salamis with all the flourish of a gunslinger.

'Hey, don't even ask,' he said, as Trinity approached the counter.

'A six-pack, that's all. He'll pay you Thursday when he gets his check.'

'That's what he said last week, and he still doesn't pay.'

'He's gasping for it, Jesús. Please.'

Jesús put down his price gun and stared at Trinity with those black-lashed eyes that put her in mind of Prince.

'I tell you what. You let me feel your pussy, I give you the six-pack.'

'*Jesús!*'

He came around the counter and walked up to her with a confident, undulating swagger, snapping his fingers. 'I'm serious, zorra. You let me give you the finger, I give you the six-pack, and I don't even charge you for it. Come on. If President Trump could do it, why not me?'

The fact that Jesús had called her 'zorra' wasn't lost on her. He knew that her surname was Fox, and 'zorra' meant 'fox'. But it could also mean a girl who partied with a lot of guys.

Trinity took a step back and looked around, towards the door. She could see Rosie sitting in the car outside, prodding at her phone. It was too dark in the store for Rosie to be able to see inside, and anyway the sunlight would be casting a reflection on the window.

She thought of her father, lying sideways on the couch, drunk and dribbling, a man worn out with grief and failure and endless disappointments. Then she turned back to Jesús. He was grinning and waggling his eyebrows up and down, as if to say, how about it then?

At that moment the doorbell jangled and a large woman in a flowery dress the size of a small sideshow tent came gasping into the store, impatiently yanking her shopping trolley in behind her as if it were a disobedient dog.

Trinity said, 'Forget the beer.' She headed for the door but Jesús followed her.

'It's okay, you can have the beer. We save the payment for next time, hunh?'

'I said forget it.'

Trinity wrenched the door open. She didn't know if she were more angry at Jesús for what he had suggested or herself for even considering it, even for a split second. Jesús shrugged and lifted both hands and said, 'Your loss, calaca! Fuck you!'

That was another word Trinity knew, calaca, because she had been called it when she was at school. It meant 'skeleton'.

She climbed back into the driving seat and slammed the door. Rosie was still prodding at her phone with her chipped orange fingernails and didn't even look up.

'I have to meet a friend,' said Trinity, trying to breathe normally so Rosie wouldn't realise that she was upset. 'I'll take you home first and when I come back I'll try and think of something different for dinner.'

'Can't I come with you? I hate being on my own with Dad these days.'

'My friend's really upset about something. I don't know what it is but she sounded like she's in bits.'

'I'll stay in the car.'

Trinity looked at the clock. It was nearly five to four in any case, so she would have been late for Margo if she had taken Rosie home first. And she knew that her father would either be asleep and snoring or else he would keep nagging Rosie to give him 'cuddles'. He never interfered with her sexually, but she was revolted by his clumsy hugging and his prickly beer-wet kisses. He missed their mother.

'Okay,' said Trinity, and she started up the engine and turned south to Peyton's Place, only five blocks south on Reseda Boulevard. She turned into the parking lot in front of the line of single-storey restaurants and bars and dry cleaners and tugged up the handbrake.

'You're sure you're going to be okay? I don't know how long I'm going to be.'

Rosie still didn't look up from her phone. 'I'll be *fine*, Trin. If I get bored I'll walk home.'

Trinity got out of the car and crossed the sidewalk to Peyton's Place. She was about to push open the heavy glass door when it was wrenched open from inside and a bulky man in a black bomber jacket and a black beanie came bursting out, swinging a large brown hessian bag. He almost knocked her over.

'*Hey!*' she said, but he ignored her, shamble-jogging down Reseda Boulevard and disappearing around the corner.

She went into the bar. It was dark in there, illuminated only by small, shaded lamps on the tables and the dim orange strip lights behind the bar. All around the walls were black-and-white photographs of Reseda in the 1920s, when it was producing more lettuce than anywhere else in the country, and Southern Pacific Railroad trains came up Sherman Way to be loaded with it.

There were only three customers in the bar, sitting in the far corner, and they were all middle-aged men who looked like Proud Boys. The bald barman was dipping into a large bag of Flamin' Hot Cheetos and staring up at a replay of a Rams game on the television. Trinity walked up to the bar and said, 'Hi. I'm supposed to be meeting my friend here?'

The barman wiped Cheeto spice from his drooping moustache with the back of his hand. He looked Trinity up and down in her faded denim jacket and her tight white three-quarter length jeans as if he were trying to decide if she was old enough to be in a bar. 'Red-headed girl? Green dress?'

'I don't know what colour dress she was wearing, but yes, she's a redhead. She hasn't come and gone, has she?'

The barman jerked his thumb towards the back of the bar. 'No. She come. But she gone to the bathroom.'

'Okay,' said Trinity. 'I'll just shout out and tell her I'm here.'

The barman shrugged and went back to cramming Cheetos into his mouth.

Trinity went to the door marked Restrooms. As soon as she opened it, she smelled acrid smoke, like varnish burning, and she could hear a sharp crackling sound. She stepped into the short corridor that separated the two toilets and opened up the door to the Women's. The whole room was swirling with smoke and transparent blue flames were leaping up over the top of the centre stall.

'*Margo!*' screamed Trinity.

She went up to the stall door and tried to push it open, but it was too hot to touch, so she kicked it. Inside, Margo was sitting on the toilet in a mass of flames. Her red hair was ablaze and her green dress was curling into blackened shreds. Her face had already shrivelled into a grimacing mask – her eyes opaque and her lips stretched back over her teeth. Both arms were held up in that monkey-like pose that was adopted by almost everybody who was burned to death – firefighters, Vietnamese villagers, saints or witches.

2

When Nemo came up to her, Trinity was still sitting behind the wheel of the Monarch with the door wide open, holding a glass of water that the barman had brought out.

The parking lot outside Peyton's Place was chaotic. A fire truck was only ten feet away from her with its lights flashing and its engine running, so that Trinity could hardly hear what anybody was saying to her, apart from feeling so numb with shock that she couldn't believe she was actually here, with all these people shouting and running around her. There were three patrol cars parked at different angles, as well as a white coroner's van and a TV truck from ABC7.

When Trinity had told her what had happened, Rosie had been excited rather than shocked. She hadn't known Margo and this was by far the most dramatic event since last November, when her classmate Mike Wollenski had been killed while racing his Dodge Caliber along Saticoy Street at over seventy-five miles an hour. Now Rosie was busy contacting all of her friends and telling them to watch the local TV news, because they would see her in the background.

Nemo had been talking to Johnny Cascarelli, the owner of Peyton's Place, a short man in a pale-blue double-breasted suit with a high black pompadour. Now and again Johnny

Cascarelli had nodded his head in Trinity's direction, and Nemo had taken off his mirror sunglasses and frowned at Trinity in the way that a father looks at his daughter when something in her life has gone badly wrong. After a while he had slapped Johnny Cascarelli on the shoulder and come across to talk to her.

'Johnny tells me that it was you who found her,' he said, in a hoarse, gravelly voice.

Trinity raised her eyes. She saw a solidly built man of about forty-five years old, with buzz-cut black hair that was beginning to show traces of grey, and a broad, squarish face with a deeply cleft chin, like a retired boxer. He was wearing a grey leather jacket with a satin emblem of some kind of black bird stitched onto the left-hand pocket, and baggy jeans.

'She was a friend of yours, right?' he asked her.

Trinity nodded. She thought she ought to be crying but she felt as if her tear ducts had dried up.

The man came a little closer. 'Johnny called me. He and me, we've been amigos for years. I'm an ex-cop, but these days I do freelance private detective work – well, among other things. Johnny's worried this is going to badly affect his business. He doesn't trust the cops any more than I do, and he wants me to double-check what really happened to your friend here. You know, in case the cops overlook something important, like they have a habit of doing.'

Trinity took a sip of her water. 'I see,' she said, although she didn't really understand what he was talking about.

'Nemo's the name,' the man told her. 'Nemo Frisby. Sergeant Weller told me that they've asked you all the questions that he needs to for now, so you can go home. I was wondering if you were okay to drive.'

At that moment, the door of Peyton's Place opened up and two investigators from the coroner's office wheeled out a gurney covered with green plastic sheeting. Trinity turned her head away and now, without warning, the tears began to run down her cheeks.

Nemo came up and took the glass of water out of her hand.

'Here,' he said gently. 'Let me drive you home. Is this a friend of yours? Does she want a ride home too?'

'I'm her sister,' Rosie told him. 'It's okay. I'll sit in back.'

Trinity stood up numbly and Nemo led her round to the passenger seat.

'It's 6844 Zelzah,' said Rosie.

Nemo climbed behind the wheel, started the engine and backed out of the parking lot. A uniformed officer gave him a familiar salute as he turned into the street, and Nemo saluted him back.

'What you witnessed there, young lady, nobody should never have to witness,' he said, as he drove. 'It's going to take you a while to get over it, believe me, so go easy on yourself. On the other hand, don't try to put a lid on your feelings, that never helps at all. I've known witnesses who've tried to pretend that they never saw nothing. You know, blank it all out. I guarantee, though, it always come back to them, mostly when they're least expecting it, sometimes months or even years later, and *bam*, just like that, they fall to pieces. And I mean they literally fall to pieces. Mentally, emotionally.'

He turned off Lindley Avenue on to Vanowen. 'You'll need to talk about it, Tina. So I'll give you my number and you can call me any time you like.'

'It's not *Tina*, it's Trinity,' Rosie put in, without looking up from her phone.

'Oh, sorry. I thought that's what Sergeant Weller told me. But really, Trinity, I mean it. Don't bottle it up. I had twenty-two years in the LAPD and I know how important it is to share your feelings with people who will listen to you and understand how traumatised you feel. It doesn't have to be me. But don't keep it bottled up, okay?'

'Okay,' said Trinity, staring out of the window. She was sure she could still smell Margo's burning hair in her nostrils.

When they arrived home, Nemo opened the car door for her and Rosie helped Trinity into the house. Kenno was waxing his Challenger now and he eyed Nemo suspiciously, although he didn't come over and ask what was going on. Nemo took out his phone and called his wife.

'Sherri? Yeah, it's me. I need a ride. I know. Yes, I know, but I left it at the crime scene and took this young woman home. No. Of course not. I would have done the same if she'd been a guy. She's traumatised. Fine. Fine. 6844 Zelzah. Just past Hartland.'

He was starting to send a text when Trinity's father appeared at the front door, blinking in the sunlight. He was still holding a can of Rolling Rock in one hand.

'Rosie just told me what happened,' he said. 'Like, Jesus Christ.'

Nemo went up to him. Trinity's father wiped his free hand on the back of his shorts and held it out, but Nemo didn't shake it.

'Nemo Frisby,' he said. 'Formerly Detective Nemo Frisby, West Valley Area. Your daughter's badly traumatised, sir. She's going to need considerable care and understanding for the next few days. If not weeks.'

'Okay,' said Trinity's father. 'I got you.'

He paused for a moment, licking his lips, and then he nodded towards the Monarch. 'You didn't happen to notice… she didn't manage to pick up a six-pack before she got trau – before she got trautamised – by any chance?'

Nemo stared at him as if he had spoken in a foreign language. Then, without saying a word, he turned around, walked back to the kerb and continued his texting. Trinity's father stayed in the open doorway for a while, holding on to the jamb for support. When he realised that Nemo wasn't going to answer him, he staggered back into the living room and Nemo heard him stumble over the rug and shout out, '*Fuck!*'

Trinity was lying on her back on her bed, staring at the ceiling, when Rosie tapped softly at the door.

'Trin? Sabina's here. She wants a word.'

Trinity sat up. On the opposite wall, over her desk, a poster of Tom Cruise playing a young lawyer in *The Firm* frowned at her seriously.

'Tell her I'm not feeling too good.'

Rosie fidgeted with the door handle. 'She said it's quite important. It's about Buddy's therapy.'

'Okay,' said Trinity, and she swung her legs off the bed.

'Have you thought what's for dinner yet?' asked Rosie, as Trinity followed her out to the hallway.

Trinity closed her eyes for a moment and stopped where she was. She didn't know if she was going to scream with frustration or collapse onto the floor and pretend to have fainted. But then she opened her eyes again and saw Buddy in the living room, sitting cross-legged on the floor in front of the TV, and he gave her a gappy-toothed grin and waved.

She took a deep breath to calm herself and waved back, although her face felt numb and she couldn't manage to smile. She could see her father's white hairy leg behind Buddy and he had obviously fallen asleep again.

'Dinner – no, not yet,' she told Rosie, who had already returned to prodding at her phone. 'If you don't want spaghetti, I'll try to think of something.'

Sabina was standing outside on the driveway. She looked like a nurse, because she was still wearing the pale-blue button-through dress that she wore when she was giving therapy to the children at the Small Talk speech-training centre. Her cornrow hair was styled into a halo braid and her lips were scarlet and glossy. Rosie had once said that she looked like Rihanna's less successful twin sister.

'Hi, Trinity! How's the world with you?'

'Well, no, not too good right now.'

'Oh, I'm sorry. What's wrong, girl?'

'It's okay. I've had a kind of a shock, that's all. I don't really want to talk about it.'

Sabina cocked her head on one side sympathetically. 'You're sure? You do look a little pale, if you don't mind my saying so.'

'You wanted to have a word about Buddy. How's he coming on? Is there a problem?'

'He's coming on *fine*, therapy-wise. I'm sure you've noticed yourself how much clearer he's talking. His resonance and his phonation have improved so much in the past three months. No – it's a behavioural thing.'

'Behavioural?' Trinity could see that Kenno had stopped waxing the hood of his Challenger in mid-circle and was grinning at her.

'He's been having fights with two of the other boys in the group. And not just an occasional scrap, you know, like all boys do. It's been ongoing for at least a week or two now. I've asked him what it's all about but he says it's nothing. I was wondering if you could get it out of him.'

'I'll try. He always has his happy face on, but he does keep his secrets.'

'Thanks. The way they've been going at each other, I'm worried that one of them's going to get seriously hurt.'

Trinity glanced behind her to make sure that her father hadn't woken up and come shuffling to the front door to see who she was talking to.

'Sabina – do you think you could do me a huge favour?' she asked. 'We're flat broke and my dad's unemployment doesn't come in till next Thursday. I have to give Rosie and Buddy something for their dinner.'

'Sure,' said Sabina. 'How much do you need?'

'Well, twenty if I get the Pizza Hut five-dollar deal.'

Sabina walked over to her red Sonic, opened the passenger door and took out her purse. She came back and gave Trinity a fifty-dollar bill.

'There. Why don't you order some chicken wings and shakes to go with them.'

'I can pay you back on Thursday, I promise.'

'There's no panic, girl. Honestly. You have enough on your plate. And that shock you had, whatever that was… well, I hope it doesn't take you too long to get over it.'

Trinity's lips were pressed tightly together and she had to blink away some tears. She wanted to say thank you but she knew that if she opened her mouth she would start to sob.

Sabina went back to her car. Before she climbed in, she gave Trinity a little wave and called out, 'Let me know how things go with Buddy, okay?'

Trinity nodded. After the death of her mother, she had always believed she could deal with any of the tragic surprises that fate had a habit of dealing out. But now she felt weak and drained of colour, almost ghost-like, and when Kenno called out to her she found it hard to believe that he could even see her.

'Hey, Trinity! You still up for tamales?'

She ignored him and went back into the house. He stood staring at her front door for a few moments as if he half expected her to come out again, but then he shrugged and said 'whatever' and went back to his waxing.

They were all sitting in the living room with their pizza boxes open on their laps when the six o'clock *Eyewitness News* came on. Trinity hadn't felt at all hungry, but she had ordered herself a Garden Party pizza with spinach and tomatoes and peppers because she knew that if she went to bed on an empty stomach, she wouldn't be able to sleep. She desperately wanted to be able to sleep deeply tonight, without dreams.

Trinity's father was sitting hunched over his pizza box with a slice in each hand, wolfing them down alternately. Whenever he ran out of alcohol he would develop a ravenous appetite, and he had started eating as soon as Trinity had shaken him awake and set the pizza box down on his lap. He hadn't said a word, not even to ask how she could have afforded it.

Buddy was still sitting on the floor in front of the TV. He was eleven, only a month off twelve, but all the same he was big for his age, and overweight. Apart from his snub nose and his dark brown crew cut, he looked just like their father. He was even wearing a Chargers T-shirt, although it was a size too small for him now, and his belly bulged over the waistband of his shorts.

Rosie had perched herself on the arm of the couch, as far away from her father as possible, while Trinity was sitting as usual in the sagging basketwork chair where their mother always used to sit, doing her embroidery. It was the family's only outright acknowledgement that she had taken her mother's place in charge of the household.

The cuckoo clock in the hallway whirred and clanked and chimed six times, interspersed with thin peeping noises because one of its bellows was punctured.

Rosie said, 'Switch over to the news! Buddy, switch over to the news! You'll be able to see me on TV!'

Buddy picked up the remote and changed the channel to the local news. The lead story was about a gas explosion in Van Nuys, but the second item was about Margo being burned alive in the restroom at Peyton's Place.

News anchor Rachel Brown said, 'The young woman's body was so badly burned that it was only because a friend had agreed to meet her at Peyton's Place that the police were able to make an immediate identification. She was Margo Shapiro, a twenty-three-year-old actress who had appeared in the movie *Hilarity Jones* and also in the TV series *Class of Angels*.

'Sergeant Weller, the lead officer of West Valley police, said it appeared that Ms Shapiro had been deliberately set alight, although who had assaulted her and why were still open to investigation.'

A screenshot of Margo in the Howard Bright movie appeared on the screen, smiling and holding a bunch of coloured balloons. As soon as she saw it, Trinity's stomach muscles clenched and she vomited half-chewed pastry and vegetables into her lap.

Rosie looked around, wrinkled up her nose and said, 'Yuck! *Gross*, Trin, or what?'

3

Over breakfast the next morning, as she was spreading butter on her toast, she said to Buddy, 'Okay then – what's this fighting all about?'

Buddy took in another spoonful of Fruit Loops and didn't answer. Rosie said, 'It's over that Imelda, isn't it? That sassy little bitch with the bangs.'

'No, it's not at school,' said Trinity. 'It's at your speech class. Sabina told me you've been fighting with some of the other boys for a couple of weeks now. She said she asked you about it but you wouldn't tell her why.'

Buddy shrugged, with his mouth full.

'She said that you and these other boys have been really going for each other. She's worried that one of you is going to end up badly injured, or worse.'

Rosie finished her cereal, stood up and stacked her bowl into the dishwasher. 'They're probably fighting over which one of them is the biggest moron.'

'It's about *nothing*!' Buddy protested, in his indistinct voice. He suffered from mild cerebral palsy because his brain had been starved of oxygen during a difficult birth. He was clever, and it hadn't affected his mobility, but he always sounded as if he were talking underwater.

'Oh come on, it must be about something,' said Trinity. 'Is it about a girl? There's that pretty Puerto Rican girl in your group, isn't there? What's her name?'

Buddy furiously shook his head. 'Clarita? It ain't about her! It ain't about *nothing*! Me and Jet and Fredo, we just hack each other off, that's all!'

'Well, if you don't like each other so much, can you try and stay away from each other? You're really upsetting Sabina and she doesn't deserve to be upset like that. And like she says, one of you is going to get hurt if you don't quit fighting.'

'I'm going over to Sally's this morning,' said Rosie. 'Can you give me a ride on your way to work?'

'Okay,' said Trinity. 'And what are you going to do, Buddy? Do you have any homework?'

'No. Me and José are going to hang out.'

'Don't get yourself into any trouble, then. I don't like that José. He's weird. None of that shoplifting.'

'You're not my mom.'

Trinity watched him as he scooped up the last of his Fruit Loops, then dropped his spoon onto the table and slurped the dregs of the milk straight out of the bowl.

'No,' she said. 'I'm not your mom. I'm not Rosie's mom, either. Or mine.'

She was carrying her mop and bucket down the driveway of the Mellors' house on Andora Avenue when a metallic red Impala appeared around the corner. It drew up behind the Merry Maids van and stopped. As she reached the van, the Impala's door opened and Nemo Frisby climbed out.

'Trinity! Caught up with you at last! I've been calling your cell for the past two hours but you didn't pick up!'

'I have to switch it off when I'm working. The customers don't like it if our phones keep ringing.'

'I just wanted to check that you were okay, that's all, and bring you up to speed on what happened to your friend.'

'I'm okay. I was thinking about calling in sick but I need the money. And coming in to work has helped me to keep my mind off it.'

'I called in at the police station earlier and had a chat with Detective Jim Bryce. He's in charge of this investigation. Long-time pal of mine, too.'

Trinity opened the back doors of the van, stowed her mop and bucket inside and snapped off her rubber gloves. It was past 3:00 p.m. now and cleaning the Mellors' house was the fourth and last job of the day. Trisha and Medallia came down the driveway to join her, both wearing the same pink cotton jumpsuit as Trinity with *Merry Maids* embroidered in red on the pocket. Medallia was lugging the vacuum cleaner and Trisha was carrying the basket of window-cleaner sprays and disinfectants.

'Are you through now?' asked Nemo. 'I was hoping we could maybe go for a coffee or something. You know, have a bit of a chat.'

'This your new *boy*friend, Trinny?' said Medallia, as she heaved the vacuum cleaner into the back of the van. She emphasised 'boy' as if to suggest that Nemo was old enough to be her father.

Trinity ignored her. The three of them were constantly bantering but today she wasn't in the mood. 'Sure,' she told

Nemo. Then, to Trisha, 'It's okay, Trisha. This gentleman can give me a ride home. I'll see you Monday.'

Nemo opened his car door for her and she climbed in. As they drove away, Trisha and Medallia grinned at her and gave her little finger-waves and she could guess what they were saying to each other.

'How are you feeling today?' Nemo asked her. 'You hungry at all?'

'A little. I had some toast for breakfast but I've had nothing since then.'

'How about a donut? Could you fancy a donut?'

Trinity smiled and nodded.

Nemo drove them to Sherman Way and parked outside Miss Donuts. They went inside and up to the glass-fronted counter, where Trinity chose a raspberry jelly filled donut and Nemo went for a cinnamon bear claw.

'I hope you don't think I'm insensitive, bringing you here,' said Nemo, as they waited for their coffee.

'No. Why should I?'

'Oh. You don't know? Well, you probably didn't see that movie *Boogie Nights*. They filmed a shoot-out right here, exactly where we're standing. A thief comes in to rob the till and *blam*! It's a bloodbath!'

'In that case, I'm glad I never saw it. *Frozen*'s about my limit.'

They sat down in the yellow bench seats by the window. Trinity watched Nemo while he emptied three packets of sugar into his coffee and stirred it.

'Oh—' He smiled, when he caught her looking at him. 'I

have a real sweet tooth. I guess that's what comes of working all those years in such a sour job.'

'When did you retire?'

'Oh, I didn't retire. I was given the bullet. I found out about some funny business going on between some of my senior officers and the Zingel crime gang. You've heard of the Zingels? Charges of fraud were quietly being dropped. Money was changing hands. After I'd reported it, abracadabra, eight thousand dollars' worth of crack cocaine was found in my car.'

'Really? They set you up?'

'My fault. I should have kept my big yap shut. You don't mess with people like the Zingels. They started in Germany, but they run so many rackets here in LA. Racketeering, loan-sharking, gambling, extortion, people-smuggling, prostitution, drug-running. Think of a crime, and the Zingels are into it.'

Trinity took a bite of her donut and thoughtfully chewed it. She found its sweetness comforting, partly because it reminded her of the donuts her mother used to make when she was little.

'I can't think why anybody would have wanted to hurt Margo,' she said. 'She was lovely. She wouldn't have hurt a fly.'

'Apart from checking that you were okay, that's one of the reasons I wanted to talk to you,' said Nemo. 'Jim told me that he's received a preliminary report from the coroner's office as to the cause of death. At first they wondered if somebody had attacked her, but now they reckon it was suicide.'

'Suicide? She was *burning*! She was on fire! That couldn't have been suicide! Who kills themselves like that?'

'Well, I don't know. Buddhist monks, I guess.'

'That's insane! Margo wouldn't have taken her own life! She had so much to live for! She was in films, she was making a name for herself on TV! And what about the man who came running out of the front door and almost pushed me over? I told the detectives about him. Why was he running away if it wasn't him who set poor Margo on fire?'

'I'm only telling you what Jim told me, Trinity. They'll have a pathologist to carry out a full post-mortem, of course, although that usually takes a few days. But one of the reasons they reckon it was suicide was because the forensic examiners found an empty plastic bottle in that toilet stall, and it still contained dregs of gasoline.'

'I didn't see any plastic bottle.'

'Apparently it was behind the toilet door, so maybe you wouldn't have. They also found a Clipper lighter on the floor, which had been dropped behind the toilet bowl. They'll test the bottle and the lighter for fingerprints and DNA, but they do kind of point to your friend having taken her own life.'

'But that guy—'

'If he'd done it, don't you think he would have picked up that bottle and that lighter and taken them away with him? I mean, leaving them there, that would be like leaving a gun or a knife behind after a murder, and you'd have to be pretty darn dense to do that.'

'But why was he coming out in such a hurry?'

'Who knows? Johnny Cascarelli told me that according to his barman, he'd come in right after your friend, ordered a beer, which he paid for. But the barman was too busy watching the Rams game on TV to see if he followed your friend to the bathroom, or when he left.'

Trinity stared out of the window. Life was carrying on as normal out on the street, cars passing by, three teenagers zigzagging across the sidewalk on skateboards. She couldn't imagine how much Margo must have suffered, burning like that. Even if she had felt suicidal, why hadn't she waited until Trinity had arrived, so that she could tell her why she was thinking of taking her own life? And if she really had killed herself, why had she done it in such an agonising and spectacular way in the women's restroom at Peyton's Place, when she could have simply taken an overdose in her own apartment?

'I don't believe it was suicide,' she said. 'I don't believe it for one second. Margo told me on the phone that she was scared. She said that she'd never been so scared in the whole of her life. That's why she wanted to meet me.'

'She didn't give you any idea what she was scared of?'

'No. But if the police are saying that she committed suicide, I'm going to find out.'

Nemo sipped his coffee, still keeping his eyes on her. 'Oh, yes. And how exactly do you intend to do that?'

'I don't know yet. But I know a lot about forensics.'

'Really?'

'I've watched almost every episode of *CSI Miami*. And I really identified with Calleigh Duquesne. You know who I mean?'

'Sure. I used to watch it too. She was the firearms specialist. Blonde, very pretty. And her dad was a drunk.'

'That wasn't why I identified with her. I liked how professional she was, and she was always positive, you know, no matter how bad things got. She believed in karma, and she never let men tread all over her. Ever since I watched that series I wanted to be a CSI. I've read three books on it already. *Practical Homicide Investigation*, and *Forensic Pathology* and *Interpretation of Bloodstain Evidence*.'

'I'm impressed. So you're seriously hoping to train as a forensics technician?'

'One day. When Rosie graduates and Buddy's old enough to take care of himself. I guess I'll be a mature student by then, but my heart's totally set on it.'

'And what about your dear old dad?'

Trinity didn't answer that, but looked away. Nemo waited for a few moments, and then he said, 'You're certain your friend didn't kill herself?'

'Positive. She asked me to meet her at four and I wasn't late. When we were at high school together, she used to tell me everything. And I mean *everything*. Even what she and her boyfriend had been up to.'

'All righty. Let's say that she didn't commit suicide, and that somebody for some reason wanted her dead. Johnny Cascarelli wants me to find out what happened. How about you and me, we track down who it was together, and why he did it?'

'You mean it?'

Nemo held up his right hand as if he were giving an oath in court. Trinity couldn't help picturing Margo at that moment, and the way she had danced at the high school reunion party, showing off the moves she was rehearsing for her brief background appearance in *Hilarity Jones*. And the time at high school when she had clung on to Trinity and sobbed because her boyfriend, Mike, had hurt her when they were in bed together. She loved him, but he had hurt her.

Trinity's eyes filled with tears. Nemo stretched out across the table to give her a high five and said, 'Yes, Trinity, I mean it. You and me together, we'll be a team Fox and Frisby. Frisby and Fox.'

4

'Your lobster rolls, gentlemen.'

Zuzana laid the plates down in front of the two men sitting at table 18 in the darkest corner of The Orange Grove restaurant, underneath the framed signed photograph of Fred Astaire.

'Can I fetch you anything else to drink?' she asked them, picking up their empty glasses.

The older of the two men repeatedly snapped his fingers, obviously trying to remember something. He had the looks of an Italian movie star of the 1960s, with shiny steel-grey slicked-back hair, hooded eyes and a hooked nose as sharp as a cheese knife. He was wearing a dark grey suit with a slight gleam to it, a purple silk tie, and a purple silk pocket handkerchief to match.

'Yes – a bottle of that Chardonnay I had the last time I was here, whatever it's called. Duck's Beak, Duck's Ass, something like that.'

'Duckhorn.'

'That's the one. I knew it had something to do with a duck's anatomy.'

The younger man snorted in amusement. He was fat and round-shouldered, with blond hair faded up the sides so that only a small divot remained on top of his head. His blue eyes were as protuberant as a frog's and his double chin had a prominent mole on it. 'Not for me,' he said. 'I'll stick with a gimlet. White wine always gives me the gripes.'

'Okay, then,' said Zuzana. 'One bottle of Duckhorn Chardonnay, one gimlet.'

She turned away, but as she did so the older man suddenly leaned over and wound the ties of her brown cotton apron around his knuckles, tugging her back.

'Hey – babe. Before you go, can I ask you a question? Did you ever audition for the movies, or for TV, maybe?'

Zuzana tugged at her apron ties and he let go of them.

'No,' she said. 'A friend and me were going to audition for *Casino*, but she got sick and I didn't want to go on my own.'

'Well, that's a pity, because you're a real looker, you know that? A peach, to be honest with you, and I'm not the kind of guy who goes around flattering young women just to take advantage. I have the contacts and I could fix you up with a part in a movie or a TV production no problem at all.'

'Serious?'

'Only something small to start with. I wouldn't kid you into thinking you could be Scarlett Johansson overnight. But I can arrange modelling work for you, too. You have the figure for it. Swimsuit, lingerie, it all pays good and it gets you noticed by the people in the movie business who matter.'

'You're really serious? You could get me a part in a movie?'

'Do I look like I'm kidding?'

'He never kids,' said the younger man. He had crammed his mouth so full of fries that some of them were still sticking out, like a cartoon vampire's teeth.

'Here—' said the older man. He took out his wallet and

handed Zuzana a business card. 'Vincent Priest, media consultant, agent and talent scout. Are you working here this evening, too?'

'No. Just this lunchtime shift.'

'Give me a call around six and I'll come pick you up. I know just the guy you need to meet. He's a producer. Where do you live?'

'You're really, really serious, right?'

'Oh, he's serious all right,' said the younger man. 'I never knew nobody so serious. He makes Chris Walken sound like a stand-up comedian.'

Vincent Priest gave the younger man the coldest look that Zuzana had ever seen, and said quietly, 'Can it, SloMo.' But then he looked back up at her, and gave her an ingratiating smile.

'See you at six, babe. Okay?'

Zuzana was sitting in front of her dressing table in the bedroom when Rod came home and slammed the front door. She heard him drop his tool bag onto the living-room floor and knew that his day hadn't gone well.

'Zooz?' he called out.

Zuzana pouted her lips in front of the mirror. She wasn't sure if the plum-coloured lip gloss that she had chosen was too dark for her pale complexion. She was happy with her hair, though. Her friend Christy had cut it for her only last weekend into a sharp dirty-blonde bob and she liked the pixie-like appearance it gave her, especially with her huge chocolate-brown eyes.

Rod came into the bedroom, stopped still and stared at her.

'What the fuck you all tarted up for? I'm staying in tonight to watch the game.'

'I met a movie agent at the restaurant. He thinks he can get me a part on TV and he wants me to meet this producer.'

'A part on what? *Sesame Street*? Miss Piggy's sister?'

'He didn't say. But he said I have the looks for it.'

'What is he, blind or something?'

'Oh, Rod. Did you have another bad day at work?'

'What gave you that idea? Yes, I did, as a matter of fact. That Lennie is driving me fucking nuts. I fix in a window like perfect, do you know? Perfect. And then Lennie comes along and says I have to take it all out again because the sealant's not even. I tell him it can't never be even because this is an old building, right, and the frame's totally out of true. But he don't listen. He says take that window out again or else *you're* out.'

'You shouldn't let him bug you so much.'

'Excuse me? He's threatening to fire me and we're a month behind with the rent and I shouldn't let him bug me? And then I come home expecting to relax and have a pizza and watch the game with my girlfriend but here she is all gussied up to go on some fancy evening out.'

'Rod – what if this producer gives me a part and I get paid good money for it? And this agent said I could do modelling too, like underwear and swimsuits.'

'Oh, sure, that's what these creeps always say. Underwear and swimsuits. And then it's why don't you take your top off, baby, and maybe your panties too, and then it's why don't you pose with this guy and the next thing you know you're in some porn movie being screwed by three guys at once.'

Zuzana fastened her silver necklace, tugged down her

white V-necked sweater, and stood up. 'It won't be like that at all. He's a proper agent. He gave me his business card and everything. And besides, I would never pose in the nude or appear in a porn movie.'

'Oh, he had a business card? Any slimeball can have a business card. You're not going, Zooz. This guy's taking you for a ride, don't you see that, or are you too fucking stupid?'

'I think he's genuine, Rod. And I'm *not* stupid. I wouldn't let nobody talk me into nothing that I didn't want to do.'

She picked up her purse and had to push past him to leave the bedroom. He followed close behind her. He was skinny and tall with hair that stuck up like a brush. He walked with a cartoon-like lope, and he had the tight-lipped look that homeopathic psychologists associated with staphysagria – the physical manifestation of repressed anger and sexual disappointment. He was handsome, though, like a starved James Dean, and when he was in a good mood he could make Zuzana laugh until she fell off the couch.

The trouble was that he hadn't been in a good mood for months now. The window business wasn't doing well and he was worried about money. On top of that, he had been smoking gage from the moment he woke up in the morning until the moment he came to bed at night, and if Zuzana hadn't wanted quick and violent sex as soon as he flung back the sheets then he would lose his temper and start throwing things, like the alarm clock and the bedside lamp.

'Don't think for one moment that you're going out because you're fucking not,' he said. He stood over Zuzana as she sat down on the living-room couch with a shoehorn to ease on her silver high-heeled pumps. She didn't answer him, so he bent down, picked up one of her pumps and threw it across the room. It hit the framed print of Kurt Cobain and cracked the glass.

'There – you see what you made me do?' he demanded. 'I try to stop you from getting yourself exploited by some scumbags and I end up insulting my hero.'

'Rod – calm down. Please. This could be the chance of a lifetime. This could be the break that I've been looking for ever since I came to LA.'

She started to stand up so that she could retrieve her shoe, but Rod smacked her across the face with his open hand, so that she gasped and dropped back down.

'*Now* see what you made me do? You just don't get it, do you? I'm trying to protect you here but you're too stupid to understand.'

'I'm going, Rod!' Zuzana shouted at him, her eyes filled with tears. Her left cheek was already swollen and turning crimson. 'You can hit me and hit me but I'm still going!'

'Why do you always have to fucking *defy* me?' Rod shouted back at her. She tried to get up for a second time, but he swung at her again. Although she ducked her head to one side, he gave her a hard smack on the shoulder and knocked her sideways across the couch.

'Stop it, Rod! Stop it!' she screamed, but he had worked himself up into one of his seething rages now and she knew that he wasn't going to stop until he had beaten her so hard he had made her nose bleed and she had dropped half-stunned onto the woodblock floor. It was only then that he would sink down on his knees beside her and beg her forgiveness.

He grabbed the waistband of her jeans and started to tug her back towards him, but at that moment the doorbell chimed, *bing-bong!* He stopped tugging and stood up straight. The doorbell chimed again, twice this time. *Bing-bong! Bing-bong!*

'Who's that?' he asked her. 'Is that him? Is that your scumbag so-called agent?'

'I don't know, Rod. Please. Please calm down. He's a really nice guy, I swear it. Please don't mess this up for me.'

The doorbell chimed again, and then again. Rod loped across the living room to the small entrance lobby and opened it. Zuzana heard him say, 'Yes? Did you want something?'

'We've come for Zuzana?' said Vincent, as if he wasn't sure that he had the right address.

'Oh, you think?'

'This is apartment eleven, two hundred De Soto Avenue?'

'I'm here!' Zuzana called out, getting up off the couch. 'I'm just coming, Vincent!'

She went across to the front door and there was Vincent, with SloMo close behind him.

Rod held out his hand like a traffic cop and said, 'Stop, Zooz! Don't even think about it! You're going nowhere!'

'Rod, I told you! I don't care what you think! I'm going!'

She pushed his hand aside but he seized the sleeve of her sweater and swung her away from the door.

'Hey-hey-hey!' said Vincent. 'What is this? If the lady wants to leave, she can leave!'

'Not with you, you motherfucker! Now beat it!'

Vincent took a step into the lobby. His lips were pursed and he had that same cold expression in his eyes that he had given SloMo back at The Orange Grove.

'I've invited Zuzana to meet an influential producer, and she's accepted my invitation, and so that's what we're going to do. So I suggest you take your hands off her, and back off, and go rinse your mouth out with Lysol, unless you want my friend SloMo here to do it for you.'

Rod kept a tight grip on Zuzana's sleeve. 'I said beat it,' he repeated, although he didn't sound so sure of himself now.

Vincent shrugged and took a step back out of the lobby. As soon as he was out of the way, SloMo stepped in. He went straight up to Rod so that his belly was almost touching him, and gave him a poke in the chest with his finger.

'You know what we prefer, me and Mr Priest here? We prefer good manners. When people treat us with respect, we're as sweet as your momma's home-baked cherry pie. But when they *don't* treat us with respect – when they use blue language and strut about like farmyard cockerels with lighted Roman candles halfway up their butt – well, that's when we have to be violent.'

Rod opened his mouth but then closed it without saying anything.

'Let the lady go,' said SloMo, leaning forward even closer, so that he was spitting on Rod's face.

Rod flinched, and then he released his hold on Zuzana's sleeve, although he didn't look at her. She turned to him, half in pity and half in disgust, and when he still wouldn't look at her she shook her head and walked out of the front door. Vincent laid his hand on her shoulders and guided her along the balcony to the stairs, talking sympathetically close to her ear.

SloMo went after them, although he stopped in the doorway and said to Rod, 'You did the right thing there, dude, and I'm grateful. I hate to tread on anybody's head before dinner, you know what I mean? It's when you see their brains squirt out their ears, it kind of puts you off your pizza.'

★

'So what's your boyfriend's beef?' asked Vincent, as they turned off Sunset Boulevard and drove in through the white-painted west gate of Bel Air. 'I'm assuming that he *is* your boyfriend, that raging orangutan who didn't want you to come out with us.'

Zuzana was sitting in the back seat of his Lincoln Continental. The air conditioning was set to frigid and the interior smelled of leather and stale cigars. She was holding up her make-up mirror, trying to mask the bruise on her cheek with light porcelain foundation.

'Rod? I don't know. His work hasn't been going too good lately. When he's nice, he's the nicest guy in the world.'

'Don't you worry. This evening you're going to be meeting some of the friendliest people you've ever come across, I promise you. And the most successful, too. You've heard of David Magellan?'

'You mean David Magellan the director? Of course! He won a Golden Globe, didn't he, for *Wanda's Weekend*?'

'Well, you sure know your onions.'

'Oh, yes. It's all I've ever wanted, to be in the movies or TV. And he had dinner in The Orange Grove the night he won it. He ordered the Wagyu steak.'

'And Arturo Funicello? The designer?'

'Oh, I *love* his dresses, they're so beautiful, but I could never afford one!'

'He'll be there. Maybe you'll be able to persuade him to give you a discount. Or even a freebie!'

Zuzana could hardly believe that this was really happening. They drove about half a mile up Chantilly Road, which was lined on either side with fan palms and eucalyptus and pink blossoming myrtle trees. Behind the trees she could see houses with pillared porticos and multiple garages, each one larger and more luxurious than the one before.

SloMo steered the Lincoln up the sloping driveway of a huge white-painted house and stopped. On one side the house had a circular tower with blue stained-glass windows and a weathervane on top of it in the shape of a hooded figure carrying a scythe. The driveway was already lined with expensive cars, including a red Porsche 911 and a yellow Bentley Bacalar. They climbed out and started to make their way up the stone steps that led to the double oak entrance doors.

Before they reached the top of the steps, though, the doors were flung open and a tall man came striding out. He was dressed all in black, with black knee-boots. His long silvery-black hair fell down to his shoulders, and he had a long angular face with a chin as sharp as a stonemason's chisel. He was followed by two girls in tiny sparkly gold dresses, one blonde and one African American, both of them giggling and tottering around as if they were tipsy or high.

'The Priest!' the man roared, flinging up both of his arms in greeting. 'And I can see you've brought me another delectable offering! What a fisher of lovely young women you are, your reverence!'

With that, he let out a bellow of laughter, and squeezed and kissed the two girls, whose breasts bulged out of the tops of their dresses.

Vincent patted Zuzana on the shoulder and smiled at her, and winked.

'Come and meet John Dangerfield. He's your future,

Zuzana. Once you've been accepted into John Dangerfield's circle, it'll be glamour all the way, I promise you. You'll be able to wave The Orange Grove goodbye. And anything else in your life that you want to leave behind.'

Zuzana looked at him. He hadn't said 'Rod' out loud, but she could see it in his eyes.

5

They were sitting side by side on the couch with their dinner trays on their laps watching *Access Hollywood* when they heard a knock at the front door.

'You're not expecting anybody, are you, Nemo?' Sherri asked him, with a forkful of lasagne poised in front of her mouth.

'Nope. Are you? Don't say it's those folks from the Church of the Holy Worship again.'

There was another knock, harder this time, and so Nemo stood up and set his tray down on the coffee table. When he went out into the hallway, he switched on the light in the porch. Through the frosted-glass panel in the front door he could see that a thickset man in a tan-coloured jacket was standing outside.

'Who is it?' he demanded. In recent weeks they had been plagued by door-to-door salesmen and evangelists, even after dark.

The man took out an identity card and pressed it flat against the glass. 'Fidel Madrazo. IAG.'

Nemo lifted the chain off the front door and opened it. The man was swarthy-looking, with shiny black hair, a heavy black moustache and rubbery lips. He looked more like the trumpet player in a mariachi band than an investigator for the Internal Affairs Group.

'What do you want?' Nemo asked him.

'Just a word, Mr Frisby, if I may. Okay if I step inside for a while?'

'Okay. Come through to the kitchen. The wife's watching her favourite programme.'

Sherri called out, 'Who is it, Nemo?'

'Business, that's all. Nothing special. I'll be back in a second.'

Fidel Madrazo followed Nemo into the green-tiled kitchen, and Nemo switched on the lights. His black cat lifted her head from her basket and looked up at him, yellow-eyed, indignant at being disturbed.

'So what do you want to know? Everything I ever found out is in the report I filed with the IAG and that was nearly four years ago. I haven't dug up anything new since I was canned.'

'This is nothing to do with your report. That's all water under the bridge. But we've been informed that you were showing an interest today in that young woman who was burned to death at Peyton's Place bar in Reseda.'

Fidel Madrazo spoke with a slight lisp, but very precisely, as if he had learned all this off by heart.

'So what?' said Nemo. 'The owner asked me to check it out, that's all. I might have been canned, but that doesn't mean I stopped thinking like a professional detective.'

'It was a suicide. She poured gasoline all over herself and set herself alight.'

'Yes. That's what the coroner's office told Sergeant Weller at West Valley. But that's only their interim report and they won't know for sure until they've carried out a full post-mortem. Maybe the pathologist's report will confirm that she killed herself, and it wouldn't altogether surprise me if it does. But then, who knows?'

'It was a suicide.'

'You just said that. I heard you the first time.'

'I repeated myself because there was no criminal act committed here for you to look into. And what I'm saying to you is, forget about it. A young woman sadly decided for whatever reason to take her own life, period. No need for you to question it. No need for you to start investigating.'

Nemo looked at Fidel Madrazo narrowly. 'If you're so sure that there was no criminal act involved, then why have you come here tonight to tell me to back off? Is somebody getting antsy about this, for some reason?'

'It's the media, mostly. When we heard that you were showing an interest, we were worried that you might encourage them to start asking questions, and that might kick off a completely unfounded and unnecessary witch-hunt. We have enough public relations problems to deal with at the moment with that jogger getting himself shot at Nickerson Gardens.'

'When you say "*we* were worried", are you talking about Captain Burovnik?'

'Of course, yes, it was Captain Burovnik who assigned me to come here and talk to you.'

'As far as I'm concerned, Captain Burovnik can shove his assignment up his ass. I intend to continue looking into the circumstances of this young woman's death regardless of what he wants. Did he give you any instructions about what to say to me then?'

Fidel Madrazo stared at Nemo for a long time, repeatedly stroking his moustache as if he had only just discovered that he had grown it. Then he said, 'No. Not specifically. I just had to tell you to back off.'

'No warning? He didn't say "tell Frisby to back off, or else he'll regret it"?'

'You know Captain Burovnik better than I do.'

'Well, I'm not going to back off. I'm a private citizen now, and if your coming here tonight constitutes a threat, either direct or implied, then I can guarantee that all hell is going to be let loose. They haven't yet invented the fan that can cope with the shit that's going to hit it.'

'Listen,' said Fidel Madrazo, raising both hands defensively. 'I'm only the messenger.'

'I realise that. But since you're the messenger, that's the message you can take back to Captain Burovnik.'

'I don't want to stick my nose in, Mr Frisby, but are you sure that's a good idea? I'm thinking about your personal welfare, that's all.'

'I appreciate your concern, Fidel. And you can call me Nemo. I like to be on first-name terms with the people who try to intimidate me. Let me show you out.'

When Fidel Madrazo had left, Nemo returned to the living room, picked up his tray and sat back down on the couch.

'Your lasagne's gone cold now, I expect,' said Sherri. 'You want I should microwave it for you?'

'It's okay. I don't mind it cold. I eat pizza cold, don't I?'

'Please yourself,' she said, and switched the TV over to *The Living Room*.

Nemo glanced at her as if he were hoping that she had miraculously changed back to how she used to look, but then he turned away.

Over the past four years, his relationship with Sherri had gradually broken down to rubble and dust. He had first been attracted to her because she was tall, almost as tall as he was, with wavy brunette hair and feline eyes and a sensual pout that reminded him of Sophia Loren, as well as a deep cleavage and wide hips and a mesmerising way of swaying when she walked. She had been a make-up artist for Summit Entertainment, and since she had spent most of her days surrounded by preening actors and fussy directors, she had been excited by Nemo's bluntness, and his masculinity, and the genuine danger of his job.

In the five years they had been together before Nemo had been sacked from the force, their time spent as a married couple had been irregular and strictly limited. Nemo could be called out without warning at any time of the day or night. and because of that almost every moment had been unpredictable and passionate. Sherri had always been immaculately groomed, and she had kept herself fit with yoga and Pilates. If she had already gone to bed when he came back off a late shift, he would always find that she had left him a tasty salad or a meal that he could easily heat up, and a sexy note. And if she wasn't asleep by the time he came into the bedroom, she always used to greet him with kisses and a warm embrace. If he had to leave the house at 6:00 a.m. for an early turn, she would always make sure she set the alarm for 5:00 a.m. so that they had time to make love before he went.

It was only when he had started to spend all day at home that they began to discover how little they had in common.

Sherri was interested only in game shows and soaps and workout videos, and it became clear to Nemo when he started to talk about crime and politics that she wasn't even listening to him, let alone trying to understand what he was saying. And when they could have sex any time they wanted, she gradually seemed to lose interest in having it at all.

She had given up exercising and spending hours on her hair and her make-up, and now she spent almost all day sprawled on the couch in a hoodie and leggings, watching TV and snacking off jalapeño cheese curls. Her stomach was bloated and her face had swollen so that those feline eyes had almost been swallowed up.

'Who was that?' she asked him, without taking her eyes off the TV screen.

'You really want to know? An investigator from IAG.'

'That's internal affairs, isn't it? What did he want?'

'He was worried because of my interest in how that girl got herself burned alive at Peyton's Place.'

'I don't even know why you got yourself involved. You're not a cop any more.'

'I got involved because Johnny Cascarelli called me and asked me to get involved – not that I told the IAG guy that, it's none of his business. Johnny's concerned that it's going to put off his customers, and he's promised to make it worth my while. Besides, it's a very intriguing case. And, come on, Sherri, I'll never stop being a cop.'

'Nemo, you stopped being a cop when they threw you off the force. Which they wouldn't have done if you hadn't been acting like Saint Nemo the Holy.'

'Oh, I see. You don't believe in honesty and integrity and not taking bribes from mobsters?'

'I believe that when you marry somebody they should come first, before everything. You were so busy being holy you didn't think how you were going to take care of me if you didn't have a job, did you? Walmart don't accept haloes.'

Nemo stood up. 'Maybe they don't. But the way you look these days, darling, nobody would guess that you're going hungry.'

'Thanks for the compliment. But since I'm the one who pays for most of the food, I think I'm entitled to eat most of it, don't you?'

Nemo was about to shout back at her and tell her yet again how hard it was for a sacked police detective to find regular employment. Only a week after he had started a full-time job at a security company at LAX, they had found out about his dismissal from the LAPD and let him go. Since then, he had been Uber driving and carrying out some part-time investigations for a law firm in Glendale and anyone else who would hire him, but that was hardly enough to cover the mortgage.

He took a deep breath. Shouting at Sherri was always a waste of effort, and it would do nothing to reassemble the scattered bits and pieces of their marriage.

'I'm going out,' he told her.

'Suit yourself. Just don't wake me up if I'm asleep when you come back. And don't breathe your second-hand JD all over me. And, Nemo—'

For the first time, she turned to look at him. When she spoke, her voice was unexpectedly gentle, and her expression was more regretful than angry.

'What?' he asked her, with one hand on the door.

'Try to accept that it's over, your being a cop. Over and done with. Dead and buried. You'll never be happy until you do.'

Nemo thought of Trinity frowning at him and saying, '*I don't believe it was suicide. I don't believe it for one second.*'

He nodded and said, 'Okay, darling. Whatever. I won't be back late.'

6

As soon as Zuzana reached the top of the steps, John Dangerfield pushed away the two girls in their sparkly dresses and came up to slide his arm like a boa constrictor around her waist, as if he had every right to. He was at least ten inches taller than she was, and the possessive way he took hold of her made Zuzana feel like a child.

'Well now, you're a hottie-and-a-half. Where did the Priest have the celestial good fortune to stumble across you?'

'She waits table at The Orange Grove,' said Vincent, following close behind them as they walked in through the double doors.

'Beats McDonald's, I guess,' said John. 'But let me tell you this, sweet cheeks, your waitressing days are behind you now. Once the Priest has spotted you, it's all the way up to the stars. What's your name, honey?'

'Zuzana. That's with two zees. It's Czech. My friends call me Zuzka.'

'I prefer Zuzana. More poetic. What's your second name?'

'Pomahačová.'

'Jesus. We'll have to think of something that the dumb public can pronounce. How about Zuzana Zilka? What do you think, Priest? Sounds pretty seductive, don't you think, Zilka? Kind of slinky.'

With his arm still around her waist, John led Zuzana across the huge air-conditioned atrium. Its floor was tiled in shiny grey marble and its fluted pillars rose all the way up to a high glass dome in the ceiling. It was lit on all sides by gilded antique sconces, and between its three archways stood giant ceramic pots with frondy palms. From the archway directly ahead of them, Zuzana could hear muted modern jazz music and people laughing, and she could distinctly smell both expensive perfume and skunk.

'I must introduce you to Dave Magellan,' said John. 'He's right in the middle of casting for a new production right now. He'll salivate when he sees you.'

'Is Bill Keller here yet?' asked Vincent.

'He's coming later. From what he told me, he's had a hell of a day sorting out CDOs at Gilded Investments. Me – I wouldn't touch Gilded with a cattle-prodder. If you ask me, he'd get into less of a mess taking a jog across the La Brea tar pits.'

'Bill enjoys taking risks. Especially with other people's money.'

John ushered Zuzana into a large low-lit reception room. It was furnished with four immense couches and numerous antique armchairs and occasional tables. Over the marble fireplace a gilt-framed mirror reflected the twenty or thirty men and women who were gathered around the room, smoking and drinking wine and laughing. In the far corner, next to the open French doors, a trio of musicians in red silk shirts were playing piano, double bass and tenor sax.

Out in the garden, Zuzana could see the glitter of an

illuminated fountain playing in an ornamental pond, with the white marble figure of a woman standing in the middle of it, her arms outstretched.

'Glass of fizz?' John asked her.

'I don't drink alcohol, thanks. It always makes me go a little bit crazy.'

'Oh come on, tonight you can let things go to your head. You're allowed. There's nothing I'd like to see more than a bouncing Czech. Get it?'

Vincent slapped him on the shoulder and said, 'John – remind me not to arrange a booking for you at The Comedy Store.'

Zuzana was looking at the people all around her. At least three or four of the men she was sure she recognised from movies or TV. One man with long raggedy hair and tattoos was sitting on the arm of one of the couches as if he were riding a burro and ostentatiously blowing out smoke from a joint. When he turned in her direction, she saw that it was Dene Bravo from the Metalliks.

'Here,' said John, and he led her across to the side of the fireplace, where David Magellan was talking loudly to a small circle of Hollywood elite, four or five men and at least half a dozen young women. The men were all formally dressed in white tuxedos and black bow ties, but the young women were wearing some of the skimpiest outfits that Zuzana had ever seen. A slim blonde was standing next to David Magellan with her hand resting possessively on his shoulder and her pink shift was completely transparent, so that her nipples and her white thong were visible. A brunette was wearing skin-tight pink satin joggers with a deep cleft that left no doubt that she was wearing nothing underneath.

'David! I'd like you to encounter the stunning Zuzana!' John announced. 'The newest and freshest catch from the Priest – our angler *extraordinaire*.'

David Magellan smiled and lifted his flute of champagne. He was years older than he had appeared in the pictures of him that Zuzana had seen in *MovieMaker*. His thinning bleached hair floated over his scalp in a thin candyfloss cloud, his eyelids drooped and he had deeply engraved lines on each side of his jaw, so that he looked like a ventriloquist's dummy.

'Well, *you're* something and no mistake,' he greeted her. 'What did John say your name was? Joanna? I've been searching for babes who look exactly like you for my next picture. It's about the early days of a whorehouse in Nevada, if you have no objection to acting a little immoral.'

He reached forward and took hold of Zuzana's hand, drawing her into the circle, although the blonde didn't release her claw-like grip on his shoulder. Zuzana thought she recognised at least two of the men: the actor Steve Murdo and the daytime TV host Walt Kasabian. She didn't know who the others were, but they all looked tanned and wealthy and pleased with themselves.

'You done any acting before, Joanna?' David asked her, still holding on to her hand.

'It's Zuzana,' she corrected him. 'Zee-you-zee, a-n-a.'

'Zuzana Zilka,' put in John.

'That's cool. I like that,' said David. 'How old are you, Zuzana?'

'Nineteen. Nearly twenty.'

'Cool. You look much younger. Great from the picture's point of view, but we have to be legal.'

'I was in two plays in high school,' Zuzana told him. 'I was in *The Princess and the Pea* and *Alice in Wonderland*. I played Alice.'

'That's wonderful, darling,' grinned David, 'although I have to tell you that this movie is going to be a mite fruitier than either of those.' Then he let go of her hand and said, 'Here – look, the Priest's fetched a glass of champagne for you.'

'It's okay, thanks, I don't drink. A soda would be fine.'

'Aw, come on. We have something to celebrate, don't we? One glass won't do you any harm.'

Vincent handed Zuzana a tall flute of champagne and David raised his own glass. 'Here's to Zee-you-zee a-n-a, and a glittering career in the movies!'

All the others in David's circle raised their glasses, too. 'Here's to Zee-you-zee a-n-a!'

Zuzana was reluctant to drink any champagne at first, but Vincent was giving her a nudging 'go on' look as if to tell her that she would be showing a lack of appreciation to David if she didn't at least take a sip.

She took a small mouthful, swallowed it and coughed. She had drunk proper champagne only once before, at her cousin Barbara's wedding, but by comparison she thought this tasted slightly salty.

'We'll be filming mostly on location in Las Vegas,' David told her. 'The finance is all set up and we should get a green light by the first week in May. I'm just waiting to hear if Lola Simmons is going to be free by then.'

'Lola Simmons is going to be in it?'

'Lola Simmons and Jed Fortune. Plus a bevy of totally delicious young women, you included.'

'Hey – so long as I can have her when you've finished with her,' growled Walt Kasabian, nudging the man next to him.

'Now then, Walt, you're old enough to be her great-grandpa!'

Vincent was standing close behind Zuzana now. 'Come on, drink up,' he said quietly. 'This is supposed to be a party. You don't know how lucky you are. David hardly ever takes his girls on just like that, at the drop of a hat. He's the pickiest director in Hollywood, when it comes to casting. But I had a feeling in my water that he'd want to snap you up the second he saw you.'

Zuzana took another sip of champagne, and then another. 'Good girl,' said Vincent, and he beckoned the waiter who was serving out the wine.

'Won't I have to take a screen test?' Zuzana asked him, as the waiter topped up her glass.

'Oh sure, he'll arrange for screen tests and voice tests and make-up tests. That's all routine. But don't you worry, he wants you, no question about it.'

David was in the middle of telling a long and complicated story about a disastrous location shoot in Brazil. 'You think *Fitzcarraldo* was a nightmare?' One of his stunt drivers had accidentally backed a Rolls-Royce off a jetty into the Paranapanema River and it had toppled trunk-first over a waterfall. His set-builders had spent more than three million dollars constructing a replica of a whole street in São Paulo in the nineteenth century but two days later almost every facade had been blown flat by an unexpected hurricane.

Zuzana stayed close by his side, trying to follow all this, and smiling and laughing when she thought she ought to. She began to feel more and more relaxed, and increasingly confident, and she thought to herself, *these are all incredibly famous celebrities, but I really like them, and they really like me, and I'm so much enjoying this.*

After she had finished her second glass of champagne, though, she started to feel a little dizzy. The faces of the people around her began to swell up, like clowns' masks, and their laughter sounded strangely mocking and blurred. The floor tilted, and she had to take a step back and cling on to Vincent's arm to stop herself from falling over.

'Vincent, I need some fresh air,' she told him, and even her own voice sounded as if she were speaking in another room. 'I feel giddy. I knew I shouldn't have drunk that champagne.'

'Let's go out into the garden, then,' said Vincent, and he put his arm around her to keep her upright. Zuzana heard him say something to David before he guided her around the antique couches to the open French doors. She saw several of the guests staring at her – the men curiously, one eyebrow raised, the girls more sympathetically.

Once outside, Vincent led her across the patio and sat her down on a bench beside a fragrant bed of evening primrose. The jazz trio were taking a break and so the evening was quiet, punctuated only by an occasional burst of laughter from John Dangerfield's friends and the high-pitched whistling of a plane landing thirteen miles away at LAX.

'Maybe you should have eaten before you came out,' said Vincent. 'Do you want me to fetch you something now? They have tacos, and I think I saw some crab cakes and some partridgeberry crostini.'

Zuzana shook her head. Her ears were filled with a singing noise and the garden around her was becoming increasingly dark. She felt chilly, too, and she rubbed her bare arms to try to warm herself up. All she wanted to do was lie down and close her eyes for a while. There was more laughter, but it sounded very far away. She wondered if she could ask Vincent to take her home.

'You're sure?' she heard him saying. Then she was suddenly overwhelmed by stifling darkness, as if he had turned on his heel like a matador and thrown a huge black blanket over her.

When she opened her eyes, it was daylight, and she could smell aftershave. She lifted her head and saw that she was lying under the sheets of a California king-size bed, in a sunny, high-ceilinged bedroom, with Impressionist prints of nude women all around the walls.

Her skull ached as if she had tripped over and knocked it against a table, and she found it hard to focus. She started to lift back the sheets and it was then that she realised she was naked. She wrapped the sheet tightly under her arms and sat up. She had no idea where she was or what she was doing here.

It was then that she heard a toilet flush, and David Magellan walked into the bedroom, and he was naked, too. He had a shaggy blond chest and his hips and belly drooped as if he were wearing a lifebelt round his waist. His circumcised penis looked like a dried damson.

'Cool, you're awake!' he greeted her, lifting up the sheets and climbing into bed next to her. Immediately, she shifted herself away. 'Now we can have some real fun and games!'

'Where am I?' Zuzana asked him. 'What am I doing here? Where's my clothes?'

'Hey, hey, hey, no need to get yourself upset! This is one of the guest apartments in John Dangerfield's house. Your clothes are all in the dressing room next door. You're here because you're going to be starring in my next picture!'

He slapped the sheets and said, 'This is your classic casting couch, and I have to say that even when you were dead to the world you passed with flying colours! Now you can give me a repeat performance, and enjoy it yourself!'

Zuzana frowned at him. 'What are you talking about, repeat performance? You don't mean you—?'

Keeping the sheet tightly tucked under her left armpit, she reached down and felt between her legs. Her lips were slippery, and her bottom felt sore, too.

David humped himself up close to her. 'This is the way that girls get famous in the world of movies, darling. This is the way it's always been and this is the way it still is today, no matter what. That MeToo stuff, that's lip service, that's all. Most of the girls are just as happy about it as the guys, believe me. In fact, most of them are gagging for it. It's only when they start getting wrinkles that women begin bitching, especially when they start being passed over for parts in major movies. Either the wrinklies, or those cranky left-wing lesbians.'

Zuzana felt numb, as if she had been tasered. She found it almost impossible to believe that she was here, in this bed, naked, with David Magellan the movie director, and that he had both raped and sodomised her while she was unconscious. Yet here he was, smiling and talking to her about it as if it were utterly acceptable. More than that, he expected her to be pleased that he had done it – so much so that she would willingly let him do it again, so that she could relish it now that she was awake.

Despite her numbness, she couldn't take her eyes away from his. Underneath their hooded lids, they were shiny and silvery, like large steel ball bearings, and they had a fascinating depth to them, as if she could see right through them to the inside of his mind, or even further, to a sparkling interstellar world beyond his mind. She started to lift herself up on one elbow, but she still couldn't look away, and she stayed where she was.

He reached out and started to curl her hair gently around his index finger.

'Listen, Zee-you-zee. I know what you want out of your life, and what you deserve. You're a strong young woman, with character, with talent, and you're bright enough to know that this is the way that you're going to get it. What you don't want is that moronic punk that you've been living with.'

'Rod?'

'Is that his name? Rod? When the Priest fetched you back inside, I couldn't help but notice the bruise on your cheek, and he told me all about him. You don't want to be staying with a loser like that. The only reason he hits you is because he knows you're going places and he never will.'

Now David was stroking her cheek. Zuzana didn't find him at all attractive. In fact, she thought he was ugly, although not repulsively ugly, more like a pug dog. She continued to stare at him and she made no move to get out of bed. In the back of her mind, her instinct for self-preservation was jangling furiously, urging her to get up at once and go, but her body refused.

David might have raped her while she was unconscious, but she desperately wanted the new life that he could offer her – free from the long and tiring hours of waitressing, free from Rod and his relentless bullying, and mingling instead with movie stars and drinking champagne. More than anything else, though, the extraordinary power in David's eyes was completely transfixing her. It wasn't so much hypnotic as overwhelming, but overwhelming in a comforting way, as if she could forget about all of her own decisions and all of her own anxieties, because David would take care of everything for her now. He was a man, but it felt strangely like being cuddled by her mother when she was little.

David leaned forward and whispered in her ear, 'You know what? Everything's going to be fine and dandy for you from now on. Fine and dandy.'

He lifted back the sheets so that Zuzana was naked, and then, with a grunt, he heaved himself up onto his knees. Somewhere in the house, faintly, a radio was playing 'Man on the Moon'. Zuzana opened her legs.

7

By eleven o'clock, Trinity had the house to herself. She was cleaning the kitchen and listening to the TV news.

Her father had been picked up in a huge Dodge Ram by three of his old friends from his building union. He had told her that they would be spending the day angling for channel catfish at Reseda Park Lake, but he hadn't even made a point of taking his fishing rod with him.

She knew that in reality the four of them would be drinking their way through half a dozen six-packs of Budweiser and telling off-colour jokes and that they would be lucky to find their way home without being stopped by the cops.

Rosie had gone off in her shortest shorts to meet some of her girlfriends at La Michoacana ice-cream parlour on Sherman Way. Trinity had given her $10 left over from the money that Sabina had lent her so she could buy herself a blackberry cheese paleta and a Coke.

Like her father, Rosie hadn't told her the whole truth. Trinity was sure that Rosie would be meeting not only her girlfriends but a gang of boys who hung around the corner of Sherman Way and Baird Avenue. They called themselves the Toreros, but Trinity found it hard to imagine any collection of young men who looked less like bullfighters. She called them the Desaliñados, the Scruffies, which always made Rosie explode into one of her tirades.

'You don't even *know* them! They're totally dope! They're goat!'

As for Buddy, he had gone off to meet his pal José. What mischief he and José got up to together, Trinity could only guess, but somehow Buddy always seemed to have pocketfuls of loose change, so he hardly ever asked her for money.

Trinity was wiping the work surface under the window when she heard the news anchor mention Margo's name. She went through to the living room in time to hear the anchor saying, '—medical examiner confirmed this morning that Ms Shapiro took her own life by pouring gasoline over herself and setting herself alight. An inquest has been opened and adjourned but in the meantime the West Valley police are not looking for anybody else in connection with Ms Shapiro's death.'

'*What?*' said Trinity out loud, staring at the television. 'She *couldn't* have committed suicide! She wouldn't have done! And that man who came running out! What about him?'

She closed her eyes for a moment and she could picture Margo sitting in that restroom stall, her face shrivelling and crinkling and both hands held up as if she were begging. She could see Margo's green dress flaking and the flames leaping up around her like dancing ghosts.

And then she thought: *the flames were blue. Transparent, but definitely blue. Surely gasoline doesn't burn blue.*

She had watched her father burning cardboard boxes and garden rubbish in the back yard, and he had splashed gasoline onto the fire to get it going. He had almost set his dungarees alight, too. But the flames had been orange.

She picked up her old Dell laptop and sat down on the couch. First of all she checked on Google what colour gasoline burned. There was even a video of a man setting light to glass jars filled with six different types of fuel, from aviation fuel to diesel, and sure enough, gasoline burned orange.

So what was it that could have given off those ghostly blue flames? She watched three more videos and read two Wikipedia entries on combustion. By the time she had done that, she was convinced that Margo had been doused not in gasoline but in methanol, or what used to be called wood alcohol. Methanol was a highly flammable solvent, but it was used in the manufacture of scores of different everyday products, from plastics to antifreeze to headache pills. Because of that, she guessed it probably wasn't hard to get hold of it.

She phoned Nemo. He took a long time to answer, and when he did she could hear traffic noises in the background.

'Mr Frisby – Nemo. It's Trinity Fox.'

'Oh, sure. How's it going, Trinity? Feeling a tad better, I hope?'

'Well, not really. I just heard on the news about Margo's autopsy. The medical examiner confirmed that first report and said that it was suicide.'

'But you – you're still quite sure that it wasn't?'

'I saw her burning with my own eyes, Nemo, and the flames were blue. They said that she set fire to herself with gasoline, but gasoline doesn't burn blue. I've been checking and I'm practically one hundred per cent sure that she was splashed over with methanol. And that guy who came running out and nearly knocked me over, I'm still sure he did it.'

'Methanol? You're sure? I once had a case when a woman

in Winnetka treated her husband to a methanol cocktail. That stuff's not just flammable, it's toxic. It can blind you or kill you if you drink it. I never saw anybody die in such agony. And all the time his wife was laughing like a hyena.'

Nemo paused for a moment, and Trinity thought she heard him talking to someone else. But then he said, 'Believe me, Trinity, I've been thinking about your friend over and over, but you see the problem we have here? You saw those blue flames, but you were the only person who did, and the forensic guys claim they found a container at the scene that still had traces of gasoline inside it. So you can understand what conclusion the ME was most likely to come to. Between you and me, he always plumps for the most obvious answer. Makes his life less stressful.'

'But did they check that container for Margo's fingerprints and DNA? And they say they found a cigarette lighter on the floor too. Did they check that?'

'I have no idea. I can ask Sergeant Weller but I'm not sure he'll know and even if he knows I'm not sure he'll tell me, and I'll tell you for why. I had an unexpected visitor yesterday evening. After what he said to me, I'm pretty much persuaded that you're right, and that your friend did *not* take her own life.'

'A visitor? Who was it?'

'Some creepy minion from the IAG... that's the internal affairs department. And guess what? He told me in no uncertain terms that the powers that be in the police force want me to forget about what happened to your friend Margo. Can you believe that? Right now I'm out running a couple of errands but I was going to call you later to bring you up to speed.'

'They want you to forget about it? Why? I'd have thought they'd appreciate any help that you could give them.'

'Well, me too. But all they've managed to do is make me ask even more questions than I had to start with. If your friend really *did* commit suicide, why should it worry them? And what makes me even more suspicious is that they've given out the results of the autopsy so soon. Like, within less than forty-eight hours. Post-mortems take *days*, as a rule. Sometimes weeks, even, depending on how the deceased was discovered, and how long they'd been dead.

'Either your friend's body was examined by the fastest pathologist in the west, or else it hasn't been examined at all. I tried to call Jim Bryce about it. Twice I called him, but he never returned my call, which is not at all like him.'

Trinity said, 'I don't know what to do now. But she was one of my closest friends and if she's been murdered I want to find out why. I can't just let it go.'

'Okay. I'm with you. I'm filling up with gas right now and I have to pick up some groceries at the Valley Marketplace or else my wife will be giving me a methanol cocktail too. But if you're free I can come meet you afterwards.'

'Yes, come round. I'm here all day, on my own.'

'I'll tell you something, Trinity – when you suspect that somebody's trying to flimflam you and cover up the real cause of death, the way to find out what actually happened is to make out that you believe them. That way, you can almost always pick their story apart and without realising it they'll help you to do it. They won't be able to remember all the details they've made up, and there'll always be important things that they've forgotten to invent. The ME's saying she committed suicide? Okay – *why* did she commit

suicide? Nobody commits suicide for no reason. Was she depressed? Was she being trolled? Did she leave any kind of suicide note?'

'All she told me was that she was scared.'

'Do you know where she lived? Do you know her parents, or her relatives, or her neighbours?'

'Yes, I know her mom and dad. And her sister.'

'Right. That's where we start. I'll see you in about an hour. And Trinity?'

'What?'

'I have a motto, and maybe it'll be good for you too. When somebody's trying to deceive you, their choice of lies is even more illuminating than the truth. I can't remember who said that. Some thousand-year-old Buddhist swami, I expect. But it's always worked for me.'

When they drew up outside the Shapiro house on Valerio Street in Lake Balboa, they saw that a group of four or five people were just leaving, all of them looking solemn, and two of them wearing black armbands.

They waited until the group had climbed into their cars and driven off, and then they went up to the front door, which was still open. Margo's mother and her sister Amira were both in the hallway, holding hands and staring at each other as if neither of them could believe that they would never see Margo again.

'Mrs Shapiro?' said Trinity. 'Remember me? Trinity Fox, from high school.'

'Of course! My goodness! Trinity! Why, look at you! Haven't you grown your hair long!'

'Trinity!' said Amira. She came up and gave Trinity a hug. 'Margo was talking about you only last weekend!'

Mrs Shapiro was short and plump with tightly curled henna-red hair, but even if her face was chubby it was almost angelic, and it was easy to see why Margo had been so pretty. Amira was red-haired, too, although she was as skinny as Trinity, and she had inherited a longer and pointier nose. Both Mrs Shapiro and Amira were dressed in black, and Mrs Shapiro was wearing a chai pendant, the Hebrew symbol for life.

'This is my new friend, Nemo,' Trinity told them. 'He used to be a police detective. We met at Peyton's Place when Margo passed. Do you think we could talk to you about Margo? Nemo believes the same as me, that there was no way she took her own life.'

Mrs Shapiro said nothing at first, but slowly nodded, as if she were silently reciting a shiva to herself, such as *Krieh, Tearing the Cloth*, or *When All That's Left Is Love*. Then she beckoned Trinity and Nemo inside the house and led them into the living room. The straw-coloured blinds were drawn, so that the room was gloomy, and it smelled of saffron and sandalwood incense. Over the fireplace stood a cluster of framed photographs of the Shapiro family, with a large smiling picture of Margo in the centre – a colour still from her appearance in *Hilarity Jones*.

'The medical examiner says that Margo committed suicide,' said Trinity. 'But Margo called me just after three o'clock, and she told me that she was scared, and wanted to meet me at Peyton's Place. She said that she had never been so scared in her life. Those were her exact words.

'When I got there I found her in the restroom, and she was

burning. I'm sure that she had passed already, so I was too late to save her. But I'm sure she didn't commit suicide. Why would she do that before she had even told me why she was so frightened?'

Mrs Shapiro and Amira listened while Trinity described the blue flames and the man who had nearly pushed her over. Both of them had tears in their eyes and Mrs Shapiro had her hand clamped over her mouth to stop herself from sobbing.

Nemo then told them about his threatening visit from Fidel Madrazo, and his suspicions about the unusually short time it had taken for the county coroner to announce the result of Margo's autopsy.

He gave them a moment to wipe their eyes, and then he leaned forward and said, 'I know these are real personal questions, and believe me I feel for your grief, but it would help us a great deal if you could give us some idea of your daughter's state of mind recently. Was she depressed? Had something gone wrong with her career? Did she have boyfriend trouble? Why do you think she told Trinity here that she was scared? What do you think she was scared of?'

Amira said, 'It was that movie crowd she got mixed up with, I'm sure of it. She was so excited at first but then something went wrong. I don't exactly know what it was because she wouldn't talk to me about it. But over the past three or four weeks she lost all of her pizzazz and she started to look so sick and twitchy. I even began to wonder if they'd gotten her hooked on molly or something like that.'

'The last time Margo came here to visit I asked her what was troubling her,' said Mrs Shapiro. 'Like Amira said, her face was white like a sheet and she couldn't sit still for a minute. Up, down, up, down, and biting her nails. I asked her again and again, what's wrong, darling, what's wrong, but in the end she said that she couldn't tell me, because she was too ashamed.'

She wiped her eyes again, and gave a helpless shrug. 'I said, Margo, you're my daughter, whatever you've done I'll never be ashamed of you. I love you. God always forgives us.'

'This movie crowd, do you know who they were?' Trinity asked her.

'When she first got involved with them, she did mention some names,' said Amira. 'She could hardly believe that she was mixing with all those A-listers. I mean, she really believed that this was the beginning of her life as a movie star.'

'A-listers like who?' asked Nemo.

'Cy Gardner was one. Ray Baccini. Tony-Joe Spearman. I can't remember all of them. But they weren't all actors. Some of them were like directors or producers or famous billionaires. She told me that Mel Kaiser was there one night, you know the guy who founded Mogul. She said they all got together in this fabulous house in Bel Air.'

'And what were they doing? Socialising? Talking business? Watching movies?'

'She said it was like one big party, at least once a week, and sometimes it would last all weekend, from Friday evening to Sunday afternoon, with different people coming and going. She said there was live music and fantastic food. I mean, she really lit up when she was telling me about it. To begin with, anyway.'

'But it didn't last?'

'No. Usually we called or texted each other almost every single day, but then a whole two weeks went by and I didn't hear from her. I called her again and again but she didn't answer. I began to think that she was off on location somewhere and hadn't thought to tell me. When she did answer, she sounded tired and weird, but she wouldn't tell me what was wrong.'

'This house where she went to all these parties,' said Trinity. 'Did she tell you who owned it, or where it was?'

'I'm sure she did tell me, but I can't remember. It was somewhere in Bel Air, but I don't know who it belonged to.'

'That agent of hers, Andy Zimmer – *he* will know, won't he?' Mrs Shapiro put in. 'It must have been him who took her there.'

'Andy Zimmer – you don't know where we can contact him, do you?' asked Nemo.

Amira took out her phone. 'Here – this is his number. He's one of the partners at Lifetime Creatives. They're at 7966 Beverly Boulevard, one floor down from Quentin Tarantino.'

'Well, listen, this is my number,' said Nemo. 'If you can think of anything that might help us to find out what happened to your sister, don't hesitate to call me, any time at all. And I mean *any* detail, no matter how small, even if you don't think it's relevant. Any more names that you can remember from those parties. Even what they were eating and drinking and what movies they were talking about.'

Mrs Shapiro stood up. 'I thank you both from the bottom of my heart for coming, and for wanting to discover how our poor Margo really passed. As soon as I hear when the coroner will let us have her, I will be arranging the funeral, and of course you are both invited. It will be at the Hillside Memorial Park because that's where her late father and her grandparents are remembered.'

They all hugged, and then Trinity and Nemo left the house and went to sit in Nemo's car.

'You got the time to go see this Zimmer guy?' asked Nemo, holding up his phone.

Trinity nodded. 'You bet. I'm beginning to have some really strange thoughts about what happened to Margo. I promise you, Nemo – I'm going to find out what scared her so much if it kills me.'

Nemo had his finger poised over his phone. 'Let's hope and pray, shall we, that it doesn't come to that?'

The offices of Lifetime Creatives were in a square black glass-fronted building in Beverly Grove. They parked in front of La Coupo restaurant opposite and Nemo took hold of Trinity's elbow as they crossed the street.

She liked that. It made her feel protected. For some reason, she was tempted to ask him if he was carrying a gun underneath his worn-out grey leather jacket, but she decided not to. She didn't want him to think that she regarded him as a cop rather than a helpful friend. Anyway, she would probably find out sooner or later if he were armed, either if he told her or if he unzipped his jacket and she saw for herself.

In the shiny reception area of Lifetime Creatives, they were greeted by a middle-aged woman with a platinum Lady Gaga hairstyle, feathery false eyelashes, salmon-pink foundation and scarlet lip gloss. Her make-up was so thick she could almost have been wearing a mask.

'Mr Frisby? Ms Fox? Andy's expecting you... Please, follow me.'

They followed her undulating hips along the corridor until they reached a large chilly office, dominated by a massive black desk and a massive black leather chesterfield. The walls were covered with at least fifty black-and-white photographs of Lifetime Creatives' clients, all autographed 'to Andy'. Trinity recognised several of them, including Cy Gardner and Tony-Joe Spearman.

Sitting behind the desk was a small round-shouldered man with a fraying brown comb-over, his eyes bulbous behind a heavy-rimmed pair of spectacles. He stood up as Trinity and Nemo came in and held up his hand in a Vulcan salute.

'Hi,' he greeted them, in a voice that sounded as if he had a blocked nose. 'We don't shake these days. Not since Covid-19. Pity. You could tell volumes about somebody from their handshake. The mighty crusher or the floppy dishrag. The Masonic finger-twiddle. Or the flirty tickle on the palm.'

He came around his desk and said, 'Please, sit down. You've come about Margo. What a tragedy. Who would have thought that she would take her own life? Such a talent. Such a future ahead of her.'

Trinity sat down on one end of the chesterfield. Nemo remained standing, close behind her.

'I was Margo's best friend at high school,' said Trinity. 'She was always so positive, and so happy. I'm desperate to find out *why* she should have committed suicide, because I have absolutely no idea. Her mother and her sister have no idea either. I was wondering if you might know anything that could help us.'

Andy Zimmer raised both hands in the air. 'I swear to God, your guess is as good as mine. She'd just finished filming the final episode of *School's Out* and I was right in the middle of negotiating for her to have a speaking part in Leonardo DiCaprio's new picture.'

'We heard that she'd been to some parties lately,' said Nemo. He said it flatly, with no expression in his gravelly tone at all.

'Parties? Well, sure, we all go to parties. That's what Hollywood is all about – parties. That's where we network. That's where the wealthy people get to meet the creative people. And that's where the wealthy people and the creative people both get to meet the beautiful people. And that's where they can all get together and hopefully mix their wealth and their creativity and their beauty all together and turn them into multi-million-dollar movies.'

Andy Zimmer said those words as if he had recited them over and over for most of his life as an agent.

'There were some particular parties that Margo had been going to, in Bel Air,' said Trinity. 'The same house, over and over. That's what she told her sister, anyway.'

'Really? That's news to me.'

'She said that there were lots of A-listers there. Actors like Cy Gardner and Tony-Joe Spearman and Ray Baccini. And billionaires, like Mel Kaiser.'

'Really?'

Nemo pointed to the photographs on the wall. 'Cy Gardner and Tony-Joe Spearman, they're both clients of yours. Margo was your client. I find it hard to believe that they were all attending some A-listers' parties every week and that you weren't aware of it. I mean, you said that's what parties are for – networking – so why weren't *you* there? Always assuming that you weren't.'

Andy Zimmer took off his spectacles. 'I don't think I want to discuss this.'

'Why not, sir? Because you really know nothing about these parties, or because you do?'

'I don't want to discuss it because I don't see that it's any of your business.'

'Of course it's our business,' Trinity put in. 'Margo was my friend, and she called me only an hour before she died to say that she urgently needed to see me.'

'I'm saying nothing. Sorry. Whatever you're trying to find out, I don't want to get involved.'

'Don't you care about her at all? She was your client. You were supposed to be taking care of her career, and that meant her well-being, too – not only the parts that you could find her. She was only twenty-three years old!'

Andy Zimmer went back behind his desk and picked up his phone. 'I don't have anything more to say to you both. Sorry, but that's it. And I'm busy now. So if you don't mind leaving.'

Nemo said, 'You know damn well where these parties were being held, don't you? Why won't you tell us? Are *you* scared of something?'

'I've nothing more to say. Look, here's our receptionist. Please go.'

Trinity stood up and approached his desk, tossing back her hair as if she were ready for a fight, but Nemo laid his hand on her shoulder and shook his head as if to tell her that it was no use pressing him any further. The receptionist with the Lady Gaga hairstyle and the mask-like face was already waiting for them at the office door.

'Some agent you are, Mr Zimmer,' said Trinity, and then she and Nemo followed the receptionist out.

Back in Nemo's car, Trinity said, 'Why do you think he won't tell us?'

Nemo took out a packet of Think Gum and offered her some.

'No thanks,' she said. 'Caffeine makes me jumpy.'

'Well, sweetheart, he could have several reasons for not telling us. Maybe he's worried about the legal aspects of it. Margo's passed away, but he might still have a duty of client confidentiality. Or maybe he's under some kind of non-disclosure contract to the people who were holding those parties. I can tell you one thing, though – I'm damn sure he knows who was holding them and where they were being held. In fact, I'd bet money that he attended them himself.'

'If the only thing that he's frightened about is breaking a contract, surely he would have told us,' said Trinity. 'I got the feeling that he's much more scared than that. Come on, Nemo, Margo was murdered. There, I've said it. And if she was murdered by the people who were holding those parties, for whatever reason, I can totally understand why he's too chicken to say anything. I'll tell you how frightened he is. He's an agent. He's a professional schmoozer, and yet he knew that he was coming over like a rat.'

'You're right. He's a chicken *and* a rat, and if you ask me there's a bit of snake in there, too.'

Trinity paused and took a deep breath. 'We're just going to have to find out some other way where those parties were being held, aren't we?'

Nemo turned the key in the ignition. As he did so, though, there was a tap on his window. He looked up and saw Fidel Madrazo standing on the sidewalk beside them. He put down his window and said, 'What the two-toned tonkert are *you* doing here?'

'You've been in that building across the street there, Mr Frisby. You paid a visit to Andy Zimmer at Lifetime Creatives. You asked him questions about Margo Shapiro.'

'What does that have to do with you? And how the hell do you happen to know that? Have you been tracking my phone?'

'Mr Frisby – I gave you a specific request from the IAG not to pursue any investigation into the circumstances surrounding the death of Ms Shapiro.'

'And if you recall I reminded you that I'm not a cop any more. I'm a private citizen and if I want to ask questions about Margo Shapiro's suicide then there's nothing at all you can do to stop me.'

'Oh, no?'

Fidel Madrazo bent down closer so that he could speak into Nemo's left ear. The expression on his face no longer resembled that of the genial trumpet player in a mariachi band, but of a Mexican hitman from Los Ántrax. Flat, and utterly emotionless.

'There's nothing we can do to stop you?' he murmured, and Nemo could smell the garlic on his breath. 'How much you want to bet?'

8

When Zuzana opened her eyes again, she saw from the digital clock by the bedside that it was 4:17 in the afternoon. She was alone in bed, with the sheets all twisted around her like a monstrous white python that had been trying to suffocate her, but had been magically turned into percale cotton with an 800 thread count. There was nobody else in the bedroom, although she could hear music playing somewhere outside. She recognised the tune. Santana playing 'Smooth'.

She lifted herself up. Her head was banging and she felt bruised all over. She unwound the sheets and saw that the insides of her thighs were mottled with crimson blotches. She sat on the side of the bed for a few moments with her head bowed. She knew what she had allowed David Magellan to do to her. She could remember every gasp and every grunt. Yet she still found it hard to believe that it had actually been *her*, Zuzana, who had consented to it. It was like remembering a story that she had read, or a movie that she had seen. She had witnessed it, in graphic detail, right up to the final climax in her mouth, but she felt that it had happened to somebody else.

She stood up and made her way unsteadily around the bed to the bathroom. It was sunlit in there, with mirrors all around, and a white bath as deep as a canyon. On the shelves beside the basin stood bottles of Chanel and Hermès shower gel, and stacks of fluffy white towels. She stared at her multiple reflections and she still found it hard to believe that this bruised and naked young woman was really her.

She sat down on the toilet and she swallowed and swallowed as if she were going to cry, but somehow she couldn't. What was she going to do now? What if David Magellan had been serious about offering her a part in his movie, but expected to have sex with her whenever he felt like it?

She wouldn't have to go back to Rod and his beating and his constant belittling her. He had hit her so many times that she had lost count. She could give up those exhausting hours at The Orange Grove, with all those arrogant and groping customers. She might even become famous. From what she had seen about the #MeToo movement, some of the best-known female stars had allowed themselves to be sexually exploited to further their careers, and it was only later that they had protested about it.

She felt sore, though, and there was a bleachy taste in her mouth and she smelled of sweat and sex. She stood up and opened the shower door and stepped inside. The first blast of water was freezing, and she jumped back so hard that she slipped and fell onto her knees. She stayed there, like a religious penitent, while the water poured down onto her head, although gradually it began to warm up. *Oh God, please take care of me. Please find somebody to protect me. Whoever I am now, I don't want to be alone.*

She managed to climb back onto her feet and start to wash herself. Between her thighs she felt so sore that she sucked in her breath and said '*ow*'. She wondered if David had pushed something up inside her apart from himself. When she had finished, she stepped out and wrapped herself in one of the huge white towels, and stood in front of one of the mirrors.

'Zuzana Pomahačová,' she announced to her reflection. The girl in the mirror stared back at her as if she didn't quite believe her. If you're Zuzana Pomahačová, what are you doing in this shining white bathroom in this luxurious mansion in Bel Air, all bundled up in this thick white Turkish towel, feeling as if you've prostituted yourself?

She was still standing there when the bathroom door opened. She tugged the towel tighter and called out, 'Sorry! Excuse me! I'm not done yet!'

'Don't panic, sweet cheeks, it's only me,' said a slightly slurring voice, and John Dangerfield stepped into the bathroom. His long silvery-black hair was tied back in a ponytail, which made his face appear even more angular, and he was wearing a loose white silk shirt with billowy sleeves and tight black jeans. Zuzana thought that he looked like Captain Hook.

'I'm not done yet,' Zuzana repeated, much more defensively. 'I can be out in a minute.'

'Are you hungry?' John asked her. 'It's getting on for five o'clock but you've had nothing to eat yet.'

'I'm – I don't know. I've only just woken up and taken a shower.'

'Well, come on out and have a late, late breakfast. Do you like pancakes? How about eggs? My cook can knock you up eggs Benedict to die for. Well, maybe that's not the right way to describe them. But you'll love them, I swear.'

'Can I get dressed first? I'm not too sure where my clothes are.'

John looked behind the bathroom door. Two satin bath-robes were hanging there, one pale green and the other pale pink. He took down the pink one and handed it to her.

'There – we can worry about your clothes later.'

Zuzana stared at him, still keeping a tight grip on her towel.

'Go on, then,' he coaxed her. 'I'm not going to bite.'

She took the bathrobe with her left hand and turned around, so that she could slide into it without revealing too much. Without hesitation he stepped up to her and wrenched the towel off her back, so that it dropped onto the floor. He held onto her shoulders with both hands and nuzzled her neck with his abrasive chisel-shaped chin.

'You're a real babe, do you know that?' he whispered. 'I've had some lookers here lately, but you're right up there in the top five per cent. You have no idea how far you're going to go. You totally don't.'

Zuzana tilted her head away from him and dragged on the sleeves of the bathrobe. Once she had fastened the sash, though, John turned her around and kissed her on the forehead. He was so much taller than she was that all she could see were the wiry grey hairs sprouting out of his open shirt.

'Come on,' he said, coiling his arm around her waist. 'Let's go find those eggs. And maybe a mimosa to sluice them down with.'

'No, no. Straight orange juice for me. I'm no good with alcohol.'

'That's what I *like*, though, sweet cheeks! Girls who are no good with alcohol! Girls who can handle their drink – they're boring.'

John led her out of the bathroom, across the bedroom and

into a dressing room, where she could see her clothes draped across the back of an armchair, her panties and her bra lying on top of her skirt. He saw her looking at them and flapped his hand dismissively.

'Nah, you can get dressed later. It's so warm out there.'

'What about my phone? Where's my phone?'

'I don't know. I'll have to ask Flora, she's the maid. Anyhow, you don't need to call anybody right now, do you? Relax, have fun. Forget about the outside world.'

They went out through the dressing-room door and into the garden. The fountain was splashing and music was playing from the open French doors. At least six or seven middle-aged men were sitting at one end of a long marble-topped table, with cocktails and tapas, some of them smoking cigars. David Magellan was among them, sitting next to Vincent Priest, and they had their heads close together as if they were sharing some dark secret that was amusing them both.

Behind them, through the arches of a leafy pergola, Zuzana could see a patio surrounded by white jasmine flowers. Three girls in dark glasses were lying there on sunloungers, two of them topless and one of them completely naked.

At the far end of the patio stood a white single-storey building with a curved roof, like a Nissen hut made out of stone, except that it had no windows. Above its door, a symbol had been painted in reddish-brown – several concentric circles with spikes radiating out from their perimeter, like a childish illustration of the sun.

John lifted his hand in salute to the men sitting at the table, and they lifted their cigars in response. One of them howled like a coyote and the others all laughed.

'You motherfuckers! You're only jealous!' John called out.

Then he led Zuzana to a secluded corner of the garden on the opposite side of the fountain, where there were two more sunloungers and a low glass-topped table.

'We can have some privacy here. And those guys are only talking business. What do you fancy to eat?'

'Eggs Benedict sounded good. And juice. Or a Mountain Dew. Anything.'

A handsome young black man with a shiny bald head and a smart blue shirt appeared, and John gave him Zuzana's food order. 'And to drink... I'll take an old-fashioned myself, but fetch an orange juice for Ms Zilka here.'

'Yes, sir, Mr Dangerfield.'

'And, Bradley. An *innocent* orange juice.'

'Yes, sir, Mr Dangerfield.'

John and Zuzana sat together in silence for a while, with Zuzana uncomfortably looking around while John continued to stare at her.

'That statue...' she said. 'Is that anybody special?'

'It most certainly is. I was going to tell you about her. Her name's Auzar, A-U-Zee-A-R, and she was the demon goddess in my most successful production to date. Didn't you see *The Mother of All Evil*? It grossed twice as much in the USA as *Exorcist Two* – over ninety-three million dollars. I commissioned that statue by way of congratulating myself.'

'She's beautiful. Who played her in the movie?'

'Kristie Turner. And she was terrific. In fact, she was nominated for a Golden Globe. Kristie really got over what Auzar was all about. Not only her beauty, and her sensuality. Not only her evil, either. But her *power* – her female power. You know what I'm talking about? That sheer power that all women have, yet so many women never wake up to the fact that they have it.'

'I heard about the movie but I never saw it. My boyfriend doesn't like to go to the movies.'

'Oh *him*, right. Yes. The Priest told me all about your boyfriend. You should have used your inner power against him, the way Auzar used to. You would have had him down on his knees, sobbing like a baby and begging you to forgive him.'

'Was Auzar a real person?'

'Auzar? Yes, she was, even though not too many people think so, even today. You know what an ethnologist is?'

Zuzana shook her head.

'Oh, clearly you don't. They're like professors who study different societies and different cultures. And almost every ethnologist except for one famous one believed that Auzar was only a fictitious character out of Tongva mythology. Even the historians at the Smithsonian thought she wasn't real. You've heard of the Tongva?'

'No. Never.'

John took a pack of Turkish cigarettes out of his shirt pocket and lit one, blowing a stream of smoke up into the air.

'The Tongvas were the tribe who lived around here before the Spanish showed up. They fished, they hunted rabbits, they built incredible houses. They had their own language and their own stories and their own moral code. Then of course the Spanish arrived and in the name of Jesus they built their missions and imposed their Roman Catholic religion and generally fucked up thousands of years of American Indian culture.

'The story goes that Auzar was the wife of a chief called Tacu. She was no obedient wife, though. She was stronger than Tacu and any other man and she knew it. She practically ran the whole tribe. When she and Tacu had their first and only son, Quaoar, she taught *him* that power, and how to use it, and when Quaoar grew up and had his own son Weywot, he passed it on to him.

'The only problem was that Weywot turned out to be an unbelievable sadist. As a little boy, he ripped the shells off turtles and spread pitch on their backs and set fire to it. When he grew up, he used to beat the living crap out of anybody who mocked him or even disagreed with him – break all their fingers or even poke their eyes out with burnt sticks and blind them.

'After years of this shit, even his three sons decided they'd had enough of him, and they gave him this drink that was part datura and part poison. It drained him of all the power that he'd inherited from his grandmother Auzar, and that was the end of him. In the movie, anyhow.'

'And that was what your movie was about?'

John was still staring at Zuzana, not blinking, and as the sunlight began to steal into this secluded corner of the garden where they were sitting, she saw that his eyes had the same highly polished metallic gleam as David Magellan's. She felt her heart beating faster, and she wondered if she had the nerve to tell him that she wanted to go back inside and get dressed, and to forget about the eggs Benedict.

It was too late, though. A smiling Bradley appeared with a tray, covered with a pink linen cloth, which he set down on the glass-topped table beside her. The tray was set with a gilt-edged plate, on which were precisely placed two muffin halves topped with Canadian bacon and two perfectly poached eggs, glistening with hollandaise sauce.

Next to the plate was a tall crystal glass of orange juice, and John's old-fashioned in a lowball, tinkling with ice.

'There,' said John. 'Paradise on a plate. If I hadn't had the crab-stuffed zucchini for lunch, I'd be jealous. Enjoy.'

Zuzana sat up straighter and picked up her knife and fork. Her heart was beating so hard now that it hurt, and she didn't know how she was going to be able to put any of this food in her mouth, let alone swallow it.

John took a drag on his cigarette, swallowed some of his old-fashioned, and then blew more smoke out of the side of his mouth.

'That was the story that was told in the legend, yes, and that was pretty much the story we told in the movie. But the real story didn't end there. When his sons gave him the poison, Weywot went into a coma for a few days, but he didn't die. When he recovered, he went to his grandmother Auzar and promised that he would never act so cruel again if only she could give him his power back.'

'And did she?' asked Zuzana, with her knife still poised.

'She couldn't. She was too old by then. A woman can't pass on her power beyond the menopause. So Weywot went along to see a shaman he'd heard of. This shaman belonged to another tribe, the Chumash. His name was Taximo, the Eagle, and he had an incredible reputation for changing the weather and mending broken bones and all kinds of shit like that.

'Taximo told Weywot that there was a way in which he could get the power out of women, if he didn't mind some pretty dramatic surgery and a little hocus-pocus. Aren't you going to start eating?'

Zuzana cut into one of the poached eggs, and the yolk poured out. She dipped the tines of her fork into the yolk and sucked it. She could feel the yolk sticking to her tongue and thought that if she ate any more her mouth would be glued shut and she wouldn't be able to speak.

'Anyhow, Weywot agreed to the procedure, and it wasn't too long before he began to get his power back. He returned to the tribe, which must have scared the living crap out of his sons, who were sure he was dead. He took over again as chief, and to begin with he was fair and reasonable, and didn't snap anybody's fingers or poke out their eyes. But it didn't take long before he was back to his old ways again. Some elder criticised him for fishing for bluefin out of season and he took a knife and cut the guy's junk off, right in front of the whole tribe.

'This time his sons gave him a drink without the datura, just undiluted poison. And when he conked out they sewed up his body in a buffalo hide and they buried him. Hey – you're still not eating. Don't you want that?'

'Suddenly I'm not hungry. I'm sorry. I feel terrible wasting it, but I've totally lost my appetite.'

'Maybe I shouldn't have told you what Weywot got up to. Look – don't worry about the eggs. Drink your juice. At least you'll have had some vitamin C.'

Zuzana picked up the glass of orange juice and took three chilly swallows. It was sharp and refreshing, and it took away the taste of David Magellan completely.

John reached across and patted her shoulder. 'That's terrific. Now, why don't you relax for a while? I need to go over and talk to those reprobates over there about David's next production. You know what a reprobate is?'

'Is it something like an attorney?'

John let out a loud bray of laughter, like a donkey. 'It certainly is, sweet cheeks! It certainly is!'

Zuzana sat in the sun for a while, sipping her orange juice and wondering why John had told her that story about Auzar and Weywot. The way he had recounted it, leaning forward and never taking his eyes off her, he must have felt that it was important for her to know about it. But why?

She looked across at the white statue of Auzar in the fountain, her head thrown back, her arms spread wide, as if she were just about to launch herself into the air. Her eyes were closed and that gave her a look of utter confidence. Her expression reminded Zuzana of what John had said about Rod.

'*You should have used your inner power against him, the way Auzar used to. You would have had him down on his knees, sobbing like a baby and begging you to forgive him.*'

Did she really have some inner power that could have made Rod cry, and apologise, and stop hitting her? Did *all* women have that power? If they did, why did so few of them ever use it?

Half an hour passed. She could hear the men talking and laughing but she couldn't quite make out what they were saying. She began to feel drowsy and she lay back on the sunlounger and closed her eyes. If she had such strength somewhere within her, perhaps she could tell David Magellan that she didn't want to have sex with him again. But then she didn't want to spoil her chances of appearing in his new movie.

She thought she could hear birds flapping their wings, high

above her. She thought she could hear raccoons, rustling in the undergrowth all around her. She thought she could hear a drum beating, soft and slow, like a heartbeat, and somebody singing in a thin, plaintive wail.

Time passed. When she opened her eyes again the sky was dark, and the only illumination came from the flickering mock-torches around the garden. She looked up and saw that all the men who had been sitting together at the table were now standing around her, silently, some of them still holding drinks and two of them still smoking cigars. She reached down to make sure that her sash was tightly fastened, and to her horror she realised that she was naked. While she was sleeping, somebody must have come and surreptitiously eased off her bathrobe.

She quickly sat up, cupping her hands over her breasts and crossing her legs.

'What's happening? Where's my robe? Please! Can somebody find my robe?'

One or two of the men grunted in amusement, although none of them spoke. It was then that a tall figure appeared, pushing his way between them. It was a man, and he was naked, too, lean and hairy, with a slight pot belly.

Zuzana kicked against the sunlounger to push herself away from him. Not only was he naked, but he was wearing a huge black bucket-shaped mask, with outwardly slanting eyes, and two curled antennae, like some monstrous insect.

He climbed onto the end of the sunlounger and crouched there on all fours. She could hear him breathing inside his mask, a low lascivious rasping sound.

'Don't be afraid, sweet cheeks,' he said, in a muffled voice. 'This is all part of the game.'

'What are you *doing*?' Zuzana squeaked at him. 'Please! Can I have my robe back? You're scaring me!'

'You're a woman. You have the power. Why are you scared?'

Zuzana started to sob. 'I can't help it. You're scaring me. I just want to have my robe back.'

John crawled further up the sunlounger. Zuzana turned her head away but she felt his stiffened penis bobbing against the side of her shin.

'Come on, sweet cheeks! Open up! This is just the beginning! This is where you start to take over the world!'

He grasped her knees and slowly forced her legs apart. The men standing around them whooped and clapped and whistled.

'You want fame, you beautiful babe? You want fortune? You want people to remember you for ever?'

He pressed her back against the sunlounger with his bristly forearm across her chest, which made her feel as if she were choking. Then he pushed himself inside her, and it hurt, because she was dry.

'Don't you love me?' he said, inside his mask, his voice breathy and hollow. His antennae jiggled up and down as he forced himself further into her. 'Don't you even *like* me?'

Zuzana squeezed her eyes tight shut and whispered the words that her mother used to spit at her father, whenever they had a serious row.

'*Neexistuje žádné slovo, které by řeklo, jak moc tě nenávidím.*'

'There is no word to say how much I hate you.'

9

Before he drove her home, Nemo took Trinity to El Rancherito restaurant on Saticoy Street, which was only two blocks away from where she lived.

'Don't try to tell me you're not hungry,' he said, as he heaved himself out of the car. '*I'm* hungry. I had a pile of buckwheat pancakes for breakfast but for some reason I'm starving again. I'll tell you – if you served it up with some salsa I could eat the back leg off of a burro. I've been meaning to come back here for months but Mrs Frisby isn't too crazy about Mexican food.'

Even though it was the middle of the afternoon, the restaurant was crowded and noisy. They went up to the counter and Nemo asked for a pork chop and rice while Trinity chose the burrito vegetariano. Then they sat down at one of the narrow Formica-topped tables.

'You must let me pay for mine,' said Trinity. 'You can't keep on treating me.'

Nemo said, 'Forget it. Like I say, Mrs Frisby isn't too crazy about Mexican food but then she's not too crazy about Chinese food, either. Or Thai food, or Korean food, or Salvadorean food. In fact, she doesn't particularly like to eat out at any place at all these days so it's a rare pleasure for me to have a dining companion.'

They sipped their drinks in silence for a while. Trinity had a guava Jarritos with tinkling chunks of ice while Nemo had a sangria crammed with fruit.

'What do we do now?' Trinity asked him. 'I mean, it seems like they're actually keeping tabs on us, doesn't it, trying to make sure that we don't look into this any further.'

Nemo held up his phone. 'That Fidel character wouldn't admit it, but they've been tracking me, no question. In fact, they've probably been tracking me ever since I met you at Peyton's Place. And like you said, why would they be taking the trouble to do that if there wasn't something about your friend Margo's murder that they were anxious to keep a secret. I've tried to get in touch with Jim Bryce again, but he still hasn't come back to me. It wouldn't surprise me if the IAG have been leaning on him, too.

'The first thing I'm going to do is go to Walmart and buy myself a burner – that's a phone they can't trace. After that, we need to find out where in Bel Air these parties were being held. Okay – so her agent refused to give us any information about them, but if your Margo found them so exciting, I can't believe that she wouldn't have told her fellow actors about them, and maybe some of the other people she was working with. You know, like her make-up artist and the camera crew.'

'Yes, but do you think they'll tell *us*?'

'Hopefully at least one of them will. I think it's unlikely that every single one of them has been individually threatened to keep their mouths shut. So on Monday let's go to Mogul Studios and see if we can find any of the cast of *School's Out*, or anybody else who was friends with Margo.'

'What if we can't? Or what if the studio won't even let us in?'

'Oh, they'll let us in all right, don't you worry about that. But if we can't find any cast members or technicians at the studio, we'll just have to do the laborious job of finding out where they live and go round to knock on their doors. After what her sister told us, I'm convinced those parties hold the key to who killed Margo. If not, at least they'll give us a scent to go sniffing after. Frisby and Fox, the human bloodhounds.'

Their food arrived, and to Trinity's surprise, she was much hungrier than she had thought. They sat looking at each other with their mouths full, chewing and saying nothing, but sharing so much with their eyes. Although she had always felt capable of taking care of herself, she was hugely reassured by Nemo's presence, and most of all by his belief in her.

Trinity had almost finished her burrito when her phone rang. She answered it, but all she heard was a blurting noise and what sounded like somebody crumpling up a newspaper. She hung up but almost immediately her phone rang again. The voice she heard was squeaky and desperate.

'Trin? Trin? It's Buddy! We're in trouble, Trin – me and José! I need you to come and rescue us!'

'What kind of trouble? Where are you?'

'We got into a beef with the Bombers and they came after us. They said they was going to jook us.'

'Yes, but where are you?'

'We're hiding in a dumpster in back of the H.K. Valley Center. But the Bombers know we're around here somewhere and if they find us they're going to kill us.'

'All right, Buddy. Stay calm and stay quiet and stay out of sight. I'll come down there and fetch you right now.'

Trinity dropped her phone into her jacket pocket and shifted herself sideways on her seat.

'I have to go,' she said. 'Do you think you can give me a ride back to my house so that I can pick up my dad's car?'

'What's wrong?'

'It's my stupid brother. He says that he and his friend have gotten themselves into a fight with some other kids and these other kids are threatening to stab them. They've hidden themselves in a dumpster at the H.K. Valley Center.'

Nemo had been gnawing at his pork chop bone. He tossed it back onto the plate, wiped his hands on his napkin and said, 'Right. Let's go get them. You don't seriously think I'm going to let you go rescue them on your own, do you?'

They left El Rancherito and drove down to the H.K. Valley Center, which was only three minutes due south on a broad and almost empty White Oak Avenue. The wind was rising so that all the tall palm trees along the median strip were leaning to the east. Nemo steered in through the arch at the centre's entrance and circled around the parking lot.

Trinity caught sight of four or five Latino-looking teenagers with headscarves and purple sleeveless T-shirts gathered outside the Greenland Market.

'Look – I'll bet that's the tagging crew Buddy was talking about. The Bombers, he called them. And see – behind that truck – there's a dumpster.'

Nemo circled around again and parked alongside the high-sided green dumpster. They both climbed out of the car and Trinity shouted, 'Buddy! Are you there?'

Almost at once, Buddy and another boy in a baseball cap

appeared over the top of the dumpster. 'Here! We're here! But, like, *quick*! They're right over there!'

Buddy and his friend started to climb down the vertical side of the dumpster, but before they had reached the ground, the tagging crew caught sight of them. They started to run towards them across the parking lot, and Trinity could see the flash of a knife.

As the crew approached, Nemo stepped forward and raised one hand.

'Hey, now! Wait up a minute, *muchachos*. What do you think you're playing at?'

The tallest member of the crew said, 'Out of the way, old man. This ain't none of your business.' He was skinny, and handsome in a very Spanish way, with a narrow nose and heavily lidded eyes. Both of his arms were blue with tattoos and there was a symbol of an atomic bomb explosion on the front of his T-shirt. He was the one who was carrying the knife.

'Well, this *is* my business as it happens,' said Nemo. 'These are my friends, and it seems to me that you're causing them some alarm.'

'Y'all *deaf* or something?' the crew leader spat at him. 'I said, out of the way. And when I say out of the way, I mean out of the fucking way, unless you want your guts spread out all over the parking lot.'

The other four gang members laughed and snapped their fingers and did little shuffling dances in their Nikes to show their approval.

Nemo turned around to Trinity and Buddy and Buddy's friend, José.

'Trinity – you and the boys get into the car, okay? This won't take a moment.'

93

'*No!* You hold it right there!' snapped the crew leader, advancing towards Nemo with his knife held high. It was a zombie knife, at least ten inches long, with a curved and serrated blade. 'We got ourselves a score to settle with those two dudes. Capping our piece like that. Like, who the fuck give them the right?'

'You *muchachos* don't seem to know the law,' said Nemo, in his steady, grating voice. 'Under California Penal Code 594 PC, it's an offence to write, mark, etch, scratch, draw or paint on real or personal property any unauthorised inscription, word, figure, mark or design, using any kind of tool. That includes you. So if these two happened to paint over what you've painted, then all I have to say to you is – tough doo-doo.'

'Are you *serious*?' the crew leader retorted, in a thin scream. 'Are you fucking *serious*?'

'Totally. For repeat offences, you could find yourselves sentenced to a year in prison or a fifty-thousand-dollar fine.'

The crew leader approached Nemo even closer.

'You know what I'm going to do? I'm going to cut your fucking tongue right out of your fucking mouth so you can't never talk no more shit to me like that. Then I'm going to cut those kids' hands off, so they can't cap our pieces no more. Like, ever.'

'Oh, you think?' said Nemo.

'Watch me, old man. I've taken down more boofs like you than you could count.'

Nemo smiled and shook his head like a patient schoolteacher. 'You know what you need to survive on the street? You need acumen. I'll bet you don't even know what that means, acumen, but it means having good judgement and the ability to make snap decisions based on what you see and what you hear.'

'I see a stupid old man standing in my way and sticking his fucking nose in my business, that's what I see.'

'Yes, but what did you *hear*? You heard me reciting Penal Code 594 word for word, and how do you think I learned to do that? I used to be a cop, and like most ex-cops I still carry.'

With that, Nemo tugged down the zipper of his grey leather jacket, reached inside and took out an automatic pistol. He clicked off the safety catch and pointed it directly at the crew leader's face.

'Throw the knife over there,' he said, jerking his head to the left.

The crew leader stared at him, obviously torn between his fear of having a gun pulled on him and not wanting to look like a wuss in front of his crew.

'I said… throw the knife over there,' Nemo repeated.

'So what you going to do, old man?' the crew leader retorted, although his knees were jiggling nervously. 'Blow my head off? They send you to jail for more than a year if you do that, bro!'

Nemo gave that patient schoolteacher head-shake again. Then he marched three steps right up to the gang leader, still pointing his gun at his face. The gang leader started to back away, but Nemo stepped forward even faster and whacked his wrist with a left-handed karate chop, so that his knife clattered onto the ground. Then he seized the scruff of his T-shirt and pulled him around in a circle, slamming him with a dull boom up against the side of the dumpster.

He pressed the muzzle of his gun up underneath the gang leader's chin and said, 'I would be more than happy to blow your head off, you pathetic excuse for a momma's boy. Like I said, I'm an ex-cop, and even if I'm not in uniform any longer, I still know all the ways to justify using deadly force against an armed suspect, which in case you're not following what I'm saying, is *you*.'

The crew leader nodded furiously. Nemo heard the sound of pattering feet, and when he looked around, he saw that the rest of the crew were running away across the parking lot.

'Now get the hell out of here,' he said. 'And if I hear that you've been threatening my friends again, I will find you. Read my lips. I will find you and I will shove your cannon where you can only paint throw-ups if you're down on your hands and knees like a dog.'

Nemo lowered his gun and the crew leader backed away. As he passed his fallen zombie knife, he started to bend down to pick it up, but Nemo said, 'Don't even think about it, *pendejo*. Vamoose.'

IO

Once the crew leader was out of sight around the corner, Nemo scooped up the knife, slung it into the trunk of his car and then climbed into the driving seat.

Trinity said, 'Thank you, Nemo. That was amazing.'

Nemo twisted around in his seat to confront the two boys sitting in the back.

'So who do we have here? And what in the name of God have you been doing to rile up a bunch of no-goods like that?'

Trinity said, 'This is my brother Buddy and this is his friend José.'

José was a small, thin boy about the same age as Buddy, with straight black hair cut in a floppy bob and soulful brown eyes. He was wearing a grey T-shirt spattered with reddish-brown paint and cargo pants, and he had at least half a dozen friendship bracelets around his left wrist.

'We're the Kumuvit Kings,' Buddy announced proudly.

'Oh, you're a tagging crew of two? But how come you call yourselves Kumuvit? Did I get that right? Kumuvit? That's what the Indians used to call themselves, isn't it?'

'I am Gabrieleño,' said José, in little more than a whisper.

'And that's what we do,' put in Buddy. 'We go around painting pictures so that nobody can forget who the land really belongs to.'

'How do you paint?' said Nemo. 'You don't have any cannon with you.'

'The Bombers, they stole them from us,' said José. 'Five new cannons of PT.'

'And how could you two afford that?' asked Trinity. 'Buddy? You didn't shoplift them, did you?'

Buddy and José glanced at each other and Buddy shook his head fiercely.

Nemo started up the car's engine. 'Well, come on, why don't you show me and your sister what all this tiffle was about? Where's this piece that you've capped?'

'It's just across the street,' Buddy told him. 'On the wall by the side of that auto place.'

'It's a good thing for you two that I'm not still a serving officer. I would have to charge you with defacing a public building. As it is, I could still make a citizen's arrest.'

He drove across the street and parked outside Reseda Transmissions. They all left the car and walked down the alleyway, and there on the concrete wall was a massive painting of a woman's face, at least seven feet high and six feet wide, and still shining wet. She had long black hair and staring eyes and what looked like dangling white earrings. Beside her was a bird with a ghostly white face, its eyes closed as if it were asleep.

The woman's face had been sprayed on top of some other graffiti, most of which was now obscured, although Trinity could still see some black clouds and lightning flashes around the edges.

'This is quite a work of art,' said Nemo. 'How long did it take you?'

'More than an hour,' Buddy told him. 'Only two people come up and asked what we was doing, but we said we was allowed to, so they didn't stop us.'

'Who's she supposed to be? Looks like Oprah Winfrey if you ask me, before she lost weight.'

'It's *Toypurina*,' said José, and it was plain from his whispery tone that he was offended that Nemo hadn't recognised her.

'Oh, sure. Sorry. Yes. Good likeness.'

Trinity knew why José had responded so sharply. In recent years, Toypurina had at last been widely recognised as a great American Indian heroine. It was only two or three weeks ago that Trinity had watched part of a TV documentary about her, before her father had woken up from a drunken snooze and changed over to *Hollywood Game Night*.

In what she had managed to catch of the programme, Trinity had learned that Toypurina was a young Tongva medicine woman who had lived in the middle of the eighteenth century. She had led a revolt against the Spanish missionaries after they had banned all tribal rituals and sacred dancing.

It was said that Toypurina had intended to use her supernatural powers to immobilise the guards at the Spanish mission of San Gabriel, so that her fellow tribesmen could take it over and expel or kill the missionaries. Her plan had been foiled because one of the guards had overheard the Tongva discussing their attack the day before, and the missionaries had been tipped off. The Tongva were all captured, including Toypurina, and she had spent a year and a half in prison.

'So this is what you and José have been up to?' said Trinity.

She had to admit that although it was so crude and so childish, she found the painting strangely moving. She was even more moved that it was Buddy who had helped to paint it. Up until now, she had despaired of him, because he had seemed to be so aggressive and monosyllabic, and she had seen his life going nowhere at all.

'You've given her quite some look in her eye. But what about this bird? Is it asleep?'

'It's a Spook Owl,' said José. 'Toypurina carried it on her arm.' He crooked up his own elbow, like a falconer waiting for a hawk to fly down and settle on it. 'If anyone looks into the Spook Owl's eyes, they cannot move.'

'But you've painted it with its eyes closed.'

'Yes. Even if it's only a painting, if you look into its eyes, you cannot move.'

'I see. Okay. Now, do you need a ride home, José? Where do you live?'

'On Texhoma. Only two blocks. I can walk.'

'You're sure? Buddy – you're coming home with us.'

'What? No, Trin! I don't want to come home yet.'

Nemo laid a hand on his shoulder. 'If I were you, son, I wouldn't push my luck any further. Those Bombers could still be hanging around, looking to jump on you, and I don't want to have saved your ass for no purpose.'

'You're not my dad.'

'I know. And you can't even imagine how pleased I am about that. Now, get in the car.'

After Nemo had dropped them off at home, Trinity went into the living room to find her father deeply asleep on the couch.

He was snoring and there was a dark wet stain on the front of his pale green Bermuda shorts.

Buddy stamped off to his bedroom, slamming the door. He would probably spend the rest of the afternoon playing *Splatoon 2*, an online game with cartoon characters spraying brightly coloured paint all over each other. Trinity let him go. He would reappear when he started to grow hungry.

As she went through to the kitchen for a drink of water, she heard muffled crying from Rosie's bedroom. She stopped to listen for a moment, and then she knocked.

'Rosie? What's wrong? You're home early.'

'Go away,' Rosie sobbed.

Trinity opened the door. Rosie was curled up on her bed in a foetal position, her face buried in her pillow.

'Rosie – what's the matter?'

She sat down beside Rosie and gently wound her tangled hair around her finger.

'I thought you were out with Sally Marshall and all the rest of the girls. What happened?'

Rosie wiped the tears from her eyes with her fingertips. 'We were in the ice-cream parlour, Sally and me, waiting for everybody else to show.'

'Okay. But why are you so upset?'

'We were sitting by the window and these two guys were walking past outside and they noticed us. They came into the parlour and one of them came up to us and said to Sally that she was so pretty she could be in movies or TV. He gave her his business card and said he could pick her up tomorrow and take her to meet some big-time movie producers.'

'Really?'

Rosie nodded, her mouth puckered with misery.

'So why are you crying? You must be pleased for her, aren't you?'

'Yes – but Sally said to him, what about my friend here? She's pretty too. And the guy looked at me and said *her* – in the movies? Not a hope. She's pretty, yes – pretty damn plain.'

'Oh, Rosie, what a terrible thing for him to say! But you know it's not true. You're not plain at all, you're beautiful.'

'No, I'm not. I'm fat and I'm ugly and I'll never have a boyfriend.'

'Rosie, you're not fat and you're not ugly. You're clever and you're funny and someday soon you'll meet some really terrific boy and he'll fall head over heels in love with you. Who was this horrible shmuck anyway?'

'I don't know. He said he was some kind of movie consultant. Sally has his card, so she'll be able to tell you. I don't know what his name is but he had this big overweight guy with him and he called *him* SloMo.'

Trinity gave Rosie a hug and said, 'Come on. Don't be upset. The way girls get treated in the movie business, you've probably had the luckiest escape ever.'

When Nemo returned home, he found Sherri in the utility room, stuffing bedsheets into the tumble dryer. She was wearing a shiny leopard-print sports bra and leggings and she was clenching a curved piece of pizza crust between her teeth as if she needed it to stop herself from crying out loud at the tedium of her existence.

Nemo waited with his arms folded until she had switched on the tumble dryer and taken the pizza out of her mouth.

'Okay?' he asked her.

'Well, hello, stranger! Where have you been? Out Ubering, I hope, and making some money. I need to go to the market tomorrow. We've run out of almost everything.'

'I was helping out a friend, that's all.'

'What friend? It wasn't anything to do with this girl who set herself on fire, was it? I would have thought you'd have the common sense to keep well clear of that.'

'It was just a young woman I met. Her kid brother got involved in some street fight with a tagging crew.'

'Oh, yes?' said Sherri, walking through to the living room with her leopard-print buttocks wobbling. 'And what's her name, this young woman?'

'Trinity. Or Trin. She was a friend of the girl who died, that's how I met her.'

Sherri sat down on the couch, picked up the remote control and switched on the television.

'Is she good-looking?'

'Sherri, for Christ's sake, she's about half my age.'

'I never knew *that* to put a man off.'

Nemo was about to reply, but realised that whatever he said and however he said it, he would sound as if he were trying to justify himself.

'I'm going out in the yard,' he told Sherri. 'I need to finish wiring up that fence.'

'What do you want to eat tonight?'

'Nothing. We had lunch at El Rancherito.'

'We? You mean you and Trinity? Or *Trin*? That sounds cosy.'

Nemo was sorely tempted to tell Sherri that she was deliberately being unpleasant, just for the sake of provoking him, when his phone warbled. He took it out into the hallway and said, 'Yes? Hallo? Nemo Frisby.'

'Mr Frisby? This is Amira, Margo Shapiro's sister.'

'Yes, of course. How are you?'

'You said that if we remembered anything that Margo told us about those parties, you'd like us to call you, even if we didn't think that it was important. I don't know if it'll help at all, but I suddenly remembered her talking about a statue.'

'A statue? You mean, at the house where these parties were being held?'

'That's right. She said it was a beautiful statue of a woman, in a fountain.'

'Did she know who this woman was supposed to be?'

'I think she mentioned the name but for the life of me I can't remember it. But she said the man who owned the house had ordered her statue to be made specially, because she was the heroine of his most successful movie.'

'Really? But Margo didn't tell you what movie it was?'

'No, she didn't. But she asked him if he'd have a statue made of *her*, when she starred in one of his movies. And she said that she was only half teasing him.'

'Amira, this could be incredibly helpful. There can't be too many sculptors around LA who can knock up a statue to order. And it wouldn't surprise me if it was mentioned in the media when he had it made. Maybe in *Variety* or *Hollywood Life* or *TMZ*. This could be exactly the lead that we've been looking for. Thanks. I'll get back to you and let you know what we find out. And if you can remember anything more – please call me whenever.'

He rang off, and then he called Trinity. She took a long time to answer, and when she did she sounded distracted.

'Trinity?' he said, and as he did so he turned around and there was Sherri, standing in the living-room doorway.

'*Trinity*,' she repeated, with utter disdain, and closed the door.

11

Zuzana was woken by a high-pitched, quavering scream. It went on and on, higher and higher, more and more distressed, and at first she thought it must be a coyote howling. When it abruptly died away, though, she heard men laughing, and then music starting to play. It sounded like the same trio of jazz musicians who had been performing yesterday evening.

She sat up and looked around her. She was in a large bedroom with four single beds in it, but apart from a small dressing table with a mirror and a stool, that was the only furniture. There were no bedside lamps and the domed ceiling light was switched off, but the purple hessian curtains were open, so that the room was illuminated by the flickering torches from the garden below.

She was wrapped up in the same pink bathrobe that John Dangerfield had handed to her, although she was still naked underneath. She sniffed her right armpit. She smelled of stale perspiration and musky perfume, and something else, too. A sour, brown odour, like cigar smoke, or even faeces. Her hair was lank and greasy and when she ran her fingers through it, she found that in places it was stuck together.

Her head was throbbing and she felt bruised all over, as if she had fallen down two flights of stairs, one after the other.

She managed to stand, but as soon as she straightened up she was stabbed by an excruciating pain in the small of her back, and she had to stand still for a few moments with her hands on her hips, breathing deeply to try and suppress it.

She had no recollection of how she had found her way into this bedroom. The last thing she could remember was John forcing himself into her, with his huge papier-mâché insect mask knocking repeatedly against her forehead, and the hollow sound of him panting inside it. While he was still on top of her she must have lost consciousness, and even now she still felt giddy and unbalanced and strangely remote, as if she weren't really here at all, but only seeing this bedroom with a virtual reality headset.

She heard another shrill scream, and this time it sounded much more human. After it died away, she heard the men laughing again. She made her way unsteadily to the window, almost losing her balance, and looked down. On the opposite side of the garden she could see the white statue of Auzar, in her sparkling fountain. Directly below her, John's guests were gathered around a long table – at least a dozen men in tuxedos of various colours, ranging from scarlet to lemon yellow. Each man was accompanied by one or more girls, some of the girls sitting on their laps, all of them dressed in clinging bodysuits or scanty dresses or the shortest of shorts.

The men were drinking and smoking and even though the bedroom window was closed, Zuzana could smell skunk fumes.

She was still looking out of the window when the bedroom door opened and Vincent Priest walked in, with SloMo close behind him. Vincent was wearing a pink tuxedo that did nothing to lessen his resemblance to a Mafia *consigliere*, but a *consigliere* who was deliberately challenging people to suggest that he was gay.

'Hey, you're awake. I just came to check up on you. How's it going? You been having a good time?'

'I don't feel too good,' said Zuzana, pulling the lapels of her bathrobe tightly together, right up to her neck. 'I'd like to get dressed and go home now.'

'What? Back to that piece of shit who hits you? Come on, it's still party time, and we're still discussing the casting for David's new picture. I was talking to him about you earlier, and it's almost ninety-nine per cent certain that he wants you for the part of a high-class young hooker. You don't have any objection to playing a hooker, do you?'

'To be honest with you, Vincent, all I want to do right now is get dressed and go back home. I feel really sick and my head's thumping. Please.'

Vincent came up to her and put his arm around her shoulders. She noticed some tiny brown spatters on the front of his tuxedo, which resembled bedbug droppings, and he had an oddly stale smell about him, like the inside of an old wooden wardrobe.

'I don't think you understand, darling. If you leave now, that will totally screw any hope you might have of being cast for David's movie. And there's two other directors here who've noticed you and asked me about you. Ray Whitton, who created the *Midnight* series, and Mike Pacholski. Yes – *the* Mike Pacholski. You must have seen *Forgotten Moon* – it got three Oscar nominations. Chances like this, they come up only once in a lifetime – if ever. There's so many girls who would *kill* to be you right now, right here, standing where you are, with such a golden future right within your reach.'

Zuzana lifted his arm away from her shoulders and sat down on the end of the nearest bed.

'You didn't warn me what they were going to do to me. David – he really hurt me. And John, he practically raped me, in front of all those other men.'

Vincent sat down next to her, while SloMo went over and opened one of the windows.

'It's always give and take in the movie business, darling,' said Vincent. 'These guys, they have power, they have influence, they have money. They have creative genius – at least some of them do. I mean, look at Harvey Weinstein. Nobody could say that he was a sex god, but he made some amazing pictures.

'These guys can make you famous and rich. But like I say, it's give and take. They want something in return. You can't finance their next picture, so how can you pay them? You can pay them with your beauty. You can pay them with your youthfulness. And those are the greatest currencies ever. No matter how many times you use them to pay those guys off – think about it – you still got them, don't you? So this evening you're feeling a little sore? Tomorrow you'll be right as rain. But David and John, they'll both still owe you.'

The smell of skunk and cigar smoke was billowing in through the open window and SloMo was having a shouted conversation with one of the men at the table below.

'Yeah, she's here! She's fine! We'll fetch her down to join you in a minute!'

'Please, Vincent, all I want to do is go home.'

Vincent laid his hand on her thigh. 'Zuzana, baby, I've done you a humongous favour bringing you here. I don't give this kind of treatment to every pretty girl I meet in LA, believe you me. How do you think I'm going to look in front of all these producers and directors and A-list talent if you walk out on me? I'll look like a total putz. Here's Vincent Priest, the most revered talent scout in the whole of Hollywood, and some waitress from The Orange Grove gives him the finger.

'I mean, *The Orange Grove*? It's not even like you were waiting table at Providence.'

Zuzana felt swimmy again. She dropped back on the bed and stared at the ceiling.

'Come on, darling,' said Vincent, stroking her thigh inside her bathrobe. 'All you have to do is sit around and smile and maybe dance with one or two guys. I know you're feeling a little blitzed right now, but once you get down there and start chatting, you'll feel fine. And when you *do* go home, you'll be able to tell all your friends that you've been cast in a movie.'

'I heard somebody screaming,' said Zuzana. 'Who was that? It sounded like a woman.'

'Oh, you heard that? Yes, she was screaming her head off, wasn't she? She was doing a sound test. David's thinking of casting her as a hooker who gets murdered by one of her johns.'

'She sounded like she was really in pain.'

'She's a terrific actress – terrific. She's been in two or three slasher movies already. That's one of the reasons I brought her here. It's a whole lot harder than you think, screaming. I mean, everybody can scream, but not everybody can scream like they're genuinely scared.'

'You want to bet?' said SloMo. 'I was woken up by this massive spider a couple of nights ago, crawling across my pillow. You should have heard *me* scream!'

Vincent took hold of Zuzana's hands and pulled her upright. 'Come on, Zuzana, let's go. I promise you, once you're back in the swing of it, you'll have a great time.'

'I won't have to do it with any more men?'

Vincent said nothing, but gave her a smile, and a wink, and kissed her on the forehead.

For Zuzana, the rest of the evening went past like a nauseating ride on a fairground carousel. She felt as if she were going endlessly round and round, half-deafened by laughter and discordant music. The men tugged her from one side of the table to the other, sliding their hands up inside her bathrobe and nuzzling at her with wet lips and breath that stank of alcohol and garlic.

John ordered her an 'innocent' orange juice, but when nobody was looking she leaned sideways out of her chair and poured it into a terracotta pot full of purple freesias.

As the hours went by, the men began to leave. Some of them took one or two girls with them. Most of them were too drunk or too stoned and their chauffeurs came into the garden to help them stumble back through the house to their waiting limousines. Zuzana ended up sitting alone at the end of the table, still woozy and unfocused. Her tongue was so dry she felt as if she had been trying to eat spoonfuls of sand.

Vincent came up to her, rattling the ice in a glass of bourbon. 'Good girl, Zuzana Zilka. You were stunning with a capital S. David adores you and he'll cast you for sure. Let me give you a hand to get back upstairs so that you can catch a few more zees.'

'What time is it?'

Vincent looked at his gold Omega watch. 'Five after two. I'll take you home in the morning, after breakfast. John always serves up an amazing breakfast, I promise you. You like waffles?'

He knocked back his drink, and then he put his arm around her and helped her to stand up. She tripped on the steps that led back into the house, but he caught her, and held her steady for a moment. As they crossed the atrium, Zuzana saw John standing beside one of the pillars, his arms folded, watching them. His expression unsettled her so much she had to look at him twice. His eyebrows were arched upward, his ball-bearing eyes were shining, and his teeth were bared in a gleeful grin. He could have been trying to imitate The Joker. Zuzana thought it was strange that he and Vincent didn't acknowledge each other. They could have been following the well-rehearsed directions in a film script. INT. ATRIUM. NIGHT. VINCENT GUIDES ZUZANA TO THE STAIRCASE.

When they reached the bedroom, they found that two other girls were already asleep there. Vincent raised his fingertip to his lips and whispered, 'Pleasant dreams, darling. You're on your way to stardom.'

He stayed by the door while she climbed into bed, and then he quietly closed it after him, like a father who has just said goodnight to his daughter.

12

Zuzana lay awake for nearly an hour, listening to the two other girls breathing. One of them started murmuring, as if she were having a dream, and then suddenly said, '*Not that! No! You can't do that!*' She said it so loudly that Zuzana was surprised she didn't wake up.

Eventually, Zuzana lifted her head off the pillow. The house was silent now, except for a clock somewhere downstairs chiming a quarter past four. She eased herself off her bed and went to the door and opened it. One of the sconces around the atrium must have been left on, because light was shining up the staircase, but the upstairs corridor was in darkness, and all the bedroom doors were closed.

She tiptoed along to the top of the staircase and looked down into the atrium. There was nobody there, and so she made her way gingerly down the stairs, stopping every now and again to listen. She prayed that the doors to the garden wouldn't be locked, and that she would be able to cross over to the dressing room next to David Magellan's bedroom and retrieve her clothes.

She had almost reached the bottom stair when she heard the sound of a door opening, and voices, and then a persistent squeaking noise. The voices and the squeaking were coming in her direction, and so she danced quickly across the atrium and hid herself behind the same pillar where John had been standing.

Bradley appeared, no longer wearing his smart blue shirt but a black Lakers hoodie and sweatpants. With his left hand he was guiding a gurney, which was being pushed from behind by SloMo. The gurney was covered with a white sheet, which had several light sepia blotches on it, like dried bloodstains. It was one of the gurney's wheels that was squeaking.

'Did you see that Lou Noveno?' said Bradley. 'Got so shit-faced he fell in the fountain.'

'Pity he didn't drown,' said SloMo. 'If they gave Oscars for acting like an asshole he'd win one every year.'

They pushed the gurney across the atrium towards the archway on the opposite side. As they passed by the pillar where Zuzana was hiding herself, she could see that a hand was dangling down from underneath the sheet. It looked like the hand of a woman of colour, with pink-painted fingernails.

Bradley and SloMo disappeared through the archway and Zuzana heard another door opening. There was a pause of nearly a minute, and then she heard the door close and Bradley and SloMo came back out.

'Right,' said Bradley. 'I need to crash. You going to be back here sometime tomorrow?'

'Yeah, most likely. The Priest is still warming up that blonde babe from The Orange Grove.'

'Hey – she's *cute*, that one! Seems a real shame, don't it, pulling in a sexy honey like that? Why can't they just use scuzzy old hoes? It wouldn't make no difference, would it?'

They continued to talk as they walked back towards the

reception room, but Zuzana could no longer make out what they were saying.

She heard a door slam but she stayed hidden behind the pillar for another three or four minutes. She would have to go through the reception room and past the music stage to reach the French doors that led out to the garden. There was probably another way to reach the dressing room without having to go outside, but she didn't want to risk becoming lost inside this house.

She was desperate to get away, but at the same time she couldn't help wondering about the gurney that Bradley and SloMo had been pushing. Was it really a woman's hand that she had seen dangling from underneath the sheet? And why had they been pushing it through the house in the small hours of the morning?

She had a cold feeling in her stomach that there was some connection between the gurney and what SloMo had said about 'warming her up'. Because why did Bradley think it was such a shame that they had 'pulled her in'?

When she was sure that the house was completely silent again, Zuzana came out from behind the pillar and crossed the atrium to the arch where they had pushed the gurney. Behind the arch there was a short corridor with wooden panelling on either side, and a dark oak door at the end of it.

She went up to the door and pressed her ear against it. There was no sound coming from inside, so she carefully pushed down the curved brass handle. To her surprise, the door wasn't locked, and it opened. Immediately, she felt a chilly draught flowing from the other side, as if she had opened a fridge, and the draught had a dry, aromatic smell to it, too, like cinnamon.

Inside the room it was totally black, and she almost lost her nerve. But when she pushed the door open a little wider, she could see by the light from the atrium behind her that the gurney had been parked up against the wall on the left-hand side. The hand was still hanging down from underneath the sheet.

She opened the door wider still and took one step inside the room. It was numbingly cold in there, so that when she exhaled her breath came out of her mouth as if she were smoking. When she took a step further, she saw that there were three other gurneys lined up on the opposite side, all of them draped with white sheets. The smell of cinnamon was almost choking and there was a sweet sulphuric smell, too, like blackstrap molasses.

'*Oh my God,*' she whispered. '*Oh my God, oh my dear God.*'

The cold was so intense that she started to shiver, but she crept slowly up to the gurney until she was close enough to touch it.

She wasn't at all sure why she was doing this, yet she couldn't remember the last time she had felt such an overwhelming compulsion to find out what was happening in her life. The inside of her mind still felt like a smashed-up kaleidoscope, but she accepted that she had been taken in by Vincent's offer of glamour and fame, and that she had given in to temptation. She wasn't naïve. She had waited table at The Orange Grove long enough to know that men routinely demanded sex in exchange for favours – especially the kind of men who were gathered here at John Dangerfield's house. She was quite aware that they had spiked her drinks, and why. But even for the hedonistic world of Hollywood, the way that she was being treated seemed more than strange. She felt horribly out of her depth, as if she were drowning in a swimming pool, and all these men were standing around watching her, enjoying her frantic struggling, and laughing.

Why had John insisted on having sex with her while wearing that huge papier-mâché insect mask, especially in front of all those other men? And that girl screaming – had she honestly been having an audition for David Magellan's new picture? To Zuzana, she had sounded as if she were suffering real and unbearable pain.

She urgently wanted to escape from this house, although she knew that could be throwing away a one-in-a-million chance of a glittering career in the movies. Maybe Vincent had genuinely brought her here to see if David Magellan would cast her, and maybe she was only being used in the way that so many would-be actresses were used. But if he had brought her here for some other reason, she needed to know what it was.

She took hold of the edge of the sheet that was draped over the gurney, gripping it tightly in her fist. She was shivering so much now that she couldn't stop her teeth from chattering.

Oh God, oh God, oh God.

She lifted the sheet and folded it over to one side. At first she couldn't understand what was lying there, especially since the light was so dim, and she was quaking so much. But gradually she saw that it was the outline of a naked woman. She was African American, life-size, but almost completely flat, as if she had been cut out of a sheet of thick brown rubber.

Zuzana stared at this figure for a long time, trying to make sense of what she was looking at. Was this a real woman or simply a representation of a woman? How could she be a real woman when she was utterly one-dimensional? Yet it looked as if her hair was real hair, all pinned up into wiry black halo braids, and when Zuzana reached out with her fingertips and cautiously touched her thigh, her skin felt slightly coarse, like real skin.

She appeared to have no skeleton. Without a skull, her face was distorted into a twisted grimace, like a crumpled-up Hallowe'en mask. Her eyelids were open but her eye sockets were hollow. Without a ribcage, her breasts lay as empty as two plastic bags. She had no pelvis, so her stomach was wrinkled, and her legs resembled dark brown leggings with nobody in them.

Zuzana slowly drew back the sheet to cover her up again – if it was a *her*, and not some weird surrealist work of art. But if she wasn't the remains of a real person, why had she been wheeled into this room on a gurney, and why was this room refrigerated, and why did it smell so strongly of cinnamon? Bezo, the head chef at The Orange Grove, had once told her that cinnamon was one of the spices used by the Ancient Egyptians to mummify their dead.

Chilled, bewildered, she turned around to leave, but then she jumped in shock. John Dangerfield was standing in the doorway, his arms folded, not grinning like The Joker now, but frowning in anger.

'What the *hell* do you think you're doing in here?' he demanded. His voice was thick from a night of smoking and drinking.

'Nothing. I saw Bradley and SloMo pushing a gurney in here and I wondered what was on it.'

'Oh, really? Oh, *really*? Why were you down here anyhow? You're supposed to be upstairs, getting yourself some rest for the morning. You don't want to be looking like some worn-out hag tomorrow, do you?'

'I couldn't sleep. I was looking for a bathroom, that's all.'

'And you saw Bradley and SloMo pushing a gurney and you decided you had some divine right to find out what was on it?'

Zuzana shrugged, and looked down to the floor, but said nothing.

'But now you know what was on it?'

'Yes, but I – no. I don't know. I don't understand what it is.'

'You're not ready to understand what it is, that's the simple answer.'

'Please… all I want to do is find my clothes and go home.'

'Are you serious?'

'I don't want to stay here any longer. I want to go home. I can pay for a Yellow Cab.'

'You have to be joking. You think that I can allow you to go home, after seeing what you've just seen? You're not done here yet, darling, I can promise you that. Not by a long shot.'

'You can't keep me here. I need to go home. My boyfriend's going to be wondering what's happened to me and I'm supposed to be working at The Orange Grove this evening. They're going to start asking where I am.'

'Maybe you should have thought of that before you let your curiosity get the better of you,' John Dangerfield retorted. He was still seething with suppressed anger. 'In a house like this, darling, everything has to run like clockwork. Everything has to be strictly, *strictly* organised – or it's supposed to be, anyhow. Everything has to be timed right down to the nano-second.'

'Well, if I've upset you, I'm sorry.'

She could have added, *that was nothing compared to what you and David Magellan did to me*, but she was desperate to escape from this house and if it meant apologising then she would apologise. If he had said to her, *you have to let me fuck you, right here and now, as the price of getting away from here*, she would have done.

John laid his hand on her shoulder and began to propel her firmly towards the staircase.

'Listen – it's twenty after three. Go back upstairs and get yourself some more sleep. We can sort this out in the morning. You can have a room to yourself, so that you don't disturb the other girls.'

'Why can't I just get dressed and go now?'

'Because we need to talk things over. And I thought David was going to offer you a part in his new picture. Don't tell me you're going to turn your back on that.'

They reached the foot of the staircase. John looked down at her and she could tell by his expression, one eyebrow lifted, that if she didn't do what he was telling her to do, he would hit her. She had been given that same look often enough by Rod.

13

Trinity was driving back from dropping off Rosie at school when her phone trilled.

'Trinity? It's Nemo. Hope I haven't caught you at a bad moment.'

'No, you're fine. How's it going?'

'I spent the whole of yesterday googling local sculptors and combing through back issues of every Hollywood gossip magazine that ever was, off and online.'

'Wow, okay. Did you have any luck?'

'Not too much. I found two sculptors – one who specialises in statues of movie characters and another who used to make busts of producers and directors and actors. The one who does the busts died last month of colon cancer. The one who makes the full-size statues is on vacation in Hawaii and can't be reached at the moment. She's a woman called Hilda Niedermeyer. She's sculpted statues for Fred Caruso, the production manager of *The Godfather*, and Michael Halperin, who scripted *Masters of the Universe*. Neither of those statues were of women, though. Halperin's was He-Man and believe it or not, Caruso's was a racehorse.'

'How about the gossip magazines?'

'Zilch. Plenty of salacious scandal but nothing about statues.'

'So what are we going to do now?'

'Like I said, we can go to Mogul Studios and talk to some of Margo's fellow actors. Do you have any spare time today?'

'I can call in sick. I'll be free just as soon as I've taken Buddy to school.'

'You're sure? I don't want you to get into any trouble with your boss.'

'Nemo, it's a domestic cleaning company. I dust tables. I mop floors. They need me a whole lot more than I need them. Besides, they pay peanuts and I've been thinking about finding a new job anyway. I'd make more money stacking shelves at the Walmart Supercenter.'

'So long as you're happy. Call me as soon as you're ready.'

Mogul film studios were sited on the north side of Century Park East. Although the Mogul lot was less than a quarter of the size of the Fox lot, which was only three blocks away, its main entrance was much more grandiose, with tall fluted pillars and elaborate wrought-iron gates.

Nemo drove up to the gates and lowered his window. A security guard in a purple uniform came up and said, 'Good morning, sir. Can I ask you what business you have here today?'

Nemo passed him an ID card. 'I have an eleven-thirty meeting with Phil Waxman.'

'And this lady?'

'She's my personal assistant. Phil knows that I'm bringing her along.'

'Wait up a moment, please.'

The security guard took out his phone and turned his back on them. Trinity heard him saying, 'Yes. Nemo Frisby. Frisby like in "frisbee". He says he has an appointment.'

Eventually, he turned around and handed Nemo his card. 'Okay, sir. You can go right ahead. Have a good day.'

The gates swung open and they drove in through the entrance. Eight sound stages lined the main road that ran down the centre of the lot, three on one side and five on the other – huge rectangular barn-like buildings with murals of Mogul's successful movies and TV shows painted on their sides. Smiling down at them was a massive portrait of Jeanette King, who was the principal character in the popular teenage series about Crompton gangs, *Loc*. She reminded Trinity of the face of Toypurina that Buddy and José had sprayed on the wall by Reseda Transmissions.

'Stage Five is the one we want,' said Nemo. 'That's where they're shooting a new episode of *Class of Angels* today.'

'I can't believe we got in so easily,' Trinity told him. 'Do you really have a meeting with this – what was his name?'

'Phil Waxman. He's executive vice-president of Mogul's business affairs. He owes me a big, big favour. Let me tell you: if favours were monkeys, this favour was King Kong. Let's just say that if it hadn't been for me, he would probably be sitting in the Golden State Modified Community Correctional Facility in McFarland right now, watching movies rather than having anything to do with making them.'

They reached the parking lot at the end of the road and Nemo pulled in next to a khaki Humvee with a white star insignia that was spattered with artificial mud. It had probably been used in a World War Two movie.

'I told Phil that you were a fan of *Class of Angels* and would love to see them shooting an episode. So try and look reasonably starstruck, if you can manage it.'

'Actually, I really like it, so that won't be too hard.'

Nobody challenged them when they walked in through the open door of Sound Stage Five. The tech crew were too busy setting up the lighting and checking the microphones and six or seven members of the cast were sitting or pacing around, rereading their scripts. It looked as if today's shoot was going to take place in one of the classrooms of Medfield High, and also in the principal's office.

Trinity recognised both sets from watching the series, but she was taken aback to see that the classroom was only half a classroom, and that the principal's office was nothing more than two walls at right angles to each other with framed diplomas hanging on them, and a desk. The windows in both the classroom and the principal's office looked out over the high school's football fields, but both views were nothing more than photographs printed onto cotton cloth.

Nemo crossed the sound stage to the classroom, where two of the actors were perched on top of the desks – a pretty brunette in a tight blue sweater, who Trinity recognised as Alice Tripper, and a lanky young man with a blond crew cut and a Medfield High sweatshirt with a big red M on it.

'Hi, folks,' said Nemo, holding up his ID card. 'Hope I'm not interrupting any last-minute line-learning. I'm a PI. Nemo Frisby's my name and this is my colleague Trinity Fox. Any objections to our asking you a couple of questions?'

The young man dropped his script onto the desk and held up both hands. 'Whatever it was, it wasn't me. I was someplace else. And even if I *wasn't* someplace else, I didn't do it. Or if I *did* do it, I don't remember doing it. I could have been drunk. Or asleep.'

Nemo grinned and patted him on the back. 'It's okay. It's not you we're interested in. It's Margo Shapiro.'

'Oh, poor Margo,' said Alice Tripper. 'I loved her. She was always such a joy to work with. It's so hard to believe that she took her own life.'

'Yes, well, that's what we're looking into.'

'Did she ever tell you about some parties that she was invited to, in Bel Air?' asked Trinity. 'I'm talking about recently. You know – only in the last couple of months or so.'

'Oh my God, yes,' said Alice Tripper. 'When she first started going to them, she hardly talked about anything else. She used to come in every morning so excited because she'd met so many producers and directors and A-list actors. I think she even spent one evening with Robin Seymour. But I don't know. After a while she stopped telling us what had happened every night, and she seemed to be kind of depressed.'

'She did, yes,' the young man put in. 'She was still going to those parties and meeting all those heavyweight producers. She told me that Dudley Kramer had promised to give her a screen test for his next picture. She thought it was going to be a speaking part, too. But Alice is right. She did start coming over all moody, and, you know, she was getting skinnier, too. I mean, Jesus. There was one scene where I had to pick her up and carry her upstairs, and she weighed like nothing at all. I could have carried four of her without breaking a sweat.'

'What we're trying to find out is *where* in Bel Air those parties were being held,' said Nemo. 'According to Margo's sister, there was some kind of statue in the garden, but so far that's all we know.'

'John Dangerfield's house, that's where,' said Alice Tripper. 'Margo told me about that statue. She said that it's modelled on Kristie Turner, who was the lead in *The Mother of All Evil*. That made John Dangerfield an absolute fortune, that picture.'

The young man said, 'Yes, he made so much he bought himself a Virgin island. Not as big as Johnny Depp's, but you know. An island is an island. I don't even own the trailer I'm living in.'

'Margo didn't happen to tell you his address in Bel Air? It's no problem if she didn't. It won't be too difficult to find out.'

At that moment, one of the crew switched on a brilliant tungsten light to illuminate the classroom set. Trinity looked around, with one hand raised to shield her eyes. Although the light partly blinded her, she saw that four men in black suits had entered the sound stage and were carefully hopscotching their way towards them over the snaking cables and dolly tracks that were laid out across the floor. One of them she recognised immediately as the man who had threatened Nemo after they had visited Andy Zimmer.

She tugged at Nemo's sleeve. 'Nemo – look who's here.'

Nemo said, 'Hold on – I just want to ask—'

'No, Nemo. Look! It's that guy who told you to stop trying to find out what happened to Margo.'

Nemo immediately turned his head. Without any hesitation, he seized Trinity's arm and pulled her away from the classroom set. Alice Tripper and the young man both swivelled around in surprise, and the young man said, 'Hey! What? Is it something I said?'

'*Run!*' Nemo grunted, still gripping Trinity's arm.

They hurried around the classroom's end wall. It was dark at the back of the sound stage, and they had to zigzag through an obstacle course of stacked chairs and tables and huge rolls of fabric and assorted LED lamps. Together they ducked under a low scaffolding framework and then ran along a corridor towards a half-open doorway.

They burst out into the daylight and Nemo turned around, slamming the door shut behind them. There was a three-tiered metal trolley only a few feet away, stacked with lengths of fibreglass coving and wooden panelling and other pieces of scenery. He rolled it towards the door and then crashed it over onto its side, so that the exit was blocked.

'Why are they after us?' Trinity panted, but all Nemo did was grab her arm again and continue to pull her along the passageway between Sound Stage Five and Sound Stage Six. They had just reached the back door to Sound Stage Six when they heard a loud clatter. Trinity saw that the men in black suits had opened the door behind them and were kicking the trolley and the fallen bits of scenery out of their way.

Nemo opened the door in front of them and Trinity followed him inside. They found themselves groping almost blindly along a dark and narrow passage between the outside wall of the sound stage and a high plasterboard wall supported by criss-cross wooden battens. It was stiflingly hot and stuffy inside this sound stage, and as they made their way further along, Trinity understood why. The plasterboard wall had windows in it, covered in thick tinted PVC, and it was obviously the back of a house on a film set. A dim light was filtering in through the windows, and from the other side of the wall she could hear several people shouting, and loud banging noises, so it sounded as if filming was in progress.

The door behind them opened, and she saw the men in black suits silhouetted against the sunshine outside.

Nemo said, 'Shit. They're serious, those bastards.'

They hurried on a few paces more, but then they had to stop abruptly. It was so dark they had failed to see that the passage in between the sound stage wall and the back of the film set came to a dead end. There was nowhere left for them to go.

Nemo turned around, opened his leather jacket and pulled out his automatic. But then he laid his hand on Trinity's shoulder and said, 'Wait. See? Is that a door there?'

The scenery house appeared to have a door in its facade – or a mock-up of a door, at least, with light shining in through the chinks all around it. Nemo went straight up to it and kicked it, hard. His foot splintered right through one of the lower panels, but the rest of the door remained intact. Taking a step back, he bunched up his shoulder, and charged at it sideways like a quarterback.

The door let out a high, hysterical squeak as he smashed it free from the screws that held it in place, and it slammed flat onto the floor in front of him. He staggered out over it, still with his automatic held high, right into the brightly lit film set. Arc lights flooded into the narrow passage behind the scenery, and when Trinity took a quick look over her shoulder she saw that the men in black suits had nearly caught up with them. As the passage was suddenly lit up, though, they came to a stumbling halt, as if they couldn't decide whether to carry on with their pursuit or give it up.

From the other side of the film set, she heard a man screaming, 'What the *fuck* is going on! Who in the name of fuck are you? Can't you see we're right in the middle of filming here? Don't you realise how much this going to *cost*? This will cost *thousands*! *Tens* of thousands!'

She came out through the doorway behind Nemo and saw that the film's director had risen from his chair – a short, bespectacled, bald-headed man in a sweaty grey T-shirt and droopy cargo pants. He bunched up both his fists as if he were going to stalk up to Nemo and punch him, but then he obviously saw that Nemo was holding a gun, and he lowered his fists, and stayed where he was.

The whole sound stage had fallen silent, apart from some shuffling and jostling and coughing. The cameraman and the rest of the crew had their eyes fixed on Nemo, and one or two of them had raised their hands, including the script girl, who was holding up the script as if it were a Bible.

Looking around, Trinity saw that the film set appeared to be a city's main square, with restaurants and shops on three sides. The centre of the square was crowded with more than seventy actors and extras, and it was clearly a slasher movie of some kind, because all of them were made up as characters from different horror films. She saw three vampires with protruding fangs and long black cloaks, and Freddy Krueger from *Nightmare on Elm Street* with a burned face and a brown fedora. Behind them she could see a family of werewolves with bristling ginger hair, including children; and at least half a dozen rotting zombies, both men and women. At the back of the crowd, a tall man in a white hockey mask like Jason from *Friday the 13th* was swaying nervously from side to side. He was flanked by two of Frankenstein's monsters, pale green, with bolts through their necks, one male and one female.

There were others. Trinity thought she glimpsed Regan from *The Exorcist* in a bloodied nightgown, with her head twisted around backwards, and Chucky the grinning doll from *Child's Play* peering out from behind her nightgown. She didn't have time to see any more because Nemo said tersely, 'Come on, Trin, let's get the hell out of here,' and reached behind him to take hold of her hand.

Stepping quickly forward together, the two of them made their way directly into the crowd of actors, who shrank back to let them through. Trinity found it surreal that she was surrounded by vampires and werewolves and zombies, who were all glaring at her with glittering eyes, but she didn't feel threatened by them. She knew that their terrifying appearance was nothing but make-up and latex prosthetics and false hair, and if anybody was frightened, it was them, by Nemo's upraised automatic.

They had nearly reached an outdoor café on the far side of the set when Trinity heard Fidel Madrazo shout out from behind them, '*Frisby! Stop where you are, Frisby!*'

Nemo pulled Trinity towards the café door, knocking over two chairs and a large oval table. He tried to open the door, but the handle broke off and fell onto the floor. He gave the door a kick, and then another kick. He split the panelling, and the window broke, but even though it looked like a door there was nothing behind it but a solid wall.

Trinity pointed to a narrow gap between the buildings in the far corner of the square, and said 'Nemo – over there!' But the men in black suits were already halfway across the floor of the sound stage, striding towards them through the parted sea of assorted monsters like the gang from *Reservoir Dogs*.

'Get down!' Nemo told Trinity. 'Down behind the table!'

Trinity dropped down behind the tipped-over table and Nemo crouched down next to her. He pointed his automatic at the four men, grasping it in both hands.

'Freeze, Fidel!' he yelled out. 'Don't you come an inch closer! Lay down flat on the floor and spread your arms and legs! And I mean all of you!'

'Drop the gun, Frisby!' Fidel retorted. He reached inside his jacket and started to lift out a revolver.

Before he could aim it at Nemo, though, Nemo fired a shot into the air, over the four men's heads. The four men immediately scattered, and the vampires and werewolves and zombies shouted and screamed and milled around in panic, bumping into each other as they desperately tried to escape from the line of fire.

Fidel had taken a knee and he aimed his revolver at Nemo and fired back. The bullet hit the remaining triangle of glass in the café door and shattered it. He fired a second shot, but at that moment a panicking teenage werewolf ran across in front of him. The young man cartwheeled across the floor with blood spraying in a fan-like shape all around him, and then thumped onto his back and lay there shuddering.

Now the screams and angry shouts from the actors grew even louder and even more hysterical. Trinity saw two werewolves seizing Fidel, pushing him over and tearing at his jacket, while a vampire was twisting the revolver out of his hand. She couldn't see the other three men in black suits because the rest of the cast had surrounded them.

Four bulky security guards in navy-blue uniforms came

bursting in through the broken door and forced their way through the monsters, adding to the chaos.

'Come on, Trin, let's hit the bricks,' said Nemo, standing up and giving Trinity a hand to stand up, too.

The two of them hurried along the back of the set and out through the gap between the buildings. They ran back around Sound Stage Five to Nemo's car, climbed in, and Nemo backed out of the parking space with a scream of tyres.

Their luck was in. As they drove towards the front of the studio, the entrance gates were opening up to let in a delivery truck. Nemo headed straight towards the front of the truck, so that it was forced to come to a juddering halt. The driver flashed his headlights and blared his klaxon, but Nemo swerved around in front of it, missing its front fender only by inches, and sped out onto Century Park East. He cut across the northbound traffic, with several startled drivers blowing their horns at him, and then slewed to the left onto Santa Monica Boulevard.

'They're really after us, aren't they?' said Trinity, twisting around in her seat to make sure they weren't being followed. 'But what will they do if they catch us? They wouldn't *kill* us, would they?'

'They'll do whatever it takes to keep us quiet,' said Nemo grimly. He turned on to South Sepulveda Boulevard, route 405, and headed due north.

'But what if they've found out where we live?'

'They know where I live already. We'll have to find ourselves someplace to hide out for a while – at least until we can convince them that we're no longer interested in what happened to your friend Margo. Even then, I know these guys – I'm not sure they're going to believe us.'

'But I have Rosie and Buddy to take care of. And my dad's in no state to do it.'

'He'll just have to rise to the occasion, won't he? I'm pretty sure I know a place where we can lie low, but let's go and give your old man a pep talk first, shall we?'

14

Zuzana woke up. She was lying in a single bed with no sheets and no pillow, covered only by a coarse open-weave blanket. A black blind was drawn down over the window, so it was impossible to tell what time it was, although she felt that she had been asleep for hours. Her throat was sore and she felt as if someone had thrown grit in her eyes.

She propped herself up on one elbow. She appeared to be lying in a small rectangular room, illuminated only by a faint light from under the door, which could have been daylight or artificial, she couldn't be sure which. She could hear music somewhere in the house, some crooning song by Frank Sinatra, and a man talking quickly and loudly, almost shouting, although she couldn't make out what he was saying.

She swung her legs onto the floor, stood up, and took a step towards the door, but as soon as she did so, a gruff woman's voice said, 'You stay! You stay on bed!'

Startled, she sat down again. Peering into the darkness, she saw the shape of somebody hunched up on a chair on the right-hand side of the door.

'Who are you?' she said. 'I can't stay in here. I have to go to the bathroom.'

'You stay,' the woman repeated, clearing her throat.

'I can't stay. I have to go to the bathroom and I need to talk to John.'

'You stay.'

'Well, I'm sorry, but I'm not going to stay. You just try and stop me.'

Zuzana stood up again and walked towards the door, but she had reached no further than the end of the bed before the woman stood up too. Not only did she stand up, she rose clear up off the floor, spreading her arms wide, and hovered over her, hissing. Zuzana screamed, and toppled backwards onto the mattress.

'You *stay*!' the woman spat at her. 'Your time with Weywot is not yet!'

Zuzana frantically kicked her way backwards up to the bedhead and curled herself up in the corner, against the wall, her arms crossed over her head to protect herself.

'You *stay*,' the woman breathed emphatically, although she spoke much more softly this time. Gradually, she sank back down to the floor and then resumed her hunched-up seat on the chair.

Zuzana was shaking with terror, and she wet herself, a warm flood that soaked her bathrobe and the mattress too, but she stayed where she was, curled up in the corner. She thought she must be having a hideous nightmare, but if this was a nightmare, why was she finding it impossible to wake herself up? Perhaps she had been dosed with so much Rohypnol that she was suffering from hallucinations.

She took several deep breaths. Her soaking-wet bathrobe was growing sticky and gradually she managed to calm down and collect her thoughts. This wasn't a nightmare, this was happening for real, and she needed to get out of here. Not just this room, but this house, even if she couldn't find her clothes. Her recollection of John bringing her up to this room was oddly disjointed, as if she had only imagined it, although she could still clearly picture the flattened-out body of the black woman lying on the gurney, and she could remember how furious John had been that she had seen her.

But who was this scary woman sitting by the door, who seemed to be able to levitate, and why wouldn't she let her go?

'I really need to go to the bathroom,' she said at last. 'Can't you call John for me – Mr Dangerfield – and ask him if you can let me out?'

'He will come,' the woman replied.

'But when? I'm wet, and I'm cold. You frightened me so much that I wet myself.'

'He will come. Until then, you stay.'

'Who are you? Why can't you let me out?'

'Your time with Weywot is not yet.'

'I don't even know what you're talking about. Please – call John for me, or somebody. Anybody.'

'He will come.'

Zuzana closed her eyes for a moment and took another deep breath. Then she swung herself off the bed, went over to the window, and seized hold of the blind. She had to tug at it three times, hard, but she managed to wrench it away from its fixings and toss it onto the floor. Although the window glass was stained pale blue, the sun was shining brightly outside and the room was instantly lit up.

She turned around. The woman had stayed where she was, sitting on her chair, but she had completely covered her head under a dark-red diamond-patterned shawl. All Zuzana could see of her was her upraised hands, with silver rings on every finger, and ragged fingernails like claws, and the brown floor-length dress that she was wearing.

'You must hide the light,' the woman told her in a muffled voice.

'I'm not going to hide the light. If it bothers you, that's too bad. I'm going to walk straight out of here and you're not going to stop me.'

'You stay!' the woman barked.

With that, she stood up, opening her shawl wide in her outstretched arms. She rose up off the floor again, floating three or four inches above the carpet, looking down at Zuzana like some huge predatory bird.

She had the face of an American Indian woman, with a broad forehead and high cheekbones and a squarish jaw. Her hair was shoulder-length, steel-grey and fastened with a beaded headband. She looked about sixty or seventy years old, because her skin was wrinkled and her lips were deeply furrowed.

Zuzana took one step backwards, and then another. It was frightening enough that the woman was hovering in the air, but what was even more terrifying was that her eyes were flaring a fluorescent green, like a coyote's caught in a headlight at night, and that she was translucent. Now that the room was lit up, Zuzana could see right through her body and her shawl to the panels of the door behind her.

'You stay!' the woman screamed at her. '*Tokoor Hikaayey command you to stay!*'

But Zuzana was panicking now. Her brain felt as if it had exploded into a thousand fragments, like a smashed window. She rushed forward, seizing the woman's shawl and pulling her downwards and off to one side. Although the woman was translucent, and bobbing buoyantly up and down in mid-air, she felt solid. As she tumbled backwards, she lashed out wildly and her ragged fingernails tore at the side of Zuzana's neck. Zuzana swung her around even harder and threw her back onto the bed.

'*You stay!*' the woman croaked. '*Your time is not yet! You cannot escape Weywot!*'

Zuzana tugged at the door handle. The door was locked, but the key had been left in the lock, and she was able to twist it open. She flung the door wide, and stumbled out into the corridor, almost falling over onto the floor. She saw the staircase up ahead of her, and she ran towards it, her damp bathrobe slapping against her thighs.

When she reached the head of the staircase, she quickly looked behind her, but the corridor was empty. For whatever reason, the woman had clearly decided not to come after her. She started to jump down the stairs, two and three at a time, snatching at the banister rail to stop herself from losing her footing.

She was only halfway down, though, before she came to a sudden and teetering stop. Down at the bottom of the staircase, the woman was standing with her shawl held out wide, or at least another woman who could have been her twin. Her phosphorescent green eyes were burning even brighter and her mouth was stretched open wide, as if she were howling, although she was making no sound.

'Don't tell me you've had enough of my hospitality already,' said a calm voice behind her, and when she turned around, Zuzana saw that John Dangerfield was standing at the head of the staircase, smoking a cigarette. Bradley and

SloMo were standing on either side of him, as well as a bald Japanese-looking man in a sleeveless jerkin, with arms like knotted ropes.

'Why don't you come back upstairs?' said John. 'Now that you're awake, darling, we can sit down together and decide what we're going to do with you next.'

Zuzana sat down on the stairs and started to cry. She had never felt so desperate or so lonely in her life, even when Rod had beaten her and blocked the doorway to stop her from leaving their apartment. She sobbed so deeply that it hurt her throat, and her tears almost blinded her.

John came down the stairs and sat down next to her.

'What are you blubbering for? You don't seem to have any idea how privileged you are! You're one of the chosen few, don't you know that? One of life's elect! So come on, how about drying your eyes and pasting a smile back onto that pretty face of yours?'

Zuzana shook her head. She couldn't speak because her throat was so constricted and she couldn't stop the tears from flowing. They were even dripping out of her nose.

The woman with the glowing green eyes came slowly up the stairs towards them, half stepping and half floating. She stood a little way below them, with her shawl bundled around her and her shoulders hunched as they had been before.

John looked down at the woman and said, 'I'd say that Tokoor Hikaayey's none too pleased with you, darling. I told her to keep an eye on you, and she never likes to disappoint me.'

He paused, giving the woman a smile that was partly indulgent and partly threatening.

'Tokoor Hikaayey, that means Ghost Woman, in case you

didn't know. In the Tongva language, they don't actually have a specific word for "ghost". You can also translate "hikaayey" as "spirit", or "wind", or "breath of air". But that's what she is, a ghost. And she's like all ghosts – she can only survive so long as she does what the real ruling forces in this world tell her to do. Those unseen forces that priests and Satanists and other ignoramuses call "demons".'

Now he stood up, and the Ghost Woman shrank back down a few stairs, raising her shawl protectively across the lower part of her face.

'You know, it always amuses me that people are afraid of ghosts. Ghosts are nothing to be scared of. It's the forces they serve – that's who you need to watch out for. The so-called demons. Now – let's get back upstairs, shall we? We need to have a little powwow later on. And don't try to run off again, will you? This time I'll tell Tokoor Hikaayey that she can give you more than just a scratch.'

Zuzana pressed her hand against the side of her neck. For the first time, she realised how much it hurt. When she took her hand away, she saw that her palm was striped with blood.

The Ghost Woman led her to a large blue-tiled bathroom at the end of the upstairs corridor. She took off her robe, dropped it on the floor and stepped into the shower. The first burst of water was freezing and it made her gasp, but it quickly warmed up, and she stood with her head tilted back, letting it cascade over her. Through the steamed-up glass she could see the dark shape of the Ghost Woman standing by the door, watching her, her green eyes glowing.

After a while she reached for the cake of white soap

in the soap dish. As she washed herself, the soap gave off a distinctive sweet fragrance that reminded her of her grandmother's garden in Bridle Path, in Simi Valley. It was moonflower, a white morning glory that blossomed at night and closed up when the sun appeared. She remembered her grandmother telling her that it could also induce the strangest hallucinations, and hippies had often used moonflower to take psychedelic trips.

When she stepped out of the shower she found a large soft towel folded up by the washbasin, as well as a pale-blue satin dressing gown. The Ghost Woman was still standing by the door, wrapped in her shawl, but Zuzana kept her back turned to her and kept silently telling herself *she's a ghost, she's a spirit, she's not really real.*

Once she was dry and had tied up the dressing gown, the Ghost Woman said, 'You come. You follow.'

'Where are we going?'

'You come.'

The Ghost Woman opened the door and started to glide along the corridor. As she passed each window, the sunlight shone right through her, in diagonal shafts, so that she seemed to flicker, like a character in a silent movie.

Zuzana reluctantly followed her, although she kept at least six or seven paces between them. She hadn't forgotten what John had said about allowing the Ghost Woman to give her more than a scratch. Although the four lacerations on the side of her neck had stopped bleeding, they were still sore. If nothing else, though, the fact that she could feel them was proof that she wasn't drugged, or dreaming.

When the Ghost Woman reached the stairs, she turned around to make sure that Zuzana was still behind her, and then she started to flow down them, towards the atrium, with an extraordinary rippling movement. As she came down the stairs after her, Zuzana wondered if she might be able to run across the atrium and reach the front doors before the Ghost Woman could catch up with her. But she was less than halfway down when she saw that Bradley and the Japanese-looking man were standing in one of the arches.

'You come,' said the Ghost Woman, once they had come to the bottom of the stairs. She crossed the atrium towards the same archway where Bradley and SloMo had pushed the gurney. Bradley and the Japanese-looking man came up to join them.

'How's it going, Zuzi-Q?' Bradley asked her. 'You frightened?'

'Of course I'm frightened. John won't let me go home. All I want to do is go home.'

Bradley shrugged, and turned his head to one side so Zuzana could see that his left eye was purple and swollen and almost completely closed. It looked like an eggplant.

'That's what you learn about this place,' he told her. 'You do what you're expected to do and if you *don't* do it then you pay the price. I forgot to lock the door to the chilling room and that's how you got in there and saw what you saw. I was whacked in the face with a metal bar for that, and it serves me right. At least I wasn't blinded.'

'All I want to do is go home,' said Zuzana, and her eyes filled up with tears again.

'Too late for that. You've seen what you've seen and you can't unsee it. But then it was always too late, from the moment you arrived here.'

'What do you mean?'

'I can't tell you, babe. I'm not allowed to tell you. If I told you, I'd get another whack, twice as hard, or worse. But you know what the name of this house is? La Muralla. That means the wall, or the dead end. That's because it's just like the Hotel California, in the song. The girls who come here, they check out, for sure, but they can never leave.'

At this moment, John appeared out of the archway. He was accompanied by another man, thin and dark, with a neatly trimmed salt-and-pepper beard. This man was wearing a white surgical jacket, buttoned up at the left side of his neck, with a large pocket in the front.

'Well, here you are, darling,' said John. 'All clean and fresh. We can have our little powwow quite soon, but first of all there's something important we need to fix. Just as a precaution, you understand.'

'What?' asked Zuzana miserably, wiping her eyes.

John smiled. 'A couple of days ago, one of you little darlings managed to slip out of here, in spite of all our security. I'm not saying that *you* would, or even that you *could*, now that we know how she managed to escape. But it's always better to take precautions rather than kicking yourself afterwards, don't you think?'

He stepped forward and took hold of Zuzana's right arm, while the Japanese-looking man grasped her other arm.

'This way,' said John. 'It'll be over before you know it.'

'*No!*' Zuzana protested. 'Whatever it is, I'm not letting you do it! No! Let go of me! *No!*'

She bent her knees so that she sagged down between the two men, but both of them were far too strong for her. They lifted her up by her elbows and dragged her through the archway with her bare feet trailing on the floor. They passed the door to the chilling room where all the gurneys were stored, and turned a corner.

Ahead of them was another door, wide open, and they heaved her through it into a large bare room with pale lime-green walls. The window let in plenty of sunlight, but it faced nothing more than the side of John Dangerfield's garage. The only furniture was two single beds, a grey metal dresser and a washbasin with a circular mirror.

John and the Japanese-looking man hoisted Zuzana onto the hard white mattress of one of the single beds, face down, and Bradley came forward to help the Japanese-looking man to hold her down.

Zuzana struggled and kicked, although she was too winded to scream. Turning her head, she saw John opening up the top drawer of the bureau and taking out two long leather belts. He came over to the bed and looped one belt underneath it, fastening the buckle tightly over her calves, so that she couldn't kick. He used the other belt to hold down her chest and trap her arms by her sides.

Now that she was pinned down, Bradley and the Japanese-looking man stepped away. The Ghost Woman had followed them from the atrium, and was standing outside in the corridor, her green eyes glowing, but John went up and closed the door.

The thin man in the surgical jacket approached the bed. He bent down sideways and said to Zuzana, in a slightly Yiddish accent, 'You will have to forgive me for this.'

Zuzana could only pant for breath and roll her eyes at him.

The thin man was holding a flat wooden board, no longer or thicker than a ruler but about three times as wide. He lifted up Zuzana's chin and wedged it firmly underneath it. Then, out of the front pocket of his jacket, he produced a pair of hole-punch pliers, the kind that were used to make holes in leather belts, as well as a small hammer, a four-inch stainless-steel nail and a scalpel. He laid these all out on the mattress, along with a thick pad of surgical gauze.

'Please, open up your mouth,' he told her.

Zuzana kept her lips tightly closed and shook her head.

'Open your mouth. Please. What's going to happen to you, it's going to happen no matter what. *Vos vet zeyn vet zeyn.*'

He beckoned to the Japanese-looking man to come closer, and then he picked up the hole-punch pliers. He pinched Zuzana's nose between finger and thumb and held them there for nearly thirty seconds. At last she had to open her mouth to gasp for air, and as soon as she did that, he used the pliers to crunch a hole through her tongue and then stretch it out of her mouth as far as he could, cupping his hand over her eyes and her forehead to give himself more leverage. Zuzana gagged and tried to twist herself free from the leather straps, but they were buckled far too tightly.

The thin man said, '*Now!*' and the Japanese-looking man carefully positioned the point of the stainless-steel nail into the furrow of Zuzana's tongue. He struck it one hard blow with the hammer and her tongue was fixed to the wooden board beneath it.

John was standing by the window, but he was intently watching everything that the thin man was doing. His shining ball-bearing eyes never blinked, but he kept his left hand pressed over his mouth as if he could feel her pain himself. His left hand was deep in his trouser pocket.

Now the thin man picked up the scalpel. Zuzana screwed her eyes tightly shut as he held it close to her lips and then sliced into her tongue. Blood immediately squirted out all over the board and onto the mattress, but he cut quickly and cleanly, and as soon as he had severed her tongue he whipped the board out from under her chin, and tossed it aside. It clattered onto the floor with her tongue nailed onto it.

He forced open her lips and stuffed the surgical gauze into her mouth, pressing it hard against the bleeding stump of her tongue. Zuzana didn't resist, because she had lost consciousness from shock.

John came away from the window and stood close to the bed. 'There's no risk of her bleeding to death, is there?'

The thin man shook his head. 'She could well do, if I applied no pressure, but you'd be surprised how quickly the deep lingual artery seals itself up. And I'll be using surgical glue and sutures to close it completely. Only a postponement, of course.'

'Pity in a way. She's beautiful. But she's like all these beautiful girls. They have so much more to give us than their looks.'

Bradley came up and looked down at Zuzana sympathetically. 'No more kissing for her, then. No more chewing her food, either. At least she won't be able to call for help.'

'I hope you haven't forgotten that this is all down to you and SloMo,' John told him. 'If you'd locked the door to the chiller room, we wouldn't have had to do this.'

'To be fair, sir, if she hadn't stopped to take a look, and you hadn't caught her, she might have gotten away altogether.'

'Well, give your thanks to God that she didn't. You would have gotten more than a black eye, Bradley, if she'd escaped. I'd have castrated you and made you eat your own junk. Without catsup.'

15

Nemo said, 'I've been trying to think where we could hide out. A friend of mine has a cabin up in Pine Mountain and I know for a fact that he's on assignment in San Diego right now. He's always said that I can crash out there whenever I want.'

He was turning off west onto the Ventura Freeway, and Trinity was twisting around in her seat to make sure that they weren't being followed.

'We can't stay there for ever, though, can we?'

'It seems to me we have two choices. We can meet up with those IAG goons and promise that we'll back off and won't investigate Margo's death any further. Or we can carry on looking into it until we can prove beyond any doubt that she *was* murdered, and if so who did it.'

'If we promise to drop it, do you really think they'll stop coming after us?'

'To be honest with you – no. The trouble is, we know what we know. It isn't much, but somebody for some reason has a major interest in it not coming out. Even if we swear on the Holy Bible that we'll forget all about it, I believe they'll still see us as a threat.'

'But if we carry on and we find out who killed her, they'll see us as even *more* of a threat, won't they?'

'Yes. But at least we'll have the evidence to have them bagged.'

Nemo left the freeway and started to drive up White Oak Avenue towards Reseda.

'I blame myself,' he said, pressing another piece of Think Gum out of its packet. 'When Fidel told me to back off, I should have realised that he was deadly, deadly serious. The IAG wouldn't have sent him to my house in person, otherwise. Me – I'm a trained and experienced cop, and I'm used to the risk that goes with it. But you – you're not, and I shouldn't have allowed you to get yourself involved.'

'Nemo, Margo was my friend and I saw her burning alive. I couldn't just pretend that never happened.'

'Of course not. But you don't want the same thing to happen to you.'

Before they reached Trinity's house, Nemo took a right into Hartland Street and parked close behind a Dodge Ram pickup so that his car was hidden from anybody who might have been tailing them up Zelzah Avenue.

They walked to the corner, pausing for a moment to make sure that there was nobody in sight. Except for parked cars and two young boys roller-skating on the sidewalk, the street was deserted. It was a hot, silent morning and a single saucer-shaped cloud was hanging motionless in the sky like a UFO.

There was no sign of Kenno or any other neighbours. Trinity unlocked the front door and Nemo followed her inside.

'Grab yourself a change of clothes and a toothbrush and

whatever else you think you might need,' he told her. 'There's a general store up at Pine Mountain so don't worry too much if you forget something.'

'Dad!' Trinity called out. She looked into the living room, expecting to see him sitting on the couch with a can of Rolling Rock, either asleep or watching daytime TV, but the room was empty.

'Dad!' she called again, and this time he called back, 'Here!' from the kitchen.

They found him standing at the counter making himself a cheese slice sandwich. His hair was sticking up and he was unshaven, and he was wearing a red polo shirt with *Winnetka Windows* printed across the back, one of several companies that had sacked him for drinking on the job.

'I got a sudden attack of the chucks,' he explained, slapping a second slice of bread on top of the cheese slices and immediately taking a bite, without cutting his sandwich or putting it onto a plate. He nodded towards Nemo and said, with his mouth full, 'So what are you two up to? Why aren't you at work?'

'I took the day off,' said Trinity. 'Nemo and me, we've been trying to find out how Margo died.'

Her father pulled out a chair from the kitchen table and sat down. 'You've been what? I don't get it. Why would you want to do that?'

Nemo pulled out the chair next to him and sat down too. 'Trinity witnessed something when Margo died that led her to believe she could have been murdered. She called me about it because I'm a former police officer and she thought I might be able to help her find out who did it.'

Trinity's father swallowed and looked at Nemo suspiciously.

'That's up to the regular cops, isn't it? Why should you two get yourselves involved?'

'Because the regular cops aren't investigating. They're saying that it was suicide.'

'Then maybe it was. They know their onions, don't they?'

'Mr Fox—'

'For Chrissakes, call me Lenny. The only time people have ever called me "Mr Fox" is when they were calling me into their office to give me the bullet or when they were hauling me up in front of a judge to explain why I was driving down Topanga Canyon on the wrong side of the highway.'

Her father winked at Trinity and took another bite out of his sandwich. Then he immediately stood up, went to the fridge and took out a can of Rolling Rock. He sat down again, popped the top of the can, and took a swig while his mouth was still crammed.

Nemo said, 'Okay then, Lenny. We're ninety-nine per cent certain that Margo was murdered because we have some people after us who are trying to shut us up. And when I say they're trying to shut us up, I mean they're probably prepared to kill us.'

Trinity's father stared with bloodshot eyes at Nemo and his chewing slowed down. 'What do you mean – *kill* you? Is this some kind of a joke?'

'No joke, Dad,' said Trinity. 'We went to talk to some of Margo's friends at Mogul Studios and they chased us. They had guns, Dad. Nemo and me – we'll have to go into hiding for a while. I've just come back home to pick up some clothes.'

'Wait a minute. If you go into hiding, who's going to take care of Rosie and Buddy? Who's going to take care of *me*, for that matter?'

'You are,' said Nemo.

'Look at me. Look at the fucking state of me. This is my third beer since I woke up this morning.'

'Makes no odds, Lenny. Trinity's life is in danger, through no fault of her own, and you're her father. In fact, you're the only father she's got, so it's up to you to protect her. You're Rosie's only father, too, and Buddy's. So while Trinity's away, you'll have to pour the beer down the sink and step up to the plate. Maybe you'll be doing yourself a favour, too.'

Trinity's father laid his sandwich down on the table. He looked horrified, as if Nemo had just told him he had only a week left to live.

'Trin,' said Nemo, 'why don't you go and collect your stuff together? If those goons managed to track us to the studios, they could well be on their way here. There's one thing, though. You'll have to leave your phone behind.'

'But if I switch it off – they can't track it then, can they?'

'I'm afraid they can. The NSA worked out how to do it. Out in Syria, they tracked hundreds of phones belonging to ISIS terrorists. And the police know how to do it, too.'

'Oh, okay.' Trinity opened up one of the kitchen cupboards and took out a black plastic bag. She had lent her only suitcase to Rosie to go on a school trip to Lake Tahoe and Rosie had broken the handle. She went through to her bedroom, sliding open the drawers of her built-in wardrobe and grabbing handfuls of T-shirts and underwear and a spare pair of jeans.

She dropped her pink make-up case into the black bag, too, and she was just about to go into the bathroom to fetch her toothbrush when she heard a slithering of tyres. She looked out of her window and saw that two grey Ford Explorers had pulled up outside the house, nose to tail. Their doors were flung open and the four men in black suits came scrambling out, heading straight for the porch.

'Nemo!' she shouted. 'Nemo, they're here!'

She picked up the black bag and hurried back to the kitchen. Her father stood up and said, 'What? Where are they?'

Trinity didn't have to answer him because the front doorbell jangled and one of the men started beating on the door with his fists.

'Can we get out the back?' asked Nemo.

'Sure, yes,' said Trinity's father. 'Those chairs at the end of the yard. You can use them to climb over the fence into the Willards' place next door.'

'Dad—' said Trinity. 'Dad, I'm so sorry to leave you like this.'

The doorbell jangled again, and again, and now the men were kicking at the door as well as banging on it with their fists.

'Listen, darling. This guy's right. I'm the only father you've got and if I can't protect you then what am I worth? I managed to bring you and Rosie and Buddy into the world and bring you up. Sure – I've gone down the toilet lately but I can look after you now, all three of you. Now, *split*! I'll deal with these palookas.'

'Dad—'

'*Go*, Trin! Just try to let me know when you're safe!'

He went out into the hallway and shut the kitchen door behind him. Trinity heard him shouting, 'All right! All right! What in the name of Jesus are you banging at my door for? Who the fuck are you? Mormons?'

Trinity opened the back door that led outside, and she and Nemo ran down to the end of the yard, where there was a wooden picnic table with a sagging parasol and four wooden chairs. Nemo dragged one of the chairs up to the fence, and helped Trinity to climb up onto it. She threw her bag into the Willards' yard first and then she lifted herself over, jumping down onto their neat green Kurapia lawn. Nemo came after her, although he almost lost his balance on top of the fence, and as he swayed and tried to steady himself, he broke one of the panels with a crack like a pistol shot.

Jim Willard must have seen them through his kitchen window, because he stepped out onto his back porch in his baggy red shorts and called out, 'Trinity? What's going on, girl? We've been in the whole morning! You could have come round to the front and knocked!'

'Sorry, Jim!' said Trinity. 'I'll tell you later!'

Jim Willard watched Trinity and Nemo in bewilderment as they crossed his yard to the Indian laurel hedge on the opposite side. There was a narrow gap between the hedge and the fence at the back, and Nemo struggled through it first, holding the prickly branches back as far as he could so that Trinity could follow him. She turned around to pull her black bag through, but it snagged on one of the branches and ripped open, so that all her clothes spilled out.

'Oh, *no*!' she wailed, trying to gather them up.

'You'll have to leave them!' said Nemo. 'Don't worry, we'll buy you some more!'

The next yard belonged to an elderly couple called the Massimos. They could see white-haired Mrs Massimo staring at them out of her window as they ran up to the house and then ducked along the alleyway where they kept their trash bins. Nemo opened their side gate and cautiously peered out into the street.

'Looks like your dad's let them in,' he said. 'Let's hit the bricks before they come back out.'

For a split second, Trinity felt like giving in, and going back to make sure that her father wasn't being threatened, or worse. But Nemo must have sensed her indecision, because he took hold of her hand and said, 'Come on, sweetheart. Your dad will be okay. But those guys will kill us if we don't get the hell out of here. Don't you have any doubt about that.'

It took them a little over an hour to drive north from Reseda to Pine Mountain. They took I-5 as far as Frazier Mountain Park Road and then snaked their way up through the pine forests.

'I'm so worried about Dad,' said Trinity. 'I pray to God those men haven't hurt him. And even if they haven't, I don't know how he's going to take care of Rosie and Buddy.'

'He'll manage, Trin, and if he can't, the two of them are old enough to take pretty good care of themselves.'

They reached Pine Mountain village, which was little more than a scattering of wooden houses half-hidden among the trees around the general store. Nemo turned up a steep side road, turned again, and parked at an angle outside a three-storey house. It was built of cedarwood, this house, stained reddish-brown, with decorative shutters and a gambrel roof, so that the snow would slide off in the winter. Nemo opened the passenger door so that Trinity could climb out, and then he helped her across to the steps that led up to a first-floor balcony.

When they reached the front door, he reached across to the windowsill on the left-hand side and felt underneath it.

'Damn. This is where Mike usually leaves the key. Maybe he's hidden it someplace else.'

He groped all along the windowsill, and then reached up and ran his fingers along the top of the door. 'No. It's not here either. I don't get it. I've stayed here twice and I'm sure he would have told me if he'd decided to move it.'

'How are we going to get in?'

'Well, fortunately, one of the specialties I was taught at the police academy was lockpicking, and even more fortunately I still keep a pick and a hook in my glovebox.'

He was just about to go back down the steps when the front door opened. Standing in front of them was a dark-haired young man in a crumpled white shirt and ripped designer jeans, with bare feet. Trinity thought that he was quite handsome in a young Johnny Depp way.

'Yes?' he said. 'Can I help you with something?'

'I'm a friend of Mike Scotto's,' said Nemo. 'He lets me stay here when he's away and that's what me and this young lady were planning to do today. Who are you?'

The young man blinked at Nemo suspiciously. 'My name's Rafael. I do odd jobs for Mr Scotto. I've been sanding the floorboards and some other stuff that needs fixing.'

'So you've been staying here, while you do that?'

'That's right. I'll be here for another three or four days at least. I'm waiting on some plumbing parts they're supposed to be delivering from Ferguson's.'

'But you don't have any objection if we stay here too?'

Rafael looked at Trinity this time. She smiled at him and brushed her hair back over her shoulder.

'If it's okay with Mr Scotto, I guess not, no. But there's only one shower working, I have to warn you.'

'I think we can live with that. Can we come in now?'

'Oh, yes. Sure. Don't go into the den, though. I only finished up varnishing the floor about an hour ago.'

Rafael stepped back and Trinity and Nemo entered the house. It was open-plan and spacious, with high ceilings, and furnished with rustic chairs and couches, all upholstered in woven fabrics in American Indian patterns. On the wall above the wide brick fireplace hung a snowscape of Mount Pinos in winter; and from the ceiling beside it hung a feathery dream-catcher. The whole house smelled of varnish and cedarwood.

'Would you guys care for a coffee or anything?' Rafael asked them. 'I was just about to make myself some.'

'I'd love a glass of water if you have any,' said Trinity.

'I'm good, thanks,' said Nemo. 'We can go across to the store later and stock up on a few essentials. Like hot dogs, and beer.'

'I don't eat meat,' Trinity reminded him.

'Oh – I forgot. Don't worry. They're bound to have something in stock that doesn't have dead animal in it. Beans, and tofu, and suchlike. Tofu doesn't have dead animals in it, does it?'

Rafael went into the kitchen to brew coffee, while Nemo slid back the glass door that led out onto the balcony, and he and Trinity stepped outside. In the far distance, beyond the forests, they could see the misty outline of Sawmill Mountain and the Eagle Rest Peak. The air was fragrant and fresh, and except for the sporadic high-pitched squeaking of hermit warblers, the silence was overwhelming.

'What are we going to do now?' asked Trinity. 'I mean, how are we going to find out how Margo died if we're stuck way out here?'

'We're not going to stay stuck out here,' Nemo told her. 'We need to cool it for today, so those IAG goons believe that we've pulled a disappearing act. I know how they work. They'll scale down their operation pretty quickly if they think they're not going to be able to find us, because they won't be able to afford to keep on looking for us ad infinitum. But starting tomorrow or the day after, we can go back into the city and start poking around and asking questions. The only thing is, we'll have to do it undercover, in disguise.'

Trinity looked back into the living room. 'There's a computer here, at least. We can start by trying to find out where in Bel Air this John Dangerfield lives.'

'I'm so sorry about all your clothes,' said Nemo. 'We can see if the store has any in stock, and if they don't, we'll buy you some more when we go back into LA. Don't ask me to take you shopping in Rodeo Drive, though. My Mastercard's nudging the limit as it is.'

'What about you?'

'Me? I always keep a change of clothes in a bag in the trunk of my car. It dates back to when I was a cop, and I never knew when I might have to stay out all night, or even longer. After I was canned I kept it up, because that's when my marriage started to get more than a little rocky. I still never know when I might have to go storming out the door at short notice.'

'I'm sorry.'

'Don't be sorry, Trin. People change as time goes by, for one reason or another. Suddenly you can look at somebody you were passionate about when you first met them, and think, what in the name of God am I living with you for? You can see them in diners, these couples, going through their whole meal from soup to nuts and not saying a word to each other.'

Rafael came out to join them, with a mug of coffee and a glass of chilled water for Trinity.

'It's Arrowhead,' he told her. 'Not out of the kitchen faucet.'

'I could never tell the difference,' said Nemo. 'Stick a fancy name on something ordinary, and you can always sell it for ten times what it's worth. My wife Sherri's been nagging me for some of them Yeezy trainers. Three hundred and sixty-nine bucks, can you believe it, when there's plenty of women's trainers for sale for thirty-two ninety-nine.'

Rafael said, 'You a cop, if you don't me asking?'

'I *was* a cop, yeah. That's how I first met Mike. I guess we must have known each other nearly fifteen years now.'

'I never would have thought that he was a cop, not at first. He's always so quiet, and so kind.'

'So how do *you* know him? Or did he just look you up online?'

'He was at the Mercy Hospital in Bakersfield when my mom died of the Covid-19. He was there to check on another cop who got hurt in a traffic accident. He saw me there in the waiting room and he asked me why I was looking so down. If you want to know the truth, I was crying my eyes out.'

Rafael looked away for a moment, towards the distant mountains. A hermit warbler made that sharp chipping sound, as if to tell him to continue.

'Mike sat with me for a while. I told him that now my mom was gone, my grandad and me would be living on our own and I didn't know how we were going to manage. My dad left us years ago. My mom had been a cook at the Lampkin Park Hotel and even though I made the odd dollar from odd jobs like carpentry and stuff, it wasn't going to be nearly enough for us to live on.'

'Tough,' said Nemo.

'Yes, but Mike was amazing. He said that he'd do whatever he could to fix me up with work, and he did. He gave me a laptop that the cops weren't using any more, and he set me up with a website, and ever since then I've been painting and decorating and plumbing pretty much non-stop. And I got support from the tribal office, too. It's only temporary, but it's helped.'

'The tribal office? You're Indian?'

'Fifty per cent Chumash, from my mom. That's enough to qualify. My grandad's one hundred per cent Indian. Like, he used to be an 'atiswinic.'

'I hope I'm not being totally ignorant, but what's an 'atiswinic, when it's at home?'

'It means "dreamer", or shaman. Somebody who has magical powers, which they got through dreams and momoy trips.'

'Now, momoy,' said Nemo. 'I know what that is. Datura.'

'I think I've heard of datura,' said Trinity. 'It's some kind of drug, isn't it?'

'It's a plant. Jimsonweed or devil's trumpet. If you eat the stems and the seeds and the leaves, it can give you some really wild hallucinations. But it can kill you, too, if you take too much of it. We had at least five cases of fatal datura poisoning when I was on the force.'

'I don't think my grandad takes it any more. You'll be able to meet him later, anyhow. He'll be coming by this afternoon to give me some of his home-made acorn pancakes. He likes to keep up the Chumash traditions.'

'Acorn pancakes?' said Nemo. 'Now they sound like something that you'd go for, Trin. No dead animals in acorn pancakes.'

16

John Dangerfield came into the room and stood over Zuzana's bed. She turned her head away and stared at the wall, her chest rising and falling because she was still finding it difficult to breathe. She kept trying to swallow but every time she did the stub of her tongue flopped back into her throat and almost choked her.

After a long silence, John said, 'It's time for you to see what your destiny looks like, Ms Zilka. Don't worry. I know you're probably feeling pretty logy, but we have a wheelchair waiting for you downstairs.'

He sat down on the bed next to her and laid his hand on her hip. She flinched, and tried to shift herself away from him.

'When you see what lies ahead of you, sweetheart, I think you'll understand why we had to make it impossible for you to talk. Too risky. Without this, half of the men in Hollywood wouldn't be where they are today. Well – maybe I'm exaggerating when I say "half". But there's a whole lot of incredibly famous names who would still be nobodies but for this.

'Okay, we could have found you a part in some forgettable B-picture. But what you'll be contributing to the movie business – it'll be far more valuable and long-lasting than that. You'll be helping to make cinema history. I'll be straight with you. When the credits roll at the end of some of the most award-winning films that come out next year, and the year after, and all the years after that, your name won't be up on the screen. But the producers and directors and talent who made those films, they'll all know that if it hadn't been for you, and all the other young women like you, they could never have created such brilliant productions. If they gave sacrificial Oscars, you'd win one for sure.'

John patted Zuzana's hip and then stood up. He nodded to the Ghost Woman, who had risen from her chair and was standing by the door with little more substance than a shadow. She opened the door and SloMo came in, wearing a red Guns N' Roses T-shirt and tight khaki shorts.

SloMo bent over, shovelling both his hands underneath Zuzana and lifting her clear off the bed. She was too weak to struggle, but she went completely limp, so that he would find her more awkward to hold on to. He jiggled her up and down two or three times to adjust his grip, and then he carried her out of the room and along the corridor, her arms and legs dangling.

Vincent Priest was waiting at the head of the staircase in his shiny grey suit. He was smiling uneasily.

'I won't join you, John, if you don't mind.'

'What? Don't tell me the Priest has turned chicken.'

'Not at all. But I'll be late for an appointment with Michael Bay.'

'Michael Bay? You have a client you want to see blown up?'

Vincent gave him a humourless laugh. Almost every Michael Bay film had an explosion in it at some point.

John clapped him on the back and said, 'Don't sweat it, your reverence. But you must be there for the grand finale, when Ms Zilka gives us her farewell performance. I'll insist on it.'

SloMo by now had carried Zuzana down to the atrium, where a wheelchair was waiting, with a tartan blanket folded over the back. He lowered her into it, tucking the blanket over her knees as carefully as a father with a disabled daughter. John came down the stairs to join them, while Vincent stayed where he was, jabbing at his phone and glancing nervously now and again along the corridor. Ghost Woman was still standing outside the bedroom door, her green eyes glowing, as if she were peeved that Zuzana had been taken away from her.

Zuzana blinked as she was pushed out of the French doors and into the sunlit garden. The stub of her tongue was still hugely swollen and sore, and since she couldn't swallow she was dribbling down her chin. The thin man had given her a massive dose of OxyContin to dull her pain, but it was making her feel that she was having a bad dream from which she couldn't shake herself awake. She heard the fountain clattering and saw the statue of Auzar and she was sure she saw Auzar slowly waving her arms as if she were alive. Then she was rolled through the pergola, between the white jasmine flowers, which smelled strongly of nutmeg. Her eyes suddenly flooded with tears, not only because her tongue was throbbing, but because she felt so hopeless.

SloMo pushed her across the patio and up to the double wooden doors of the building with the sun symbol painted on it. Bradley had joined them now, and he went up to the doors with a large bunch of keys and unlocked them. He opened them wide so that SloMo had enough space to tip the wheelchair up over the doorstep and into a small, chilly vestibule.

John came into the vestibule and stood beside the wheelchair with his hand on Zuzana's shoulder. Bradley switched on a single overhead light and then closed the double doors behind them, and locked them. Facing them were two more doors, although these doors appeared to be made of metal, and painted olive green. Bradley sorted through his bunch of keys, and then unlocked these doors, too.

Zuzana was pushed into a large gloomy room that was illuminated only by three low-wattage light bulbs hanging from a branch-like chandelier. The room was stunningly cold, so that her breath poured out of her nostrils in two smoking tusks.

'We have to keep the temperature at a constant three degrees,' said John, as if he were a tour guide. 'Now you can understand why we lent you a blanket.'

Zuzana looked around. Every wall was densely covered with black and orange pictographs. She could see dancers and hunters with spears, as well as rattlesnakes and frogs and scorpions. There were dozens of abstract figures, too – circles and triangles and pinwheels and what looked like comets flying through the sky.

The centre of the room was dominated by a massive stone or concrete plinth. On either side of this plinth stood two metal posts, with horizontal bars across them about two feet from the floor, so that they looked like inverted crucifixes. Resting on top of the plinth was a long, lumpy sack, which appeared to be made of some hairy animal hide. It was sewn together up the middle with thick leather stitches, apart from a small gap at the far end, where it was folded into a point like a hood.

John went up to the end of the plinth, his head wreathed in his exhaled breath. He beckoned to Zuzana and said, 'Come on, sweetheart. Come and take a look. The boys will help you.'

Zuzana shook her head. Whatever it was, she didn't want to see it. But SloMo and Bradley folded the blanket aside, took hold of her elbows, and lifted her bodily out of the wheelchair. With her bare feet sliding on the floor, they carried her along to where John was standing, and held her there. She was quaking with cold.

'Look,' said John. 'This is your destiny.'

Zuzana closed her eyes tightly and turned away.

'*Look!*' John demanded. 'This is your future! Because of this, you'll never be forgotten!'

He reached up and gripped her chin between his thumb and two fingers, forcing her to face towards the plinth.

'Open your eyes, damn you! Open your eyes and see the glory that's waiting for you!'

John kept up his hold on her chin until she felt as if her jaw would crack open and drop off. Her elbows were hurting, too, where SloMo and Bradley were still propping her up. Her brain wanted her to scream but all she could do was gargle.

She opened her eyes, and looked. Anything to stop the agony.

In the gap that had been left in the animal hide sack, she saw a man's face. He was either sleeping or dead, because his skin was a soapy white, and she could see pale greenish tinges around his lips. He had a high forehead, with a tight twisted band around it, and deep-set eye sockets. His cheeks were sharp and angular, and he had a thin, prominent nose like the end of a sickle.

His lips were slightly parted, so that she could see his broken, irregular teeth.

'There,' said John, releasing his hold on her chin. 'Nothing and nobody in this world can equal that. *That*, sweetheart, is what you can only call a living legend. And that will make *you* a legend, too.'

Zuzana was so cold now that she was shaking violently, and all of a sudden she was overwhelmed by darkness, and sagged down onto her knees. SloMo and Bradley dragged her back to the wheelchair and tucked her back in. John stayed where he was for a few moments more, staring down at the man's pallid face, almost as if he envied him.

'*Mopuushtenpo xaa mochoova*,' he said, so quietly that only the man himself could have heard him, so long as he wasn't sleeping, or dead. 'May the force be with you.'

17

Trinity and Nemo came back from the general store with a cardboard box full of bacon and coffee and cans of beans and cookies. Trinity had found a blue check lumberjack shirt that was only one size too big for her, as well as three pairs of thick size 7 socks.

When they entered the house, they heard Rafael upstairs, making clanking noises. He had told them that he would try to get another shower working. Nemo carried the box into the kitchen and set it down on the pinewood table.

'How about tomato soup?' he suggested.

'I'll fix it,' said Trinity. 'I'm an expert when it comes to heating up canned soup.'

'I should have had a wife like you. Or a daughter like you, anyhow.'

'Don't you have children?'

'Never got around to it. I was always too busy chasing after scumbags and Sherri loved her movie make-up work too much to give it up and raise kids. Besides, I don't think she wanted stretch marks, although it wouldn't surprise me if she has a few now, the size of her.'

Nemo unpacked the groceries while Trinity pinged two mugs of soup in the microwave. Then they went through to the living room and sat down on the couch in front of the television. On ABC7 News they saw that a Confederate monument in the Hollywood Forever Cemetery had been vandalised with the word *Racists* in red paint. This was followed by an update on a massive sixty-five-vehicle pile-up on the Ventura Freeway, in which two drivers and a small child had been killed.

After that, the anchor announced that a young actor who had been accidentally shot on a movie set had died in the early hours of the morning.

'He was playing the part of a werewolf in a multi-million-dollar production at the Mogul film studios called *The Throng*. We understand that it's a spoof horror movie featuring a mass get-together of all the monsters from the most famous horror movies ever made. Its cast includes vampires and zombies and werewolves, plus Freddie from *Nightmare on Elm Street*, Jason Voorhees from *Friday the 13th* and Chucky from *Child's Play*.

'Police officers from the Internal Affairs Group were in pursuit of two suspects who gatecrashed the film set in the middle of a take. One of the suspects opened fire on the officers and when the officers returned fire, the actor was struck in the chest by a stray bullet. His name has not yet been released until his next of kin have all been informed.

'Eyewitnesses say that the suspects were a middle-aged white male and a white woman in her mid-twenties. Both managed to make good their escape. The IAG have so far declined to release their names or descriptions or why they're wanted, but so far the two of them remain at large.'

'That's us,' said Nemo. 'So why won't they give out our names, or say what we're supposed to have done?'

He drained the last of his soup, wiped his mouth on a paper napkin and set down his mug.

'Do you know what I think? I think they're keeping the details under wraps because it would incriminate *them*. It makes me even more certain that your Margo was murdered. It's the way things are done in this country these days. If you have evidence that could bring down somebody important, you don't get the chance to testify in court. You get bumped off.'

'But we don't *know* anything that could bring down somebody important, do we?' said Trinity. 'At least, not yet. All we've managed to find out is that Margo went to parties at John Dangerfield's house and that for some reason she started to get depressed about it.'

'Right. So the first thing we do now is we pin down where John Dangerfield lives. Then we snoop around and try to find out *why* she got so depressed.'

'That's not going to be easy, though, is it, snooping around? What if we get caught?'

'I'm not pretending that it's going to be easy. But you'd be surprised the places you can get into if you have the nerve. I once joined a dinner party at the Penthouse at Mastro's with about a dozen of the top fraudsters in the whole of LA. None of them asked who I was or what I was doing there, and the information I got from their conversation saw three of them jailed for a minimum of ten years. Not only that, the Wagyu Tomahawk chops were to die for.'

Rafael came into the living room, still holding a wrench and looking pleased with himself.

'I've mended the shower in the master bedroom. I guess that's the one you guys will be using?'

'We don't sleep together,' said Nemo. 'We're what you might call business partners, that's all.'

'Oh, sorry. I just assumed. These days you see so many older dudes with younger women, specially around LA. You know, like that Leonardo Di-what's-his-face.'

At that moment the doorbell chimed and Rafael went to answer it. He came back followed by a short elderly man in a light grey three-piece suit. The man's shirt was fastened up to the top button but he wore no tie. Instead, a beaded and fringed medicine bag was hanging around his neck. Trinity guessed that he must be at least eighty years old. His face was wizened, his nose was flat, and his mouth was deeply creased. His hair was woven into shoulder-length braids, and it was as white as the Pine Mountain snow.

All the same, he stood very straight, and he had a commanding presence that Trinity could sense as soon as he walked in.

'This is my grandfather, Teodoro Kip'omo,' said Rafael. 'Grandad, these are friends of Mike who have come to stay for a few days. Nemo and Trinity.'

Teodoro Kip'omo nodded and pressed his hands together by way of greeting.

'Any friend of Mike is also my friend,' he said, in a dry pipe-smoker's voice. 'He was our saviour, after my dear daughter passed.'

Rafael held up a brown paper bag that his grandfather had given him. 'Anybody for acorn pancakes?'

They took drinks out onto the balcony and spent the afternoon talking. Teodoro told them about the history of his tribe and how those Chumash who had resisted the Spanish missionaries had been scattered and lost their lands; and how they had later been betrayed by the federal government, who had never given them back the territory that had been taken from them, where they used to hunt and fish.

'I trust nobody from the government,' he said emphatically. 'They pretend that they are not racist, but nothing would please them more than if the last of the Chumash died out. Like all Indian tribes, we are a constant reminder that this nation, which boasts so proudly that all people are equal, was founded on genocide.'

He stared narrowly at Nemo and Trinity, as if he were daring them to contradict him.

'And you?' he asked at last. 'You are father and daughter? But you are not here on vacation, are you?'

'Shall we tell him?' said Trinity.

'Well, I don't see why not,' Nemo told her. 'He doesn't seem like the kind of guy who's going to rat on us to the authorities, does he?'

'You have done something wrong?' said Teodoro, although it hardly sounded like a question. 'You are hiding out here?'

'How did you guess?'

Teodoro tapped his forehead. 'From the moment I first saw you I knew that you both had shadows behind you. And you are not father and daughter, are you? You have been brought together only by those shadows, whatever they are.'

'That's some intuition,' said Nemo. 'Rafael said that you used to be a shaman. What was the word for it?'

''Atswinic,' said Teodoro. 'And I am still an 'atswinic. I no longer practise medicine because I no longer have my fellow tribespeople around me who need me to treat them when they fall sick. But I have not lost the powers that my dreams used to give me. I can still heal. I can still foretell what the future will bring. I can still make people see things that do not exist, and I can also make things disappear. Watch.'

With that, he set his half-empty beer glass down on the small round table beside him. He closed his eyes and raised both hands and started to recite a repetitive rhyme in what Trinity assumed was Chumash. He droned on and on for nearly two minutes.

After he had finished his intonation, he hummed, and then he whispered a single word. When they looked back at the table, the beer glass had vanished. In its place was a green soapstone figurine, hunchbacked and grinning like a malevolent goblin.

'That's incredible,' said Trinity. 'How did you do that? That was even better than that Dynamo.'

'It is not a magic trick. The glass has changed into a demon because I have made you believe that it has changed into a demon. It is what in Chumash we call "sudden dream", or "*anyapakh*", which means "mirage". Our hunters used the sudden dream as a way to catch all kinds of animals, mostly deer and rabbits. They could make the animals see them as a tree, or a bush, or even another animal, so that the unsuspecting creature would come up close enough for them to be killed with one single cut of a knife.'

'So how the hell does that glass still look like a demon even when you've told us that it isn't?' Nemo demanded.

'Because you are still dreaming that it's a demon. I would say that the nearest effect in the white man's culture is hypnosis. My words and the power that I have in my mind have made you hallucinate.'

Teodoro waved both of his hands from side to side and spoke some more words in Chumash. The green figurine vanished and in its place the beer glass reappeared. Teodoro held it up and said, 'Let us drink to good health, and to dreams.'

Nemo shook his head in disbelief. 'That is totally nuts. You sat there and sang a little song and that was all it took for you to make me have a dream. And I was convinced that I was the most hard-headed guy on the planet.'

'Everybody can be made to have a sudden dream. It is much like the dreams you have when you are almost awake. Sometimes those dreams can seem so real that for a few moments after you have opened your eyes, you can believe that they have actually happened.'

Trinity and Teodoro carried on talking, and Rafael went inside to fetch out a plate of acorn pancakes, along with a pot of chilli and tomato chutney. Nemo remained silent and thoughtful, but after about ten minutes he said, 'Can anybody do that? Make other people think that they're a tree or an animal or whatever?'

'Of course, it takes a little training,' Teodoro told him. 'You have to learn the right words, and you have to find out how to dream in such a way that you can make others dream. But if you are open-minded about such things, then yes.'

'So I could do it? And Trinity – she could do it, too?'

'I see no reason why not. But for what purpose?'

'I'm wondering if we could make people believe that we're somebody else? I mean, could we use these sudden dreams to disguise our faces?'

Teodoro smiled. 'Who do you two want to look like?'

'It doesn't really matter. Anybody who isn't us.'

★

For the rest of the afternoon, Teodoro helped Trinity and Nemo to learn the words of the *anyapakh* incantation that could induce a sudden dream. The rhyme was only four lines, repeated over and over, but both of them found it difficult to get their tongues around the Chumash pronunciation, especially words like *vsqvnv*, to ask.

Trinity was the first to be able to say it correctly, but after more than ten attempts, Nemo at last managed to recite it to Teodoro's satisfaction.

'We should smoke a pipe together to celebrate,' said Teodoro.

'Don't tempt me,' Nemo told him. 'It took me two years of nicotine patches to give up Camels.'

'When will you teach us how to dream?' asked Trinity.

'Tonight, after the sun has gone down, and you are growing tired. I will make you a drink of white sage and momoy and the dreams will come to you. In one of your dreams you will recognise a friend, a helper, and you can ask that friend to come whenever you need them, even if you are awake.

'You will be able to call on that dream friend to enter the minds of anybody you meet, and make them dream that you are different than you really are, in the same way that I made you dream that my glass was a demon.'

'Oh boy,' said Nemo. 'When this is all over I'm going to go back to West Valley and make those conniving bastards who sacked me dream that I'm the chief of police. I'll give them such a hard time that they'll crap their pants, pardon my Chumash.'

'It will depend if your dream friend allows you,' said

Teodoro. 'He will be very protective not only of you but of anybody whose identity you have taken on. For instance, he would not permit you to injure or murder somebody while you appear to be this chief of police.'

'All right, then. I'll make them all dream that I'm a tree. Then, when they come and sit under me, I can steal their billfolds.'

Darkness fell over Pine Mountain like a warm black blanket. It was a cloudy night and so there were no stars visible. The four of them sat in the kitchen for a supper of cheeseburgers and Caesar salad, although Rafael made Trinity a tofu burger with soy sauce and maple syrup.

They spoke very little while they ate, but somehow they had all formed a bond, and felt relaxed with each other. Rafael kept glancing at Trinity and smiling at her, and nodding to make sure that she was enjoying her burger. Trinity couldn't help smiling back. She liked the way he looked, but more than that she liked the way he talked to her as an equal and treated her with respect. She had never experienced that with a boy before.

Nemo and Teodoro got on well together, too, as if they were veterans who had known each other from way back.

At ten-thirty, when they were sitting in the living room half-watching *Doctor Merritt*, Trinity yawned and said, 'I'm really tired now, Teodoro. Do you want to do the dreaming thing? I won't be able to stay awake much longer.'

'Sure,' said Teodoro. 'Let me go to the kitchen and fetch your drink.'

Rafael stood up too, and said, 'I'll show you to your room.'

They went upstairs and along the corridor. Trinity's bedroom was right at the end, facing the back of the house. It was small, with a sloping ceiling, but it had a king-sized bed with a patchwork quilt and a washbasin with a mirror and a bookcase that was crammed with dog-eared crime novels.

On the wall next to the bed hung an oil painting of a young Native American woman in a fur robe, standing on a hilltop and shading her eyes with her hand as she looked towards the far distant mountains. Trinity thought that it illustrated almost exactly the way she was feeling right now – afraid of what was going to happen to her next, but knowing that she couldn't turn back.

Rafael left them and Teodoro said, 'Here... drink this first.'

He had brought a glass bottle from the kitchen with a pale greenish liquid in it. He measured some carefully into a mug and handed it to her. It was still warm and it smelled fragrant and almost too sweet. Trinity hesitated for a moment and then drank it.

'It's a tea, brewed of momoy seeds and white sage. It will bring you strange visions and you may begin to wonder where you are and why you are here. You may wonder *who* or even *what* you are, human or animal. But when you fall asleep, it will take you to places where you will find people who love you and who can take care of you. Dream people. Ask those people which of them is prepared to be your companion and to remain with you for as long as you need them.

'When you wake up, and when the effect of this tea has worn off, go to the mirror and speak the name of your new dream friend. Call on him, or her, or whoever it is. If you have been successful, they will appear to you, and you will know that you can rely on them to help you at any time.'

'This is seriously going to happen?' Trinity asked him. 'I'm going to find a friend in a dream who stays with me when I'm awake?'

'I have had the same dream friend for nearly fifty years,' Teodoro told her, with a puckered smile. 'His name is Shu'nu, which means "sleepyhead". I called him that because I often have to shake him awake so that he can assist me. But today he woke up quickly enough when I wanted you to dream that my beer glass was a demon. Now… lie down, relax, and let the visions rise inside of your mind.'

Trinity eased off her trainers and dropped them onto the floor. Then she tied her hair back in a knot and lay down on the bed. The patchwork quilt was soft and slightly damp and smelled faintly of the same perfume that Trinity's grandmother used to wear. It gave her a strangely mixed feeling of sadness and reassurance, like hearing a familiar song from long ago.

'I will leave you now,' said Teodoro. 'But I will be listening, and looking in on you, in case you show any signs that you need me. I don't expect that you will, though, because the amount of momoy that I gave you is quite safe, and the white sage will clear your mind and help you to sleep. I used to give it as a cure for insomnia.'

'Your people must miss you.'

Teodoro had one wrinkled hand raised against the door, with a silver ring on every finger. 'I miss my people. The spirits miss my people, the First Ones who were here on this earth before we were. The land and the sea, they miss my people too, because my people treated them with care, and respect.'

Once he had gone, Trinity lay with her eyes open, looking up at the sloping ceiling. After a while, she began to feel that the bed was gently wallowing from side to side, and up and down, as if it were floating on the ocean. She lifted her head up and looked around. The bedroom was still the same, but the wallowing sensation continued. She looked up at the ceiling again, and saw that the cedarwood boards were starting to open up, right above her head, and were rolling apart with a clattering sound to reveal the night sky. She saw stars, and comets, and then the moon passed overhead, huge and bright.

Once the moon had gone, the sky darkened again, and the light in the bedroom dimmed too. She heard a clicking, scurrying noise, and when she strained her eyes she could just make out that hordes of spiders and cockroaches were swarming into the bedroom through the opening in the ceiling. There were thousands of them, and they came pouring down the walls, completely covering the painting of the young woman on the hilltop, and filling up the washbasin so that they overflowed and dropped out onto the floor.

Trinity crossed her arms tightly over her chest and drew up her knees. She had always hated spiders and cockroaches, and now the whole bedroom was alive with masses of them, glittering and rippling, covering the floor and crawling up the sides of the overhanging quilt. She could hear them, and she could even *smell* them, that sickening brown stench of cockroach.

This is not real, she told herself, with her eyes tightly shut. *This is a mirage*. Without knowing why, she thought of the word *anyapakh*, and then she said it out loud.

'*Anyapakh!*'

The bedroom instantly fell silent, and the bed stopped floundering up and down. Cautiously, she opened her eyes. The spiders and the cockroaches had all vanished. The ceiling was boarded up again. Gradually, the bedside lamp grew brighter.

She relaxed, and straightened out her legs. Teodoro had warned her that she would have hallucinations, and she was relieved that he hadn't dosed her with so much momoy that she hadn't been able to realise that those scurrying insects had been nothing more than a drug-induced delusion. She sat up and looked over the side of the bed, just to make sure that there were no spiders or cockroaches still crawling around on the carpet. Then she flopped back on the quilt and closed her eyes. She was overwhelmingly tired, and the flavonoids in the white sage had emptied out her mind of any resistance to sleep.

If she slept, she would dream; and if she dreamed, she would meet those people who could help her, and find a dream friend.

Yet she wasn't asleep. She was walking around Reseda Park Lake on a warm afternoon, with ragged white clouds floating north-eastwards overhead. As usual, the path around the lake was crowded with geese and ducks, and they were so reluctant to move out of her way that they brushed against her ankles.

Her legs were bare because she was wearing nothing but a waist-length crop top printed with big red poppies. Nobody stared at her and she felt no embarrassment. In fact, she felt comfortable and attractive – more assured of her appearance than she had felt for a long time.

As she came around the north side of the lake, past the pump house, she saw that a group of eight or nine people, both men and women, were sitting on the grass on blankets, enjoying a picnic. They were all dressed formally in white – the men in blazers and the women in ankle-length dresses.

They had propped up white parasols to shield themselves and their plates of food from the sun, and they had ice buckets crowded with bottles of champagne and white wine. It was like a scene from a 1930s' Hollywood movie.

Several of them stood up as Trinity approached, smiling and raising their glasses to her. A tall man with a straw boater and a neat ginger moustache came up to her and said, 'Trinity! We've been expecting you! Come and join us!'

'I'm looking for a friend,' she told him, in a whispery voice. She couldn't understand why she was speaking so softly, but then it occurred to her that she didn't want to wake herself up.

'Yes, we know you are,' the man replied. 'That's why we've all gathered here. It's always our pleasure to meet a dreamer who's looking for somebody to take care of them. In your case, we've been waiting for quite a long time, but we had a feeling that you'd come sooner or later.'

Trinity shyly joined the group, kneeling down on one of the blankets. Their faces were all blurry, as if they had been pixilated, but she could see that they were all smiling at her warmly, and one of the women said, 'You can see the resemblance, can't you? Quite striking!'

The man with the ginger moustache stood beside her and laid his hand on her shoulder. 'Most dreamers find it quite challenging when it comes to choosing a dream friend. But your dream friend has selected herself already, and who better?'

Trinity frowned as she looked around. The picnickers' faces were all so out of focus that she couldn't recognise any of them. Who could have chosen to be her dream friend already, and why?

It was then that she saw a woman leave the shade of a tree about fifty yards away and come walking towards them. She was wearing an ankle-length white dress, like all of the other women, as well as a white wide-brimmed hat that cast a shadow over her face so that at first Trinity didn't recognise her.

Only when she came walking between the tilted parasols did Trinity realise who the woman was. She burst into tears and jumped up onto her feet, and as the woman came nearer her legs were trembling like a newborn foal.

The dream friend who had been waiting so long for her was Valerie Fox. She was her mother.

18

'Not tomorrow night but the night after,' said John Dangerfield. 'That's when you'll be meeting your destiny.'

Bradley had hung the blind back over the window of Zuzana's bedroom so that it was dark once again, and John was standing silhouetted in the open doorway, wearing a silky grey shirt and high-waisted black trousers.

The Ghost Woman was hunched up on her chair, although she had draped her shawl over her head so that Zuzana was unable to see the smouldering greenish glow of her eyes.

'Before then, though, there are certain necessary rituals that have to be performed,' John continued, in the same tour-guide tone that he had used before, when he had taken her to see the white-faced figure on the plinth. 'Everything that has happened to you so far in this house has been part of your preparation for your great final moment. Your *coup de théâtre*, as it were – although it would probably be more accurate to call it your *coup de grâce*.'

Zuzana lay on her left side, staring at the wall. She could hear John speaking, but his words made no sense to her at all, and all she wanted to do was fall asleep, and wake up somewhere else, even if it was back in her apartment with Rod.

'First, of course, David Magellan took you. That was only to make sure that your last intimate encounter before you began your initiation had not been with some unbeliever from outside our circle – that your insides were purged of any trace of him. Then I took you myself, in the mask of *'ałxałtisqom*. The purpose of that was to introduce you not only to the physical symbolism that you will be celebrating the night after next, but to the spiritual symbolism, too. *'ałxałtisqom*.'

Although John repeated the name slowly and with much more emphasis, Zuzana didn't want to know what it meant. She just wanted him to go away and leave her in peace.

'*'ałxałtisqom*,' the Ghost Woman repeated, in a muffled but reverent voice from under her shawl.

'I'll be back later, when the moon has gone down,' said John. 'You should rest, in the meantime. Sleep if you can. You're going to need it.'

Zuzana closed her eyes. She heard the door close, and the bedroom was left in total darkness. All she could hear now was the soft whistle of the Ghost Woman breathing and the faint monotonous thumping of some heavy guitar riff from downstairs. It sounded like ZZ Top playing 'La Grange'.

She tried to sleep, but after about ten minutes she opened her eyes again. She couldn't sleep. She couldn't escape. All she could do was wait here until John returned, and suffer whatever he had planned for her.

He came back soon after the clock had struck midnight. He was accompanied by SloMo and another man she hadn't seen before, a lanky African American in a grey hoodie. This man had a shiny shaved head and his lower lip was pierced with stainless-steel studs.

'Ah, good, Zuzana, you're awake,' said John. 'DaShawn – help SloMo to carry her downstairs, will you?'

DaShawn stepped into the bedroom but when John switched on the overhead light he caught sight of the Ghost Woman sitting behind the door and he stopped abruptly and turned around, his eyes bulging.

'Yo! What is *that*, bro? That frighten the livin' shit out of me!'

'Oh, *her*,' John told him calmly. 'You don't have to be afraid of her. Well, I say that, but for the love of God don't rile her up for any reason. If you do that, all I can say is – hold on to your cojones.'

DaShawn continued to keep a wary eye on the Ghost Woman as he and SloMo lifted Zuzana off the bed and carried her out through the door. As before, Zuzana went completely limp, so that they would find her harder to carry, her arms and her legs dangling and her head tilted to one side.

'This bitch acting awkward on purpose,' said DaShawn. 'Come on, bitch, why don't you co-operate and straighten yourself up?'

SloMo grunted. 'Are you kidding? She'd act even more awkward if she knew what was coming.'

They carried her down the stairs to the atrium and then through to the entertainment room. Zuzana still kept her eyes closed but she could hear that the room was crowded. The music had stopped but there was subdued conversation and nervous laughter and the tinkling of wine glasses. As she was carried across the floor a woman let out a little breathless scream, as if she were close to an orgasm.

SloMo and DaShawn sat Zuzana down in what felt like a heavy wooden chair. She felt them fasten her wrists tightly to the arms of the chair with leather straps, and it was then that she opened her eyes. There must have been at least fifty or sixty people gathered around her, mostly middle-aged men in tuxedos of varying pastel colours, but young girls, too, in sparkly revealing dresses and skin-tight camel-toe leggings and impossibly high-heeled shoes.

Everyone in this crowd was staring at her as if she were some rare and unusual animal on display in a zoo. They spoke to each other, and nodded confidentially, and sipped at their champagne flutes, but not one of them came up to speak to her or find out if she needed any help. She tugged at the straps holding her wrists and shook her head from side to side and when she pressed the stub of her tongue up against the roof of her mouth she managed to produce a gargling, hooting sound, but none of the crowd asked her if she was in distress.

As she looked around, desperately trying to communicate with her eyes the words that she was unable to speak without her tongue, she saw that almost all of the men had the same eyes as John Dangerfield – silver and shining, expressionless yet somehow triumphant, like robots' eyes. She recognised some of them, too, from her evenings serving at The Orange Grove: Ward Briscoe, the director of *Shark Tsunami*; Robert Manzetti, the producer of the Flying Frogs cartoons; and T.B. Fawkes, the scriptwriter for the horror movie *Twelve Terror Street*.

Four black jazz musicians were standing on the stage, and they struck up a slow and dirge-like tune, like 'St James Infirmary' played at half speed, punctuated by a monotonous thumping drumbeat. As they started to play, the crowd parted, and John Dangerfield appeared, wearing a long leather butcher's apron. He was followed by SloMo and Bradley and DaShawn and a white-haired man who was another one of John's staff. They were carrying a stretcher between them, at shoulder height, like pall-bearers carrying a coffin to a funeral.

As they reached the chair where Zuzana was sitting, John stepped aside so that the four of them could lower the stretcher onto the floor. Lying on it was a full-grown female coyote, with cinnamon-grey fur and a dark-tipped tail. The coyote was semi-comatose but clearly still alive. Her tongue was lolling out between her teeth and she was softly panting. Zuzana could only guess that she had been drugged, just as she had been herself.

John raised his hand and the music stopped. Then he looked around at his assembled guests and said, 'In the name of 'ałxałtisqom, you are assembled here tonight for the preparation of Zuzana Zilka for her ultimate sacrifice. She will be taken to meet her destiny not tomorrow night but the night after that, when the full moon is watching.

'Tonight, she is here for her blooding, and for her merging with the gods who roamed these plains and these mountains long before man and woman made their appearance. When this is done, she will have reached the stage of transcendence that Weywot expects, and all she will need to do then is take the five potions that will finally prepare her for the momentous journey on which she is about to embark.'

There was a general murmur of approval from the crowd, and some of them lifted their glasses to salute him.

John held out his hand, and DaShawn came up to him and

gave him a broad-bladed knife. He raised the knife up high so that it flashed in the light of the chandeliers and everybody could see it, and then he turned to Zuzana. Panicking, she struggled even harder against her straps, and twisted herself from side to side on the seat of the wooden chair.

He said nothing as he approached her, although she could see that his nostrils were flaring. It was impossible to read any expression in those shining ball-bearing eyes. She managed to make another hooting sound, but the only effect that had on him was to make him lick his lips with the tip of his tongue, as if he could taste her blood already.

Oh God, he's going to cut my throat. He's going to murder me and all those people are going to watch him do it, and they're going to enjoy it. Oh please, dear God, please let it be quick if he's going to do it, and please don't let it hurt.

John leaned over her chair, face to face, so close that she could smell the alcohol and the garlic on his breath, even over the antiseptic-soaked gauze that filled her mouth.

'Don't be frightened, sweetheart,' he told her, in a low, seductive tone. 'You're by far the most beautiful young woman that we've ever been blessed with. Even that lovely girl that DeShawn brought us – the one you saw – she couldn't hold a candle to you. You'll be given all the respect that your beauty entitles you to, and more. I can promise you that.'

With that, he took hold of the hem of her bathrobe, lifted it up, and sliced it open all the way to her neckline. She moaned, and jerked her head to one side, but he didn't cut her throat. Instead, he slit open each of her sleeves, one after the other, all the way down to the cuffs, and then stepped away. Bradley came forward, gripped the ends of her nightgown, and wrenched it out from under her, a few inches at a time, until she was sitting on the chair naked.

Again, there was murmured applause from the crowd, and Zuzana heard somebody close beside her say, 'What a *babe*, John! I mean, wow! Where the heck did you find *her*, if you don't mind me asking?'

'Ask the Priest. It was the Priest who fetched her here. You can't match the Priest when it comes to sniffing out hotties.'

Zuzana turned her head and saw the comedy actor Bill Nugent leering at her. He winked and gave her a thumbs up. All she could think of was how much older he appeared in real life than he did on the screen. In movies he had a shock of blondish hair, like Donald Trump, but apart from a few stray wisps he was almost completely bald.

John beckoned to SloMo and Bradley and DaShawn. Between them, SloMo and Bradley heaved the coyote up off the stretcher and held her upright so that her hind paws were clear of the floor. Her head slowly sank back into the fur around her neck and her muzzle pointed up towards the ceiling. She didn't struggle at all and her yellowy-green eyes were glazed over so Zuzana could tell how deeply she had been sedated.

John bowed his head to the crowd. Then, without any hesitation, he went up to the coyote and slashed her throat wide open, left to right, so fast that Zuzana didn't realise at first what he had done. It was only when she saw blood spraying across the polished oak floor and heard the coyote let out a high breathy squeak that she understood that he had killed her.

He didn't stop with cutting her throat. He stuck the point of the knife into the gaping wound in her neck and then he dragged it slowly downwards, cutting apart the fur on her ribcage so that it wrinkled and then opening up her belly so that her stomach and her liver and her intestines slid out between her legs in a bloody jumble.

Zuzana turned away again, only to find Bill Nugent still leering at her. He smacked his lips at her lustfully and so she turned her head the other way, only to find herself looking at a red-haired girl who was letting out little squeals of excitement as John dragged out the coyote's bowels and dumped them on the floor. She had one hand squeezed between her thighs and was hopping from one foot to the other.

John raised his hand again for silence, and then he said, 'This is the ritual that shows that Zuzana Zilka is accepted by the animal gods – that she takes on their form, and shares their blood, and that their spirits are sisters.'

When he had said that, the four musicians struck up again, this time with a discordant tune that sounded as if they were all screaming, punctuated by irregular beats on the bass drum and crashes on the cymbals.

John swiftly cut the coyote's intestines away from her body, and then SloMo and Bradley carried her empty carcass around to the back of Zuzana's chair, dripping with blood. John joined them and guided the furry body as they lowered it on top of her, wedging her head into the neck cavity so that she was wearing the coyote's head on top of her own, like a monstrous crown.

John laid a paw on each of her shoulders so that the coyote appeared to be embracing her from behind. Blood was already sliding down her forehead and droplets were getting caught in her eyelashes. Then John came around to admire her, and to give her a beatific smile. Then he stepped away, walking backwards and bowing to her as if she were a queen, or a minor deity, and this had been her coronation.

'There!' he cried out. 'Now she's blooded!'

Zuzana was too shocked to weep. She sat in her chair with the thirty-pound weight of the coyote pulling her head back and pools of blood congealing in her collarbone, staring at the ceiling. All around her the crowd drank and talked and laughed, growing more and more raucous, and the smell of skunk smoke grew stronger. The screeching music came to an end, and the musicians started playing a slow, creepy-sounding rumba.

Several men came to look at her and they all had those silvery eyes. It was only when the sky began to lighten outside the French doors that a stocky man in a dark blue tuxedo approached her and stood staring at her for much longer than the rest. He was ugly in an oddly attractive way, with a widow's peak and narrow eyes and a bulbous nose. He stared at her for so long that she tilted her head forward a little and stared back at him. Unlike the other men, his eyes were pale blue, like an angel in a medieval painting. He was holding a cigar, and the smoke was curling around him in the dawn sunlight.

'If you only knew how much you mean to me,' he said at last.

Zuzana could only continue to stare at him in silence. Her neck was aching now and she felt exhausted.

'Maybe you don't recognise me,' he told her. 'Joe Bellman. No? Did you ever see a movie called *Death By Laughter*? I directed it. Two thousand and seventeen, that was.'

Bradley came up and said, 'Joe? You want another drink? We'll be serving breakfast in about a half-hour.'

'Sure, yes. I'll be with you in a minute,' said Joe, without taking his eyes off Zuzana.

When Bradley had gone, he came up closer so that his trousers were almost touching her bare knees.

'I've had a long run of bad luck since then, although I don't expect you to know that. What I badly needed was some extra chutzpah, to say the least. And you're going to make that possible. So if I don't have the chance to tell you again – thanks. I mean it, darling. I really do. Thanks from the very bottom of my heart.'

With that, he turned and rejoined the crowd, and Zuzana let her head drop back. The musicians were playing a faster rumba now, and some of John's guests were dancing.

19

When Trinity came downstairs in her blue check shirt, Rafael was already in the kitchen, frying bacon.

'Hey, sleep well?' he asked her.

She nodded, and sat down at the table.

'Dream?'

'Yes.'

'Care for a coffee? You bought some soy milk, didn't you?'

'Yes. Yes, please.'

He poured her a mug of coffee, dropped a spoon in it, and brought it over. 'Was it the right kind of dream? Like – did you find yourself a friend?'

She smiled tightly and her eyes filled with tears. 'Yes. I found a friend. And I can't tell you how happy I am. It's my mother. She died three years ago, but now I have her back again. I can feel that she's with me, even now. It's like she's sitting right here next to me.'

Rafael went back to his frying pan. 'That's amazing. Your mother? I never heard of that before. I mean, usually it's some total stranger and all they want is the chance to come back out into the world where people are awake.'

'They're always dead people?'

'Mostly. Sometimes people in comas, you know? People who aren't going to wake up for years, or maybe never.'

'It's such a good feeling. But do you think it's going to work? Do you think she's going to be able to make anybody think that I look like somebody else?'

'You saw what my grandpa did with his beer glass. But you could always try it out, if you want to. You can try it out on me, but let me finish frying these rashers. I don't want to set fire to the place.'

Once he had scraped the bacon onto a plate and put it in the oven to keep warm, Rafael stood by the window and said, 'Okay. I'm all yours.'

Trinity had no idea how this dream disguise was supposed to work, but she closed her eyes and she could sense her mother's presence as strongly as if she were actually there, beside her.

I want Rafael to see me differently, she told her mother, inside her mind. *I want him to see me with short blonde hair and looking much older, maybe about forty, with a pointy nose and a pointy chin and wearing a chunky green sweater.*

She visualised the woman that she wanted Rafael to see, as vividly as if she actually knew her. It wasn't difficult, because she closely resembled her math teacher from John R. Wooden High School, Ms Novak, and her mother had known Ms Novak too.

She recited the words that Teodoro had taught her, and when she had repeated them five times she hummed and whispered '*anyapakh*'.

At first she felt nothing, but then she had a sliding sensation inside her mind, as if her head had been covered in a black cloth hood and somebody had drawn it off. She opened her eyes and saw that Rafael was staring at her as if he couldn't believe what he was seeing.

'Well?' she said, and she reached up and tugged at her hair. It was still long, and it was still brunette. 'It hasn't worked, has it?'

'Are you *kidding* me? You look totally different. You don't look like you at all.'

'Really? You're not just saying that?'

Trinity pushed back her chair and stood up. 'Go on, then. Tell me what I look like.'

'You have short fair hair and you look kind of like a witch.'

'A *witch*? Oh, thanks!'

'Well, sorry, but it's your nose. You could open a can of beans with that nose!'

Trinity couldn't help laughing. She came around the table and stood right in front of Rafael and said, 'You'd better watch out, then. I might stab you with it! So, go on, what am I wearing?'

'You're wearing this thick woolly sweater. And black stockings.'

'All right. What colour is my sweater?'

'Green. Same green as that pond, out there in the yard.'

Trinity didn't know what to say. Her dream friend had made Rafael dream. Her mother had entered his mind and changed his perception of her so that she couldn't be recognised.

'Is that what you wanted to look like?' he asked her. 'Did I get it right?'

'Exactly. It's incredible. I didn't believe that it would work, but it does. But what happens now? How do I stop you dreaming? How do I get back to looking like myself?'

'I don't know. Maybe just close your eyes and imagine it.'

Trinity closed her eyes and tried to think of her reflection in a mirror. After a few moments she opened them again and said, 'Well?'

'You're still witchy.'

'But I'm not really witchy. You're just dreaming that I'm witchy.'

'Then maybe it's down to me.'

Rafael put his arms around her waist and held her closer. Then he leaned forward and kissed her on the lips, very lightly.

'You don't feel like a witch,' he said, staring into her eyes.

Trinity raised her hands onto his shoulders and kissed him back, just as lightly. Then they kissed harder, with passion, holding on to each other as if they were lovers who had been reunited after months of separation. Rafael's tongue slid between her lips and their tongues fought each other. His left hand cupped her breast and he pressed his hips harder against her so she could feel that he was aroused already.

There was a dry cough, and they instantly parted, and looked around. Nemo was standing in the kitchen doorway with a grin on his face.

'Hate to interrupt your powwow here, folks, but I smell bacon.'

A few minutes later Teodoro came downstairs, his long white hair hanging loose, and they all sat down for breakfast. Rafael served up bacon and fried eggs and hash browns for himself and Nemo and Teodoro. For Trinity he filled a bowl with granola and topped it with blueberries and honey yogurt.

As they ate, Rafael told Teodoro how impressed he had been with Trinity's sudden dream disguise.

'And do you know what? Her dream friend turned out to be her mother, who died of cancer. You've made her incredibly happy.'

'And *you*?' asked Teodoro, turning to Nemo. 'Did *you* dream, and find yourself a friend?'

Nemo prodded at his bacon. 'I did, yes, except it was more of a nightmare than a dream. I was back in uniform, carrying out a drugs bust behind the Dog Haus in Canoga Park. There were five other cops there – six, including the undercover cop who had blown the whistle on the drug dealers. Jim Moretti, his name was.'

'And he was the one you chose to be your friend?'

'Well, to be honest, we kind of chose each other. We'd always worked close together when he was alive, and we were good buddies. He was undercover in the Bryant Street gang when somebody ratted on him. They shot him in the back of the head and dumped his body on the sidewalk outside the West Valley station.'

'Do you want to try and see how well he can disguise you?' asked Teodoro.

Nemo looked around the table. 'That would mean making the three of you dream.'

'That's right. But once it has begun, the sudden dream affects everybody who sees you. When you go to investigate this young woman's death, you will probably find that you have many more people than three to delude, and all at the same time. But very few people are on their guard against dreaming, or resistant to it. It's the same as hypnosis. You've seen these stage hypnotists who can make a dozen volunteers fall asleep with a snap of their fingers. Sudden dreaming is similar, except that you're calling on the spiritual power of your chosen friend.'

Nemo laid down his fork. 'Okay... I'll give it a shot. Let me think who I want me to look like, instead of me.'

He closed his eyes for a moment, and then he said, 'Okay. Jim and me, we've decided.'

He closed his eyes again and recited the Chumash incantation. He stumbled on the words once or twice, but repeated them in order to correct himself. Then he gave a low hum and pointed to Teodoro first, and then Rafael, and finally to Trinity.

His appearance changed right in front of their eyes, as if his face were made of soft melted wax that an invisible sculptor was remodelling into the likeness of someone else altogether. He looked younger, and thinner, with a high forehead and long swept-back hair. His eyes were much deeper set, but they had a devilish look in them. His lips were thinner, and they were curled in a sly, irreverent smile.

'You know who you remind me of now?' said Trinity. 'Clint Eastwood, when he was in those spaghetti westerns.'

'Yeah, me too,' said Rafael. 'Definitely Clint Eastwood.'

'Well, you're not far wrong,' Nemo told them. 'Actually, I've modelled my dream on my old firearms instructor, Sergeant Boyle. He was always being mistaken for Clint Eastwood, excepting that he was about six inches taller, and I'll bet he was a darn sight handier with a .44 Magnum than Clint Eastwood. Bullseye Boyle, that's what everybody called him.

He could shoot the heart out the ace of hearts from a distance of forty-five metres.'

'In a way, then, it's a pity that you're not really him,' said Teodoro. 'But you have succeeded in making us all dream that you look like him. Even me, although I deliberately relaxed my mind to allow you to change how I saw you.'

'It's unbelievable,' said Trinity. 'But if we disguise ourselves with these sudden dreams, can we go visit my dad and Rosie and Buddy? I've been so worried about them.'

'Sure,' said Nemo. Although he looked so different, he had the same gravelly voice, which Trinity found quite eerie. 'As soon as we've tracked down where this John Dangerfield character lives, we'll drive directly back down to LA. We'll make a point of calling on your family first, okay?'

'You were trying last night to find out where he lived, weren't you? Did you have any luck?'

'Not yet, no. I found his previous address in Malibu, but he hasn't lived there for five years now. Then I remembered this guy called Dean McCloskey. He used to be a cop but he quit to be a personal security guard for Universal because the money was so much better. He wasn't home but his wife said that she was expecting him back later this morning, so I'll try him again. I'd say there's a good chance that he knows where Dangerfield is living now, or at least knows somebody else who knows. I wish I'd thought of him before.'

Trinity said, 'So long as I can make sure that my dad's managing to take care of Rosie and Buddy, and that they're all safe. And – can you please stop me dreaming that you look like Bullseye Boyle? If you really *were* him, I'm not too sure that I'd like you. You look – I don't know – kind of *sly*.'

*

Trinity was out on the balcony with Rafael when Nemo came to tell her that Dean McCloskey had found John Dangerfield's new address for him.

'Chantilly Road, Bel Air. Once we've checked up on your dad, we can go up there and scout the place out. It's a pretty elite street, Chantilly Road, I can tell you. You might be lucky and find yourself a house there for as little as seven-and-a-half million, but it would only have five bathrooms.'

Trinity stood up. 'Are we going to go right now?'

'I have to call Mike and ask him if we can borrow his Acadia. I've borrowed it before so I know where he keeps the keys. But I don't want to risk us going back to LA in my own car. We'd get picked up by ALPR cameras before we could find someplace to park, and I kid you not.'

Trinity looked baffled, so he said, 'Automatic license plate readers. They have this amazing Palantir software that can pick out any vehicle the cops are looking for, and even ones they're not. When I was in the force I used it maybe twenty or thirty times a day, and that was only me and my team. Believe me, there's nowhere you can drive in LA without your vehicle being under surveillance. Absolutely nowhere.'

'You've made me feel worried now. Sometimes when I've been late to pick up Rosie and Buddy from school I've really put my foot down and driven like a maniac.'

Nemo went back indoors to try and get in touch with Mike. When he had gone, Rafael came up to Trinity and took hold of both of her hands.

'You'll be careful, Trin, won't you? You won't do anything too risky?'

'You mean like barging into another movie studio full of monsters? I'll try not to.'

'No, I'm serious. I don't want anything to happen to you.'

'I don't want anything to happen to me, either, Rafael. But Nemo – he'll look after me. I know he will. We're a team. Fox and Frisby. Frisby and Fox.'

Nemo drove slowly past Trinity's house on Zelzah Avenue but didn't stop. Only a few houses further on, he said, 'There… that blue Malibu. Don't turn your head to look at it. But that's one of the cars that the IAG uses. And – see – there's two guys sitting in it. I'll drive around the block just to make sure but I doubt if they have more than those two staking your house out.'

'So what do we do?'

'From what Teodoro told me, all we have to do is park right up close behind them and say the words and they'll start dreaming. Of course they'll see us when we cross the street and walk up to your house, but with any luck we won't be matching our descriptions.'

'What if they take pictures of us? We can't make their cameras dream, can we?'

'That's a chance we'll have to take. We won't be staying more than a few minutes, will we, and if they *do* take pictures, hopefully they won't check them out until after we've gone.'

Nemo drove up as far as Hart Street and then U-turned and drove back down Zelzah so that he could pull in close behind the blue Malibu.

'Okay… we're going to recite the words together?' said Nemo. 'You're better at it than me.'

They chanted the Chumash rhyme. Nemo said it slowly, but this time he was word-perfect.

'Fingers crossed this is going to work,' said Nemo, unbuckling his seat belt. 'I have my heater if it hasn't, but let's hope it doesn't come to that.'

They climbed out of the Acadia and crossed over to the opposite sidewalk, not even glancing at the two IAG officers. Next door to Trinity's house, Kenno had the hood of his orange Challenger lifted, and was tinkering underneath it with a wrench. He turned around and looked at them as they passed but he showed no sign that he recognised Trinity. Teodoro had been right: the sudden dream effect appeared to work on everybody who saw them. To him, Trinity would have looked like Ms Novak, her math teacher, with her short blonde hair and her frumpy green sweater.

Trinity had a key to her front door but Nemo had cautioned her not to use it. The IAG investigators might see her and wonder how this strange woman was able to let herself in. She rang the doorbell and waited, and when nobody came to answer it, she rang again, and again.

Eventually they heard somebody stumbling inside, and the door was opened. Her father was standing there, blinking, unshaven, wearing a grubby fawn T-shirt and drooping boxer shorts and one sandal. The other sandal had dropped off halfway down the hall.

'Whatever you want, I gave already,' he told them, his voice slurring. 'And if I didn't give already, I'll give next time. But not today. I'm cashless in Gaza.'

'Dad, you're not going to believe me, but I'm Trinity, and this is Nemo.'

'*What?* No, you're not. What the hell are you talking about?'

'Dad, just let us in and we'll show you. We're wearing this kind of disguise.'

'Disguise?' He peered at them narrowly. 'I don't believe you. Get the hell off of my porch before I call the cops.'

He started to close the door but Nemo stepped forward and pushed it wide open again, forcing Trinity's father back into the hallway.

'Hey – what the fuck!'

'Quick – *in*,' Nemo told Trinity, and once she had stepped inside, he slammed the door shut.

Trinity closed her eyes for a moment, and said, '*anyapakh!*' When she opened them again, her father was staring at her as if she had hit him on the side of the head with a baseball bat.

'Trin? *Trin!* Is that you? How the hell did you do that?'

Nemo repeated '*anyapakh*', and he too melted back into his normal appearance.

'Oh, now – no, this is too fucking much,' said her father, backing away towards the kitchen. 'I've had a beer or three this morning, but this is insane.'

Trinity went up to him and caught hold of his hand. 'Dad, don't worry. The way we both looked – it's a trick, that's all. A really clever trick, like an optical illusion. This really is us.'

Her father stopped, breathing heavily. Trinity leaned close to him and said, very quietly, 'There once was a lady whose head was made out of currants and bread.'

His bloodshot eyes widened. That was the first line of a rhyme that he had made up when Trinity was little, and which he used to recite to her almost every night when she was tucked up in her crib. The last line ended, '—nothing but crumbs in her bed.'

'Jesus Christ, it *is* you,' said her father. 'And you, too, mister. Sorry, I forget your name.'

'Nemo. Same as the captain of the *Nautilus*.'

'Well, I sure as hell don't know how you fooled me into thinking you looked like two other people, but you sure as hell did. How'd you do that? *Why*'d you do that?'

'The house is being watched by those same guys who came looking for us before,' said Trinity. 'The same guys we ran away from.'

'Come into the kitchen and sit down. They were pretty damned aggressive, those guys. They said I should call them if you ever came back. As if I would. So they're still out there, are they? Give them a call my ass.'

'How have you been coping, Dad? Where's Rosie and Buddy?'

'Oh, I've been managing not too bad. We had a Hungry-Man chicken dinner last night. And this morning Rosie made waffles. And I've even done some laundry.'

'Where is Rosie? And Buddy? I was hoping to see them.'

Her father went to the fridge and took out a can of Rolling Rock. He popped the top and took a swig and sat down. Then he said, 'Okay, okay. Give me the disapproving look, why don't you? But I'm weaning myself off it. And what else am I supposed to do, sitting in this house all on my ownsome?'

'So where are they?'

'Rosie's friend came around. You know that real pretty one, Sally? Her dad fetched them both back from school. She said that the movie agent who had spotted her in the ice-cream parlour had invited her to meet some director. It seems like there's a good chance that he could cast her in a new movie he's putting together. But he said this director was looking for a twosome, so could Rosie come along too.'

'Rosie told me he was really insulting about the way she looked, and said she'd never get a part in a movie in a million years, or something like that. She was real upset, as you can imagine.'

Her father swallowed more beer, and shrugged. 'Sally said that he was sorry about that, and in fact she had exactly the type of face this director was looking for.'

'Really? That sounds kind of fishy to me. How did this director know what she looked like?'

'I'm only telling you what Sally told Rosie. And Rosie was real excited. This agent guy was waiting outside in his car and they both went off with him.'

'What? And you didn't ask where he was taking them, this agent? Do you even know his name? Or when he's going to fetch Rosie back home?'

'Rosie's a big girl now, Trin. She can look after herself. And she has her phone.'

'Dad, she's only fourteen. She's not even old enough to see an R-rated movie on her own.'

'She'll be okay. Sally's parents wouldn't have let her go off with this guy if they didn't think he could be trusted.'

'Maybe Sally's parents don't even know that she's gone off with him. You know how ditsy they are. Anyhow, what about Buddy? What's he up to?'

'He went off to play with that José kid. He promised he'd be back by five at the latest. We're having hot dogs.'

'Okay...' said Trinity, without much confidence. 'How

are you doing for money? You said just now that you were cashless.'

'That's when I thought you two were collecting for charity. My unemployment came through, so I'm fine for now.'

Nemo looked at his watch and said, 'Trin – we should get moving. There's so much we need to look into.'

Trinity's father stood up. 'That's what this disguise is for, is it?'

'It keeps us safe from the bad guys, Mr Fox,' said Nemo. 'It's an old Indian trick that we've been taught.'

Trinity was tempted for a moment to tell her father that her mother was now her dream friend, but she caught Nemo frowning at her as if he could guess what she had in mind, and was advising her not to. She knew that he was right. Her father would only be confused. He wouldn't be able to feel or see or talk to her mother and he had suffered enough pain from losing her without being hurt any more.

'Oh, Trin – before you go!' her father said, snapping his fingers. 'Sandy Willard from next door came around last night. She collected up all your clothes from their garden and packed them in a suitcase for you. She said it's only an old one so she's in no particular hurry to have it back.'

He went into the living room and returned with a battered blue suitcase.

'How about that,' said Nemo. 'There are some good people in this world after all. And that means we won't have to go clothes shopping for you now.'

'Oh,' said Trinity.

'Hey, darling! Don't look so disappointed!' said her father, putting his arm around her and giving her a hug.

'Dad – you will take good care of Rosie and Buddy, won't

you? I know it's hard, cutting down the drinking, but please try. I'll keep in touch with you as often as I can.'

Her father kissed her. 'Your mom would have been proud of you, Trin. You know that, don't you?'

Trinity and Nemo repeated their Chumash incantation while Trinity's father stood and watched them with his beer can in his hand, shaking his head slowly in semi-drunken wonder. Once their appearance had changed, they left the house and crossed back over the street.

'First stop, Chantilly Road,' said Nemo. 'Let's take a look at where this John Dangerfield lives.'

As they approached the blue Malibu, the two IAG investigators opened their doors and climbed out. They held up their badges and one of them said, 'Pardon us, folks. Okay if we ask you a couple of questions?'

'Questions? What about?' said Nemo.

'You've just paid a visit to the Fox household. Can I ask you what the purpose of your visit was?'

'Sure, you can ask. But I'm under no obligation to tell you.'

'Do you happen to know Ms Trinity Fox, who lives there?'

'What if we do?'

'Do you happen to know Ms Fox's current whereabouts?'

'What if we did?'

'Ms Fox is wanted for questioning regarding a serious criminal case. We'd very much appreciate your co-operation in locating her.'

'So you have no idea where she is?'

'Not right now, sir, no.'

Trinity was standing less than six feet away from this investigator, and facing him. She could tell by the tone of Nemo's responses that he was relishing how ironic this was.

The other investigator stepped closer to Nemo and looked at him quizzically. 'Don't I *know* you?' he asked. 'You're not Sergeant Boyle, by any chance? Didn't you give me my firearms training? Bullseye Boyle?'

'No,' said Nemo. 'You must be dreaming.'

20

'This place is *urr*-mazing!' said Sally, as Vincent led them into the entertainment room at La Muralla. She had to speak loudly because a maid was vacuum-cleaning the floor.

'Everybody's out in the garden right now,' said Vincent. 'Come and meet them. It's David Magellan who's interested in casting the two of you. Did you ever see a movie called *Wanda's Weekend*?'

'No, but I've heard of it,' said Rosie. 'Was it him who directed it? And he wants to cast us? No way!'

'Way,' grinned Vincent. 'And – like I told you on the way here, Rosie – I apologise one hundred million per cent for what I said about you when we first met. I was having an off day, that's all. Every girl's pretty in her own way, and you're much prettier than most.'

He led them out into the garden, where David Magellan and two producers were sitting under a large striped sunshade, along with three actors. Although all the men were wearing sunglasses, Rosie recognised one of the actors as Beano from *The House Next Door* TV series, and she couldn't stop herself from letting out a little squeal and whispering to Sally, '*It's Beano!*'

'David – guys – this is Sally and this is Rosie,' said Vincent.

'I'll let you all introduce yourselves if they don't know you already. I found them in La Michoacana on Sherman Way, would you believe? It's not often that an ice-cream parlour can offer you something a whole lot more exciting than chocolate sprinkles.'

'Here, come and sit down next to me,' said David Magellan, standing up and scraping out two chairs. 'I was right in the middle of discussing my latest picture with Mr Zetter here.'

Rosie and Sally sat down on either side of him. There was nothing that Rosie could do to stop her heart beating so fast and she could feel herself blushing. She envied Sally for looking so composed, but then Sally had shining blonde hair that reached down to her waist and dreamy blue eyes and she was used to men staring at her. She was used to telling them to take a hike, too.

'You girls care for a drink?' asked Vincent. 'I'll go tell John Dangerfield that you're here. That's John Dangerfield the producer. This is his house.'

'I'd like a Coke if you have some,' said Rosie.

'Oh, come on, how about a glass of champagne? I think we have something to celebrate, don't you?'

Rosie and Sally looked at each other and giggled.

'My parents will go *nuts* if they find out!' said Sally.

'My dad won't even notice,' said Rosie. 'That's if he's still awake when I get home.'

Vincent went indoors and a few minutes later he came back out again, followed by John Dangerfield and Bradley. John Dangerfield was dressed all in black with one black leather glove, and his eyes were hidden behind mirror sunglasses. Bradley was carrying a tray with three flutes of champagne.

'Here they are, J.D.,' said Vincent. 'Sally and Rosie.'

David Magellan stood up and moved to another chair so that John could sit down between the two girls.

'Well, now,' he said, hooking an arm around each of them and giving them each a wolfish grin. Rosie could see in his sunglasses that her cheeks were still flushed. 'Perfectamundo! A perfect pair, in more ways than one! The Priest has excelled himself once again! Worth drinking a toast to celebrate, I'd say!'

He lifted his glass and clinked it against Sally's glass, and then Rosie's. Both of the girls took a mouthful but Rosie almost choked because she had never drunk champagne before and it fizzed straight up her nose.

'Hey – that's why they call it bubbly, sweetheart!' John laughed, patting her on the back. 'But you'll get used to it when you're famous. David – have you told these two beauties what parts they'll be playing?'

'Not yet,' said David. 'My new picture, it's hard to describe, because nothing like it has even been done before.'

'Well, go on, why don't you tell them all about it?'

David hesitated, and crossed and uncrossed his legs like a schoolboy repeating something that he had learned by rote. 'It's what you might call a post-apocalyptic Western. It's like Covid-19 has caused the total collapse of the US economy and decimated the white population. So now the American Indian tribes are launching attacks to get their old territories back. Like manifest destiny in reverse. Do you understand what I'm talking about?'

Rosie looked across at Sally uneasily. She was beginning to grow uncomfortable with the way that John had moved his hand down from her shoulder and was now holding her under her armpit, and occasionally giving her a squeeze.

'The whole crux of the story is that the Indians know how to live off the land much better than the white man, and it's like the land kind of welcomes them back. The working title is *Revenge of the Spirits*. You two – you two would play young Indian girls from one of the local tribes.'

'The Tongva, they're called,' John interrupted, taking over. 'They used to worship spirits, the Tongva – those of them who weren't forcibly converted to Christianity, that is, and even some of them who were. They believed that all animals had spirits – bears, coyotes, raccoons, you name it. They believed that trees had spirits, too, as well as rocks, and rivers, and lakes. Even today, a fair number of them still do.'

'Creepy,' said Sally, and she reached behind her back to lift John's hand away.

'In this picture, you two would play girls who can talk to the spirits,' said David. 'That's because you're related to one of them.'

'What do you mean, "related"?' asked Rosie. 'How can you be related to an animal? Or a rock?'

John nodded at her champagne flute and said, 'Come on, sweetheart, drink up. The spirits weren't all animals and rocks. Before the Spanish arrived and drove the Tongva off their native territory, some of their spirits had human form. They looked just like ordinary men and women but they had incredible supernatural power. I mean, forget about the Fantastic Four.'

'That's right,' David put in, as if he had suddenly remembered what he was supposed to say. 'And in my story, you two girls are the great-grand-daughters of a Tongva woman who wandered into the woods and got lost. She ran into one of these human-looking spirits who really took a fancy to her. He put her into a trance and seduced her and, to put it bluntly, he knocked her up.'

'So what happens next?' Rosie asked him. 'What do these two girls do?'

David lifted his sunglasses and looked across at John. 'We don't want to give away too much, do we?'

'No, we don't, and anyhow the script is still being rewritten. But at the end of the picture, these girls help to save the day. Without them, the American Indians would carry on fighting for their land right to the bitter end, and thousands would be killed. But these two give up their lives to make peace.'

'We *die* in the end?'

'Don't worry about it!' John laughed. He waved to Bradley to bring them fresh glasses of champagne. 'We'll give you both a wonderful funeral!'

John stood up now and went around the table so that he could join the rest of the men. They lit up cigars and started to talk finance and streaming and the latest developments in LED sets and game engine software. The only part of their conversation that Rosie and Sally could understand was an off-colour story that the actor who played Beano told about his first nude scene, and they had to try hard not to laugh.

Rosie and Sally were left to chat to each other and look around the garden. Rosie was fascinated by the shining white statue of Auzar. She couldn't take her eyes off it; and she could almost believe that it turned its head slightly so that it was staring back at her. The ceaseless clattering of the fountain made her feel drowsy, too.

Sally yawned and stretched and said, 'I don't know why I

feel so *tired*. I went to bed early last night but I can hardly keep my eyes open. Maybe it's the heat, or this champagne.'

'Me too,' said Rosie. 'I feel *weird*. Like I know I'm really here, in this garden, but it's like I'm dreaming it.'

'Come on, Rosie. We're going to be famous. Can you believe it? We'll be able to go to the movie theatre and see ourselves right up there on the screen – *us*! I guess that's what makes it all seem like a dream. I don't know what your dad's going to say but my folks are going to be over the moon. Sissy Huntsman will be spitting blood!' She was referring to another girl in their class who had always boasted that she was going to be a movie star.

Rosie finished the last of her champagne. She was beginning to like the taste of it and she felt as if she could happily drink another glass. While she was waiting for Bradley to reappear, however, she thought that she would close her eyes for a moment and listen to the fountain and the endless chirping of cicadas.

She heard Sally saying, 'Rosie? Rosie?' and she said '*mmmh?*', but she didn't open her eyes because she felt warm and relaxed and the darkness inside her mind was so comforting. The men were talking and laughing among themselves and she knew that Sally was tired, too, so it wouldn't matter if she slept for a minute or two.

When Rosie opened her eyes, she saw at once that she was no longer sitting in the garden. She was indoors somewhere, in a chilly room with lime-green walls, lying on a hard single bed. Her skin felt scratchy all over, and when she tried to sit up she realised that she was naked, but tightly wrapped up from her neck to her ankles in a hairy animal hide. Not only was she wrapped up in it, with her arms pinned against her sides, but it had been sewn together all the way down with criss-cross stitches.

The hide smelled strongly of whatever beast it had been cut from, and faintly of vomit. She tried to sit up again, finding it hard to believe that she was actually here, bundled up like this, in this bare air-conditioned room. She was able only to lift her head, but when she did she saw that there was another single bed next to hers, and that Sally was lying on it. She too was wrapped up in an animal hide, cinnamon-brown and bristly, so that only her face was showing. Her eyes were closed and Rosie had never seen her look so pale.

Rosie cleared her throat and cried out, '*Help! Somebody help us!*', although her mouth was dry and her voice sounded thready and weak.

She thought she could hear footsteps and a door opening and closing, and voices, but nobody appeared.

'*Help!*' she called again. '*Please, somebody help us!*'

She shrugged her shoulders up and down and wriggled her hips and tried to bend her knees, hoping that she could break the stitches, but even though she managed to loosen them a little they were cut from thick strips of leather and they were far too strong.

She threw herself even more violently from side to side, and the third time she did it she tumbled off the side of the bed and dropped heavily onto the floor. She lay on her side, gasping and sobbing, still tightly wrapped up in the animal hide like a giant chrysalis.

She heard the door open again, and rubber-soled footsteps

squeaking on the floor, and then a bearded man in a white surgical jacket was kneeling down beside her, his head tilted to one side, looking at her sympathetically. He smelled faintly of Lysol.

'Say, you haven't hurt yourself, have you?' he asked her.

'Yes,' Rosie wept.

'No bones broken, though?'

'No. Why am I all sewn up in this skin? What's happening? Where are my clothes?'

'You're sure no bones broken?'

'No! But why am I all sewn up like this? And Sally too? What are you doing to us?'

The bearded man stood up. 'I'm sorry. You'll have to ask Mr Dangerfield about that.'

'Then fetch him, please! And take this horrible skin off me. I want my clothes back. I want to go home.'

'I'll fetch him, okay? Here – let me pick you up. I can't leave you lying on the floor.'

'No, leave me alone, don't touch me!'

The bearded man ignored her. Even though she jerked and wriggled in protest, he hefted her up off the floor and laid her back down on her bed.

'Mr Dangerfield shouldn't be too long,' he told her, panting from the effort of lifting her, and walked off. Rosie let out a thin, high howl of despair.

'Sally!' she called out. 'Sally, wake up! *Sally!*'

Sally groaned, and said, '*What?*' She opened her eyes and then there was a long, bewildered silence while she gradually took in where she was and what had been done to her.

At last, in a panicky voice, she said, 'Rosie? *Rosie!* What's going on? Why are we all sewn up like this?'

'I don't know,' said Rosie. They were both crying now. 'There was this man and he said that Mr Dangerfield was coming, but that was all he would tell me.'

'They must have drugged us. They must have put something in that champagne. I was reading about men doing that. They drug you and then they rape you.'

'You don't think they've raped us?'

'I don't feel sore or wet or anything, do you?'

'I feel *itchy*, that's all. It's this horrible skin. It's so itchy, and it *stinks*.'

They were both silent for a few moments, except for sniffling. Then Rosie said, 'They were lying to us, weren't they, about that movie? I don't think there even is a movie.'

Minutes went by. Eventually they heard footsteps and the door opened up. John Dangerfield appeared between their beds, tall and smiling, still wearing his mirror sunglasses. Behind him came SloMo and DaShawn, each of them pushing a squeaky-wheeled hospital gurney.

John said, 'I hope you ladies are not too uncomfortable.'

'Why are we all sewn up like this?' Sally retorted. 'What have you done with our clothes? Have you raped us? Is that what you've done – drugged us and *raped* us?' Her voice rose higher and higher, until she was so shrill that she ran out of breath.

'*Raped* you, sweetheart? Of course not. You're far too young. Having sex with you would be illegal, even if you enjoyed it.'

'Enjoyed it?' Sally spat at him. 'With *you*?'

John smiled even more broadly. 'I'll admit we did originally have something on the carnal side in mind, and that was partly why the Priest recruited you. But when you told him how old you weren't, I decided that you could be part of our grand design in another way. You're going to be equally important, I might add. But that was why we needed two of you, rather than one, and why your looks weren't so critical, after all.'

'What are you going to do us?' sobbed Rosie. 'We just want to go home. We won't tell anybody about any of this, we swear to God.'

'Let me explain it to you, darling,' said John, coming up closer so that he was standing right over her. 'Some men are like automobiles. They're well-engineered, technically clever. They're the kind of men who have a clear idea where they're going and don't care who they run down in order to get there. It's men like these who change history and create great music and great art and great movies, too. But even talented men like these rarely have the natural energy to fulfil their potential on their own.'

Now he hunkered down beside her bed and took off his sunglasses, so that she could see his gleaming silvery eyes. She blinked through her tears, both horrified and fascinated for a second, but then she shuddered and turned her head away.

He stayed where he was, his breath against her cheek; so close that she felt he might infect her.

'The thing is, sweetheart, that however well-engineered these automobiles might be, they need fuel. They're like Teslas, they need to be charged up with electricity every few hundred miles. But most men simply aren't born with that kind of power, no matter how gifted they are. Whereas *all* women have it, whether they realise it or not. Women are this world's electricity!'

'I don't know what you mean,' said Rosie, without turning back to look at him. 'I don't *want* to know, either.'

'That's why I'm here now. I'm here to take you to see what a wonderful contribution you're about to make to the glorious history of Hollywood.'

'My parents are going to miss me if I'm not back by six,' said Sally. She was trying to sound fierce, but her voice was shaking.

'Don't you worry about that,' John told her smoothly. 'We have that covered.'

'How? How can you have that covered? My dad goes ape if I'm even half an hour late! And what are you going to say to them when they find me like this? "Oh, we thought we'd drug her with champagne and take off her clothes and stitch her up in a cowhide." You know, just for laughs.'

'In actual fact, it's buffalo hide,' John corrected her. 'And they won't find you like this, I promise you.'

'What do you mean?'

'Better if I show you,' said John, and he beckoned to SloMo and DaShawn to wheel the gurneys up to the sides of the beds.

The two girls were rolled across the sun-dappled garden, passing close to the table where the men were sitting. The actors had left now but David Magellan and Paul Zetter and another producer were still there, drinking champagne and smoking. They were all wearing dark glasses but Rosie could see that they were following them with their eyes. Even so, none of them seemed to be at all surprised by the sight of two girls stitched up in buffalo hides being wheeled through the garden on gurneys.

They were pushed past the fountain and through the pergola, until they reached the building with the sun symbol on it. John unlocked the outer doors so that SloMo and DaShawn could drag the gurneys into the vestibule. Then he opened up the inner doors and the gurneys were pushed with their wheels squeaking into the dim, chilly sanctum where the concrete plinth stood.

Even though she was folded up in her buffalo hide, Rosie started to shiver, and couldn't stop shivering. She looked up at the walls, all of them teeming with black and orange images of hunters and deer and shooting stars and arrows and scorpions. She felt completely detached from reality, as if she were dreaming that she was dreaming. Yet she could distinctly feel the scratchy hairs of the buffalo hide against her bare skin, and she could see her breath rising like smoke in the bitterly cold air, and she could hear John talking to SloMo and DaShawn. If she could feel and see and hear everything around her so vividly, how could this be a dream, let alone a dream about a dream?

John came and stood close beside her, and said to SloMo, 'Lift her up. Let her get a good look at what she has in store.' Then, to DaShawn, on the other side of the plinth, he said, 'Her too.'

SloMo and DaShawn cranked up the back rests on both of the gurneys, and as Rosie was raised up, Sally appeared, too, looking drained and frightened and bewildered. They both saw the pallid man with the sharply curved nose, wrapped up in the same way that they were, in a buffalo hide. His deep-set eyes were closed and it was impossible to tell if he was breathing or not.

'Do you know who this is?' said John. 'No, well you

wouldn't, of course, but this is Weywot, the last surviving spirit of the Tongva tribe. Can you believe that? The last surviving spirit who isn't hiding himself inside a coyote, anyhow, or a cherry tree, or a lump of granite.'

He bent over the plinth, so close to the man's face that Rosie thought for a moment that he was going to kiss his green-tinged lips.

'We have a deal with Weywot. It's the kind of deal that the white man should have made with all of the Indian tribes right from the very beginning, instead of wiping them out – but then most white men heap fucking stupid. The deal is, you see, we keep him alive, and take good care of him, and in return he gives us – well, you can hardly imagine what he gives us. The power of Greyskull doesn't even come close.'

Rosie looked away. She had no idea what John was talking about and she had no interest in him explaining himself, either. If this were a dream, all she wanted to do was wake up, and be back at home, doing her history homework on the dining table and listening to her father snoring on the couch.

John said, 'Whenever we need Weywot to give us power, we have to perform this special ritual, and there are certain offerings that he expects. Well, *demands*, to tell you the truth. Like he wants bluefin and crab and acorn mush and manzanitas and prickly pear pads. That's to get his strength up after weeks of fasting.

'On top of that, when he's doing the business, he has to have fire, and light, and living sacrifices.'

He went over to one of the two metal posts that stood on either side of the plinth, and clanked against it with his signet rings. 'That's what these posts are for. Fire, and light, and living sacrifices. And that's why I've fetched you in here to see what you can expect. It's important for you to know well in advance, so that you have plenty of time to reflect on how much you're going to be giving for the greater good. And maybe have time to pray, too.'

'What are you *talking* about?' Sally demanded, in a screechy whisper. 'I don't understand anything you're saying.'

'It's very simple to understand, sweetheart,' John replied. 'Weywot needs light and fire and living sacrifices, and we can give him all three at once. Now do you get it? Now do you see why we've wrapped you up in those buffalo hides? We're going to tie you two up to these posts and set you alight. You'll both be going out in a blaze of glory.'

Rosie started to scream, and went on screaming. She didn't realise that she was doing it, because she had gone deaf with fear, in the same way that survivors from a doomed airliner report that they heard nothing at all as their plane went plunging towards the ground. The seamless silence of approaching death.

21

Nemo parked the Acadia on the opposite side of the road from John Dangerfield's house, under the shade of a fishtail palm.

He and Trinity then sat there for over a quarter of an hour, watching to see if anybody would arrive or leave or if there were any deliveries. That would give them an idea of La Muralla's security procedure: whether it looked as if visitors had already been spotted on CCTV as they approached the front doors, how quickly the doors were opened, who opened them, and whether it looked as if visitors were expected to show some ID before they were let in.

Three guests arrived, parking their cars in the sloping driveway next to the house. A shiny black Cadillac Royale limousine was chauffeur-driven, and when the chauffeur opened the door to let the passenger out Nemo recognised him immediately – a short, bald man with thick-rimmed glasses and a beard.

He gave Trinity a nudge. 'That's Robert Bassani. He's the director of all those *Black Hole* movies. Probably a billionaire by now. Looks like this is definitely the place where the Hollywood elite get together for a schmooze.'

They could see that when every guest arrived the front

doors were opened even before they had reached them, and that there were two men waiting to receive them, one of whom was muscle-bound like a bouncer. When Robert Bassani approached the front doors, John Dangerfield himself came out, his arms flung wide in greeting, accompanied by two bosomy young women in glittery shorts.

'Hmm. It doesn't look like it's going to be too easy to sneak in there and check out what goes on,' said Nemo. 'I was toying with the idea that we could disguise ourselves as actors or agents or something like that, but it looks like they make a pretty close check on everybody who comes to the door. Man, I'm thirsty. Any of that drink left?'

Trinity handed him a warm can of Diet Pepsi and he popped it open and took a swig.

'Maybe there's a way we could get in around the back of the house,' she suggested.

'We could try. Let's get out and take a look.'

They stepped out of the Acadia and walked a short way up the road, so that they had a side view of La Muralla. Around the north side of the garden there was a dense Texas privet hedge, at least thirteen feet high, but it was possible that there might be a gap in it somewhere, or even a back gate, although it was almost a certainty that a gate would have an alarm attached.

They were about to cross the road when a man appeared from the driveway of the house next to them. He was wearing a yellow silky top like a kimono and he had a small furry löwchen dog on a lead. He was fortyish, blond, suntanned and quite handsome, like a young Peter O'Toole, and he had the same pale-blue eyes as Peter O'Toole.

Trinity didn't realise at first who he was, because he was

much shorter than he appeared on the screen, but as he came closer she saw that it was Ned Wallace, who played the lead in all the *Hot Chase* spy movies.

'Help you folks?' he challenged them. But before Nemo could reply, the löwchen yapped and tugged at its lead, straining to reach Trinity.

Trinity bent down and stroked the löwchen and tugged gently at its ears, and the little dog jumped up at her again and again, as if it were trying to entertain her with a *Riverdance* jig.

'Well, Ticktock's sure taken a liking to *you*,' Ned Wallace told her, raising one eyebrow. 'Never seen him act that flirtatious before. Do you own a dog yourself?'

'No, never. I always wanted one but my dad wouldn't let me. He said that I'd soon grow tired of it and he'd be the one who would end up having to take it for walks.'

'That's such a pity. You definitely have something special about you that appeals to Ticktock. It's amazing but dogs can tell instantly if somebody's a pooch lover or not. Maybe they like the smell of our bones. Who knows?'

He watched Ticktock jumping and dancing around Trinity for a few moments, and then he said, 'Look, folks – I'm sorry if I sounded suspicious. You can probably understand that we tend to be kind of wary around here. There's a regular security patrol but we've had a couple of break-ins lately. Not that I'm suggesting for a moment that you two look like robbers.'

Nemo grunted in amusement. 'Thanks for the compliment, I'm sure. Actually, we've been checking out properties around here. The trouble is that none of the houses that we've really liked so far are up for sale. Take that one across the road, for example. In my business we're always entertaining, so a house of that size would suit us down to the ground. And it's a stunning building, too. That turret, and those blue windows.'

'It's a fantastic house, I agree, but I don't think there's any chance of John Dangerfield selling up anytime soon.'

'Oh, John Dangerfield lives there, does he? Is that John Dangerfield the producer?'

'That's right. But, like I say, I don't think he'll be putting it on the market for quite a while, if ever. He's spent an absolute fortune on modernising it and landscaping the gardens. Apart from that, he's always holding parties. In fact, he seems to be having one non-stop party, twenty-four hours a day, seven days a week. He'll be holding a real monster of a party tomorrow night, so he tells me.'

'Are you invited?'

'No, but I wouldn't have gone anyway. Half of Hollywood is going to be there from what he told me, but it's not really my scene. He warned me in advance because there's going to be a massive firework display and he doesn't want Ticktock having a nervous breakdown.'

'Very neighbourly of him,' said Nemo.

Trinity gave Ticktock one more tickle under the chin, and then Ned Wallace tugged him away, his claws skidding on the sidewalk because he was so reluctant to leave her.

'I think he's fallen in love with you,' Ned Wallace grinned, shaking his head. 'You folks take care now.'

As they watched him walk away, Trinity said, 'That was a good lie. I mean about us looking for a house.'

'Shame we don't have that kind of money. But what he said about that monster party – that could be just the break we need. I'll check up on which actors won't be able to be there, because they're shooting movies someplace on location, and then you and I can disguise ourselves to look like them.'

Trinity thought about that, but then she said, 'Yes, but the other guests are bound to *know* those actors, aren't they, and what if they start asking us questions? They'll realise at once that we're not really them, won't they? I mean, our voices are different, for a start.'

'That's a risk we'll have to take, Trin. I guess we can both pretend that we've caught a dose of laryngitis, and that we can only speak in a whisper.'

Trinity looked across at La Muralla. A woman had appeared in one of its upstairs windows, with what looked like a dark shawl around her shoulders. It may have been a trick of the sunlight, but she appeared to have luminous green eyes.

'I'm frightened,' said Trinity. 'I can't pretend that I'm not.'

'We could always call this whole thing off. But those IAG goons will still be after us, even though we don't know why.'

'No, Nemo, we can't stop now. We have to find out why, because it's something to do with Margo being murdered. And I believe the answer's in that house. I can feel it in my bones.'

Nemo put his arm around her. 'Those same bones that Ticktock had such a taste for? Come on, let's go back to Pine Mountain and fix ourselves something to eat. Talking of bones, I could kill for some barbecued ribs.'

Nemo was in luck. When they returned to Pine Mountain, they found that Rafael had set up a barbecue in the back yard. He hadn't yet lit it, but he was in the kitchen marinating rib-eye steaks and chicken wings and ribs, and he had made a beetroot and halloumi slider for Trinity, as well as some courgette lollipops with honey and lemon sauce.

Teodoro was still there, sitting on the balcony smoking a long-stemmed pipe and staring out at the distant mountains.

'I had planned to go back home this afternoon,' he told Trinity and Nemo, as they came out to join him. 'But then I thought that it would be best if I stayed, to see what experience you two had with your sudden dreams. I was reluctant to tell you before, but for some people they can have disturbing side effects, like seeing figures from other people's nightmares, or believing that they themselves are dreaming.'

'Well, thanks for warning us – not,' said Nemo, sitting down next to him with a glass of beer. 'But as it turned out, the disguises worked pretty well, and we didn't have any side effects like that. *You* didn't, did you, Trin?'

Trinity shook her head. 'I did feel a little weird, especially when we went to see my dad and he didn't recognise me, but that was all.'

Nemo could see that Rafael was shaking out a paper sack of charcoal into the barbecue.

'Ah – what he needs is an expert,' he said, and so he left them and went down the steps into the back yard to help Rafael to light it.

'It's amazing, this sudden dream thing,' said Trinity. 'And most of all, it's made me feel that my mom's back with me, like she's right inside my head.'

'That is good, and that is because you are a good person,' Teodoro told her. 'I was not seriously worried about you two having those side effects, because both of you are honest and truthful people, and usually it is only tricksters and deceivers who have a frightening experience when they disguise themselves in an *anyapakh*. They can be haunted by their own lies.'

'We're going to do it again tomorrow,' Trinity told him. 'I think it's going to be a whole lot more risky this time, though. We're going to try and gatecrash a Hollywood party with all kinds of celebrities. I can't imagine what will happen if they guess who we really are. Nemo's sure that they want to get rid of us. You know – actually kill us.'

Teodoro said nothing for a long time, steadily puffing on his pipe. At last he looked over at Trinity, and she found the expression on his face unreadable. It was caring, in a way, but determined, too, yet there was also some hint of regret in his eyes, as if he were about to tell her something that should have been forgotten a long time ago.

'Listen to me, Trinity. Your friend has a gun, so he can take care of himself if his life is in danger. But you have nothing. What I am about to tell you, I beg you not to share with him, because I think it is important that he continues to believe that he is your protector, and that he never lets down his guard. There are three words that the Chumash wonder-workers used in order to kill anyone who threatened them. My grandmother taught me these words. They had been told to her by my grandfather on his deathbed, so that even when he had passed into Šimilaqša, the house of the sun, she would always be able to keep herself safe.'

Trinity felt deeply uneasy. It was hard for her to believe that any of this afternoon was real. Yet here she was, and she could smell the pine forests all around her, and barbecue smoke, and the smoke from Teodoro's pipe, and hear the birds chirruping.

'You can kill people just with words?'

'It was important for us in the days before the Spanish came. This middle world where we Chumash lived we called Hiashup. But underneath Hiashup is a lower world called C'oyanishup, and in this lower world lived terrible creatures we called the nunashush. As soon as the sun set, and it was dark, the nunashush would crawl up from their world and come looking for humans to eat.'

'But that's only a story, surely.'

'There are stories and then there are stories. Maybe the nunashush were not as our people imagined them. But there is no question that whenever night fell, *something* was hunting us, because the next morning half-eaten bodies would be found scattered around our villages. Maybe in reality it was bears, or mountain lions. But many people claimed to have seen the nunashush lurking in the forests, and that they were like hunchbacks, with green eyes that glowed in the dark.'

'Spooky, or what?' said Trinity. 'But those people could have been drinking some of that momoy, couldn't they? After you gave me that momoy tea, I saw millions of roaches running down the walls – millions of them! – but *they* weren't real.'

'I accept that is a possibility, yes. But in any case, a Chumash shaman named Chnawaway devised these three mystical words that could instantly stop the heart of any creature – human, animal or nunashush. If there was any sign of a raid at night by the nunashush, he would stand outside the village and if he saw their green eyes shining in the dark, he would repeat these words, over and over. He would also cross his fingers in an X shape – like this. He would do this twice, because it showed them that he knew they were nunashush, after the most evil nunashush monster of them all, Xolxol.

'After that, Chnawaway's people were never troubled by the nunashush again. And not by any other enemies, either. When the Spanish soldiers arrived at their village, Chnawaway spoke the words and made the sign at each of them, one after the other, and so many of the soldiers dropped dead on the spot that they ran away and never returned. The Spanish missionaries even gave that village the name Corazón Parando – the heart stopper.'

Teodoro puffed away at his pipe for a while, waiting to hear what Trinity would say next. He knew, and *she* knew, and yet she hesitated. It was so hard to accept that what he had told her might actually be true, and that he could tell her those fatal three words. No matter how dangerous her investigation into Margo's murder might be, did she really want the power to stop people's hearts from beating?

But then she heard Nemo, down in the back yard, laughing, and she felt the warmth of her mother's presence inside her. Nemo was taking care of her now, but supposing something happened to him, and she was left to fend for herself? She remembered her mother giving her advice on how to protect herself when she was younger, and she could almost hear her now, saying, *hope for the very best, my darling, but always be prepared for the very worst.*

'So,' she said to Teodoro, 'what are the words?'

Teodoro set down his pipe and reached into his shirt pocket. He took out a folded scrap of paper and passed it over to her.

'Whatever you do, do not read these words out loud,' he told her. 'If you do that, my heart will stop.'

Trinity opened up the paper and saw the words. They were all Chumash, and meant nothing, but he had spelled them out in Roman characters and she could see that they weren't difficult to pronounce.

Teodoro picked up his pipe again. It had gone out, and he had to relight it. As he flicked his Zippo and sucked repeatedly at the stem, he didn't take his eyes off Trinity once.

'You understand what you are now – now that you know these words? You are more dangerous than anybody with a gun. You are a killer.'

22

John Dangerfield opened the door of the bedroom and stood looking at Zuzana for a few moments before he turned to the Ghost Woman.

'She's totally out now?'

'Yes. She will sleep now for many hours. And she will dream her last dreams.'

'Great. Everything's ready now for waking up Weywot. Do you want to come on down?'

That wasn't a question. The Ghost Woman wrapped her shawl more tightly around herself and stood up. John started to walk away, along the corridor, and she followed him.

It was dark outside now. Not even the mock-torches in the garden were lit. This was a night of intense preparation, and La Muralla was unusually quiet. There was no music, no laughter, only the staff speaking quietly to each other as they went in and out of the kitchens or hung elderberry branches around the walls of the entertainment room, by way of decoration.

John led the way across the garden, with the Ghost Woman close behind him. The doors of the white building were wide open and at least twenty men were waiting for him, silhouetted against the dim light that was falling across the patio from inside, so that they looked like a gathering of shadows. Vincent Priest and David Magellan were both there, as well as Paul Zetter and Randy Stavriano. Most of the men were wearing black tuxedos, but instead of bow ties they had multi-stranded necklaces of Tongva beads strung around their necks.

'Are we ready?' said John, and there was a general murmur of assent. He looked at his watch and said, 'The moon's about to show her face, and so is our benefactor Weywot. Let's go make him welcome.'

The men all shuffled through the vestibule and into the room where Weywot lay on his plinth. Although the doors were open to the night, the cold inside the room was still intense, and several of the men chafed their hands together and stamped their feet, trying to keep themselves warm.

Six of John's serving staff were standing at the far end of the room, with dark brown Tongva blankets draped over their shoulders and headbands with zigzag patterns of beads on them. Five of them were holding wide pottery bowls, one of which was heaped with seared fish fillets, and one with orange boiled crabs, still in their shells. The other bowls were filled with prickly pear pads and acorn mush and red manzanita berries.

The sixth servant was holding a fully grown tortoiseshell cat, with thick matted fur. Its legs were dangling down, but he was repeatedly stroking it to keep it calm.

On the right side of the room, three elderly Tongva Indians were waiting, with haughty expressions on their faces. This was their mythology and their god, after all. Their grey hair was tied back in horsetails and each of them had a moon symbol daubed onto his forehead. John clapped his hands in their direction and they began to tap out a repetitive rhythm on rain sticks – four-foot-long instruments made of dried cactus stalks and filled with small pebbles, so that they made a soft trickling sound like falling rain.

One of the old Tongva Indians started to chant, and when he did, John beckoned to SloMo, who weaved his way between the men in their tuxedos until he reached the opposite side of the plinth. Weywot was still stitched up in his buffalo hide, his eyes closed, his face luminously white. But then the old Tongva raised his rain stick up high and smacked it against the palm of his left hand, faster and faster, in an ever more complicated pattern, and then started to screech out, '*Muwaar! Muwaar!*', over and over. He was calling the moon.

Weywot opened his eyes. They were completely bloodshot, except for the irises, which were a poisonous yellow. As soon as he did that, SloMo reached over, took hold of the stitching that held his buffalo hide together, and started to tug it loose. He quickly unlaced it as far as Weywot's waist, exposing a narrow white torso with pierced nipples and prominent ribs, and two arms no thicker than the rain sticks, with eagle-claw hands.

Now John turned around to the Ghost Woman, who was standing behind him. The Ghost Woman came forward, her green eyes gleaming, and bowed her head to Weywot.

'Tell him the seventh full moon has risen,' said John.

The Ghost Woman bowed her head again, and then spoke to Weywot in a reverent whisper.

'Tell him we have fetched him food.'

The Ghost Woman whispered again, and now Weywot turned to face her, and then to look up at John. He licked his green-tinged lips with the tip of his powdery white tongue, and then he said something to the Ghost Woman in a voice that sounded like an unoiled hinge. The rain sticks had stopped tapping now, but there was an audible frisson of excitement among the men gathered in the room. Joe Bellman had edged his way along the side of the plinth to get a closer look at Weywot.

'Jesus,' he said. 'I mean, Jesus X. Christ. This is something else.'

'Weywot asks if you have a woman ready,' said the Ghost Woman.

'You know darn well we have,' John replied. 'And you can tell him that she's an outstandingly beautiful woman. The most beautiful woman we've found for him yet. A goddess, almost. And yet she'll be silent, because she has no tongue.'

Weywot's lips curled up into a smile.

'He says that the screaming gives him pleasure.'

'Then tell him that he won't be disappointed tomorrow night by the torches that we'll be lighting for him.'

'He says that he had a dream in which you brought him more than one woman.'

'Really? Tell him that this one woman should easily satisfy him as much as two women, if not more.'

'He says his dreams always come true.'

'Tell him that we have plenty of food. And manzanita cider.'

Weywot stared at John for a long moment with his bloodshot eyes and it was clear that he was irritated that John had changed the subject. But a month in this chilly room in suspended animation had left him ravenously hungry, as it always did, and his throat was so dry that he found it difficult to speak. He said nothing more, but raised his head, and craned his neck around to see what they had brought for him to eat and drink.

John waved his servants forward, and they came up to the plinth one by one, carrying their bowls of food and a flagon of cider. They had done this before, several times, but they couldn't conceal how frightened they were, and the hands of the man who was holding the bowl of bluefin fillets were shaking so much that John was worried he would drop them onto the floor.

SloMo helped Weywot to sit up. He was so emaciated that his shoulders looked as if the back of an angular chair had been forced up underneath his skin, but he was unusually tall, with a narrow, elongated head. He could have modelled as an alien for the cover of a 1950s' science fiction magazine.

'Tell him that we are privileged to be giving him this food,' said John. 'We continue to honour him as the last surviving god of the Tongva to be living in the land of the first people. We acknowledge his power, and we respect his authority.'

The Ghost Woman whispered these words to Weywot, but Weywot was more interested now in cramming his mouth with bluefin fillets. As soon as he had finished the fish, but still had shreds of it dangling from his lips, he reached out for the bowlful of crabs. He picked out the largest one and bit into its shell, breaking it open with a crack like a pistol shot. He devoured it whole, crunching into its claws and its legs, and then reached out for another crab, and another.

Now the Tongva with their rain sticks started up their tapping rhythm again, while John's guests in their tuxedos could only stand and watch Weywot wolfing down his tribute meal in awe. Not only did he eat each crab in its entirety, with its broken shell and its purse and its ligaments and its dead man's fingers, but he ate the cactus pads uncooked, with their prickly spines still attached, and the manzanita berries complete with their rock-hard seeds.

John clapped his hands again, and the old Tongva stopped rattling his rain stick. When the room was quiet, he looked around with a self-satisfied smile.

'As you know, gentlemen, I came across Weywot soon after I bought La Muralla and started to landscape the garden. And there he was, as you see him now, buried deep in the clay, wrapped in the same buffalo hide that his vengeful sons had wrapped him in. But he's a god, a spirit, and however many years he'd been buried for, he'd survived. When the moonlight fell on him, he was revived.

'That's what we're celebrating here tonight – Weywot's revival. And most of all we're preparing for tomorrow night, when Muwaar the moon is at her height. That's when we'll be bringing Weywot our monthly sacrifice, and Weywot in return will reward us for resurrecting him and caring for him.'

John looked around at the assembled men like a pastor giving a sermon to his flock.

'All of us here have achieved incredible dominance in the motion picture business, and in so many of the companies associated with the motion picture business – financial and legal and promotional. We're the Genghis Khans of Hollywood. The Napoleons. The Hitlers. And we owe that dominance almost entirely to Weywot.'

The men clapped, and shouted out, '*Weywot!*', and one or two of them whooped. John stepped back, lifting his hands to acknowledge their applause. It was then that the servant holding the tortoiseshell cat carried it up to the side of the plinth, and held it out. Weywot took it, digging both of his thumbnails deep into its chest so that it yowled in pain and wriggled and twisted and scrabbled at him with its claws.

Weywot shifted his hold on the cat so that he was squeezing its throat with his left hand, just below its jaw, and using his right hand to grip it by the root of its tail. It was frantically pedalling its legs and scratching his wrists, but if he felt any pain he didn't show it. He stretched his mouth open wide and buried his face into the cat's brindled flank, biting it so hard that it let out a half-choked scream.

The old Tongva men started up their rain stick rhythm once again, very slowly this time, so that it sounded like rain falling on a dreary afternoon. The men in the room stood silent, unable to take their eyes off Weywot as he bit into the cat again and again. Unlike the pistol-sharp splitting of the crab shells, the cat's hind legs made a soft crunching sound as his teeth broke them apart, and then an almost inaudible crackling as he chewed them.

The cat was still alive as he stuffed it inch by inch into his mouth, its green eyes staring in pain and desperation at the men who were watching it, but Weywot was holding its throat too tightly now for it to make any sound. He tilted back his narrow head in order to drag out its internal organs, its looped intestines and its liver. It died, and its eyes misted over, but after it had died its deflated lungs and its glossy prune-coloured heart were still hanging on Weywot's chin, dripping with blood.

Weywot grasped the cat's ribcage with both hands and

levered it wide apart with a sound like somebody breaking the spine of a book. It took him about five minutes to force the rest of the cat into his mouth. At last there was nothing left but its head, although it was still staring out blindly from between his lips before he bit down on it hard. He crushed its skull between his jagged teeth, and as he closed his mouth its brains squirted out on either side.

Weywot chewed, and chewed, and eventually swallowed. He used the back of his hand to wipe away the brains and the fur that were still sticking to his lips, and then he looked around for the flagon of cider. The rain stick beat continued, and in quavering voices the three old Tongva began to chant. The men in their tuxedos remained silent.

SloMo helped Weywot to lift the flagon of cider to his lips, and Weywot swallowed and swallowed until he belched and cider came gushing back out of his mouth and running down his emaciated chest. After that, he lay back down, and closed his eyes. SloMo waited until he was sure that he was sleeping, or at least that he wouldn't need help to sit up again, and then he laced up his buffalo hide, as far as his chin.

Although John had not asked her, the Ghost Woman started to translate the song that the old Tongva men were singing. She said it flatly, with no expression, but clapping her hands in the same irregular rhythm.

'I am Weywot, the spirit, and I did not die. Tsuqqit may have created you humans and Chinigchinich may have given you the dreams that brought you food, but I am the only survivor and now you will live by my rules.

'If you look with lust at a man or a woman who does not belong to you, the raven will pluck out your eyes and drop them in the ceremonial quiver made from young coyote skin.

'If you steal food or weapons or jewellery that do not belong to you, the bear will bite off your hands and drop them in the ceremonial quiver.

'If you speak a single word that defies my rule, the tarantula wasp and the rattlesnake will poison you so that you swell and die.

'And be warned: if you are a woman and you try to imitate Tsuqqit, the sacred scorpion will sting you for your blasphemy, and you will be left as empty as the space between the stars.'

The singing and the rain stick tapping suddenly stopped. The assembled men looked at each other as if to say 'is that it?' and one or two of them laughed, but there was a feeling of intense unease in the room, as well as anticlimax.

John called out, 'Right, everybody! Time for a drink, I think. But let's go easy, shall we? We've a hell of a night ahead of us tomorrow.'

He turned to the Ghost Woman. 'You can go now, Tokoor Hikaayey. You'll need to do some meditating, won't you, even if you never sleep.'

'The morning after tomorrow night, seven times seven moons will have come and gone,' she said, in a strangely seductive tone, and her eyes glowed brighter green.

'Yes, and so what?'

'When tomorrow's moon sinks behind the mountains, my debt to you will finally be settled. That was your promise.'

'So? What difference is that going to make? If you don't stay here, where are you going to go? You don't have a hope of finding anybody to take care of you the way I do. You'll probably run into some priest and he'll exorcise you. You wouldn't fancy that, would you?'

The Ghost Woman continued to stare at him. Then, without saying anything else, she walked off into the garden, and the darkness swallowed her up.

'What was that all about?' asked SloMo, watching her go.

'Oh, nothing. You make a promise to an Indian and they're stupid enough to think you're going to keep it.'

23

About an hour after she had gone to bed, Trinity was jolted out of her sleep by an ear-splitting rumble of thunder, directly overhead. It shook the whole house and made the shutters rattle like dancing skeletons. It was followed by a dazzling flash of lightning, and then another rumble, even louder.

Rain began to hammer down on the roof, and within only a few seconds the gutters were flooded, and water clattered onto the balcony outside her bedroom window. She buried herself in her thickly woven Indian blanket and put her fingers in her ears. It had thundered for hours on the night that her mother had died, and she could never rid herself of the feeling that electric storms were an omen that something dreadful was about to happen.

Lightning flashed again, lighting up the whole of her bedroom, and although she had her fingers in her ears she heard Nemo shouting in the corridor outside her door. There was another devastating rumble of thunder, and she waited until it had banged and bumbled away before she climbed out of bed to find out why he was shouting.

Both Nemo and Teodoro were standing next to the window that overlooked the driveway in front of the house. As Trinity went along the corridor to join them, she could see that a tall pine tree was on fire, like a gigantic Roman candle, and that blazing branches were dropping onto the ground below.

'Got hit by lightning,' said Nemo. 'Teodoro's truck was parked right underneath it, so Rafael's gone to move it for him.'

Lightning flashed again, and again, and the next burst of thunder was so loud that Trinity felt as if her ears had been boxed.

'I believe Shnilemun is giving us a warning,' said Teodoro solemnly. Now he could see that Rafael had parked his truck on the opposite side of the driveway, he turned away from the window. 'Shnilemun is the Sky Coyote who takes care of us, but he is like any father. He will also punish us if he thinks that we are becoming too arrogant.'

Rafael came up the stairs, brushing the rain from his shoulders and shaking it out of his hair.

'I think we can count ourselves lucky. If that tree hadn't been so tall, the lightning might have hit the house.' He smiled at Trinity. 'Hey, don't look so worried. It's only an electric storm.'

'I know. But I don't happen to like storms, that's all. They shouldn't scare me, I know, but they do.'

She was going to tell him why, but then she felt her mother inside her mind, her dream friend, soothing her and calming her down. *What's past is past, Trinity. No matter how much we grieve for them, nothing can bring back the people we've loved and lost. Think of the future, and be brave.*

'Listen,' said Rafael. 'Why don't I make us some tea, and I can stay with you until the storm's passed over.'

'I know what I'm going to have, and that's a JD,' said Nemo. 'Teodoro, you going to join me?'

Lightning flashed yet again, followed by thunder so violent that a framed etching of Eagle Rest Peak dropped off the wall, and its glass was cracked from side to side.

Trinity and Rafael sat on the bed together, propped up by pillows. Trinity was cupping the mug of tea that Rafael had made for her in both hands and sipping it occasionally. The storm was still prowling around Pine Mountain like an angry bear and the rain was lashing across the balcony but she felt much safer now, and less frightened by the prospect of what she and Nemo were planning to do tomorrow. She thought that was probably what had been making her so anxious, rather than the thunder and lightning.

'Better now?' Rafael asked her.

She nodded. 'This tea's lovely. What is it?'

'Mango and bergamot flavour. At least, that's what it said on the package. It's Mike's.'

'I can't believe that my life has fallen apart like this. Only a few days ago I was cleaning houses and taking Rosie and Buddy to school and thinking how boring everything was. But at least I knew what was going to happen from one day to the next. At least I didn't have people trying to kill me.'

Rafael leaned across and kissed Trinity on the cheek, and then lightly on the lips. He looked her in the eyes and said, 'Don't be afraid. Everything is going to work out for you. For good people it always does. There was a story my grandmother used to tell me. I always thought of that story whenever I felt that everything was going wrong for me and that nothing but bad things were going to happen.'

Trinity put down her mug and reached up to stroke his

cheek. She had never felt as relaxed as this with a man before, not even with Ted, who had been her only serious boyfriend, and who had even asked her to marry him. 'Go on then, tell me, if you think it'll help.'

'A woman went to her chicken house and came back with a basketful of eggs. All of the eggs were good except for one, which kept hiding under the other eggs and saying, "You go and get yourself boiled, or fried, or scrambled. I'm staying here." But this egg managed to dodge being cooked for so long that it went bad. Its shell turned a horrible green, and so the woman threw it out into her yard.'

Trinity laughed. 'How old were you when your grandmother told you this story? Did you believe that eggs could talk to each other?'

'I guess so. But talking eggs are no more ridiculous than talking puppets or talking crickets, like in *Pinocchio*, are they? Anyway, this bad egg was lying in the grass when a centipede came up to it. This centipede was a real tough guy, a real gangster, and it had been in so many fights that it only had fifty-one legs left. It took one look at the bad egg and fell in love with it.'

Trinity snuggled up closer to him, looking up at him and smiling. 'Go on. A criminal centipede fell in love with a rotten egg, what could be more natural than that?'

'The egg fell in love with the centipede too, and so they decided to get married. They couldn't find a priest so the wedding was carried out by a banana slug. Don't ask me where they went for their honeymoon. Maybe Lake Tahoe. But after only a couple of months, the egg got pregnant.'

'A pregnant egg? Now I've heard everything!'

'Well, that's what happened. I guess centipedes don't use

condoms. But when the bad egg's time came, and she was ready to give birth to the gangster centipede's baby, she cracked wide open, and guess what came out?'

Trinity shook her head. 'I don't have a clue. A chicken with a hundred legs?'

'Good guess, but nope. What came out was the most beautiful butterfly you ever saw in your life, with gold and purple wings, and it flew off into the sky. And that's the point of the story. Out of the worst situations that you can think of, when everything looks ugly, incredibly wonderful things can get born. All it takes is a little love.'

Trinity laughed, and kissed him, and he kissed her in return, tangling his fingers into her long brunette hair. He ran his hand up her bare leg, underneath her blue check shirt, and caressed the small of her back. She looked intently into his eyes and said, 'You can make love to me if you want to.'

'I don't have a condom.'

'You never know. I might give birth to a beautiful butterfly.'

He kissed her again, and then he rolled off the bed and stood up, unbuttoning his shirt and unbuckling his belt. At the same time, she pulled her shirt over her head and underneath she was naked. He climbed back onto the bed, lean and muscular, with tattoos on his shoulders of dragons and tigers. He was already hard, and Trinity was already slippery. She parted her legs wide, and held herself open with her fingers, and he slid himself into her so deep that she gave a little jump.

Trinity had never had a lover like Rafael before. He felt powerful, and yet he was gentle, and he took his time, kissing her lips and her breasts as if he were a pilgrim kissing a beautiful religious figure that he had travelled for weeks to worship. Before he climaxed, he took himself out of her, and she felt blobs of warm semen dropping onto her stomach. She smoothed it around and around and massaged her breasts with it.

He didn't leave her unsatisfied, though. He lay down beside her and kissed her and stroked her clitoris with his fingertip until she felt that the whole bedroom was growing dark. She shuddered, and let out a little yelp of pleasure. At the same time, lightning crackled over the distant mountains, and thunder gave a last sulky rumble before the storm moved away.

They lay there silently for almost half an hour afterwards, simply holding each other and kissing and touching each other's faces.

'I think the gods must have brought you into my life,' said Rafael at last. 'I just pray that they protect you.'

Trinity sat up. He had reminded her that she and Nemo would be going back to LA tomorrow to try to infiltrate John Dangerfield's party.

'What?' Rafael asked her. 'What's the matter?'

She didn't want to tell him that he had unknowingly broken the spell. She reached across for her mug and said, 'Nothing. My tea's gone cold, that's all.'

The next morning was sunny and warm, and they took their breakfast out onto the balcony. As he poured syrup over his pancakes, Nemo said, 'I think I've found a couple of actors who we can use to disguise ourselves. One of them's on location in Alaska and the other's currently attending some movie convention in France. Toby Carter and Clarissa Keyes. They're both about the right age and they're not so devastatingly famous that everybody will suss at once that we're not really them.'

'I've heard of Toby Carter. I'm not so sure about what's-her-name?'

'Clarissa Keyes. She's had quite a few bit parts in horror flicks. Running around and screaming mostly. There's dozens of pictures of her on IMDb and Google Image, so you'll be able to get a good idea of what she looks like.'

Teodoro came out and lit his pipe. He stood by the railing looking out over the mountains and placidly puffing smoke. He waited until Nemo had gone back inside to refill his mug of coffee, and then he said to Trinity, without turning to look at her, 'Those words I gave you. You will guard them with the greatest care, won't you? They are more powerful than poison. You should only use them if you are faced with the choice between life or death.'

'I hope I never have to use them at all.'

'None of us knows what our fate will be, from one minute to the next. Death is always waiting for us. He is like a black wolf in the forest, and all we can try to do is avoid him for as long as we can.'

24

DaShawn came into the bedroom and handed the Ghost Woman a blue ceramic bowl, with a ceramic ladle in it. He looked at Zuzana lying on the bed, covered in her blanket, and said, 'Is she asleep?'

'No. She has been given guaraná to keep her awake. As you know, it is important that she does not dream.'

'Mr Dangerfield says it's time for you to make her ready.'

'There is no hurry. It is not dark yet.'

'I'm only telling you what Mr Dangerfield told me.'

The Ghost Woman stood up and set the bowl down on top of the chest of drawers. 'Mr Dangerfield does not always have to be obeyed. We are not his slaves.'

'Maybe not, but it's not a great idea to cross him. I wouldn't cross anybody who set fire to living women, just for the sake of some god.'

'Weywot is not "some god". Weywot is the last living deity of the Tongva. He is heartless and cruel, but then every tribe has its dark side. If Satan was found alive, do not doubt for a moment that there would be white men to feed him and worship him and offer him living sacrifices.'

DaShawn was silent for a few moments, watching the Ghost Woman lift the blanket off Zuzana and fold it up. Then he said, 'I didn't never have the nerve to ask you this before, but what *was* you? Like *before*, I mean.'

The Ghost Woman turned and stared at him with her luminous green eyes. 'Before I died?'

'Well, yeah. I guess so.'

'I was a wonder-worker. I could cure many illnesses, from fevers to snake bites to the plagues that the Spanish brought with them. To the Tongva, it did not matter if a wonder-worker was a man or a woman. All that was important was their power to heal the sick.'

'And that was why Mr Dangerfield raised you up?'

'Now and again we all take the wrong path. Sometimes we have no choice, because there is no other way to go.'

'But, like, what does it feel like, being the way you are now? It blows me away that you can say stuff and you can move around and you can pick up solid things like that bowl and all, but I can see right through you.'

'Imagine that you are walking through a thick fog but you too are made of fog. You do not know where the fog finishes and you begin. That is what it feels like.'

DaShawn slowly shook his head. 'You are something else. That's all I can say. I never believed in ghosts until I met you, and I'm still finding it hard to get my head around you being real.'

'All I can say to you, my friend, is that you should not try to test if I am real or not. You would regret it.'

'Hey, no, I wasn't intending to. But can I ask you one more thing? Jahmelia, she didn't suffer, did she? I mean like, she didn't feel any pain at all, did she?'

'Do you care if she did?'

'Well, yes and no. God wanted women to suffer pain, didn't

He, which is why He made it hurt so much to have babies. And Jahmelia's in a better place now, isn't she? Much better. There's no more privileged place for a woman to be, is there, excepting inside a man. That's what women are for, after all, giving their strength to the men in their lives. It says so in the Bible, again and again.'

'I know nothing of your Bible. Only that it was used to justify the theft of our lands and the wholesale murder of those of us who resisted.'

DaShawn was about to respond to that, but the Ghost Woman turned her back on him and he changed his mind. Instead, he said, 'Okay. I can tell Mr Dangerfield that you've started to make her ready, can I?'

'You can tell him whatever you like.'

DaShawn hesitated for a moment longer, but despite telling himself that she was only a woman, and only a ghost of a woman at that, he found her deeply unnerving, and he decided to leave before she turned back around and screamed at him.

He had heard her scream before, when he was downstairs, and it had chilled him down to the soles of his feet.

When DaShawn had gone, the Ghost Woman went up to Zuzana's bedside and stood over her. Zuzana was facing the wall, but she could feel the Ghost Woman on her bare shoulder, like the draught from a bedroom window on a winter's night.

'Lie on your back,' the Ghost Woman told her. 'It is time for me to anoint you, ready for Weywot.'

Zuzana stayed where she was, clutching the sheet

underneath her tightly with both hands, in case the Ghost Woman tried to turn her over. She was exhausted, more tired than she had ever felt in the whole of her life. Every muscle in her body was aching. Her knees and her elbows were actually creaking with tiredness, and yet her mind was wide awake, clear and bright and pin-sharp. Her eyelids refused to close, and she was acutely sensitive to everything around her. She could hear planes passing over the house on their way to land at LAX, and she could even hear John Dangerfield's servants talking to each other downstairs, and the kitchen doors swinging open and shut.

The root of her tongue felt even more swollen than before, which made it difficult for her to breathe and almost impossible to swallow, so that she felt as if she were choking.

The Ghost Woman laid her hand on Zuzana's bare shoulder. 'I am going to anoint you to give Weywot more pleasure, and to calm him. If he is calm, and you please him, you will feel nothing but pleasure yourself.'

Zuzana continued to cling on to the sheet. Without her tongue, she couldn't ask the Ghost Woman what she meant by calming Weywot, or to please him, but she guessed that even if she could, and the Ghost Woman told her, it would terrify her even more.

'I promise you that this anointing will make your ordeal easier to bear,' the Ghost Woman told her. Unlike the way she had shrilled at her before, she spoke patiently, and Zuzana could hear regret in her voice. Although her sharp-nailed hand was resting on her shoulder, she had so far made no attempt to turn her over by force.

Another plane flew over the house, and she couldn't help thinking about the passengers sitting comfortably in their seats, staring out of their windows as the sun went down and the lights of LA started to sparkle as far as the eye could see. She thought of the one time she had done that herself, not thinking of what might be happening in the darkness of all the houses down below her.

'I ask you as a healer,' said the Ghost Woman. 'I ask you as a woman. I ask you as somebody who was once a mother.'

Zuzana at last released her grip on the sheet and turned over onto her back. Although she was naked, any embarrassment she might have felt had long been overwhelmed by fear. The Ghost Woman was leaning over her, her shawl around her shoulders, her green eyes gleaming. The expression on her face was unlike any that Zuzana had ever seen before, on anybody's face – an extraordinary look of power, but of sadness, too.

She picked up the ceramic bowl and sat down beside Zuzana on the bed, with the bowl in her lap. When Zuzana lifted her head a little, she could see that it was filled with a jellyish red paste, which the Ghost Woman stirred with the spoon several times while muttering some words in Chumash, repeatedly emphasising the word *'aqiwo*.

When she had finished stirring and chanting, the Ghost Woman scooped up some of the paste in her fingers and held it up close to Zuzana's face so that she could smell it. It had a sweet scent that was almost erotic, but it was spicy and astringent, too, and it also had a musky undertone, as if fruit and flowers had been mixed up with tobacco.

'It is bearberries, crushed with devil's claw, and momoy,' said the Ghost Woman. 'It has one more herb, which is my secret. I call it *wištoyo*, which means rainbow. Many hundreds of years ago, our people were brought to this land on a bridge made from a rainbow, and so we see the rainbow as the way from one world into the next.'

Zuzana managed to make a gargling sound in the back of her throat, to tell the Ghost Woman that she had heard her, and understood.

'Close your eyes now. Think of a good time in your life, when you were happy. When the sky had no clouds and your friends were dancing all around you.'

At first, Zuzana kept her eyes open. Her brain was still dazzlingly bright inside, overlit like a film set, so bright that it was giving her a headache. But then the Ghost Woman started to massage the paste into her shoulders, and around her neck, and she began to relax. The paste was slightly sticky, and cool, and occasionally she was scratched by the Ghost Woman's ragged fingernails as she smoothed it into her skin, but the more she breathed in its fragrance, the more dreamlike the experience became.

She closed her eyes and her mind was still bright, but this brightness was sunshine, and she was sure that she could hear the sea. She breathed in again, and she could hear laughter. Her mouth still felt clogged up and dry, and she was frustrated that she couldn't cry out to her friends that she was here, but she was happy for them, because she knew that they were dancing in the surf, and that they loved her.

As she smeared the aromatic paste all over her, the Ghost Woman began to hum under her breath, and then to sing.

'This is the sour dock song,' she said, smoothing paste over Zuzana's thighs and around her buttocks. 'The sour dock itself is not a medicine, but it has an acid in its leaves that helps all the other herbs to release their energy.'

Gently, she parted Zuzana's legs and smeared paste between them, all around her vulva and then deep into her vagina. Zuzana shuddered, because it felt cold at first, but after a few moments she felt a warmth rising inside her, and despite her fear she began to feel aroused.

The Ghost Woman carried on singing and humming, her hands sliding around Zuzana's calves and down to her feet, carefully rubbing paste between each toe. When she had finished, she stood up and said, 'You will see things now. Birds flying around the room, spiders crawling all over you, coyotes coming up to you to sniff at you. You will think that they are real, because they *are* real. They are visitors from the spirit world, not dreams. You will never have a dream again.'

Zuzana stared up at her. The Ghost Woman was gradually growing darker, and yet she could still see the outline of the door right through her. She was more like a shadow than a ghost. Only her green eyes shone as brightly as before.

'You are ready for Weywot now,' she said softly. 'In a few hours, the last and greatest moment of your life will have arrived.' With that, she covered her head completely with her shawl.

Zuzana lay on her back, taking in quick, anxious breaths through her nostrils. She could feel the paste drying on her skin, as if she were shrinking, and its smell gradually began to fade as it dried. She knew that she wasn't dreaming. Her senses were all too aware. Yet it was hard for her to believe that any of this was real, and she still couldn't understand what the Ghost Woman meant about her being 'ready for Weywot'.

After only a few moments, she felt something prickling on

her right shoulder. She turned her head to see what it was, and was confronted with a hairy dark-brown ebony tarantula.

She couldn't scream out loud, but the scream inside her head was piercing.

25

Rod was already in a bad mood when a huge Skylite Logistics semi-trailer stopped right in front of him at the intersection of Roscoe Boulevard and De Soto Avenue and then remained stationary, so that he was unable to take a right turn on red.

He blasted his horn but the semi-trailer stayed where it was, even when the lights turned green. He could bet that the driver was checking his route map or phoning his girlfriend or had decided that this would be a good place to stop and eat a Subway.

On the corner of the intersection, on his right, there was a 76 gas station. As he sat there fuming, his eye was caught by a fat young man with a divot of blond hair on top of his head who came out of the gas station's shop, and then waddled across the forecourt to open the door of a white Lincoln Continental and climb behind the wheel. Rod recognised the man immediately. It was SloMo, who had threatened him on the evening that Vincent Priest had taken Zuzana away.

'Shit,' he breathed. 'I don't fucking believe it!'

Zuzana still hadn't returned to their apartment, not even for a change of clothes or to pick up her mail. She hadn't even called or texted him to say that she would never be coming back.

The Lincoln pulled out of the gas station and into the road alongside him. Its rear windows were tinted so Rod was unable to see if there was anybody sitting in the back, but one of the windows had been lowered an inch, and as he waited for the lights to change again he saw a puff of smoke wafting out of the gap. When the lights changed, the Lincoln turned left down De Soto Avenue and so he swerved his Colorado truck out from behind the Skylite semi-trailer, ignoring the angry tooting from a woman in a Golf, and followed it.

The Lincoln cruised at a leisurely speed south on De Soto as far as the Ventura Freeway, where it headed east. Then it cruised south again on I-405 to Sunset Boulevard, and at last it turned in through the gates of Bel Air. Rod kept at least five car lengths behind it all the way, in case SloMo and his passenger realised that he was tailing them. When the Lincoln eventually pulled in to the driveway of La Muralla, he deliberately overshot and parked outside the house next door.

He jumped out of his truck and hurried back to La Muralla, in time to catch SloMo and Vincent Priest as they were walking up the stone steps to the front doors.

'Hey!' he shouted out. 'I want a goddam word with you!'

Vincent stopped and turned around. He was still puffing on his cigar. SloMo stopped too.

'Do I *know* you?' asked Vincent.

'Of course you fucking know me. I'm Zuzana's boyfriend. You took her off for some meeting with movie producers and I haven't seen her since. I want to know what the fuck you've done with her!'

Vincent frowned and shook his head. 'Sorry. I have no idea who you're talking about. What did you say her name was?'

'You know damn well who I'm talking about! Zuzana! Where the hell is she?'

Vincent turned to SloMo. 'Do you remember a girl by that name? I certainly don't.'

Rod went right up to Vincent and prodded him in the chest with his finger.

'Hey, easy,' said SloMo, and he came back down the steps.

'What do you mean, "easy"? It's my girlfriend we're talking about here, so you can stop jerking me around. If you don't tell me where she is, I'm going to call the cops.'

'Be my guest and call them,' said Vincent. 'I'll only tell them the same as I've told you. I know no girl of that name and never have.'

At that moment, the front doors opened and John Dangerfield came out wearing a piratical shirt with billowing sleeves, his long hair tied back in a man-bun.

'What's the problem, your reverence?' he called out. 'I thought you were fetching me that new cutie from Bottega Veneta.'

'She was off sick today. Maybe tomorrow.'

Rod looked at Vincent sharply. 'Oh. You fetch girls for this dude, do you?' Then he turned towards John Dangerfield. 'Did he fetch you a girl called Zuzana? A waitress from The Orange Grove?'

'I just told him!' said Vincent. 'We've never heard of any girl called Zuzana!'

'There! You got her name right that time, didn't you?' Rod challenged him. 'You think I'm some kind of fucking moron or something? I was there when you took her away.'

He shouldered Vincent aside and started to climb the steps.

'Is she here? She's here, isn't she?'

John began to back away, and at that moment DaShawn and Bradley came out to see what all the shouting was about.

'Come on, tell me!' Rod raged. 'She's here, isn't she? And if she isn't, then what the fuck have you done with her, you big faggot?'

'Cool it, young feller, if you don't mind,' said John. 'I don't know how you've got it into your head that this girl that you're talking about is here, but I can assure you that she's not. And there's no call for you to be insulting.'

Rod pointed angrily at Vincent. 'He took her away! *He* knows where she is! He took her away and I haven't seen her now for two days! If you won't tell me what's happened to her, I'm calling the cops!'

'Listen,' said John. 'It so happens that we have a senior police officer here today as our guest. Deputy Chief Brogan, from Van Nuys. Why don't you come inside and have a word with him? I'm sure he'll be able to give you all the reassurance you need about your – what was her name? Wizzana?'

Rod hesitated. He looked back at Vincent again, and Vincent shrugged as if to say, *why not, if it calms you down and makes you feel better?* The look on SloMo's face was one of tightly suppressed amusement.

'Okay,' said Rod. In truth, he had no idea what he was going to do next. If all these men persisted in denying that they had ever known Zuzana, he had no way of proving that they were lying. Neither could he prove that Vincent and SloMo had come round to their apartment and taken Zuzana away with them. Even if he could, he had no way of verifying that they had brought her here, to this particular house.

John stepped forward and put his arm around Rod's shoulders. 'Come on, I'll introduce you to Deputy Chief Brogan. I'm John Dangerfield, by the way. I don't know if you ever saw that movie *The Mother of All Evil*? Yes? Well, I produced it. Me, yes, really. So what's your name?'

'Rod. Rod Ferris.'

'Like in the wheel? Forever going around and around?'

Rod didn't answer that. He was overawed by the atrium, with its domed ceiling and its pillars and its gleaming marble floor. John led him across it and through the entertainment room, its walls now densely decorated with elderberry branches. Out in the garden, five men were sitting around the table, drinking and smoking and scooping up handfuls of pecan nuts.

'Ned,' said John, walking up to a balding man with a round belly and Ray-Bans and a distinct resemblance to Ernest Borgnine. 'This young man has a missing person problem. For some reason he believes that Vincent here took his girlfriend away and that he might have fetched her here, to La Muralla. Of course he's mistaken, but she's pulled off a vanishing act and he doesn't know where she's disappeared to. Rod – this is Deputy Chief Brogan. Hopefully he can advise you.'

'Here, take a seat,' said Deputy Chief Brogan. He was wearing a tight yellow polo shirt with dark semi-circles of perspiration under his armpits. 'How long's she been gone, this g.f. of yours?'

'Two days. And not a word. I called her folks and her brother and they haven't seen her either. Zuzana, her name is. She's a waitress at The Orange Grove.'

'Has she shown up for work?'

Rod shook his head. 'This Vincent guy spotted her at the restaurant and told her she could be a movie star. She was real excited about it. I mean, like over the moon. Vincent came around to our apartment and picked her up and that was the last I saw of her.'

Vincent was standing close behind Rod. 'I think he's mistaking me for somebody else. I've eaten at The Orange Grove, sure, but I don't know any girl by that name. I mean, that's a name you'd remember, right?'

'How well have you two been getting along?' asked Deputy Chief Brogan. 'Any arguments lately? You think maybe she could have just wanted a break?'

'Well, we fight now and again, of course we do. What couple doesn't? But she's never walked out without a word before. Not like this. She's left everything behind. Her clothes, her make-up, her shoes. Even her toothbrush.'

'If I was you, I'd give her another day or two. You know what young women can be like, especially at certain times, if you follow me. If she hasn't shown up by then, you can call into your local police station and file a missing person's report. But I wouldn't worry too much. We had a fellow recently in Winnetka whose wife disappeared for a month. She came back but she never told him where she'd been, or why she'd gone, but he said that their marriage was a whole lot feistier after that.'

Deputy Chief Brogan took a handful of pecans and started to feed them into his mouth one by one, still talking as he chewed. 'Women need to feel validated sometimes, do you understand what I mean? They need to know that they're still attractive to other men. I'll bet you a hundred bucks that's why your g.f.'s gone off.

'As for these guys here... John Dangerfield here and Vincent Priest. I know these guys well and I can vouch for their integrity one hundred and ninety-eight per cent. They value women, these guys. More than you'd ever believe.'

'Happy now?' asked John Dangerfield.

Rod stood up. 'I don't know. I guess so. But I still don't know where she is.'

'You'll find out, sooner or later,' said Deputy Chief Brogan. 'There's not many people who go missing for ever without a trace, and most of the time it's because they want to. You wouldn't want somebody back who didn't want *you* that badly, now would you?'

He took off his Ray-Bans and looked up at Rod, and Rod saw that his eyes were shining silver, with no irises. He had never seen eyes like that before, and he assumed that he must be wearing some kind of contact lenses.

'I'll see you out,' said John, and he led Rod back through the entertainment room. As they reached the atrium, though, Rod saw that SloMo and DaShawn and Bradley were lined up across it, blocking the way to the front doors, their legs apart and their hands clasped in front of their crotches, the classic pose of bouncers.

'There's something I want to show you before you leave us,' said John, taking hold of Rod's elbow.

'What?' asked Rod.

'This way. You'll see.'

John led him through the left-hand archway and along the short oak-lined corridor to the second door. He opened it and Rod found himself inside a chilly room with lime-green walls and no furniture except for a metal dresser and two single beds.

'So what do you want to show me?' he asked, turning around, but it was then that he saw that SloMo and the other two men had followed close behind.

John stepped back, and as he did so the three men rushed forward. They grabbed hold of Rod's arms and one of his legs and pitched him sideways onto one of the beds, jarring his spine.

'Get the fuck off me!' he screamed at them, but Bradley stuffed a dirty crumpled-up duster into his mouth, while SloMo and DaShawn reached under the bed for the leather belts that were dangling underneath it, and strapped them over his legs and his chest, pinning his arms by his sides. He tried to bounce up and down to work himself free, but he was buckled too tightly.

John came up to the side of the bed and looked down at him. He delicately licked his lips with the tip of his tongue, and then he said, 'Did you seriously think that you could come to my house and make such serious accusations against me and that I would simply let you go?'

Rod could do nothing but stare back at him.

'As it happens, your accusations were well founded. The Priest *did* take your Zuzana and bring her here. She's been with us ever since. And what a gorgeous girl she is. Zuzana Zilka, we call her. She *could* have been a movie star, yes, and in a way she will be, although not quite in the way that she expected.

'Whatever Deputy Chief Brogan told you, Rod, I can't risk you reporting Zuzana's disappearance to the police, not in two or three days' time – not ever. But you'll be reunited with her, I promise you that – and much sooner than you think. Tonight is the great night, the great coming-together – the gala! Tomorrow, the celebration breakfast. The feast!'

A thin man with a salt-and-pepper beard entered the room, buttoning up a white surgical jacket. He was frowning as if his train of thought had been interrupted while he had been trying to think of something else altogether.

'Ah, Jacob,' said John. 'Sorry to call you down at such short notice. We have here an unexpected guest. But not totally unwelcome, under the circumstances. It will save us looking around the streets for some derelict.'

He turned back to Rod again and said, 'Rod – if we take out that cloth, do you promise not to scream, or blaspheme, or accuse me of any more transgressions?'

Rod didn't really understand what he was talking about, but he nodded all the same. Bradley reached across and pulled out the duster, and Rod spat to get the taste out of his mouth.

'How did you get here?' John asked him. 'I assume you drove.'

'Yes,' Rod croaked. 'I couldn't have walked here, could I?'

'So where's your vehicle? And what kind of a vehicle is it?'

'It's a grey Colorado. I parked it down the street a ways. But listen—'

'And those are the keys, hanging out of your pocket there?'

Rod didn't answer, although he said, '*hey!*' when Bradley tugged the bunch of keys out of the front pocket of his jeans. Bradley tossed them over to DaShawn, and as soon as DaShawn caught them, John pointed to the door with a pistol finger and DaShawn immediately walked out.

'Listen, listen – I'll go,' said Rod. 'I'll just go and I won't say nothing about this to nobody. I swear it. I'll even forget about Zuzana if I have to.'

'Do you know what you sound like?' said John. 'You sound like you've lost your balls. First of all you show up here, shouting at me like you've got the biggest pair that ever was. But the way you're talking now, you could be a gelding.'

'For fuck's sake, man, I only wanted to know where she'd gone. She's my girlfriend and we've been living together for nearly three years. I care about her.'

'From what the Priest told me, you knocked her around quite a bit. You call that caring? Men who knock women around, they don't have balls. So what we're going to do now, we're going to give you a taste of balls.'

'What are you talking about? I've just told you I'll go. I swear on the Holy Bible I won't never breathe one word about this to nobody. I won't even say Zuzana's name again. Not once. I'll forget that she ever existed.'

'Jacob,' said John, and he beckoned him to come forward. John nodded to Bradley, too, and Bradley stepped up closer to the side of the bed. Bradley unfastened Rod's cowboy belt buckle, twisted open his fly buttons, and wrenched down his jeans as far as the middle of his thighs. After that, he pulled down Rod's blue-striped boxer shorts to expose his genitals.

'*What are you doing?*' Rod panted, trying to lift up his head to see what was happening. '*What the fuck are you doing?*'

John put his fingertip to his lips. 'Shh, quiet! From now on, Rod Ferriswheel, you're not going to utter a word. Do you understand me? Not one single syllable. Because you have a choice, see? Jacob here has a surgical scalpel in his hand, and you can either lie quiet and let him operate on you, which shouldn't cause you too much pain, or else you can shout and struggle and generally make a nuisance of yourself. In which case we'll have to forget about the surgery and cut your throat. And you'll die.'

Rod stared at him in disbelief. But then John took hold of Jacob's wrist and held up his hand so that he could see the scalpel.

'I feel for you, I truly do,' John told him, in a warm, mock-sympathetic voice. 'But then you *rushed* in, didn't you? You rushed in where even demons fear to tread. If there's one lesson that the people in today's world need to learn, it's to mind their own business.'

Rod let his head drop back onto the bed. Although the room was so chilly, he was sweating with fear, and he had to keep blinking the drops of perspiration out of his eyelashes. What were they going to do? Cut off his cock? Or cut off everything? He started to make a humming sound in the back of his throat, out of sheer terror.

The thin man leaned over him and fastidiously lifted up his penis with his latex-gloved fingers. Then, with great precision, he sliced open the left side of his scrotum and peeled back the skin to expose his testicle. It took five careful slices to cut that free from its artery and the fine ductules that clung to it. Bradley held out a stainless-steel dish and he dropped the testicle into it.

Rod stopped humming and started to quake uncontrollably. The incision had hurt so much that it had gone beyond pain, and was more like a high-pitched screeching in his brain. The thin man said to Bradley, 'Try to hold him still, would you, please? I don't want to hurt him more than I have to.'

'Do you know, Jacob,' said John, standing back watching with his arms folded, 'you have a heart of gold.'

The thin man pressed a thick pad of gauze against Rod's left thigh to stem the bleeding from his severed artery, and then he proceeded to slice open the right side of his scrotum and cut out his other testicle. It took him less than a minute to remove it and drop it into the dish.

John now came closer again, and beckoned to Bradley to bring the dish nearer.

'We're giving you a rare opportunity, Rod. An opportunity that is given to very few men, if any. We're not only giving you the chance to see what your manhood looks like, but to discover what it *tastes* like. And to nourish yourself with your own virility.'

Bradley took a cocktail stick out of his pocket and pierced one of the testicles with it. Then he lifted it up like a pale pink plum and held it, dripping, an inch above Rod's lips. Rod closed his mouth tightly and could only stare at Bradley in agony and utter disbelief. He felt as if somebody was holding the pointed flame of a welding torch between his legs.

John seemed to grow calmer as Rod's pain and terror increased, his eyes half closed. In fact, he looked almost blissful.

'Eat,' he said, so quietly that Rod could hardly hear him. Then he screamed, '*Eat!*' and although he didn't say so, Rod had no doubt that if he didn't, John would order his throat to be cut.

Rod opened his mouth and Bradley dropped the testicle into it. Rod chewed and chewed, gagging with every bite. The testicle was tough, like gristle, and made a squeaking noise between his teeth. He managed to swallow it while it was still all strung together.

'Only one more to go,' said John. 'Don't you feel the sheer naked power that's giving you? And soon you can share it!'

SloMo watched in appalled fascination as Bradley pushed the second testicle into Rod's half-open mouth. 'If you eat yourself, does that make you a cannibal?'

26

As they drove south on I-5, with the sun setting off to their right over Cobblestone Mountain, Trinity said, 'There's something I have to tell you, Nemo.'

'Oh, yes? Let me guess. You don't like my aftershave? I found it in Mike's bathroom, so you can't really blame me.'

'Teodoro said that I shouldn't let anybody know. But he gave me three words in the Chumash language, and he said that those three words could stop anybody's heart.'

Nemo looked away from the highway for a moment and frowned at her. 'Are you serious? Was *he* serious?'

'I don't know. But he told me the story about them, how one of his people had spoken these three words and a whole lot of Spanish soldiers had dropped stone dead on the spot. He said these words could kill anybody, or anything. Human, or animal, or even demon.'

'Maybe he told you just to bolster your confidence. But – hey – don't repeat them! Teodoro can make beer glasses turn into statues and he showed us how to make ourselves look like other people. It could be that they actually work, these words.'

'I couldn't keep it to myself. I wouldn't ever want to use them, believe me, but if we find ourselves in a really desperate situation – like, if we're being threatened with our lives – well, I wanted you to know about them.'

'If you say these words, though, how come everybody around you doesn't drop dead?'

'I have to make an X sign with my fingers, like this, and hold it up towards the person I want to kill. I suppose it's a bit like aiming a gun.'

Nemo was silent for over a minute. Then he said, 'This is all so crazy, this whole thing. I mean, it's like a dream. I keep thinking I'm going to wake up back at home any minute with a hangover, with Sherri yelling at me to haul my ass out of bed and put out the trash.'

'Me too, Nemo. Well, not with a hangover. But this isn't a dream. It's real.'

They drove first to Zelzah Avenue. Trinity wanted to check that Rosie had come home, and also that her father had fed Buddy and made sure that he had finished his homework. There was no sign of the blue Malibu that had been waiting there previously, nor the grey Ford Explorers, nor any other vehicle that was used by the IAG. Once they had parked, though, they recited the words that would change their appearance. It was still possible that the Fox house was being watched from a surveillance camera, or from another property across the street.

With every word that they recited, Nemo's hair darkened, and his jaw became squarer, and his eyes turned to swimming-pool blue. Trinity's hair turned curly blonde, and tangled, like Rosie's. Her nose lengthened and her lips plumped up into a provocative pout.

Once they had melted into Toby Carter and Clarissa Keyes, they sat and stared at each other, giving themselves a few moments to become familiar with their dramatically altered appearance.

'Well, wow, you're quite a babe magnet, if you don't mind my saying so,' said Trinity, and she couldn't help smiling.

'Looking pretty good yourself, blondie,' grinned Nemo. 'But come on, we'd better get moving.'

Trinity had to ring the doorbell three times before the door opened. Buddy stood blinking at them, in a grubby Steven Universe T-shirt and droopy boxer shorts and bare feet. He was holding a half-eaten peanut-butter HoHo.

'Yes?' he said. 'Do you want to see my dad? He's asleep.'

'Buddy, I know you don't think that I look like me, but it's Trin. And this is Nemo.'

'What? You're not Trin. Is this some kind of a trick?'

'It is in a way, but it's like a magic trick. It's an Indian magic trick, like José does, you know, when he paints those pictures of Toypurina and her Spook Owl.'

Buddy shivered. 'You *know* about that? I don't get it. How do you know about that?'

'I know about that because I'm your sister and you're only dreaming that I look like somebody else. It was me and Nemo who came down to the H.K. Valley Center when you were hiding in that dumpster and rescued you.'

'For *real*? You're really Trin for real?'

'I'm really Trin for real and this is really Nemo for real. You say that Dad's asleep? Has he been drinking again? Where's Rosie?'

Buddy still appeared to think that Trinity and Nemo were two strangers playing some elaborate prank, but he said, 'Rosie hasn't come home yet.'

'Did she come home last night?'

'No. I think she was having a sleepover with her friend Sally.'

'Has she called to say she's okay?'

Buddy shook his head. 'Nobody's called.'

Trinity looked around. The only signs of life along Zelzah Avenue were the flicker of televisions in living-room windows and an elderly man slowly walking his elderly Labrador along the other side of the street. 'Nemo... I don't think there's anybody watching. Shall we...?'

'Sure, okay.'

They both said softly '*anyapakh*', and as soon as they had, Buddy came out of his dream and saw them for who they really were. Immediately, he burst into tears, dropping his HoHo onto the floor and jumping up to hug Trinity as if he hadn't seen her for months.

'It's horrible, Trin, it's horrible! I came home from school and Dad was drunk and there was nothing to eat and Rosie wasn't there and I didn't know what to *do*!'

Trinity and Nemo stepped into the hallway and Nemo closed the door behind them. They went through to the living room and found Trinity's father lying face down on the floor, wearing nothing but a pair of yellow-stained underpants, snoring. The coffee table was crowded with empty Rolling Rock cans, and four or five of them had tipped over onto the couch, so that the cushions were soaked in beer.

Trinity knelt down beside her father and shook his shoulder. 'Dad? Dad! It's Trin! Wake up, Dad, it's Trin!'

Her father snorted, but he was so drunk that his tongue lolled out and his eyes remained closed. Trinity shook him again, but it was useless, and so she stood up.

'It's no good. He'll have to sleep it off, that's all. It looks like he's lashed out all of his month's unemployment on booze.'

'So what about young Buddy here?' asked Nemo. 'We can't take him with us. Too damn risky, for starters.'

'We can't leave him here, though. Buddy – do you think you could stay with José for tonight? His mom and dad wouldn't mind, would they? You've slept over with him before, haven't you?'

Buddy nodded, wiping the tears from his eyes with the back of his hand. Trinity said, 'They don't live far, Nemo. I'll pack him a bag with his pyjamas and his toothbrush and his school clothes for tomorrow.'

'And what about your sister?'

'Rosie? I'll leave her a note and could you spare ten dollars for a cab? She'll just have to spend the night with Sally or some other friend.'

'Where are you going?' Buddy asked her. 'Why can't I come with you?'

'There's some bad guys who want to hurt us, Buddy,' said Nemo. 'That's why we put on those funny faces, so they wouldn't recognise us. Don't you worry. Once we've sorted them out, we'll come back for you, and the first thing we'll do is treat you to a slap-up meal at McDonald's.'

Buddy bit his lip. He was too upset to say anything, but he looked down at his drunken slumbering father and then up at Trinity, and he nodded again, as if he understood how dangerous the situation was, and how uncertain, and that being brave would be the only way out of it.

*

They drove across to Texhoma Avenue, a short straight street of single-storey homes in Encino Village. José lived in one of the smaller houses, with no garage. A red Chevrolet pickup truck was parked in the driveway, with *Pérez Tree Trimming* and a picture of a red-shouldered hawk on the driver's door.

After they had stopped outside, Nemo twisted his head around to make sure that nobody had been tailing them, and then he said, 'Okay. This is only for tonight, Buddy. With any luck, we'll have this all done and dusted by tomorrow.'

They all went up to the front porch and knocked. After a moment, the door was opened by a tall, stringy-looking man wearing a headband and a loose brown T-shirt, with a necklace made of coloured clamshells. There was no mistaking from his hawklike features and his long grey ponytail that he was a Gabrieliño-Tongva Indian.

'Well, if it isn't Buddy!' he said, and then he turned to Trinity and Nemo and said, 'Yes? You must be Buddy's dad, and one of his sisters. Can I help you with something?'

At that moment, José appeared behind his father. 'Buddy! *Cool-a-doola!* I'm just about to play Pokémon Sword! We can play it together!'

'Hey, hold your horses, Jo,' said his father, taking hold of José's shoulder.

Trinity stepped forward. 'I'm so sorry to show up on your doorstep like this, Mr Pérez, without giving you any warning. I'm Buddy's older sister, yes – Trinity, or Trin you can call me. This isn't his dad, though. This is a friend of mine, Nemo Frisby. The thing is, we're in a spot of bother, Nemo and me, and we badly need to find someplace for Buddy to spend the night.'

José's father looked from Trinity to Nemo and back again, as if he couldn't be sure if he could take them seriously.

'To tell you the truth, sir, it's a whole lot more than a spot of bother,' said Nemo, in his hoarse, gravelly voice. 'For one reason or another, which I won't go into right now, Trinity and me have some particularly unpleasant characters chasing after us. Unfortunately, this means that Trinity can't stay home to take care of Buddy. That wouldn't matter but Buddy's dad is totally stinko and his other sister hasn't come home, so we're appealing to your good nature to take him in.'

'I've fetched my pyjamas, Mr Peréz,' said Buddy, holding up his bag.

José's father thought for a long moment, and Trinity was afraid he was going to turn them away, but eventually he nodded and said, 'Okay, you'd better come in.'

He led them into the family room, where another son was sprawled on the floor watching TV. 'Leon, give us some time, would you? Go help your mom in the kitchen.'

Leon gave them a disgruntled frown, but did as he was told, and climbed to his feet, and left the room. José's father switched off the TV and said, 'Sit. Tell me what this is all about. Jo, Buddy, go off and play your game, why don't you?'

Trinity looked around the room. The shelf over the fireplace was crowded with black-and-white photographs of Tongva villagers and willow huts, while the walls were hung with paintings of rainbows and cacti and clouds, and the blissful faces of people who seemed to be dreaming. The side tables were decorated with pebbles and Tongva pottery.

At the end of the room, the whole wall was painted with the same face of Toypurina that Buddy and José had sprayed onto the wall at Reseda Transmissions, along with her Spook

Owl. The owl's eyes were covered with duct tape, although Toypurina herself had a haughty, slightly menacing stare.

'So, you are Trinity and Nemo, yes?' said José's father. 'José told me that you rescued him from another tagging crew.'

'You know about his tagging?' asked Nemo.

'Not only do I know about it, I encourage it. The white people of Southern California should never be allowed to forget whose land it is that they are trespassing on.'

His speech was slow and measured, as if English were his second language, and he was weighing up the possible effect that each word would have before he allowed it out of his mouth.

'My name is Red Bird Gabriel Peréz. Well – you probably saw that on my truck. I am a tree surgeon by trade, but as you can see by this room, I spend much of my time preserving and reviving the traditions of the Tongva.'

'So José is following in his father's footsteps?' said Trinity. 'He and Buddy painted an amazing picture of Toypurina and her Spook Owl, almost identical to the one you have there. That's what got them into trouble with those other taggers… they'd painted it over one of *their* tags.'

'I tell José to be respectful and not to deface anybody's property. That is something of a joke, of course, when you consider that we were driven off our own land and our houses were torn down and thousands of us were killed or died from diseases against which we had no immunity. I really should tell him to paint the words "thieves" and "murderers" on every wall and window in Encino.'

'Well, Red Bird, you can be assured that Trinity and me, we have the greatest sympathy for you and your people,' Nemo told him. 'Right now we're hiding out with a couple of Chumash, and they've been giving us support like you couldn't believe. Not only food and shelter, but what you might call magical help too.'

Gabriel Peréz raised an eyebrow. 'Really? You should be cautious with Chumash magic. They say that they learned it from their gods and their demons, and sometimes it can prove too powerful for humans to handle. They also say that it has a way of rebounding on those who use it, especially if they use it selfishly or unwisely.'

'Thanks for the warning, but right now we need all the magic we can get.'

They heard José and Buddy laughing on the other side of the hallway.

Gabriel Peréz gave Trinity and Nemo the ghost of a smile. 'Don't you worry. My wife and I will happily take care of Buddy while you deal with these people who are giving you so much grief. One night, two nights, whatever. I have to say that Buddy can sometimes act a little strange, but then José can sometimes act a little strange too, and it is like they both live in the same strange world together.'

'Interesting guy, Red Bird,' said Nemo, as they drove away from Texhoma Avenue and headed south on the freeway towards Bel Air. 'He's a tree trimmer, but he speaks like a college professor. And, boy, does he have one Godzilla of a grudge about the way his people were treated.'

An SUV roared past them with one rear light missing and smoke billowing out of its exhaust. Nemo jammed his foot down on the gas pedal so that they started to surge after it, but he slowed down again, almost at once. Trinity glanced across at him and she could see by his expression that he had reminded himself that he was no longer a cop.

'Mind you,' he continued after a while, 'sometimes I wonder why the Indians aren't even angrier about what was done to them than they are. If somebody had turned up out of nowhere and thrown *my* ancestors off their own land, believe me, I'd be madder than all hell.'

'Maybe they are,' said Trinity. 'But maybe they know there's nothing much they can do about it. Maybe they're just being ultra- ultra-patient and waiting for us to self-destruct. You know – burn ourselves to death with forest fires or freeze ourselves to death because we never took any notice of climate change. Or infect ourselves with Covid or some other horrible virus because we thought they were a hoax and never wore masks. Or simply because we're so out-and-out stupid that we think assault rifles are more important than Medicare.'

'Yeah, maybe you're right. Although I'd rather have a pistol in my pocket tonight than a prescription for indigestion pills.'

By the time they reached Bel Air, it was dark. They drove in through the west gate and then up to Chalon Road, where Nemo pulled up under an overhanging sycamore, so that they could recite the words that would change their appearance into Toby Carter and Clarissa Keyes. As they sat there, three cars passed them, all of them heading up Chantilly Road – a white Cadillac limousine, a red Ferrari California and a dark maroon Bentley.

'What's the betting those are all guests at John Dangerfield's party,' said Nemo. 'Pity Teodoro didn't give us a spell to make this crappy old Acadia look like a Rolls-Royce. Or a Lamborghini, at least.'

Trinity said nothing. She could feel her mother's presence

inside her, almost as if she were softly singing her to sleep, the way she used to do when she was little.

Nemo looked across at her and frowned. 'Hey, Trin. You're not crying, are you?'

Trinity wiped her eyes with her sleeve. 'It's that dream feeling, that's all. It makes me kind of emotional.'

'Sweetheart – I wish I could say that we could call this whole thing off. If we did, though, we'd have to leave LA and never come back, and even then I wouldn't be too sure that we'd be safe, no matter where we went. There's some powerful people involved in this, and whatever they're up to, they don't want anybody to find out about it, ever.'

He started the engine again and they drove up Chantilly Road until they reached John Dangerfield's house. The Bentley was turning into the driveway just ahead of them, and they could see a security guard talking to the passengers in the back. After a few moments, the Bentley was waved through and directed to a parking space.

Now the security guard beckoned Nemo forward, and Nemo put down his window. The security guard's face immediately lit up.

'Hey, *Toby*!' he exclaimed. 'How's it going, dude? Didn't I hear you was up in Alaska?'

'Oh, yeah, I was,' Nemo told him. 'Well, I am still, because we haven't wrapped up shooting yet, but I needed a couple of days' break from all that freezing-cold weather. Not to mention all that reindeer. Reindeer steak, reindeer soup, reindeer hot dogs. Jesus, I tell you. They even mix reindeer fat into their fucking ice cream.'

'Pukesville! But I must say you're looking well on it, whatever.'

The security guard ducked his head down so that he could see who was sitting in the front passenger seat. 'And is that Clarissa Keyes? I never realised you two knew each other! Hi, Clarissa! *Cómo lo llevas?* You remember me, don't you?'

'Sure, hi,' said Trinity, and she gave him a little finger-wave.

'No, you don't. Fernando! I was on security on *Bloodbath 2000.* I lent you a borrow of my jacket when you got all shivery after that swimming-pool scene. *Fernando*, now do you remember?'

'Oh, yes, Fernando. Hi, Fernando.'

Another of John Dangerfield's staff waved them to a narrow parking space at the far end of the driveway, behind a thick holly olive bush.

'I think he's trying to hide our beaten-up SUV from the neighbours,' said Nemo, as he climbed out. 'Now look – I'm going to leave the keys under the seat here, in case anything happens to one of us and we have to hit the bricks in a hurry.'

'What do you mean, "in case anything happens to one of us"? Anything like what?'

'Trin – you've already seen how determined these guys are. They'd only have to have the slightest suspicion that we're not the people we're pretending to be and we could be in serious shit. So this is a precaution, in case one of us gets hurt, or one of us has to leave the other one behind.'

'I wouldn't leave you behind, not for anything.'

'Well, me neither, but there's one lesson that being a cop teaches you, and that's always prepare for the worst, and then some.'

They climbed the steps to the front doors. Two more security guards were waiting there, standing in the time-honoured pose of all security guards, with their hands clasped together over their crotch. One of them could have been Mike Tyson's brother and the other had a tattooed cobra rearing out of his collar.

'See your invites, sir?' asked Mike Tyson's brother.

'Excuse me, you don't recognise us?'

'Still need to see your invites. Mr Dangerfield emailed every guest an invite.'

'Well, we forgot to bring ours. Sorry.'

'They'll be on your phones, sir.'

'I'm sure they will be, but we didn't bring our phones. We wanted an evening off, without being pestered, if you get what I'm saying. I mean – are you kidding me here? You don't know who I am? Didn't you ever watch *Home Is Where The Heart Is*?'

The security guard appeared to be unmoved, but at that moment one of the front doors opened and John Dangerfield stepped out, smoking a cigar. He was wearing a shiny silver suit with black silk lapels, and his ponytail was tied back with a floppy silver ribbon.

'Hey, Toby!' he called out. 'And Clarry, baby! What are you two doing out here? Come on inside! We're just getting started!'

'They don't have no invites, Mr Dangerfield,' said the security guard.

'Oh, shoot! Never mind. They wouldn't be here, would they, if Myrtle hadn't sent them one? Come along in. We've a margarita punch to die for!'

The security guards reluctantly stepped to one side, and Trinity and Nemo followed John into the marble-floored atrium. From the archway ahead of them, they could hear loud conversation, although nobody was laughing and it sounded more like tons of gravel being slowly poured from the back of a truck. They could hear music, too, extraordinary scraping music. Trinity's father would have said it was the kind of music that set his teeth edgewise.

'Didn't Dan Magellan tell me you were shooting that sled-dog racing movie, up in Alaska? That was a pretty quick wrap.'

'Oh, yes, no,' said Nemo. 'We still have quite a few takes to finish off. There's a scene that takes place in a blizzard and we're still waiting for a blizzard.'

'You couldn't rent a couple of snow machines? Who's directing now, anyway? I heard Joe McCormack was taken off it, or quit. Something about artistic differences, or the studio wouldn't pay for his boyfriend to join him.'

Nemo started coughing, slapping his chest and waving his hand to indicate that he couldn't speak. He was saved from having to answer by SloMo, who came out of the entertainment room with Bradley close behind him.

'We've fixed that trouble we had with the refrigeration system, Mr D. The fan was sticking, that was all. Goddam fence lizard left his tail snagged up in it. So we'll be ready to go when you are.'

'Great. Excellent,' said John, looking at his Rolex. 'We can start in exactly... fifty-five minutes from now. But meanwhile, why don't you down a margarita or two, and mingle with the mighty.'

He led them into the entertainment room, which was crowded with at least two hundred people in evening dress – the men in black tuxedos and the women in floor-length gowns by Oscar de la Renta and Alexandre Vauthier or dresses that left them almost naked.

The lighting had been turned down low, and all the walls were thickly hung with pungent elderberry branches. John Dangerfield's staff were weaving in and out of the guests with silver trays, bringing them margaritas and glasses of champagne, and there was a strong smell of cigar smoke and weed in the air, but the atmosphere was tense rather than sociable. It was less like a Hollywood party than a gathering of relatives and friends before a funeral service, especially since the room was so dark.

'Toby, Clarry, you know almost everybody here, don't you? Toby – there's J.D. Marshall over there. And Clarry, look, there's Nina Truffino. I'm delighted that you two could join us. You had a ball the last time you came here, didn't you, Clarry? But tonight we'll be having so much more than just fun. Tonight is going to be a real eye-opener. Tonight you're going to see where the *real* power in Hollywood comes from!'

27

Vincent came through the crowd, took hold of John's sleeve and whispered something into his ear. John nodded and said, 'Really? Okay. Well, talk to Bradley. He'll know what to do to keep her quiet.'

Vincent caught sight of Trinity and gave her a little salute. He obviously knew Clarissa Keyes but not that well, because he didn't stop to talk to her. Instead, he made his way back through the crowd to talk to David Magellan, who was looking unusually edgy, and kept turning around like a man whose suitcase went missing at the airport and he's anxiously waiting for somebody to bring it back.

John said, 'Okay, you two, there's a few things I have to check out before the ceremony starts, so I'll leave you to socialise. You'll remember, though, won't you – what you see here tonight at La Muralla, it stays at La Muralla. We don't call it "the wall" for nothing.'

Both Trinity and Nemo nodded and smiled, and John left them beside the stage, right next to the scraping, discordant musicians. They saw him go outside into the garden, where he met up with SloMo and DaShawn. Trinity tugged Nemo's sleeve and said, 'Look. The statue.'

'Wow – kind of spooky, isn't it?' said Nemo. The moon had

risen now, and it had given the white marble statue of Auzar an unearthly shine, as if she were illuminated from inside.

A waiter came up and asked them what they wanted to drink.

'A Coke will do for me,' said Nemo. 'I'd love a margarita but I'm not allowed alcohol right now. I'm on nitropazychlorofestarol.'

Trinity asked for a Coke, too, and when the waiter had gone, she said, 'What's *that*?'

'Nitropazy-what's-its-name? Search me. I just made it up.'

For most of the next hour Trinity and Nemo circled slowly around the room, moving all the time and pretending to keep each other engaged in a serious conversation, so that any of the other guests who recognised them as Toby Carter and Clarissa Keyes would find it awkward to stop them and interrupt them. It was nerve-wracking, because so many of the actors and producers and movie publicists in the room recognised them, and waved to them, and called out 'Toby! Clarissa! What's the story, you two?', and more than a dozen people asked Nemo why he was here in LA, and not filming in Alaska.

Each time, Nemo pointed to his throat and croaked out, '*Laryngitis!*'

The darkness helped, because they could keep to the shadowy corners of the room. The music helped, too, because it was so loud and so jarring that it was almost like listening to a woman continually screaming in pain, and the guests were having enough trouble talking to each other as it was.

After an hour, though, the music abruptly scraped to a stop. An expectant murmur rippled through the guests, along with a tinkling of glasses as they hurriedly finished their drinks. John climbed up onto the stage with the musicians and held up both hands for attention, although everybody was already looking at him.

'Welcome, folks! Welcome! Tonight is a most significant night, as many of you know already and some of you are about to witness for the first time. Tonight is the seventh full moon of the year, and in the calendar of the Tongva Indians, this was the night when sacrifices were offered to their gods and their ancestors, and especially to Weywot, their immortal and much-feared chief.'

None of the guests applauded, but from somewhere outside Trinity heard the rattling of rain sticks, like a late-summer shower suddenly falling into the garden.

'I think we're all aware of the overwhelming power that women possess,' John continued. 'Some of us have found out about it to our cost – both emotional and financial.'

This time, four or five of the men in the crowd grunted in bitter amusement. Joe Bellman was standing close beside the stage, and he blew out cigar smoke and said, 'John – you never spoke a truer word. Fifteen-and-a-half million, that's what the judge gave her! *And* my fucking house!'

'Come with me now, all of you,' John continued. 'Come with me now and see for yourselves how Weywot draws out the power that all women have within them. A little of that power he keeps for himself, so that he can go on living here in a state of suspended animation. Most of it, however, he gives to us, as the reward he pays us for having revived him, and the price he pays us for continuing to take care of him, and guarding him.

'I know that most of you are Christians, and that you

believe that the Lord God will always protect you and give you the strength you need to be successful in life. But as *I* know and many of you have now been fortunate enough to find out, Weywot can share out the disproportionate power that God gave to women much more equally between the sexes. Weywot can do it immediately, and it's one hundred per cent guaranteed, with no need for you to offer up prayers and hope for the best.'

He turned now to the archway that led from the atrium into the entertainment room, and beckoned, and called out, 'Bring her on, Tukuut!'

As he did so, the musicians started to play again – piano and saxophone and violin and drums – a slow, tortured march with unbearably shrill notes and bass notes that made the stage reverberate, accompanied by a leaden drumbeat that sounded like the last heartbeats of a dying horse.

One of the three Tongva elders came through the crowd, and they all stepped back like the Red Sea to let him through. He was dressed in the same traditional robes and beads that he had been wearing yesterday evening, when Weywot had been offered his preparatory feast, but instead of his rain stick he was carrying a tall painted spear with the head of a female coyote impaled on top of it. He was barefoot, and he walked at the same leaden pace as the drumbeat, but with a slight hesitation before he put each foot down, as if he were walking across a firepit.

Behind the elder came SloMo and Bradley and DaShawn, and all three of them now were wearing black bandanas tied around their heads and black three-piece suits like morticians. Between them, Bradley and DaShawn were guiding the Ghost Woman, Tokoor Hikaayey. Her head was covered by a multi-layered brown hood, fold upon fold, so that her green eyes were hidden and she resembled a nun from some mystical medieval painting rather than a Gabrieleño ghost.

Next came four young men, and between them they were carrying a wooden litter, shoulder high. Each of them wore a red lacquered mask with a sharp hawklike beak, like plague doctors, and their bare chests had been painted with blue and red herringbone patterns. Zuzana was lying on the litter, completely naked except for a clamshell necklace and clamshell bracelets around her wrists and her ankles, and she had been smeared all over in golden glitter. Her head lolled from side to side as she was carried through the crowd, and Trinity could see that she was semi-comatose, and probably drugged.

Trinity gave Nemo a quick, worried look, but Nemo shook his head, as if he were telling her to stay calm and wait to see what was going to happen next.

The Tongva elder led the way through the open French doors and into the garden, slowly circling the coyote's severed head around and around in time to the drumbeat. Once Zuzana had been carried outside on her litter, John beckoned to all the assembled guests to follow. They crowded out of the entertainment room, trying not to look as if they were pushing to get to the front of the line, but those guests who had seen one of these ceremonies before were eager to make sure that they secured themselves the best vantage point. There was some jostling as they elbowed their way out through the French doors, and one woman in four-inch Jimmy Choo stilettos stumbled over, although David Magellan helped her up onto her feet.

Trinity and Nemo held back. 'Oh my God,' said Trinity.

'That poor girl. What do you think they're going to do to her?'

'Whatever it is, Trin, I pray that they don't do her an injury.'

The guests made their way past the fountain and through the pergola to the white building with the sun symbol painted on it. Trinity and Nemo went after them. As they passed by the statue of Auzar, Trinity looked up at her, and she had the disturbing sensation that Auzar turned her head very slightly to look back at her. She knew it was probably an optical illusion caused by the fountains refracting the light, but as they walked through the pergola she still couldn't resist looking back to see if Auzar had turned her head round even more to see where she was going.

'What?' said Nemo.

'Nothing. I got a weird feeling that statue's alive, that's all.'

'Ha! That wouldn't surprise me! *Nothing* surprises me in this joint! Some of the parties we raided when I was a cop, they'd have made your hair stand on end. But this little get-together – this takes the biscuit. Look – there's Herman Friedman right in front of us. What the hell is he doing here? He's only just finished a remake of *The Ten Commandments*.'

The doors of the white building were open wide and the guests were being ushered into the vestibule. Then they all filed into the cold gloomy room with the massive stone plinth in the centre. Since they came in last, Trinity and Nemo had to stand at the back of the crowd, pressed against the wall with its murals of rattlesnakes and scorpions and frogs and strange distracted faces.

The room was so frigid that Trinity couldn't stop herself from shivering, and even Nemo had to rub his hands together.

'Why is it so *cold* in here?' she whispered, but Nemo could only shrug.

She stood on tiptoe so that she could look over the shoulders of the men standing in front of her. She saw that there was somebody lying on the plinth, wrapped from head to foot in what looked like a hairy buffalo hide. On the opposite side of the plinth, the Tongva elder had joined the two other Tongva, and they were chanting and making shushing noises with their rain sticks.

'What are those?' said Nemo, and he nodded towards the end of the plinth. There were two posts, one on either side, and hanging from each of these posts was a large bulging sack of mottled brown animal hide, similar to the hide that wrapped up the body on top of the plinth. Both sacks were sewn most of the way up with large criss-cross stitches, but small gaps had been left open at the tops. From the top of one of them, long strands of brunette hair were hanging down, and out of the other a few blonde wisps were curling out.

'I think there are *women* in those sacks!' Trinity hissed into Nemo's ear. 'If I didn't know better, I'd say that one of them could be Rosie! Look at that curly blonde hair!'

'Bizarrer and bizarrer,' said Nemo. 'I'm almost tempted to call Sergeant Weller, except that he'd probably haul *us* in, you and me, instead of this crowd of gawpers.'

The four young men in their red beak masks were standing at the foot of the plinth now, still patiently holding the litter on their shoulders. Trinity saw that Zuzana was stirring, and that she lifted her head for a moment, as if she were waking up from a dream, but then she slowly lowered it again, so that she was staring up at the ceiling.

The three Tongva began to chant, and to beat out an insistent slushy-sounding rhythm with their rain sticks. SloMo approached the plinth and started to drag out the stitches that held the buffalo hide together, and gradually Weywot's elongated head appeared, with his crimson bloodshot eyes and his greenish lips.

'Holy Saint Joseph,' said Nemo, under his breath. 'And look, Trin, he's moving. He's *alive*!'

SloMo continued to open up the buffalo hide, gradually exposing Weywot's narrow ribcage with his pierced nipples, and his stomach that was still bloated from the sacrificial meal he had devoured the night before, including the cat.

The Ghost Woman came forward now, and lifted her hood a little with one hand so that Trinity could see her gleaming green eyes. She leaned close to Weywot and murmured something in his pointed ear, and in return Weywot nodded, and closed his eyes to indicate that he had understood.

'What did he say?' asked John. He had to raise his voice so that the Ghost Woman could hear him over the rain sticks. He was standing a little way behind her, as if he were cautious about coming too close to Weywot.

'He wanted to know if you had fetched the Tokoor. I told him yes.'

'Ask him if he is ready to begin.'

The Ghost Woman spoke to Weywot again, and again Weywot nodded.

John said to SloMo, 'Okay, go for it. But watch yourself. Remember what happened last time.'

'Are you kidding me?' said SloMo. 'You think I'm ever going to forget it?'

He started to yank at the stitches that were holding the

buffalo hide together below Weywot's waist, but each time he pulled one open, he whipped his hand back as if he were afraid that something was going to jump out and bite him.

'See that?' said Nemo, close to Trinity's ear. 'What the hell's he afraid of?'

SloMo drew out the last stitch and dropped the leather lacing onto the floor. He peeled back the sides of the buffalo hide, and it was then that Trinity and Nemo could see why he had been so cautious. It took Trinity a few seconds to understand exactly what she was looking at, but when she did, she gripped Nemo's hand in horror and disbelief.

'*Holy kamoly*,' breathed Nemo. He was clearly just as shocked as she was.

Between Weywot's stringy, emaciated thighs, they had expected to see a penis. Instead, the jointed tail of a huge scorpion was rearing up, and waving slightly from side to side. The scorpion's head and pincers and its eight-legged body were buried deep in Weywot's groin, with his papery white skin stretched over them.

Its tail was at least twenty centimetres from its root to the sharp curved stinger at its tip, and its six sections were a pale amber colour, almost translucent, although its stinger was a dark varnished brown.

Trinity dropped back down onto her heels, so that Weywot with his scorpion tail was hidden by the men standing in front of her. Almost at once, though, she stood up on tiptoe again. However gruesome it might be, she knew that if she was going to have any chance of understanding what had happened to Margo, she would have to witness what was going to happen next.

The three Tongva elders beat their rain sticks louder and

faster and began to screech at the top of their voices, calling out *Weywot! Weywot!* over and over.

Now the four young men in their red beak masks lowered Zuzana to the floor. The guests who were crowded around the plinth started to stamp their feet and clap in time to the rain sticks, and two or three of them let out whoops of excitement. Despite the bitter cold, so that their breath was puffing out in little clouds, their faces were flushed and their eyes were bulging, as if they were feeling sexually rampant.

Weywot said something to the Ghost Woman, and she beckoned to SloMo, who was standing close beside her. SloMo came over and lifted Weywot's head a little, and kept it lifted, so that he would be able to see Zuzana as the four young men bent down and picked her up off the litter. They turned her over so that she was face down, and then carried her forward, until she was suspended horizontally about fifteen centimetres above Weywot, toe to toe and eye to eye.

Zuzana was completely limp, so that the young men had to keep a firm grip on her shoulders and her thighs for her to stay in that position, and they were shaking with the strain of it. Although she appeared to be drugged, her eyes were open and she was staring down at Weywot as if she were trying to remember who he was.

Weywot stared back up at Zuzana for nearly half a minute. Then he nodded and said a few words to the Ghost Woman. His greenish lips were glossy with saliva, and the tip of his tongue darted out to lick them, like a white rat darting out of its nest. The Ghost Woman turned to John and said, 'The grandson of Auzar approves. You may start the harvesting.'

John Dangerfield's surgeon, Jacob, was standing close beside the plinth in his white surgical jacket, snapping on a pair of blue nitrile gloves. He had the same unfocused look as always, as if he were thinking about something else altogether, like where he was going to play golf tomorrow. But when John gave him the thumbs up, he beckoned at once to the four young men, and gestured that they should bend Zuzana's knees and open her thighs wide so that she was kneeling on either side of Weywot's bony hips. The scorpion's tail was standing up rigidly now, with its quivering stinger almost touching the lips of her vulva.

With his left hand, Jacob took hold of the scorpion's tail, pressing his thumb down just below the stinger. The scorpion struggled to break free, and it was obviously strong, but its head and its body were buried too deeply in Weywot's pelvis and Jacob's grip was too firm, and after a while its tail stopped waggling from side to side. Once he had steadied it, Jacob used two fingers of his right hand to part the lips of Zuzana's vulva as wide as he could.

John was close behind him, so close that he was almost breathing down the neck of his white surgical jacket. John's eyebrows were raised high in anticipation and his mouth was half open, as if he were ready to let out a triumphant shout. The rest of the guests were crowding in around them, elbowing each other to get the best view of Zuzana being penetrated.

'You might be interested to know that a scorpion's stinger has a scientific name,' said Jacob calmly, as he guided it into Zuzana's vagina. 'Biologists call it a telson.'

As soon as he had inserted it, and released his grip on it, the young men gently but firmly pulled Zuzana's hips back and down so that the rest of the scorpion's tail disappeared inside her, joint by joint. Zuzana jolted, and shook, and let out a strangely haunted cry, but the young men kept her pinned down in that position while Weywot immediately began to lift his scrawny buttocks up and down, awkwardly but persistently, and in time to the slushing of the rain sticks.

Trinity was shivering in sheer horror, but Nemo had wrapped his arm around her shoulders and was holding her close. She couldn't believe what she was witnessing. It was more frightening than a nightmare because it was real, and she could see and hear and feel everything. She felt trapped by the crowd of guests all around her in their evening finery, whooping and clapping and shuffling their feet. She was almost choked by the smell of Joy and Bulgari perfume in the freezing cold air, as well as skunk and burning jimsonweed leaves. She was almost deafened by the screeching Tongva elders and their endlessly chugging rain sticks. And then there was the sight she knew she would never be able to unsee for the rest of her life: the slippery amber joints of the scorpion's tail sliding in and out of that helpless woman's body.

She prayed that this ritual couldn't get worse, and that it would soon be over. But how would it end? Would the scorpion climax, and ejaculate a squirt of its venom, so that this young woman was stung to death?

But what happened next was even more horrifying. Zuzana's naked body began to shudder, all the way down her back. Her shuddering grew stronger and stronger, and at first Trinity thought she might be reaching some kind of hideous orgasm.

Instead, she saw that Zuzana's muscles were shrinking, so that her skin was stretched tightly over her ribcage and her pelvis, and her spine protruded from her back like a long knobbly centipede. Even above the sound of the rain sticks, Trinity could hear her bones crackling as her chest collapsed. Far from filling her up with its own venom, the scorpion was relentlessly sucking everything out of her: her brain, her lungs, her stomach, her intestines, even crushing and dissolving her skeleton. The very essence of Zuzana was being emptied, leaving nothing but a flaccid bag of skin, sprinkled with glitter. Even her head was flattened, so that it looked as if a tangled blonde wig had fallen onto Weywot's emaciated chest, with a grotesque rubber mask attached to it.

John clapped his hands and shouted, 'Time for the sacrifices! Time for the fire! *Chaavot! Chaavot!*'

Trinity saw that SloMo was manoeuvring his way through the crowd, swinging a green plastic jerrycan. When he reached the two metal posts that stood at the head of the plinth, each with its bulging buffalo-hide sack suspended from it, he waved his arm to indicate that the guests should stand well back. Then he unscrewed the lid of the jerrycan and started to splash the two sacks with sparkling clear liquid, until both of them were soaked.

Nemo sniffed twice and said, 'That's not gasoline. But Dangerfield's called out for a fire, so it won't be water, either. It could be methanol – the same stuff you reckon they used to burn your friend Margo.'

'But there are living women inside those sacks – they can't set light to them!'

'I think we've seen enough, Trin. We need to get out of here and call the fire department fast.'

Nemo took hold of Trinity's hand and they started to edge their way towards the vestibule, keeping well back against the wall. When they reached the doors to the plinth room, though, they found that DaShawn and the four young men in red beak masks were standing in front of them, with their arms folded, and it was obvious that they had been posted there to prevent anyone from leaving.

'Clarissa's not feeling too well,' Nemo shouted, over the clapping and the screeching. 'She needs some fresh air.'

DaShawn shook his head. 'Sorry, man. Nobody leaves till it's over.'

'Have a heart, for Christ's sake. She's going to faint if you don't let us out.'

'I can't. Those are my orders. It's something to do with the ceremony. Like, nobody's allowed to turn their back on Weywot.'

At that moment, Trinity heard a sharp crackling sound. She turned around and saw that both buffalo-hide sacks were on fire. Lurid blue flames were leaping out of them, almost up to the ceiling, and the hairs on the hides were shrivelling up. The guests were chanting, 'Chaavot! Weywot! Chaavot! Weywot!' and punching the air.

As the hides burned, the laces holding them together began to snap apart, one by one, so that they gradually opened up. Their sides curled back, to reveal the women inside them. Although they were both tied to their posts, the women were throwing themselves from side to side and screaming in agony, but Trinity could hardly hear them over the chanting of the guests and the screeching of the Tongva elders.

She couldn't hear them, but she recognised them, and she had to cling on to Nemo's arm to prevent her knees giving way with shock. Sally appeared first, her long hair rising from the top of her head in a spire of flames, and then Rosie, her curls already burnt off and her face bubbled up with blisters.

28

Trinity shouted out, '*Rosie!*' and started to push against the men in their tuxedos standing shoulder to shoulder in front of her.

Nemo seized her arm and said, 'Trin! What's going on? What are you doing?'

Trinity twisted around, pulling her arm free. She was almost hysterical.

'That's Rosie! That blonde girl! That's my little sister! And the other girl, that's her friend!'

'Jesus Christ!' said Nemo, and he threw his whole weight against the backs of the men who were blocking their way.

'*Hey!* Who the fuck do you think you're pushing?' one of the men protested. But then he recognised Nemo's dream disguise and said, '*Toby!* What the hell? Are you busting for the bathroom or something?'

Nemo said nothing but shoved the man hard in the chest with the flat of his hand, and when the man staggered back, Nemo dragged Trinity past him. He forced more and more guests to one side, and three or four of them shouted at him angrily, but most of them were too enthralled by the sight of the two fiery girls hanging in front of them, and the spectacle of Zuzana's empty carcass lying draped on top of Weywot.

Apart from that, almost all of them were high on coke or weed or datura, or so drunk on margaritas that they barely knew where they were.

At last Trinity reached the metal pole on which Rosie was suspended, but by then the last of the blue flames were flickering out and she could see that she was too late. The buffalo-hide sack had been charred black and dropped apart like the wings of some giant dragonfly. Although she was still fastened to the post with wire, Rosie's naked body had sagged down between them, her skin crinkled and charred. Nothing was left of her blonde curls but stubble, her eyes were hollow, and her lips were stretched back across her teeth in a silent howl.

Trinity looked across at Sally, and saw that she was dead too, hanging from her post with her head forward. Smoke was drifting across the crowd of guests from both of the sacrificed girls, and some of them were ostentatiously breathing it in, as if it were incense.

Trinity sagged to her knees in front of Rosie and held on to the post. She was too shocked and distressed to cry, but in her mind's eye she could see a flicker-book of images – Rosie pushing her doll's pram stuffed with teddy bears – Rosie running into the sea in her sunhat when she was only three or four – Rosie standing by the window when their mother died, her cheeks shining with tears.

She started to shudder, as if she were slowly sinking into an ice-cold lake, inch by inch, and would eventually drown. She tried to whisper 'Rosie', but her lips felt as if they were frozen.

'Trin,' said Nemo. He laid his hands on her shoulders and said, 'Come on, Trin. There's nothing more we can do here, not you and me. If I'd had any idea, I would have gotten in touch with the cops before we even thought of coming here, no matter what I thought they might say to me. But we need to get in touch with them now.'

He helped Trinity onto her feet. When they turned to leave, though, they found that the guests had gathered around them in a silent semi-circle, no longer whooping or shuffling their feet, but staring at them suspiciously. The Tongva elders had stopped singing, too, and laid down their rain sticks. The doors to the vestibule had been opened and the smoke was slowly shuddering outside.

The four young men in their hawk masks had lifted Zuzana's empty skin back onto their litter, while SloMo was starting to stitch up Weywot's buffalo hide. He had already tucked the scorpion's tail between Weywot's thighs, but Weywot's belly was grossly swollen and he was straining to pull the sides of the hide together to cover it.

Nemo took Trinity's arm and led her towards the line of guests, but then John stepped forward and held up his hand like a cop holding up traffic.

'Here now. Wait up, you two.'

'What for?' asked Nemo. 'Come on, we need to get out of here. Clarissa's not feeling too good. She has asthma, and there's all this smoke.'

John smiled. 'I might believe you if she really *was* Clarissa Keyes. Somehow she managed to look just like Clarry, and convince me that she was. I can't imagine how in the world she did it, but she did, except that now she doesn't look like her at all.'

'I still need to get her out of here,' Nemo insisted.

'If you were really Toby Carter, then maybe I'd say okay. But you're no more Toby Carter than she's Clarissa Keyes.

Maybe you dropped something in our margaritas, who knows? Maybe there's something like Rohypnol that makes you see people different.'

'Look – why don't you just let us leave?' asked Nemo.

'If I didn't know who you really are, then I still might have said okay. But you've been recognised, my friend. You've been ID'd!'

John turned around and laid his hand on the shoulder of a short, big-bellied man in dark glasses. The man stepped forward and took off his glasses, and even though his eyes had a strange silvery look about them, Nemo knew at once who he was. He was one of the senior police officers he had reported for taking bribes in exchange for dropping prosecutions – one of the senior police officers who had made sure that he was sacked from the force and stayed silent for the rest of his life, under the implicit threat of not-so-accidental death.

'You remember Deputy Chief Brogan, I'm sure,' said John.

Nemo said nothing, because he couldn't yet be certain if he had stopped looking like Toby Carter. But he glanced across at Trinity, and there was no question that she no longer looked like Clarissa Keyes. For some reason their dreams had faded, and everybody in the room had woken up to who they actually were.

He wondered if the powerful aura of Weywot's mystical ritual had overwhelmed Teodoro's spells. Or maybe Trinity's dream guide had been too distressed by Rosie's death to continue her illusion. After all, Rosie had been her daughter too.

Maybe Nemo's own dream guide had come out in sympathy, or to make sure that he protected Trinity in his real identity as a one-time police officer, and not as a minor movie actor.

Whatever had happened, Deputy Chief Brogan came up close to him and said, 'Nemo Frisby. The snitch of the century. I mean, who'd have thunk it? This is the very last place on earth I thought I might come across *you* again. And so who's this young lady? And what's *she* been screaming and shouting about?'

'Her sister has been burned to death right in front of her,' Nemo retorted, his voice shaking with rage. He pointed up at Rosie's smoking body and shouted, 'That's her sister! That's her sister, you fucking savages!'

'Now then,' said John. 'Sometimes less valuable lives have to be given up for the benefit of other, more important people. That's happened throughout history. It's the story of humankind.'

He pointed to the plinth. Weywot was completely sewn up now, except for his face.

'Do you have any idea who that is? That's Weywot, one of the greatest chiefs who ever ruled over the Tongva Indians. This land is his land, but in return for us taking care of him, he has generously granted us the power that he can take from women. But he always needs some kind of sacrifice. Some kind of acknowledgement that his life is more important here than any other.'

'Are you out of your mind?' Nemo shouted at him, so hoarse now that he could scarcely be heard. 'All of you! Look at you! Have you gone crazy or something? Whatever that thing is lying there, it's just killed a woman and you've just burned two innocent young girls to death! You're nothing but a bunch of psychos!'

'SloMo,' said John, and nodded towards Nemo.

As soon as SloMo came around the end of the plinth, Nemo reached inside his jacket for his automatic, but he had tugged it only halfway out when his arms were seized from behind by Bradley and DaShawn. They twisted his hands so viciously behind his back that he dropped the gun with a clatter onto the floor.

'Trin!' gasped Nemo. 'The words! Say the words that Teodoro taught you!'

But SloMo had grasped Trinity's arms, too, and pinned them behind her back.

'I can't,' she sobbed. Then, 'Ow, that hurts! *Ow*, that really hurts!'

'Say the words, for Christ's sake!'

'I can't! I have to make the sign with my fingers! *Ow!* If I don't, *everybody* will die, including you!'

Both Nemo and Trinity were forced down onto their knees. The crowd of guests clustered around to stare at them, as if they had been exposed as freaks, but then John spread his arms wide and began to usher them all out.

'Time for some more margaritas, my friends. And a barbecue to die for. Well, not literally! Not like this one!'

Soon, the last of the guests had shambled back through the pergola to the entertainment room, and the music had started up again, although this time it was relaxing middle-of-the-road jazz. 'I Can't Get Started', on the piano.

Trinity and Nemo were left in the freezing cold room with John and SloMo and Bradley and DaShawn and the Ghost Woman. The four young men carried Zuzana's flattened body outside and swung it onto a gurney, her arms and her legs flopping, before wheeling her away. One of them returned only two or three minutes later with two black nylon zip ties, which Bradley and SloMo fastened around Trinity and Nemo's wrists.

'You are *not* going to get away with this,' said Nemo, with a grimace.

'Well, we'll have to see, won't we?' John smiled. 'Deputy Chief Brogan isn't the only friend we have in high places. Meanwhile, let's get you inside and settled down and then we can decide what we're going to do with you.'

Trinity and Nemo were hoisted up onto their feet and led through the garden. As they walked past the fountain, Trinity looked up at the statue of Auzar, but this time she didn't see her head move. Perhaps it did, but Trinity's eyes were too blurry with tears. Perhaps Auzar didn't recognise her, now that she looked like herself, and not like Clarissa Keyes.

The Ghost Woman was walking beside Trinity, with her head completely covered by her hood. As they came close to the house, she came so close that her shawl was brushing against Trinity's shoulder.

'The full moon sets in one hour,' she said, in a muffled voice.

Trinity turned to stare at her.

'In one hour she sets. Then tomorrow, she starts to wane. Only one thin slice will have vanished, but the debt will be settled.'

'What? What debt?'

But the Ghost Woman walked away without saying anything more. Trinity was pulled by SloMo towards a side door, which John was holding open for her. Stepping inside the brightly lit corridor, she couldn't help noticing that John was looking not at her, but at the Ghost Woman, as she disappeared into the darkness. She thought the expression on John's face was one of mistrust, and dislike. Maybe she was mistaken, but she thought she could also see apprehension, as if he were afraid of what the Ghost Woman might do next.

They were taken upstairs and along the corridor. Nemo was pushed into one room and Trinity was led along to the next room, which was where Zuzana had been kept. Before SloMo pulled her through the door, she glanced out of the window that overlooked the garden. She could see the statue of Auzar, gleaming white, and she could also see that the moon had sunk behind the trees that bordered the north-west side of John Dangerfield's property.

'Come along, for God's sake,' said SloMo. 'I don't have all night.'

'You murderers,' Trinity spat at him, although she was so distressed that she could barely speak. 'I hope you never sleep again, ever.'

'Just shut up and get inside, will you? I don't make the rules around here.'

'You're still a murderer. That was my sister you burned. My younger sister. But you'll burn too, when your time comes. You'll burn in Hell, for all eternity.'

SloMo didn't answer, but pushed her roughly onto the bed. He left, closing and locking the door behind him.

Trinity lay in the darkness, on her side, her wrists still painfully ziplocked behind her back. She let out a long wavering howl of grief and then she fell silent, although her lips were still juddering and tears were still dripping onto the mattress. She had felt that nothing could hurt as much as losing her mother, but seeing Rosie consumed by flames in front of her eyes had made her feel as if her brain were burning too.

An hour went past. She could faintly hear the long-case clock chiming in the atrium. She could also hear the jazz music from down in the entertainment room, and people laughing. They had watched Rosie and Sally being cremated and that other girl being raped and reduced to nothing but an empty bag of skin, and they were laughing.

It was air-conditioned in this room, and cold, and she was starting to shiver. The mattress was damp and cold, too, and reeked of urine. She shouted out, '*Nemo! Nemo, can you hear me?*' but there was no reply. She tried kicking against the wall, but she had lost her shoes when SloMo had first made her kneel down, and she could manage only a few dull thumps.

The room had already been dark when she was first locked up in it, because the blind was drawn down, but now the moon set and it became even darker. Another hour went past. Her bladder was so full that it was hurting and she could understand now why the mattress smelled the way it did. She found herself thinking of Jinko, a friend of her father's who had served out in Afghanistan. He had said that bursting to go to the toilet but having nowhere to relieve themselves had been far more traumatic than shooting people.

Her shoulders were aching and the zip ties had been fastened so tightly around her wrists that both of her hands had become completely numb, as if they had been amputated.

'*Nemo!*' she cried out again, even though she was sure he wouldn't be able to hear her, and even if he did, there would be nothing that he could do to save her. His hands had been bound behind his back, just like hers, and he was probably lying on a stinking mattress, too, in total darkness, with the door locked.

'Nemo,' she whispered, because she knew it was no use calling for him, and she couldn't even imagine what these people were going to do to them. Was she going to be given to that Weywot to be raped, or wrapped up in a buffalo hide and set on fire?

'He cannot answer,' said a breathy voice. 'They have struck him on the head and for now he is lost to the world.'

Startled, Trinity twisted herself around. She had not heard the door being unlocked, nor opened, nor anybody coming in, and the room was so dark that the door must still be closed. But then she heard the faint swish of fabric, and two luminous green eyes appeared, hovering beside her bed.

'Hush,' said the voice. 'Do not be afraid. I am Tokoor Hikaayey, the one these vagabonds call Ghost Woman. The moon has gone and my debt is paid and I am free to leave. But before you came I had nowhere to go if I left. If I can come with you, wherever you live, then I will help you to escape.'

'How did you get in here?'

'My name means spirit, which means that I can pass through any door or any wall. Of course, you cannot. You are still flesh. But if you say you will take me away with you, I will open this *ahuunon*, this door, and we can leave together.'

Trinity tried to raise her head from the mattress, but her neck hurt and she had to drop it back down.

'I'm dreaming this.'

'No, this is no dream. Before vagabonds came, this land was always shared between living and dead. Spirits could come back to meet their sons and their daughters and to tell them that they were happy after death. Please – if you promise me that you will find somewhere for me to shelter, I will open this door and release you.'

Trinity closed her eyes for a moment. All right, maybe this was a dream. But if she agreed to help the Ghost Woman in a dream, where was the harm? And if it *wasn't* a dream, if it was actually really real, she would be able to escape. She could take the Ghost Woman to Pine Mountain, and she was sure that Teodoro would know how to take care of her.

'What about my friend?' she said. 'What about Nemo, can you free him too?'

'He is not yet awake. They hit him very hard. Maybe he will never awaken.'

'Oh, God. All right, then. I think I know where I can take you. You don't have anything against the Chumash, do you?'

'After death, everybody is a friend. There is nothing for us to fight over. Not land, not gold, not gods. Only the living are possessive about such things.'

The Ghost Woman leaned over, put her arms around Trinity and helped her to sit up.

'You *feel* real,' said Trinity. 'You feel just as solid as me. How did you walk through that door?'

'I am as real as I wish to be,' said the Ghost Woman. 'After you die, nothing is impossible.'

Trinity heard her robe softly swishing on the floor as she returned to the door. Then there was a complicated series of clicks and the door opened, so that she could see the corridor outside. The Ghost Woman came back and eased her onto her feet.

'That's amazing,' said Trinity. 'How did you unlock that door?'

The Ghost Woman held up a key. 'In life, I was a

wonder-worker, but this was not magic. I stole it from the one they call SloMo.'

She ushered Trinity into the corridor. It was still dark outside, although the sky to the east was beginning to grow lighter.

'All visitors have left now,' she said. 'Almost everybody else is asleep. If we meet anybody, say nothing, but walk like you have every right to go where you go.

'Here,' she added. She stopped and turned Trinity around, and hooked her fingers under the zip tie that was binding Trinity's wrists. She gave a sharp tug and the zip tie snapped. 'Now, *mire 'eyoomar*! We are leaving!'

The Ghost Woman led the way swiftly along the corridor and down the stairs. The house was eerily silent, except for the clattering of plates and saucepans in the kitchen, where the catering staff were clearing up after last night's barbecue.

They crossed the atrium and the Ghost Woman opened up one of the double front doors. Immediately, somewhere in the house, an alarm began to beep.

'Quick,' said the Ghost Woman. 'We will have a little time. They will be looking for a thief breaking in, not for anybody breaking out.'

She closed the door behind them and then they ran down the steps to the parking lot. Trinity panted, 'That Acadia, behind the hedge!', although it occurred to her that the ghost of a Tongva Indian woman might have no idea what an 'Acadia' was.

She opened the passenger door so that the Ghost Woman could climb into her seat. Once she had slammed the door she ran around and sat down herself behind the wheel, ducking down to pick up the keys that Nemo had left under the seat.

Thank God, she thought – *Nemo, you must be some kind of clairvoyant*. She started up the engine and swung the Acadia out from behind the holly olive bush. She snagged some of the bush on the front fender and ripped it up.

They sped out of the parking lot and turned south on Chantilly Road. As they passed the front of La Muralla, Trinity could see that lights were coming on in the upstairs windows.

The Ghost Woman said nothing until they reached the freeway and started heading north. The sky was a pale rose colour now, with planes twinkling in it as they headed in to land at LAX.

'Where do you take me?' she asked.

'To the future, I hope,' said Trinity. 'Both of us. I can't bear the past any longer.'

'I am so sorry about your sister. There was nothing I could do to stop it. I was bound by my promise to John Dangerfield, and John Dangerfield has the power of Weywot.'

'What was the promise?'

'I was Weywot's wonder-worker, his shaman, and when he was buried, I was buried with him. John Dangerfield found out from histories of the Tongva people who I was, and how I could be made to serve him. He freed me from my grave, if I would serve him without question for seven times seven full moons. If I did not, I would be returned to my grave for ever. But now the last full moon has set, and I am free.'

'You speak English. I mean, you speak it real well.'

'I spoke Tongva when I was alive. But John Dangerfield made sure that I was taught to speak English so that he understand me. More important, he want me to understand *him*, and all that he demand that I do for him.'

'And what did he demand?'

The Ghost Woman turned towards Trinity and for the first time Trinity could see her wrinkled face, as well as her luminous green eyes.

'I will tell you when I am sure that I am safe, and that he does not know where I have gone to. As I said to you, John Dangerfield has the power that Weywot has given him, and Weywot forgives nobody.'

They drove in silence for a while, and then Trinity said, 'What will they do to my friend Nemo? Like, what were they going to do to the both of us? They couldn't let us go, could they?'

'I am afraid to say that he will be offered to Weywot as a sacrifice, like your sister. It will happen tomorrow in the early morning, before the sun rises. It is to honour Weywot when he gives a share of what he has taken from that young woman to the man who has been chosen by John Dangerfield to receive it.'

'It looked like he took everything out of her. Her bones, her blood, her entire insides. I mean, my God.'

'He took her greatest possession. He took what women are born with, and men have always hungered for, even more than women's bodies, even though they never admit it. He took her strength. He took her soul.'

29

Nemo was woken by angry shouting in the corridor outside his room.

'She's gone! How the hell did she get out of there? Didn't any of you see her? And where's that goddam Ghost Woman? Jesus Christ! Can't I trust any of you morons to do *anything* right?'

Nemo struggled to sit up. The zip ties were still cutting into his wrists behind his back and his head felt as if it had been split in half. He remembered now. When John Dangerfield's thugs were dragging him towards the bed, he had struggled free from them and charged, head down, towards the door. Either he had struck the door frame or one of the thugs had coshed him on the head.

Now it sounded as if Trinity might have been able to get away. He prayed that she had, because that would dramatically increase his chances of survival. The IAG may be after him, but he doubted if they would risk the media scandal and the official investigation that could follow if he was murdered here in John Dangerfield's house, and John Dangerfield couldn't risk the police searching La Muralla to try and find him.

He stood up. He still had double vision and he staggered a

little. He knew a technique for escaping from zip-tie handcuffs, but it involved removing his shoelaces. Maybe twenty years ago he might have been flexible enough to reach down behind him, but there was no possibility that he could do it now.

He heard more shouting, and then his door was unlocked and flung open, and John Dangerfield stalked in, wearing nothing but a quilted dressing gown in turquoise satin, and slippers. His hair was sticking up as if he had just got out of bed.

'Where is she?' he demanded, so furious that he was spitting. 'Where would she go?'

'Where would who go?' asked Nemo, shaking his head.

John pushed him in the chest so that he sat down abruptly on the bed. 'You know damn well who. Your partner. Your friend. She's managed to leave us. God knows how, but she has.'

'Well, full marks to her. Pity I was out cold, I would have gone with her.'

'If she lived with her sister then we know where she lives. But if she isn't there, and I doubt that she will be unless she has shit for brains, then where would she go?'

'How the hell should I know?'

'Because you came here together and in some crazy way you both managed to look like other people when you first arrived.'

'I didn't know that we looked like other people. You must have been smoking something.'

'You looked like Toby Carter and Clarissa Keyes. So far as I was concerned, you *were* Toby Carter and Clarissa Keyes. I have no idea how you did it, but do you think I would have let you in to Weywot's ceremony if you hadn't?'

'I still think you must have been smoking something. That jimsonweed, that can play some real weird tricks with your perception. A pal of mine smoked some once and thought he was Marilyn Monroe, returned from the dead.'

SloMo had come into the room. John turned around and jerked his head towards Nemo. SloMo went up to Nemo with three short strides and punched him hard on the cheek. Nemo fell back onto the bed and lay there, feeling as if his head had been knocked clear off his body.

John approached the bed again and leaned over him. 'We can do a whole lot worse to you than that,' he said very softly, almost as if it were an invitation to come out for a walk.

'I have two words for you, Mr Dangerfield,' said Nemo. 'They're only short words, both of them, but between them they have three effs.'

SloMo came up behind John with his fist clenched, but John said, 'No. Leave him. He's obviously not in the mood to be helpful just yet. But let me tell you this, Mr Frisby, we have another ceremony planned for tonight, when Weywot will be giving us some of the power that he took from that beautiful young lady last night. We will need two more sacrifices when that happens, to show Weywot how much we appreciate his generosity. We have one sacrifice already, but if you continue to be so uncooperative, you will be the other.'

'And you don't think the cops are going to come looking for me?'

'I very much doubt it. From what Deputy Chief Brogan told me about you, almost every officer in the Los Angeles Police Department would be more than delighted to hear that some civic-minded citizen had disposed of you, for good and all.'

Nemo said nothing. His head was still throbbing and now his right eye was closing where SloMo had hit him on the cheek. He was quite sure that many of his former colleagues would be secretly pleased to hear that he had come to a gruesome end – especially some of his senior officers. His whistle-blowing about their bribery had meant that they had been abruptly deprived of a reliable and tax-free source of income. But there were still some who liked him and supported him, even if they believed that he should have kept his mouth shut, and maybe they would come to rescue him. 'Turn a blind eye, Nemo,' Sergeant Weller had advised him. 'You're not a goddam priest.'

Rod was woken up by an unbearable pain between his legs. His tongue felt fat and furry, as if a hamster were sleeping in his mouth. He was lying on his side on a canvas camp bed in a small room that looked like a store cupboard. Shelves on both sides were crowded with files and manila folders and cardboard boxes. Up above the shelves there was a small window, so he could see that it was still bright daylight outside.

He tried to sit up but the pain lanced right up his spine as if he had been stabbed in the groin with a bayonet. He shouted '*aahhhh!*' and dropped back down onto the creaky bed, spraining his shoulder. He lay there panting and licking his lips, trying to stimulate some spit. He remembered now what had been done to him, and what he had been forced to do. The thought of it was so sickening and so overwhelming that he closed his eyes tightly and prayed that this was nothing but a nightmare and that he wasn't here at all, but back in his bed in the apartment that he shared with Zuzana.

The pain, however, wouldn't allow it. He had to open his eyes and face up to the reality that he had not only been gelded, but had eaten his own testicles.

His shirt and his jeans had been taken away and he was dressed in nothing but his T-shirt and his blue-striped boxer shorts. His shorts were spotted with dried blood and they were stuffed inside with a thick pad of white surgical gauze, like a geriatric diaper, and that was stained with dried blood too.

'Zoozy,' he whispered. 'I swear to God I didn't mean it. I swear to God. Please – if you're anyplace here in this house, get me out of this, will you? I'll make it up to you, I swear.'

He lay there for more than another hour, whispering and softly sobbing. Then he heard voices outside the store cupboard door, and a key turning in the lock.

John Dangerfield came in, smelling strongly of Chanel Bleu aftershave and wearing one of his white pirate shirts. He bent sideways so that he could look Rod in the face, but for a long time he didn't speak. His expression was one of curiosity, as if he were staring at a creature in a zoo and couldn't work out what it was.

Eventually he said, 'Sorry for the state of this accommodation, my dear boy. All of the luxury bedrooms were taken. But you won't have to put up with this any longer. We'll be taking you downstairs now to make you ready for tonight's celebration.'

'Zuzana's here, isn't she?' said Rod, his voice rasping for lack of saliva. 'You were lying to me, weren't you, you bastard? You and that cop.'

'I admit it, yes,' John replied. 'But I can assure you that

there was a valid reason for it. The same reason that we're keeping *you* here. We needed her, you see. And as it happens we needed someone like you, too, and by good fortune you turned up, uninvited.'

'What are you talking about, what reason?'

'It's the never-ending story of human society, *muchacho*. The high and the low. Great and powerful men could never be great and powerful without the adoration of the humble masses. And their sacrifice, too. No war was ever won without millions of ordinary people willingly throwing away their lives. The great bus of human progress can never roll forward without people like you and your Zuzana being tossed under its wheels, so that it has traction.'

'If you've hurt her—!'

John smiled. 'She's feeling no pain, your Zuzana, I can vouch for that. But I expect that you are. You can have another shot of morphine when we get you downstairs.'

'You can shove your morphine up your ass. I just want to get out of here, that's all. And I'm going to take Zuzana with me. And then I'm going to call the cops and have you busted, you and all of your skanky friends.'

'I don't think so, my emasculated friend. Bradley – SloMo – do you want to tote our guest here down to the surgery? It's time we made him ready.'

Bradley and SloMo had been waiting in the corridor outside the store cupboard, and now they came in.

'Don't even think about it!' Rod screeched at them, in his rasping whisper, as Bradley bent down to take hold of one end of the camp bed and SloMo took hold of the other.

'Dude, we're *not* thinking, I promise you,' said SloMo. 'We're doing what we're told, that's all.'

Rod tried to roll himself off the bed and onto the floor, but the pain stabbed him in the groin again, and he could only roll back and lie there, biting his lower lip so hard that it bled, his eyes blinded with tears. *Oh Christ, oh holy Christ, this hurts so much. I never knew that pain like this could even exist.*

SloMo and Bradley manoeuvred the bed out of the store cupboard and along the corridor. As they made their way down the stairs, Bradley raised his arms and held his end of the bed up high so that Rod wouldn't slide off. They carried him across the atrium and back to the pale-green room where he had been castrated. When they set him down on the floor, Rod could see that a hairy brown animal hide was spread wide open on top of one of the two beds.

He could also see that Jacob was waiting on the other side of the bed, abstractedly looking at his fingernails, as if he were wondering if he needed a manicure.

John followed them into the room. He stood watching as SloMo and Bradley hoisted up the camp bed next to the bed with the animal hide and tilted it sideways so that Rod tumbled off it. He cried out like a child as he fell onto the hide and lay there on his back. The hide was parched and rough, and it had a strong musty smell.

John lit a Turkish cigarette and blew smoke out of the side of his mouth. 'Once we've made you ready, you'll be fed,' he said. 'Do you like toyon berries? When it comes to the ceremony that we're going to be holding tonight, we always feed our sacrifices with plenty of toyon berries.'

Rod was unable to answer. He could only whimper. Jacob had dragged his shorts down to his ankles, and was peeling off the bloodstained surgical gauze that had dried over his empty scrotum.

'We do it for the same reason that you stuff a turkey at Thanksgiving,' John went on, in the same conversational tone. 'When the meat starts to burn, the toyon berries lend it a very bitter aroma. The Tongva have always believed that this bitter smoke pleases their spirits. In the same way that incense tickles God's nostrils, I should imagine.'

Jacob had now cut apart the front of Rod's T-shirt with a pair of surgical scissors and dropped the pieces onto the floor, so that Rod was completely naked. Bradley then helped Jacob to fold over the sides of the animal hide so that he could start to sew them together, starting at the feet and slowly stitching his way up. It took about fifteen minutes before Rod was completely enclosed in the hide, except for his face. He hadn't struggled, or protested. He was in too much pain, and his mind was a jumble of electric flashes and thunderous noises and black geometric shapes, like falling grand pianos.

When Jacob had finished his stitching, John leaned over Rod and stared down at him in satisfaction, with smoke leaking out of his nostrils.

'Now you can rest for a while. We'll feed you in an hour or so, and then we'll take you to meet your destiny, the great Weywot. You should be thankful. It's not often that we get the chance to meet our destiny, face to face.'

'Where's Zuzana?' Rod croaked back at him.

'Oh, you'll get to see her, too. After all, it's her life that you'll be celebrating.'

'Where is she? You haven't hurt her, have you?'

'Rest. Sleep, if you can. You'll find out everything soon enough.'

John and Jacob walked out of the room together. Rod heard SloMo and Bradley talking, but he couldn't make out what they were saying, although he thought he heard the words 'wired up'. Then they walked out, too, and he was left lying on the bed on his own, sewn up tightly in his dry animal hide.

How had his life come to this? Was this his punishment for being arrogant, and careless, and not fitting windows properly, and abusing Zuzana? Wasn't there any way in which he could show that he was sorry, and that he wouldn't make the same mistakes again?

But all he could do was lie in that pale-green room, hurting and helpless, and wait for whatever the destiny was that John had promised him.

30

Trinity turned into the driveway in front of the house in Pine Mountain, and stopped.

'This is where you have been hiding?' asked the Ghost Woman. 'This was once Chumash land.'

'Yes, and like I said, Rafael and his grandfather Teodoro, they're Chumash. That's not going to be a problem, is it? I mean, Tongva and Chumash, they get along together okay?'

'Do not worry. Before the Spanish came, we lived a peaceful life, both tribes. There was no fighting between us. It is because of Chumash that my spirit is still here on earth.'

'How's that?'

'When the Spanish came I caught their breathing disease, and I was dying. My father and my brothers took me to a Chumash wonder-worker, the Eagle they called him, to save my life. The Eagle was the greatest of all wonder-workers, greater than any Tongva shaman.'

'He couldn't save you, though?'

'Not my earthly body, no, but he made a bargain for me, with Chumash magic. He made a spell so that when I died my spirit rose up, and so long as I served Weywot I could go on walking the earth for ever.'

'But now you've left Weywot.'

The Ghost Woman nodded. 'Yes. Because I have seen again and again how Weywot makes men cruel and greedy and hurt other people for nothing but their own pleasure. And I have seen too many young women tortured and killed in terrible ways. You can say that I have seen the light at last. I have served Weywot for far too long, and now it is time for me to make amends for what I have done and find peace with my ancestors.'

Trinity sat silent for more than a minute, looking up at the house. She could see the lights in the living room, and Rafael walking past the window. He came back, and peered out. It was obvious that he had caught sight of the Acadia parked in the driveway. He hesitated for a moment, and then he disappeared.

'Oh, God,' she said. She could see the front door open and Rafael walking towards them. She was suddenly overwhelmed with panic. She would have to tell Rafael and Teodoro about Rosie, and in her mind's eye she saw a sudden explosive image of Rosie in flames, screaming. It made her feel as if she were falling to pieces, not only mentally but physically – as if her arms were going to drop off and her head was going to roll off onto the floor and hit the pedals.

She let out a cry of absolute grief and doubled up so that her forehead hit the steering wheel. The Ghost Woman draped her arm around her to comfort her, although her arm felt no more substantial than if she had settled her shawl over her shoulders.

Rafael knocked at her window.

'Trin? What's up? Where's Nemo? Who's that you've got with you?'

Trinity sat up straight and put down the window. 'It all

went wrong, Rafael,' she told him, and in spite of herself she started to cry. 'It all went so wrong.'

Rafael opened her door and held out his hand to help her out. 'Come on, babe. Come inside and tell us what happened.'

He frowned at the Ghost Woman, whose eyes were hidden by her hood. 'I guess your friend had better come inside, too.'

Teodoro was sitting in the living room, watching the Los Angeles Angels playing the St Louis Cardinals on television and eating pecan nuts. As soon as Rafael and Trinity entered the room, with the Ghost Woman trailing behind them, he switched off the television and stood up, still juggling a handful of nuts.

'Trinity? What has happened? Is something wrong? Where is Nemo? And who is this?'

Trinity sat down. The Ghost Woman stood behind the couch and folded back her hood, so that they could all see her wiry grey hair and her crinkled face with its phosphorescent green eyes.

'Holy shit,' said Rafael. He stepped back and nearly tripped over the coffee table.

Teodoro raised his left hand in a cautious salute. Trinity could see that he was wary, but not afraid.

'You are a walking spirit,' he said. 'From your many necklaces, I would say you are Tongva.'

'Yes,' said the Ghost Woman, in a voice that was scarcely any louder than the rustling of the trees that they could hear through the open balcony door. 'They call me Tokoor Hikaayey, Ghost Woman, servant of Weywot. In life I was always called Toovit because I was shy like a rabbit.'

'They've killed – they've killed my sister, Rosie, and her best friend,' Trinity blurted out, exploding with tears. 'Tokoor Hikaayey helped me to escape. Otherwise they were going to kill me too, I'm sure of it. They've still got Nemo locked up, and she says they're planning to kill him, like some kind of human sacrifice. She thinks they're going to do it tonight.'

'Peace, Trinity, peace,' said Teodoro. 'Sit down, Tokoor Hikaayey, and rest yourself. I know that you spirits need rest, like all of us do, even if you have no substance. Trinity – tell me everything. Tell me from the beginning. We must see if we can rescue Nemo before any harm comes to him.'

He looked over to Rafael and said, 'Please, Rafael, make us some dream sage tea, will you? I think it will be good for all of us.'

Rafael glanced at the Ghost Woman once more and went off to the kitchen as if he were glad to go. Trinity then explained to Teodoro how she and Nemo had disguised themselves to gain entry to La Muralla, and how they had mingled with all the guests. She described the ceremony in which Weywot had raped Zuzana with his scorpion tail, and how he emptied out her bones, her blood, her brains, and her very soul.

Teodoro slowly shook his head. 'I have heard stories about men being given great desert scorpions instead of penises, so that they can draw out the strength from the women they lie with, but I had always thought that they were nothing more than myths.'

Trinity wasn't able to stop herself from sobbing again as she described how Rosie and Sally had been burned alive in their buffalo hides. The Ghost Woman held her close, staring at Teodoro all the time with her luminous green eyes. Her face was little more than a reflection, as dark as a face seen in a bedroom mirror at night, but Teodoro could see by her expression and by the way she was holding Trinity that she was pleading with him to help.

'I guess that you could call the police,' he said. 'From what you have told me, though, the police may not show up until it is far too late to save Nemo's life. More likely they will not show up at all. Even if they *do* decide to go to the house, this John Dangerfield could turn them away if they had no search warrant, or he could make sure that Nemo was hidden from them. They might force their way in, but Weywot has survived for hundreds of years and he is said to have powers that shamans can only dream of. Even if he chose not to kill the police or injure them, he could wipe their minds of any memory of him, or drive them mad.'

'So what can I do?' asked Trinity. 'There's no way I can rescue him on my own.'

'Can *you* go back with her to help her, Tokoor Hikaayey?' asked Teodoro, turning to the Ghost Woman.

The Ghost Woman's hood flapped from side to side to tell him no. 'My time to walk the earth is almost done. I have paid my debt in full to John Dangerfield and I have turned my back on Weywot. As soon as the moon climbs down below the world tonight, I shall be joining those who went before me.'

'You're sure?'

'Even if I could stay on this earth another day, Weywot will not forgive me for leaving him. If I go back, he will tear my spirit into a thousand shreds in his anger, and scatter them into the wind like dead leaves. My spirit must be whole when I go to meet my fathers and my mothers. If Weywot tears me apart, I will be left in pieces and in pain until the very end of time.'

'Very well,' said Teodoro. 'But Rafael can go with you, Trinity. You can use dream disguises to gain entry to the house, like before, except that you will have to be different people this time, not Toby Carter and Clarissa Keyes. We must look up some more movie actors who are out of town on location somewhere.'

'But even if they let us into the house, what can we do then?' Trinity asked him. 'John Dangerfield has that whole bunch of heavies that I was telling you about – that one called SloMo and at least a dozen more. How can Rafael and me rescue Nemo when he's guarded by people like that? We wouldn't stand a chance.'

'You haven't forgotten the three words I taught you? I taught them to Rafael, too.'

'I don't want to kill anybody.'

'Of course you don't. But by the same token you don't want Nemo to die, do you? Sometimes you need to take a life to save a life. But after what you have told me, I will give you one more spell.'

He reached across to his worn-out leather pouch, untied it, and rummaged inside.

'You must handle these with great care. But I will show you what they can do.'

He produced two silver discs, tied together with a cord. He handed them to Trinity so that she could examine them closely. On one disc, the face of the sun was engraved. On the other, the face of the moon. The reverse sides were patterned with zigzags.

Trinity handed them back. 'What do they do?'

'Rafael knows, because I have shown him before. Come outside, onto the balcony.'

He stood up and Trinity followed him outside. The sky was dusky pink now, and it was beginning to grow cooler. The Ghost Woman stayed inside. Perhaps she already knew what the silver discs could do, or perhaps she knew how little time she had left before she had to fade away from this earth and join the ghosts of her ancestors.

Teodoro pointed to a small manzanita bush on the far corner of the garden. He held up the two silver discs and pointed them in its direction, rubbing the zigzag faces against each other, around and around.

He said, '*Qsi, Qsi, Qsi*,' and then, ''*Awa'y, 'Awa'y, 'Awa'y*.'

Instantly, the bush crackled into flame, and started to burn fiercely. Its leaves curled up and its branches snapped, and after only a few minutes it was nothing more than a blackened, smoking heap of ashes and skeletal twigs. A strong smell of charcoal drifted across the garden.

Teodoro handed Trinity the silver discs. 'Take these with you. Qsi is the Sun and 'Awa'y is the Moon. We call these medallions the Faces of Fire. I doubt if you will forget their two names, but in any case Rafael knows them, and can call them if you need them to set light to anything. Or anybody.'

They went back into the living room. Teodoro said, 'Tokoor Hikaayey – how long do we have before they start the ceremony?'

'It will be held tomorrow morning, before the sun appears.'

'And Trinity – how long will it take you to drive down to Bel Air?'

'About an hour and a half, so long as the traffic on the freeway isn't too bad.'

'Good... You have plenty of time in hand, so that you can rest and make yourselves ready. But Rafael, you had better switch on that laptop of yours and start looking for some new disguises for you and Trinity to wear.'

Trinity sipped her dream sage tea, although it was still scalding hot. It was brewed with mugwort leaves and tasted like hay and aniseed. Rafael had made some for her last night and she had found that it had cleared her mind and helped her to sleep. It also settled her stomach. She was hungry but she knew that if she tried to eat anything she would think of Rosie, and be sick.

Trinity took a long shower and changed into a silvery knitted sweater with big pockets and a short black skirt, with black tights. Even if John Dangerfield's security guards didn't recognise her new dream disguise, they might remember the clothes that she was wearing when she had looked like Clarissa Keyes.

She lay on top of her quilt in semi-darkness, her eyes closed, unable to sleep but resting. She knew she would find it impossible not to think about Rosie, so she allowed herself to picture her sister's last terrible moments in flames, over and over. She prayed that her agony had been over quickly, and that she was at peace. She knew that there would be many times when she would shed tears for Rosie again, but this evening she could feel only hatred for the people who had set fire to her as a sacrifice, and poor Sally too. At some point she would have to tell Sally's parents what had happened to her, and that would be almost unbearable.

She thought of Nemo, and how much he cared for her, and

protected her. If she were to lose him, she didn't know what she would do. She had begun to think of him almost as an uncle, more than a partner.

There was a soft knock at her door and Rafael leaned inside.

'Trin? Are you awake?'

'No. I'm having a nightmare.'

He came into the room and sat on the bed beside her.

'I've found two actors that we can turn ourselves into. I can be Jeff Baker. You remember him – he was in that TV series *Bikers*. You can be Olivia Jones.'

'Oh, I know her. She's been in loads of those historical costume movies, hasn't she?'

'That's right. *Chesapeake* and *Washington's Wife*. Jeff's in Italy right now, shooting a picture with Sergio Astorino, and Olivia's visiting her grandparents in Florida because there's been some kind of a hold-up on her next movie. I have plenty of good pictures of both of them on my laptop, so that our dream partners can see what they look like.'

Trinity sat up. 'I'm not often scared, Rafael, but I am this time. I can't pretend that I'm not. Like, I mean really, *really* scared. It's only going to be you and me, on our own, and supposing we have to use those words and kill somebody? I don't want to kill anybody, no matter how horrible they are, and what if we end up in jail? And what about that Weywot?'

'I know it's scary, babe. But the way you've described that house, we may be able to sneak Nemo out of there before anybody realises that we've gone. We'll be looking like Jeff Baker and Olivia Jones, remember, and not like us. And even if we do have to zap somebody, who's going to be able to prove that it was one of us who did it? We won't be carrying heat, will we? Who's going to believe that we spoke three little words and crossed our fingers and whoever it was fell down dead?'

'Do they really kill people, those words?'

'Teodoro says that he's seen it done. I get the feeling he might have done it himself, once upon a time, but he's never said so.'

'So why didn't the Chumash use them against the Spanish, and all the other white people who killed them and drove them off their land?'

'Because for every Spaniard that the Chumash killed, the Spanish sent in their soldiers and killed a hundred Chumash – men, women and children. It was the same when the Mexicans came, and then the Americans. It was just like the Nazis, if a German soldier got killed. They burned down whole villages and shot everybody who lived there.'

Trinity sat up and switched on her bedside lamp. 'All right. Let me have a look at those pictures of Olivia Jones and then we can go.'

Rafael took hold of her hand, leaned over and kissed her. 'You're really brave to do this, do you know that? You could call the cops, or you could forget about Nemo altogether. He knew what a risk he was taking, after all.'

'I've lost too many people that I love already. I'm not going to lose any more.'

She kissed him back and for a few moments they sat staring at each other, as if they always wanted to remember each other like this. Then they went downstairs.

Teodoro was sitting on the couch in front of the fire with the Ghost Woman, and their heads were bent close together in conversation. Trinity could actually see the flames of the fire flickering through the Ghost Woman's translucent silhouette, but Teodoro didn't seem to find her at all intimidating.

He looked up, and smiled at Trinity. 'Excuse us. We were just talking about *tipea*. That's heaven, the kingdom of Tameat, the sun, where this woman will soon be dancing and singing with her ancestors.'

'We're ready to go, Grandfather,' said Rafael.

Teodoro stood up. 'I wish I could come with you. If I was twenty winters younger, I would, but I would only slow you down. As the Tongva say, you need to be as quick as the lightning that made Chukit pregnant.'

Trinity turned to Rafael, but Rafael simply said, 'I'll tell you all about it later. Chukit was a goddess who fell in love with a bolt of lightning and got knocked up. It was either the lightning that did it, or one of her four brothers.'

The Ghost Woman stood up too, and almost floated towards Trinity. She held out her hands and took hold of Trinity's hands. Trinity felt that she was being held by two gloves whose fingers were puffed up with nothing but warm breath.

'I will be thinking of you when the moon drops and the darkness takes me away.'

Trinity looked into those phosphorescent green eyes but she could see nothing to explain what the Ghost Woman really was, or what she was feeling. It was like looking at the stars.

31

They arrived at Chantilly Road a few minutes after midnight, but Trinity turned into the gateway of a large Spanish-style house that was over half a mile to the north of La Muralla. This house was in darkness, and looked unoccupied, at least for tonight, and she parked tight up against the boxwood hedge, so that the Acadia couldn't be seen by anybody looking out.

Although she had been driving, she left the keys under the seat in case one of them failed to make it back here. Then they walked down the road until La Muralla came into sight, and then stopped, and listened, and looked.

They could hear jazz music coming from the garden at the back of the house, and occasional bursts of laughter. They saw barbecue smoke rising up, and they could faintly smell pork ribs and weed. Again, Trinity couldn't stop herself from visualising Rosie, her face blistering as it was licked by those leaping blue flames. The same blue flames that had immolated Margo.

One of the oak front doors was half open, but there was only one security guard standing outside, a big-bellied black man with a shiny bald head, and all of his attention was on his phone.

'Shall we chance it?' said Rafael, and Trinity said, 'Yes. Let's chance it.'

They climbed the steps. The security guard glanced up from his scrolling as they came up to him, and Rafael said, 'Jeff Baker and Olivia Jones.'

'Sure,' said the security guard, and waved his hand to indicate that they could go in.

'Phew,' said Rafael, as they stepped into the atrium, pretending to wipe beads of sweat from his forehead. 'I guess he must know them. Or us.'

Trinity nodded towards the other side of the atrium. 'You see that staircase? That leads up to the corridor where they were keeping us. Nemo's room was on the right, the last room but one.'

'Do you want to go up and take a look? If he's still up there, maybe we can be in and out of here before anybody realises we've been.'

They went across to the staircase, but before they had reached it, David Magellan came out from the entertainment room, walking unsteadily, with a champagne flute in one hand and a chicken fajita skewer in the other.

'Olivia, darling! And Jeff! I didn't know that you two were coming tonight! John never mentioned it! How are you, Olivia? How about a kiss for your old uncle David? How's your grandma? Is she better now?'

David Magellan came up to Trinity and tilted towards her with his lips puckered. She gave Rafael a surreptitious look of disgust, but she allowed David to kiss her on both cheeks. His lips were greasy and he smelled strongly of garlic, but she resisted the urge to wipe her face until he had turned to Rafael.

'Has Netflix greenlighted that Civil War series? What's it called again? I think it's a mistake, myself. This isn't the time to stir up BLM all over again. They'd be better off making a drama about rigged elections. *Hoax*, they could call it. And I'll bet they could get Donald Trump to take a walk-on part.'

He laughed, and jerked up his arm, so that some of his champagne splattered onto the marble tiles. 'Listen,' he said, 'come inside and join the party. You know that this is Cy Gardner's night, don't you? This is the night that Cy gets the silver eyes. And the power.'

He jerked up his arm again, and shouted out, 'Eat your hearts out, Iron Man!' and then laughed again, until he started coughing and couldn't stop. Rafael rolled his eyes at Trinity and gave David three hard slaps between the shoulder blades, probably harder than he needed to, until he coughed up some half-chewed fragments of chicken fajita.

David weaved his way back into the entertainment room, still coughing and punching his chest, and for a moment Trinity thought they might have a chance to run upstairs and see if they could find Nemo. But it was then that they were spotted by the Fox presenter Lydia Marsh, and she frantically waved, and blew kisses to Trinity, and pointed out 'Olivia Jones' and 'Jeff Baker' to her circle of friends, including the director Mimi LaVerne. She beckoned them to come over, and Trinity knew that they had no choice, not if they were to stay in disguise. It would only take one of the guests to query why the two of them had ignored their invitation to join them and gone upstairs, and John Dangerfield might send his heavies up after them, and that would be the end of them, as well as Nemo.

They went into the entertainment room. Like the previous

night, it was crowded with more than two hundred guests, but unlike the previous night, when the atmosphere had been expectant and subdued, tonight was festive and noisy. Black tuxedos had been replaced by yellow and blue and pink, and Trinity saw women wearing plumes of coloured ostrich feathers and hardly anything else, as if they were burlesque dancers. Almost everybody was drunk or high, or both.

Waiters brought champagne for Trinity and Rafael, and they lifted their flutes in salute to the actors and directors and scriptwriters gathered around them, who all raised their glasses in return.

'Here's to Cy!' screamed Mimi LaVerne, over the deafening roar of shouting and laughter, and the discordant warbling of the jazz band. 'At last he'll be able to Cy in relief!'

Trinity found the noise was so deafening that there was no need for her and Rafael to carry out any kind of coherent conversation, or explain what they were doing here in La Muralla tonight when Olivia Jones was supposed to be taking time off in Tampa and Jeff Baker was filming in Cinecittà in Rome. Most of the time they simply stood there, smiling and nodding and pretending that they were listening.

They circulated around the room, too, so that they appeared to be socialising, although all they were doing was attaching themselves to one group after another, and smiling again, and nodding, and then moving on to the next. In between they discreetly emptied their champagne flutes into the marble planters around the wall, so that they always looked as if they were ready for a refill.

Hours went past, and Trinity was beginning to feel exhausted and overwhelmed by the endless noise. Eventually, she had to sit down on a carved wooden chair next to the French doors, and Rafael stood beside her.

'I know just how you feel, babe. Totally bushed. Okay if I sit on your lap?'

She smiled and reached up and stroked the back of his hand. 'I feel like this night is never going to end. I mean, where's poor Nemo?'

At that moment, though, the jazz band fell silent, and all the guests stopped talking and laughing. John Dangerfield climbed up on the stage, along with Cy Gardner. There was a smattering of applause, and a few whoops.

'Friends, colleagues… last night we witnessed another amazing demonstration of the supernatural influence that the American Indians still hold over this land, even though they were banished from it so many decades ago. We saw the extraction of power from a female donor, in order to donate it to a man whose creativity and flair deserve all the energy that a woman's spirit can give him.

'This morning, I give you that man – Cy Gardner, one of the most talented actors ever to grace a movie screen. His Captain Ahab in the remake of *Moby Dick* was stunning. His lead role as Jim Keiller in *Death By Dancing* would and should have won him an Academy Award, if he hadn't been pipped at the post by Joaquin Phoenix playing the Joker, and we all know why that was.

'Next year, with the benefit of this morning's donation from Weywot, I promise you that the Oscar will be his for the taking… and he hasn't even made the picture yet!'

There were cheers and clapping. The jazz band struck up the theme from *Death By Dancing*, and John Dangerfield and Cy Gardner climbed down from the stage.

'Come along, everybody!' John Dangerfield called out, and he led the way through the French doors into the garden, one arm held up like a tour guide. Outside, the clouds had only a sulky reflected glow from the lights of Los Angeles. The moon had set behind the trees and the sun had yet to rise.

As she followed the crowd past the fountain of Auzar, Trinity thought to herself that Tokoor Hikaayey the Ghost Woman must have left this world by now to join her ancestors. Hopefully she would now find peace for herself, and redemption for the cruel acts she had committed in her service of Weywot. She had been forced into them, after all.

Trinity looked up at Auzar's serene white face, but this time Auzar didn't appear to be turning her head to look back down at her.

Rafael stayed close behind her, one hand resting on her shoulder as if to reassure her that he would protect her, no matter what. That gave her a little more confidence. As they approached the open doors of the white building in which Weywot lay, she could feel already the chill of his deeply refrigerated chamber. She shivered, not only because of the cold, but at the thought of seeing Weywot again.

They followed the guests through the vestibule and into Weywot's dim and freezing chamber. Trinity managed to push her way to the front of the crowd, even though several of the other guests frowned at her and said '*hey!*' She ended up standing so close to the left-hand side of the plinth that she could have reached over and touched Weywot's face. Weywot appeared to be asleep, his turquoise lips curled up in the slightest of smiles, as if he were dreaming that he was doing something sadistic.

Trinity looked back to see Rafael elbowing his way through

the guests to join her. It was only when he had reached her that she turned around and saw Nemo.

'Oh, dear Jesus,' she said, cupping her hand against the side of her mouth so that nobody else but Rafael could hear her. 'That's the same post they hung Rosie from, when they burned her, and they've wrapped him up in just the same way.'

Nemo had been stitched all the way up to his chin in his buffalo hide, and he was sagging limply from the metal pole. His eyes were closed and Trinity thought that his face looked bruised.

Rod was suspended from the other pole. He was tightly stitched up, too, although he was wriggling and kicking inside his buffalo hide. His eyes were open and he was looking desperately around the room like a trapped raccoon.

'What if Nemo's out for the count?' Rafael hissed into Trinity's ear. 'I might be able to cut him down, but how are we going to get him out of here? And what about that other guy? Do you know him?'

'No. But we're here to save Nemo. Maybe we could carry him between us. That's if nobody tries to stop us.'

'That's what I was thinking. But I don't fancy our chances. I mean, look at the size of that gorilla over there.'

He nodded towards SloMo, who was ushering the three Tongva elders into the opposite corner of the room.

'Let's hold off a while,' said Trinity. 'Last night, everybody went crazy when that poor girl was being raped. If they go crazy again tonight, maybe that would be the best time to try and get him free. The Ghost Woman told me there's going to be some kind of ritual, but I don't exactly know what it is.'

Rafael said something back to her, but his voice was drowned out by a shout from one of the Tongva elders, immediately followed by the furious rattling of their rain sticks, and a deafening sound like a rough wind blowing through a tunnel. One of the elders was whirling a bullroarer, a thin wooden slat on the end of a cord.

'He is doing that to wake up Weywot!' Rafael shouted, although Trinity could hardly hear him. 'It summons the spirits!'

The roaring went on and on. SloMo went up to the plinth and started to unlace Weywot's buffalo hide, unhurriedly, because Weywot still seemed to be asleep. SloMo opened up the two sides of the hide as far down as Weywot's bony knees, exposing the curled-up scorpion tail between his thighs. Trinity had told Rafael about the scorpion, but Rafael still turned to her, his eyes wide, obviously shocked to see something in reality that he had heard about only in legend.

After a few more minutes of bullroaring, Weywot's bloodshot eyes flickered open, and he lifted his head and spoke. The bullroaring stopped, and he spoke again, and this time Rafael could hear what he was saying, even though he was speaking in Tongva, and Rafael was Chumash.

'I think he's saying that he's ready to pay what he owes.'

SloMo and Bradley took hold of Weywot's bony arms and helped him to sit up. Weywot looked around the crowded room with the satisfied but contemptuous expression of an aging emperor viewing his subjects. After all, he had ruled over this land before any of the overfed men and half-naked women clustered devotedly all around him had even been imagined, let alone born.

John Dangerfield stepped up to the end of the plinth with Cy Gardner and lifted Cy's hand, like a referee declaring the winner of a boxing match.

'Friends and colleagues, I give you the actor's actor Cy Gardner – soon to be the best-known actor since Brando! Cy has already won himself a sound rep in Hollywood for all his great supporting roles… now we're going to see him in leading parts that make him famous worldwide. Tonight, La Muralla. Tomorrow – a star on the Walk of Fame.'

All the guests clapped and whooped, and the Tongva elder whirled his bullroarer. Now Jacob stepped forward, wearing a single blue nitrile glove, and took hold of the flopping segmented scorpion tail that was hanging between Weywot's thighs. While Weywot watched him, unblinking, Jacob started to massage the tail up and down until it stiffened, and stood up as rigid as an erect penis, with its curved stinger trembling as if it were aroused.

John draped a red Tongva blanket over Cy's shoulders. Cy then leaned over the side of the plinth until his lips were almost touching the stinger. Jacob was maintaining his grip on the tail to keep it steady.

Nobody moved. Nobody spoke. The guests were clutching each other's hands in delighted dread, and the only sound was their breathing. Clouds of vapour rose into the freezing air from every one of them, so that it looked as if the chamber were filled with dandelion puffs.

The leading Tongva elder croaked out, '*Chaavot! Chaavot!*' and John slapped SloMo on the shoulder. SloMo went to the side of the room and picked up two plastic jerrycans. He made his way through the crowd towards the poles where Nemo and Rod were hanging, and Trinity could see from the undulating way that he was swinging the jerrycans that they were both full up. He set them down on the floor and unscrewed one of their lids.

'*Chaavot! Chaavot!*' croaked the Tongva elder again. He could have been a crow calling from a broken-down fence.

'That means "fire!"' said Rafael. 'Holy shit! He really is going to set them on fire!'

SloMo sloshed clear liquid from one of the jerrycans all over Rod's buffalo hide. Rod tried to shout out, but the liquid splashed into his face, and all he could do was splutter, and draw in a long, agonised breath.

SloMo took out a Zippo lighter, flicked it, and Rod was instantly engulfed in a cloak of rippling blue fire. His buffalo hide crackled and shrank, and for a moment his face was completely swallowed up by flames. When he reappeared, his scalp was blackened and smoking, both of his eyes were blinded, and his cheeks were as red as raw meat.

The crowd let out a huge shout of excitement. Not only was Rod on fire, but now Cy had opened his mouth and taken the scorpion's stinger onto his tongue. Trinity glanced over at him, and saw him close his lips around it, and start to suck, but she turned back immediately to see what SloMo was doing. He had picked up the second jerrycan and was carrying it across to the pole where Nemo was hanging.

'*Rafael! Stop him!*' she squealed, and she didn't care who heard her.

Rafael pulled out his sheath knife and pushed against the two overweight guests who were standing between him and the end of the plinth. One of them shoved back at him and snarled, 'What's your problem, bro?'

Trinity could see that SloMo was unscrewing the lid of the second jerrycan. For a split second, she thought of shouting out the three fatal words that Teodoro had taught her, but Rafael and the two bulky guests were jostling from side to side in front of her, and she was terrified that she might kill Rafael by mistake.

She fumbled in the front pocket of her sweater and took out the two silver discs that Teodoro had given her, the Faces of Fire. She held them up as high as she could and pointed them at SloMo. He had taken the lid off the jerrycan now and was lifting it up, ready to splash over Nemo.

'*Qsi! Qsi! Qsi!*' she cried out, and her voice was nearly a shriek. "*Awa'y! 'Awa'y! 'Awa'y!*'

Instantly, SloMo exploded in a huge ball of orange flame, and then his jerrycan of methanol blew up, too, in a weird hourglass shape of pale-blue fire. For one moment it looked as if he were dancing with a ghost.

All the guests screamed and shouted, and the ones who were gathered nearest to SloMo staggered back and collided with the guests behind them, and at least a dozen of them toppled onto the floor. Others fell sideways against the plinth, bringing down everybody who was standing next to them.

SloMo was blazing fiercely from head to foot. He shuffled around and around, flapping his arms, before dropping to his knees. Rod was still burning, too, and the heat that was rippling up from SloMo made his blue flames leap even higher, until they were licking the ceiling, with its suns and its moons and its painted wolves. Over the screaming of the guests, Trinity heard John yelling, '*Out! Out! Follow me! Everybody out!*'

The air was rapidly filling up with acrid brown smoke, so that Trinity felt she could hardly breathe. But Rafael ducked around the two men who had been blocking his way and circled around SloMo's blazing body, one hand held up to shield his face from the heat. He went up to the pole where Nemo was hanging and gripped the ragged edge of his buffalo hide, shaking it hard. Nemo opened his eyes, and Trinity could see that Rafael was shouting something to him. He must have been telling him that he was Rafael, even though he looked like Jeff Baker, and that 'Olivia Jones' was really Trinity.

Whatever Nemo said back to him, Rafael didn't hesitate. He started to slash at the stitches that held the buffalo hide together, and when the two sides flopped apart, he reached behind Nemo to untwist the wires that had kept his nylon handcuffs fastened to the pole. When Nemo dropped down heavily onto the floor, Rafael cut the nylon ties, too.

SloMo was lying right at their feet, burning so ferociously that his fat was crackling and his ribs were already starting to appear through his blackened flesh.

'Let's go! Let's go!' Trinity shouted, and she reached out for Nemo's hand. The three of them pushed their way through the smoke and the panicking crowd until they reached the doors. They were held up for a moment because two women in stiletto heels had tripped over in the vestibule, and several more guests had stumbled over them.

Trinity looked quickly behind her. The plinth chamber was now filled up with such dense brown smoke that Rod's burning body appeared only as the faintest flicker. But then, with an ice-cold prickle of utter fright, she saw a white figure stalking towards them through the smoke – a figure that was walking with the stilted gait of a Martian tripod from *The War of the Worlds*.

A figure that was tall, and almost skeletal. A figure with a scarf wrapped around its head, but otherwise naked. A figure with a rope-like appendage swinging between its legs.

'*Nemo!*' she screamed at him. 'Nemo – Rafael – look! It's Weywot!'

Nemo and Rafael turned around. Weywot was making his way unsteadily towards them, swinging his arms to knock the other guests aside.

'It's *you*, Nemo,' said Rafael. 'He must be coming after *you*.'

'Me?' said Nemo.

'You were supposed to be sacrificed. He needs you.'

'In that case, let's get the hell out of here.'

They stepped over a red-headed woman in a shiny evening gown who was lying on the vestibule steps, partly hysterical and partly drunk. Then, without a word, they started to run through the pergola towards the house. Trinity glanced over her shoulder as they reached the fountain and saw that despite his stilt-like way of walking, Weywot was catching up with them. He was so tall and his arms were so long that he was followed by a storm of white jasmine flowers.

The rest of the guests were scattering in panic all around the garden, and some of them were trying to clamber over the fence to the next-door property.

'Through the house!' Trinity panted. 'We're parked a little way up the road!'

They ran towards the open French doors, but before they could reach them, John stepped out of the dark interior, flanked by Bradley and DaShawn, and the leader of the Tongva elders. The Tongva elder had one hand raised, like a traffic cop. John was holding up Nemo's automatic.

'Hold it, you people!' John barked at them. 'Just hold it! Stay right where you are and don't even *think* about moving!'

Panting, Trinity and Nemo and Rafael came to a stop.

Immediately, they looked behind them, but they saw that Weywot had stopped too, and was standing beside the fountain, swaying slightly. He was staring at them malevolently with his bloodshot eyes, his bony chest rising and falling as he breathed and his scorpion's tail curling and uncurling between his emaciated thighs.

In a high, warbling voice, the Tongva elder chanted a long and repetitive incantation, ending again and again with '*Mopuushtenpo xaa mochoova!*'

John walked up to Trinity and Rafael and peered at them both intently, still holding the gun raised.

'You sure *look* like Jeff Baker and Olivia Jones. But I was fooled like this last night. Maybe you really are Jeff Baker and Olivia Jones. But on the other hand, maybe you're not. You're not behaving in the way that the real Jeff Baker and Olivia Jones would behave, and you've just fucked up one of the most important ceremonies in the entire history of motion pictures.'

He paused, still staring at them, and then he went over to Nemo. '*You* – you were supposed to be a sacrifice. You were supposed to give your life for something really worthwhile. Well, you'll be happy to know that you still have the chance to do that. The sun doesn't come up for another half hour, and that means we still have time to finish the ritual. So why don't you walk back the way you've come, and we can carry on where we left off.'

'And supposing I won't?' Nemo challenged him.

'If you won't, then I'll have no option but to shoot your two friends here in the head and have my helpers carry you back down there by force. This is the great god Weywot you're messing with, *compadre*, not some two-bit demon.'

'You're out of your mind.'

'Oh, you think? I'm the single most successful independent producer in Hollywood, and there's a reason for that. Everybody knows that success only comes at a price, but not everybody dares to pay the *ultimate* price. *I* dare, and that's why nobody else in this town will ever be able to come close.'

'So you're going to sacrifice me to this—' Nemo looked back at Weywot, who was trembling now and whose breathing was coming in tight, suppressed whistles '—walking clothes horse?'

'Don't insult Weywot,' John warned him. 'If he gets the idea that you've disrespected him, you can't even imagine what he might do to you. By comparison, you'd enjoy being burned alive.'

Nemo caught Trinity's eye, and he gave her three winks. She knew what he was telling her, but she had already decided to do it. There was, after all, no other way out.

There was a strange moment when the only sounds were the fountain plashing and the chipping song of a mockingbird in a nearby sycamore tree, apart from the occasional snapping of branches as the rest of the guests tried to fight their way through the bushes.

Trinity crossed her fingers, holding them up so that John Dangerfield was caught like a sniper's target in the cross hairs of a gunsight. Then she spoke the three lethal words, a little shakily, but clearly.

The Tongva elder screeched out, '*Noooo!*' Even though the words were Chumash, he obviously knew what they were, and what effect they would have.

John had heard them, and he turned towards Trinity with

a puzzled frown. For five heart-stopping seconds, she thought that the words had failed to work. Then, with a loud crack, John's head burst apart like a broken jug, with fragments of his skull flying in all directions. His entire brain shot more than fifteen feet upwards into the air, with his spinal cord trailing after it like the tail of a kite. It dropped with a splash into the fountain behind him, and floated, staining the water with blood.

The rest of his body toppled backwards, and thumped onto the paving stones. Nemo's automatic dropped out of his hand, and Nemo scooped it up.

Bradley and DaShawn and the Tongva elder were making for the French doors, but Nemo pointed the gun at them and shouted '*Freeze!* None of you move a goddam muscle!'

Bradley and DaShawn put up their hands, but the Tongva elder cried, '*Weywot!*' He started to blurt out a warbling incantation, stamping his feet in a complicated little dance. '*Weywot!*'

'Just quit that crap, will you?' Nemo snapped at him.

He was too late. Weywot took in a high-pitched whistling breath, and they heard his elbows and his knees creak as he started to stalk towards them again.

Nemo swivelled around and fired at Weywot. The bang was so loud that the mockingbird flew up screaming from the next-door tree. They could see the bullet puncture Weywot's chest, and he hesitated. After only a few moments, though, he steadied himself and continued to walk towards them.

'Let's just *go!*' Rafael shouted, and he grabbed Trinity's hand.

Except for the Tongva elder, they all ran towards the

open French doors. But they had only just scrambled into the entertainment room when Bradley and DaShawn both skidded to a stop. Bradley gasped out, 'Jesus Kerr-*rist*!'

He was staring back outside. Nemo said, 'What?', and he came to a halt too. Trinity and Rafael were halfway across the room by now, but they turned around to see why Nemo had stopped running.

Weywot had nearly reached the house, but once again he had come to a standstill. His feet seemed to be rooted to the paving stones, but he was teetering from one side to the other, as if he were finding it difficult to remain upright.

He was facing the fountain. When Trinity saw why, she whispered, '*no*'.

The white statue of Auzar was no longer leaping joyously upward. She had turned around so that she was staring at Weywot, and both her arms were raised, with her index fingers pointing at him accusingly. Her ecstatic smile had disappeared. Now her brow was furrowed, and her jaw was jutting out. She looked deeply angry.

'That's impossible,' said Nemo. 'That's a statue.'

'I thought I saw it move before, but I didn't believe it,' Trinity whispered. 'I thought I must be seeing things.'

'Right now, I think we're *all* seeing things. That is absolutely one hundred per cent not possible. That's a statue made of solid marble and statues made of solid marble can't move. I reckon there's something in the smoke that's making us hallucinate. Jimsonweed or something like that.'

Rafael said, 'Nemo – I see it too. We can't all be having the same hallucination.'

Weywot bowed his misshapen head. The Tongva elder came up and stood beside him, and started to chant, and although they had no idea what he was saying, it looked as if he were begging the statue of Auzar to be lenient.

'I can't believe this,' said Trinity. She was still trembling with shock from setting fire to SloMo and killing John Dangerfield. 'I can't believe any of this.'

Rafael put his arm around her and hugged her, although he said nothing more. None of them spoke. Trinity felt that they were gathered in a collective nightmare from which they were waiting to wake up.

Slowly, the statue of Auzar spread her arms wide. She looked almost as if she were going to take off and fly. The Tongva elder dropped onto his knees, repeating his chant over and over.

As he was chanting, Trinity began to be aware of a high hissing sound, as if she had tinnitus. But it grew louder, and louder, and it was clear that it wasn't inside her own head. It was the statue of Auzar who was hissing, her lips parted and her teeth clenched together. The hissing reached a pitch when it blotted out every other sound in the garden, and the guests who were still trying to climb up the neighbouring fence looked around in bewilderment to see what was causing it.

Weywot's feet were sinking into the paving slabs, up to his ankles. He threw back his head and let out a long, anguished howl. Trinity could hear him, even over the hissing. Gradually, inch by inch, his legs started to disappear downwards, until he had sunk into the limestone right up to his bony knees.

As he sank, the scorpion tail between his legs started to whip frantically backwards and forwards. His belly bulged, and his upper thighs rippled. He howled again, and as he howled the skin of his crotch suddenly burst open in a welter of blood. The scorpion struggled out – the whole yellowish scorpion, head, eight legs and huge pincers. It dropped onto the ground, paused for a second, and then scuttled off into the darkness.

The hissing continued, and Weywot began to slide down into the paving slabs faster and faster. When he was buried up to his chest, he held out his hands towards the Tongva elder, silently pleading with him to pull him out. The Tongva elder climbed to his feet and backed away, and when Weywot sank right up to his neck, he hobbled off as quickly as he could and disappeared around the side of the house.

Soon, only Weywot's head remained above the paving stones. He was staring up at the statue of Auzar with an expression on his face that Trinity thought was strangely resigned. He seemed to be accepting his fate as if he deserved it. The limestone crept up to cover his mouth, and then his nose, until there was nothing left of him but his bloodshot eyes and the scarf around the top of his head. Then, within seconds, he was totally gone.

The hissing died away, and with a soft grinding sound the statue of Auzar turned around to face the house again. Her head was lifted and her expression was triumphant, as it had been before.

'It's over,' said Nemo, in his thickest voice. 'I can't believe it. I don't know if I just dreamed all of that, but it's over.'

'Auzar sent Weywot back down where he belonged,' said Rafael, although he, too, sounded as if he couldn't believe the scene that he had just witnessed.

'What do we do now?' Trinity asked him. Smoke was still billowing out of the building where Rod and SloMo had been burning, and John Dangerfield's brain and spinal cord were still wallowing in the fountain.

'I know what *I'm* doing,' said Bradley. 'I'm going to vamoose and I'm never coming back. And don't you try to stop me.'

'I'm with you, bro,' said DaShawn. 'And don't try to stop *me*, neither. I mean, I'm gone.'

'We should get out of here too,' said Nemo. 'The cops'll be here before we know it.'

'Shouldn't we stay, to tell them what's happened?' Rafael asked him.

Nemo shook his head. 'Unh-hunh. The last thing we want to do is get ourselves involved in any of this. I don't, especially, the way the cops think of me. In any case, what can they prove? Trinity, Rafael – you two bear absolutely no resemblance to the way you really look, so you can't be identified. And forensics will never be able to work out how one guy spontaneously combusted and the other got his brains blown out by three little words.'

Rafael looked down at the paving stones where Weywot had disappeared from sight. 'I guess you're right. Let it stay a mystery. All that anybody should ever know is that a white man tried to mess with Indian magic.'

Trinity nodded numbly. She was beginning to shiver with the post-traumatic stress of what they had been through, and what she had done. She let Nemo and Rafael take her by the hands and hurry her out of the house, like Cinderella being hurried out of the palace on the stroke of midnight.

32

With Rafael driving, they headed first for Texhoma Avenue, to pick up Buddy. Dawn was only just beginning to break, but they didn't want to have to drive all the way back down from Pine Mountain to collect him later. Trinity had decided to take him with her, since it was depressingly clear that her father wasn't going to stop drinking. He was in no condition to look after himself, let alone Buddy.

Rafael did most of the talking, as he drove. Almost as soon as they had turned out of the gates of Bel Air, his dream disguise of Jeff Baker had melted away, and only a few minutes later, when they reached the freeway and started north towards Encino, Trinity's disguise melted too. For a brief sad moment, she thought she could smell the flowery perfume that her mother always used to wear.

'Auzar, you know, was Weywot's grandmother,' said Rafael. 'That's what comes of bringing your family into disrepute, I guess. Sooner or later your old folks will give you a hard time for it.'

'But for God's sake,' Nemo protested. 'That was only a statue of her.'

'Makes no difference. Among the Tongva, any figure that looks like a person or an animal can have their soul hiding inside them – their manitou. It's the same with the Chumash, and some other tribes, too. It's like voodoo dolls, in a way. You make a voodoo doll to look like somebody you don't like, and when you prick it with a pin, that person feels pain. In Tongva magic, the spirit of a dead person can go on living inside a photograph or a painting or a statue, like Auzar. You've heard of Indians refusing to have their photographs taken, because they believed that cameras would steal their souls.'

'So where is Weywot now?' asked Trinity. 'Has he been buried forever?'

'I have no idea. He's incredibly powerful, so it goes to show you how powerful Auzar must have been. Then again, Auzar was a woman, so it goes without saying.'

They had almost reached the turn-off to the Ventura Freeway when Nemo said, 'What's that scraping noise?'

Trinity listened. It sounded as if a branch had got caught somewhere underneath the Acadia and was trailing along the road.

'I must have picked up a bit of that hedge when I parked. We can have a look when we get to José's.'

They reached Encino Village and turned into Texhoma Avenue. The street was silent and deserted and in the Peréz house all the blinds were drawn down. The three of them climbed out and closed the Acadia's doors as quietly as they could. Trinity went up to the front door and rang the bell while Nemo and Rafael bent down to see if they could find out what had been causing the scraping noise.

'I can't see any twigs or anything like that,' said Nemo. 'It was probably a disc brake rubbing.'

There was no answer from the house so Trinity rang the

bell again, three times. Eventually a light was switched on in the hallway, and the door was unlocked and opened. Red Bird Gabriel Peréz was standing there in a loosely tied bathrobe, blinking at them.

'Do you know what time it is?' he said. He had obviously seen who was ringing with his video doorbell. 'Buddy's still asleep. Well, we all were.'

'I'm sorry that we woke you up, Mr Peréz. I realise it's desperately early but we're on our way back to Pine Mountain and we thought it made sense to pick up Buddy now.'

Red Bird digested that for a moment and then he said, 'Okay. Why don't you come on in? I'll shake him awake and have him get himself dressed.'

Trinity, Nemo and Rafael followed Gabriel Peréz inside, and he showed them into the living room and switched on the lights. Rafael saw the mural of Toypurina on the wall and said, 'Wow.'

'Please, take a seat,' said Red Bird. 'Buddy shouldn't be too long.'

Trinity and Nemo sat on the couch but Rafael circled around the room, admiring all the paintings and photographs of Gabrieleño-Tongva villagers, as well as the pebbles and the jugs.

'It's great to see all this stuff preserved. So much Chumash jewellery and pottery got lost for ever. Well, let's face it, so many Chumash got lost for ever.'

From one of the bedrooms, they heard Buddy and José talking, and then laughing. After about five minutes, Red Bird led both boys into the living room – Buddy dressed in his jacket and his jeans, while José was still in his pyjamas.

'Do I really have to go?' said Buddy, pulling a sad face. 'I've been having such a cool time with José. And Red Bird has taught me how to shoot a bow and arrow.'

'I'm sorry, Buddy, but yes,' Trinity told him. 'But I won't be taking you back to Dad just yet. You'll be coming up to Pine Mountain with me and Nemo and Rafael. You'll have a great time there too, I promise you.'

They went out into the hallway and Red Bird opened the front door.

'Thank you for looking after him for us,' said Trinity. 'You don't know how much of a help you've been, honestly.'

'Any time,' smiled Red Bird. 'Any boy who helps my son to paint Tongva pictures all around the neighbourhood is welcome here.' But then he frowned and said, 'Are you all right, Trinity? I hate to say it but you look like you're kind of stressed.'

'Let's just say it's been a difficult night, and I'm more than glad that it's over.'

She laid her hand on Buddy's shoulder and was about to usher him out of the front door when they heard a sharp rattling sound, like castanets. The rattling came closer and closer, and then the scorpion came scuttling into the hallway, running between their legs and jumping up at Nemo, clinging on to his grey leather jacket.

Nemo shouted out and tried to beat it off, but he lost his balance and staggered into the living room, falling backwards onto the carpet.

'Get it off me!' he shouted. 'Get this fucking thing off me!'

The scorpion had fastened itself to his jacket with its pincers, and now its segmented tail was rising up and curling over so that it could sting him in the face. Red Bird grabbed it in both hands and tried to pull it off him, but it twisted its body violently from side to side and its legs scratched at him in such a vicious flurry that his fingers were instantly smothered in blood. He stood back, shocked, holding up his hands like two dripping red gloves.

Nemo managed to seize the scorpion's tail in his left hand and hold it tight, so that its stinger was quivering only an inch from his left eye. He was grunting with effort because the scorpion was so strong. With his right hand he tried to reach down to his belt, to pull out his automatic, but the scorpion's legs lacerated his fingers too, like Red Bird's, and ripped his thumb right down to the bone.

Rafael pushed Red Bird out of his way, picked up a rain stick that was propped up against a side table, and started to hit the scorpion on its tail and on its back. He hit it again and again, harder and harder, but the scorpion clung on, and at last the rain stick burst open and the carpet was showered in thousands of tiny pebbles.

Red Bird's wife had come out of their bedroom in her nightgown and she started to scream when she saw the scorpion and Red Bird's bloodied hands. Trinity was ready to go into the living room and batter the scorpion with anything she could lay her hands on – a book, a jug, a poker from the fireplace.

But before she could move, Buddy squeezed past her. He bounded across the living room as if he were leaping in slow motion, until he reached the painting of Toypurina. Without any hesitation, he tore off the duct tape that covered the eyes of the Spook Owl on Toypurina's arm.

'Nemo – don't look at the owl!' he shrilled. 'Nobody look at the owl!'

'What?' said Nemo. It had been taking all of his strength to stop the scorpion from stinging him in the eye, and his arm was trembling now with effort.

'Don't look at the owl!' José repeated. 'Nobody must look at the owl!'

There was a long moment of silence, but the scorpion's legs had stopped their frantic scratching at Nemo's jacket. Its pincers gradually opened up, and it stiffened, and then it dropped sideways off Nemo's chest and onto the floor. Nemo quickly climbed onto his feet, holding up his bloody right hand to shield his eyes from the Spook Owl's stare.

'Is it dead?' asked Trinity.

'No,' said Red Bird. He was wiping his bloody hands on his bathrobe. 'It's paralysed, that's all. If you look into its eyes, the Spook Owl freezes you, the same as a hypnotist. Not for ever, but long enough for you to be killed.'

With that, he left the living room. He said some reassuring words to his wife, and then he stepped out of the front door. He went over to his van, opened up the back, and returned carrying an electric chainsaw and a hessian sack.

Rafael had pushed an armchair across the living room to cover up the painting of the Spook Owl. Nemo and Rafael stayed in the room while Red Bird started up the chainsaw, and Red Bird's wife took Trinity and Buddy and José into the kitchen.

'I would have done this outside in the yard if it hadn't been so early in the morning!' Red Bird shouted. 'I don't think my neighbours would have appreciated the noise, even if I told them that I was cutting up a giant scorpion!'

Nemo and Rafael looked down at the paralysed creature.

It was lying on its back now with its pincers and its legs splayed out and its tail curled up. Red Bird's wife had given Nemo a towel to wrap around his bleeding thumb but it was throbbing now.

'Just give it what's coming to it!' he shouted back.

Red Bird lowered the chainsaw and cut the scorpion's body in half. It jerked and twitched as if it could feel it, and its tail straightened out, quivering, as stiff as Weywot's penis. With all the expertise of a professional tree trimmer, Red Bird cut off its head, its pincers, and its eight claw-like legs.

When he had finished dismembering it completely, he picked up the pieces and dropped them into the sack. He was careful not to touch the stinger or its bulb, which was still swollen with venom.

'You should burn it now,' said Rafael.

'I intend to. The last thing I want is for all these bits to join together again and the scorpion to come looking for its revenge.'

'Oh come on,' said Nemo. 'You're not serious.'

Red Bird tied up the neck of the sack and looked at him gravely. 'You are a white man. You know so little of Indian magic.'

'I know that I nearly got myself stung to death by a three-foot scorpion. Believe me, my friend, I don't want to know any more than that.'

Trinity appeared in the living-room doorway, with Buddy. She looked worn out.

'Is it finished?' she asked.

'Yes, sweetheart,' said Nemo. 'It's finished.'

*

As they drove north to Pine Mountain, Buddy suddenly piped up and said, 'Is Rosie there, where we're going?'

Trinity looked across at Nemo. He gave her a quick shake of his head and said, 'Later.'

'She's not there, Buddy, no,' said Trinity. 'She's with Sally.'

'Oh, okay,' said Buddy, and he continued to play Yooka-Laylee on Nemo's phone.

When they reached Pine Mountain, they climbed wearily out of the Acadia. Teodoro must have heard them arrive, because he was waiting at the front door for them.

Shakily, trying to smile, Trinity said, 'Teodoro, this is my brother, Buddy. Buddy, this is the great Teodoro I was telling you about on the way here. The man who does American Indian magic.'

Buddy raised his hand to give Teodoro a high five. 'Me and my friend José, we do it too.'

Teodoro smiled at him and then looked at Trinity with narrowed eyes. 'You used the words, didn't you? And the Faces of Fire.'

'We wouldn't be here if she hadn't, Grandfather, believe me,' said Rafael. 'Come on, Trinity. Come and sit down.'

'Just give me a minute,' Trinity told him. 'I need to get myself together.'

While he and Nemo and Teodoro and Buddy went into the living room, she went upstairs to her bedroom and switched on the lamp on the dressing table.

She sat down in front of the dressing-table mirror and stared at herself. She thought she looked pale and tired, and her eye make-up was blotchy, but otherwise her face told nothing of what she had lost and what she had been through.

She couldn't think how Teodoro had guessed that she had killed John Dangerfield and SloMo.

Staring at herself, she started to tremble uncontrollably, and tears rolled out of her eyes and ran down her face. She felt as if an agonising moan was rising up inside her, but she kept her teeth clamped tightly shut so that Rafael and Teodoro and Nemo and Buddy wouldn't hear her.

She couldn't imagine that anything in the world could hurt more than losing Rosie – actually watching her burn, when she was still alive – and she couldn't imagine anything more horrifying than speaking the words that had made John Dangerfield's skull explode, or setting fire to SloMo.

The dark feelings that were churning around in her mind were so complex that she thought she would never understand them. She was overwhelmed with grief, as well as guilt, and revulsion, and the terrifying weirdness of Auzar's statue coming to life. She was sure she would have nightmares for months to come.

She sat in front of the mirror for almost five minutes before there was a gentle knock on the door.

'Trin?' said Rafael gently. 'Are you okay?'

Hastily, she wiped her eyes with the backs of her hands and switched off the lamp.

'No, I'm not. But I'll live. I'll have to, won't I?'

'Why don't you come downstairs? Teodoro's made some lizard tail tea and I've told him everything that happened.'

'What did he say?'

'He didn't seem to think that it was such a big deal. You know – a statue forcing a demon to sink down through solid paving stones. Or a giant scorpion clinging on to our SUV because it didn't want to let Nemo go and miss out on its sacrifice. As if things like that happen every day.'

'I'll just come down for a minute, but I won't stay. I'm totally bushed.'

She followed Rafael downstairs. Nemo and Teodoro were talking together and Buddy was playing some video game with dancing rabbits on the television.

Teodoro stood up and said, 'How are you now, Trinity? Would you like some tea, or something to eat?'

'No, no thanks. I'd only bring it straight back up again. I need some rest, that's all.'

'I'll come back up with you,' said Rafael. 'I feel like I've just gone fifteen rounds with Mike Tyson, and lost.'

'Well, I think I'll stay up for a while,' said Nemo. 'I could use a drink of something a bit less politically correct than lizard tail tea. And I think I should sterilise this thumb and bandage it properly. You never know what diseases a giant scorpion might be infected with.'

Trinity and Rafael went back up to Trinity's bedroom, undressed and crawled under the covers. Rafael held Trinity close and kissed her neck.

'You're a princess,' he whispered.

'I'm an exhausted princess. I hope I don't have nightmares about Weywot, that's all.'

'I'm here for you, if you do. I'll jump into your nightmare and knock him back down under the ground.'

Trinity heard the floorboards creaking as Nemo went downstairs, and then she heard Teodoro and Buddy talking to each other. Buddy had already slept for most of the night, so he sounded bright. Teodoro sounded as if he were telling him a story.

'I'll have to tell Buddy about Rosie tomorrow,' said Trinity. 'I can't face doing it. He's going to be in bits.'

She closed her eyes, and when she opened them again the sun was shining through the bedroom blinds and it was half-past noon.

Rafael was in the kitchen brewing coffee and making waffles, and Nemo was out on the balcony talking to Teodoro. Her heart beating hard, Trinity sat down in the living room with Buddy and explained to him quietly that Rosie had died, along with Sally, and that neither of them would be coming back.

'How? How did they die? What happened?'

'It was at a party, in Bel Air, with lots of famous movie people. We haven't been told the full story yet.'

'Was it drugs?' asked Buddy. He could barely get the words out, and his face was a picture of misery. 'Like an overdose or something?'

They were both crying now. Trinity shook her head. She couldn't bring herself to tell him that his sister had been burned alive, or why.

'We don't know yet,' she told him, and hugged him. 'All I know is that Rosie wouldn't have wanted you to feel sad for ever.'

It was still sunny and warm so they sat out on the balcony with coffee and waffles. Nemo and Teodoro continued to talk quietly, but Trinity and Rafael remained silent and thoughtful. Buddy sat on his own in the corner with Nemo's phone, playing with his dancing rabbits again, and Trinity could understand why. Anything to take his mind off Rosie.

They had switched on ABC and CBS and Fox News, but there had been no mention on any TV channel of what had happened at La Muralla. No report of John Dangerfield being killed, or the two men who had been incinerated in Weywot's chamber. Not a word about two hundred celebrity guests fleeing from the house in a panic.

'They're going to put a lid on it,' said Nemo. 'The same as they did when I blew the whistle on their bribery. You wait... give it a week or so and you'll hear that John Dangerfield died of a heart attack, or something like that.'

They kept the television on, in case there was any news update about La Muralla, but all they heard was a report about Vankwish Pictures filing for bankruptcy and Madonna's latest performance.

Without looking up from his dancing rabbits, Buddy said, 'It's a good thing that Spook Owl was painted on the wall. We never could have zapped that scorpion if that wasn't there.'

'Hey – it's a good thing that you and José knew what it could do,' Nemo told him. 'One thing that's been kind of puzzling me, though. You painted a Spook Owl yourselves, didn't you, on that wall off White Oak Avenue? But yours had its eyes shut, so that you wouldn't get paralysed when you looked at it. The Owl at José's place, it had its eyes open, even though they were covered up with duct tape. So how did Red Bird paint it without being paralysed as soon as he'd filled in its eyes?'

Teodoro smiled and said, 'There is a simple answer to that, Nemo. In the Tongva language, there are three words that you can use to bring something inanimate to life, just as there are three words in Chumash that can kill something living. The picture will not have been possessed of any power until those words were spoken, so the Spook Owl's eyes could have been painted as open without any risk to the artist. Only when the words were spoken would it have been necessary to cover them up.'

'Amazing. I'm learning something new about this country every day, and I thought I knew everything there was to know about it. My family have been here for three generations, but I feel like I'm a stranger in a nation that doesn't belong to me.'

Teodoro shrugged and said, 'Well...'

They sat for a while watching the sun go down behind the clouds. Then Trinity said, 'What are we going to do now, Nemo? Do you think it'll ever be safe for us to go back? I'm really worried about our dad. I don't want him drinking himself to death. And I want to arrange some sort of memorial service for Rosie.'

'I don't know, Trin. If there's one thing I've found out about the people in power in this country, it's that they're utterly corrupt, and utterly ruthless, and that they'll lie and cheat and even kill to hold on to that power, and the wealth that goes with it. The only way that you and I are going to be able to lead a normal life again is if we expose the people who are after us and bring them down.'

'But *you* have a power now that no white men possess,' said Teodoro. 'You have shown that you believe in the reality of Chumash and Tongva magic, and you can use it to defeat those who wish you harm. You have already used it to win one great victory. You can use it again.'

Trinity looked at Nemo, and at Buddy, and for the first time since she had walked in to find Margo in flames, she felt strength, and hope, and the courage of being ordinary.

*

That night, Rafael took Teodoro home, and so Trinity slept alone. It took her nearly three hours to get to sleep, because she was unable to think about anything but John Dangerfield's head exploding and his brain flying up into the air, with his spinal column flailing behind it.

Eventually, though, she fell into a sleep as deep and dark as the well in *The Ring*. She was woken up only by the distant rumbling of thunder, and the flicker of lightning across the ceiling. She sat up in bed and saw from the digital clock on the nightstand that it was 10:17.

Before she took a shower, she wrapped herself in the thick brown towelling bathrobe that was hanging on the back of the door. She went along to the bedroom next to hers and quietly opened the door. Inside it was dark and Buddy was still fast asleep, in spite of the thunder. She closed the door again and went downstairs. Nemo was sitting in the living room drinking coffee and watching the news on television.

'It's so *late*!' she said. 'You could have woken me!'

'I reckoned you needed your sleep, sweetheart. Young Buddy too. And besides, there's nothing to wake up for.'

'Rafael's not back yet?'

'No, not yet. He called and said that he was going to be spending some time with his relatives. He may make it back sometime this afternoon.'

Trinity nodded towards the television. 'And still no news about John Dangerfield?'

'Absolutely zilch.'

There was another flicker of lightning, followed by a burst of thunder that made the window rattle. It started to rain, large random drops that plopped onto the balcony outside, and then harder and harder.

Nemo stood up. 'Let me fix you some coffee. What would you like for your breakfast? I'm not much of a cook but I could whip up some pancakes.'

Before Trinity could answer, they heard the doorbell chiming. Nemo frowned and said, 'Who the hell could that be? Rafael has his own key, and he didn't tell me that he was expecting anybody.'

He went into the hallway and looked at the doorbell video. There were three men standing on the porch outside, all three wearing black raincoats with pointed hoods, so that they looked like three giant rooks.

It was only when one of them turned to face the camera so that he could press the button again that Nemo said, 'Shit. It's that Fidel guy from the IAG. They've found us.'

He went back into the living room, picked up his grey leather jacket from the back of the couch and yanked out his gun.

'Get back upstairs,' he told Trinity. 'Find yourself a closet to hide in.'

'I'm not going to leave you.'

'They're ruthless, these guys. I mean it, Trin, get upstairs and hide. Wake up Buddy if he's still asleep and hide him too.'

Trinity was only halfway across the living room when they heard Fidel Madrazo shouting from behind the front door.

'Mr Frisby! Nemo! It's me, Fidel Madrazo from the IAG! I've come to tell you that you're not on our hit list any more! I'm telling you the truth, I swear it! But we need to talk!'

Nemo looked at Trinity. 'What do you think? You think he's serious, or just bluffing?'

'I don't know. We saw everything that happened at John Dangerfield's house, didn't we? They might want us out of the way even more than they did before.'

Nemo stood in the hallway, holding up his automatic. He clicked off the safety catch but he stayed where he was, biting his lip, undecided. Yet another burst of thunder made the whole house shake, and they could hear the rain spouting torrentially from the gutters.

'Mr Frisby! We know you're in there! I swear we haven't come to do you any harm! But we're not going away until you talk to us!'

Trinity said, 'Maybe we should trust him. They're never going to stop coming after us, are they? How are we ever going to live a normal life, otherwise? And I need to bury Rosie. Even if I never get to do anything else, Nemo, I need to say goodbye to my sister.'

Nemo went up to the door and shouted out, 'Fidel? I'm going to open the door. I want your hands where I can see them, all three of you. I get the slightest indication that any one of you is going for a weapon, I'm going to blow your fucking head off.'

'I swear to you, Nemo! I want to make a deal with you, that's all.'

Nemo unhooked the chain off the door and slowly opened it, with his gun pointing directly at Fidel Madrazo's head. Fidel and the other two investigators all had their hands lifted and their fingers spread.

'Push those hoods back,' said Nemo. 'Let me see your faces. Okay. Come on in. Take those coats off and drop them on the floor over there.'

The agents unbuttoned their dripping-wet raincoats,

shook them, and tossed them into the corner. Fidel even had raindrops on the ends of his moustache.

'Right, now take out your weapons between finger and thumb, and set them down on that side table.'

The agents did as they were told. Nemo then went up to each of them and quickly patted them down for any other guns they might have concealed, lifting up their jackets at the back and feeling their trousers around their ankles. Finally, he said, 'Okay, fine. Come through. This is my friend Trinity Fox, by the way. Trin, you remember Fidel. The guy who threatened us after we'd talked to Andy Zimmer.'

'I remember,' said Trinity. She stood behind the couch, looking at the three investigators suspiciously, holding her left elbow in her right hand like a student waiting to hear if she can go home for the weekend.

'Well, you found us,' said Nemo.

'We wouldn't have done, if John Dangerfield's neighbour hadn't come home to find you parked in his driveway and taken a picture of your vehicle. Once we had your number, it was just a question of "follow that CCTV".'

'Goddam it. We thought the owner was away.'

'*Mala suerte para ti*, Mr Frisby, *buena suerte para nosotroso*. Bad luck for you, good luck for us.'

'So, okay. What's this deal you want to make?'

'There were more than two hundred guests at John Dangerfield's house the night before last, and the night before that. Almost all of them were famous, or influential. What you might call movers and shakers. We've interviewed as many as we've been able to identify.'

'There's been nothing on the news about it.'

'No, there hasn't. And there won't be. Not ever. You're not

a stupid man, Mr Frisby, and you know as well as I do that there are too many reputations at stake here. What happened is very hard to believe. But even if it's true – even if what some of these guests have told us about an Indian American figure of some kind, it will still ruin some of the most powerful men and women in Hollywood. *Especially* if it's true.'

'Trinity's sister was murdered there, Fidel. She was hung up and cremated alive, along with her best friend, and we saw another guy burned to death, too. Not to mention a woman who was raped to death in front of all those powerful men and women. And who knows how many other innocent people John Dangerfield and his cronies have killed, for nothing but their own sadistic pleasure?'

'My sincere condolences for losing your sister, Ms Fox,' said Fidel. 'As it happens, there was actually a genuine reason why those victims' lives were taken. It wasn't solely for their pleasure.'

'What?' Nemo demanded. 'What genuine reason could there possibly be for setting fire to helpless young girls?'

'Mr Frisby, I'm not at liberty to tell you that. And it's part of the deal that I'm offering you here this morning that you never ask again, or make any attempt to find out.'

'So what *is* this dark and devious deal?'

'I know you'll never be able to forget what happened, but you have to promise never to mention it again to anybody, not as long as you live. In return, the IAG will agree to leave you alone and allow you to carry on your lives without being followed, or monitored, or threatened, or harassed in any way.'

'What's our guarantee that you'll stick to that agreement?'

'Your guarantee is that you were both seen by numerous

guests at those parties. Maybe most of them would never admit that they were there, but if anything untoward should happen to you, and only one of them voiced suspicions about it, the IAG will be at risk of being charged with lethal misconduct.'

'Oh, you might lose your pension?'

'Well, it would probably turn out a whole lot worse than that. An official investigation would want to know why we wanted you eliminated, and then the entire John Dangerfield mess could come out into the open. There would be so many heads rolling that Wilshire Boulevard would look like a bowling alley.'

Trinity said, in a trembling voice, 'What about my sister, Rosie? How am I going to give her a funeral if I can't tell anyone what happened to her? And where is she now?'

'I was coming to that,' said Fidel. 'The official explanation for the fatalities that occurred at John Dangerfield's house that night is that a fire was caused by a faulty propane gas tank when they were lighting up a barbecue. The fire department are prepared to confirm that.'

'So the fire department are liars and cheats too?' asked Nemo.

'They know like we do that there's no point in causing total devastation to this town's economy, especially for the sake of someone who's paid the price already.'

'But what about Rosie, and Sally, too? Sally was burned right beside her.'

'Their remains have been respectfully removed from John Dangerfield's house and taken to the Costello Funeral Home on Santa Monica Boulevard. I've brought one of their cards for you here, so that you can contact them about making all the necessary arrangements. We've already informed Mr and Mrs Marshall about Sally. They've accepted the story that both girls went to a glamorous Hollywood party and met with a tragic accident. I hope you can accept that, too. It will make your life much easier, and our lives, too – and the lives of some of the most famous people in the world.'

Nemo went around the couch and put his arm around Trinity. She looked up at him with tears in her eyes and said, 'We'll have to, won't we?'

Nemo gave Fidel and his two investigators his hardest stare. He was so angry, his nostrils were flaring.

'It's a deal?' asked Fidel.

'Yes, you piece of shit. Now put your coats back on and get out, so that we can disinfect the place.'

At that moment, Buddy appeared, rubbing his eyes. 'Where's a piece of shit? I don't want to tread in it.'

Rafael decided to stay over with Teodoro that night, so Trinity had to sleep alone again. She was glad of it, though, because she was tired and emotionally exhausted and she needed to sob quietly into her pillow. She felt that she had betrayed Rosie by agreeing not to tell anybody how she had really died, not even their father. On the other hand, she was relieved that she would be able to give her a proper funeral, with flowers, and a eulogy, and her favourite song, 'The Circle of Life' from *The Lion King*.

She had been asleep for less than half an hour when she felt that somebody was gently laying a hand on her shoulder. At first she thought she was dreaming it, but then she heard a voice say 'Trinity?', and the voice was so familiar that she opened her eyes.

'Trinity?' the voice repeated, and it wasn't a dream. Standing beside her bed, barely visible in the darkness, were Rosie and Tokoor Hikaayey, the Ghost Woman. Both were wearing simple grey robes, and bead necklaces, so that they looked like members of a holy order. Trinity could see that they were holding hands, and smiling at her.

'I have come to show you that I have found your sister, and that I will take care of her now for all time,' said the Ghost Woman, in a voice as soft as the draught blowing under the door. 'And your sister has come to say goodbye, and that one day she will meet you again. You have shown my soul a place in these mountains to shelter, and your sister will shelter here with me. You can come here at any time to find us.'

'Rosie,' said Trinity, and her eyes were almost blinded with tears. 'Rosie, I'm so sorry.'

'You mustn't feel sorry, Trin. I'll always be with you, just like Mom. They stole my life, but they could never steal my soul.'